I0699649

F. FOX NORTH

The Tender Familiar

A novel of Baron & Eddie, their children, grandchildren, and various cats.

Fretboard Press

For Jordan, who knows why.

I do not talk of the beginning or the end.

Walt Whitman

Contents

Preface

Here is another book I never intended to write. A diversion, I thought, between other projects. I told myself I'd write a short story about Baron Templeton's guitar. I thought maybe I'd get to the bottom of where it had gone in 2017. I let myself make the story smutty, because no one was ever going to read it. This was just fan-fiction, you see - since no one is a bigger fan of my own work than me.

I wrote a story about that guitar's birth. I wrote a story about the first time Eddie and Baron fucked. And then, I thought, why not write another story? Because they still hadn't told me where that guitar had gotten to.

Before I knew it, I had 40,000 words. A short story sequence. 50,000. A novella, then. Before I knew it, my sciatica was flaring up. Before I knew it, I had a 93,000 word sequel to a book no one had read but me.

Crap.

It was good, though. And I finally knew what became of Baron's guitar.

Think of this book as "ten times Baron and Eddie fucked and one time their kids did." It includes some (very) raunchy bits. But we're all adults here. Baron's not ashamed, and he says you shouldn't be, either.

Yours this winter, and every winter until Baron is done with me,
Fox

P.S. The "familiar" in question is named Alonzo.

Acknowledgement

For those who live in my den with me: DB, JD, SW, EM, KLA, CS, RZ, TM, LT, MD, and especially Kristin Muller, who gave Cymbeline her last name. For VM and AG, for being the first fans of these books, and LJ, for being the second.

Chronological Note

These short stories takes place before, and after, the novel *The Chaos Agents* and the chapters may be read in the order as presented, or chronologically, as follows:

The Tender Familiar

The guitar was pink.

Pink, pearlescent, shot with gold, glittering beneath the overhead lights of the Steinway Haus, as they all glittered in those days, four wan and underfed boys in black leather, their curls unwashed and overgrown and come loose from their Vaseline binding. But the boys, the four of them, glittered only like sweat glittered. This pink, pink guitar?

Glittered like something else.

It was one of only eight guitars in the shop. The place was packed with pianos mostly. All angles and ivory. Whereas this was pink pink pink and hippy. Floral. Feminine. Fruity.

Baron stood beneath the guitar wall, his hands behind his back. He knew, he knew, that was the one. Herr Sinkler had not yet paid them a single Kroner or whatever it was that passed for money here in Deutschland, keeping the only record of their wages to come in a ledger book behind the bar, and so Baron had no idea how he could possibly make this dream *manifest.* Couldn't pay for it in swill beer and pretzels and prellies, anyway. And yet Baron knew he would have that guitar. Had to. If the band were going to make this work - make themselves heard over the din of bar voices, make themselves bigger, better here in Hamburg, he needed it. Him. His guitar.

Liam paused in his studious browsing beside him. The child was looking downright gaunt now, practically a reanimated skeleton. His eyes were squirrel-bright and neverslept. He'd been taken, lately, with one of the barmaids, a zaftig maiden named Gretel, and she kept feeding him prellies, more than the rest, and so he ate even less than the rest of them. When he climbed down from the bunk they shared in the morning, clad only in his BVDs, Baron could count every rib, every single vertebrae. Liam leaned in close, spoke smoke-shot words into his ear.

"She's the one you've been achin' for? A Ricky, really?"

He, Baron wanted to say, but didn't. Liam was right, anyway. It was ridiculous, in its way. A Rickenbacker Combo 800, an American guitar, in Germany, but not a Fender or anything like a Fender, which is what any sane boy would want. That's what Liam's mum had gotten him, right before they left, a gift for his seventeenth birthday. An egg blue Stratocaster, shipped in by an auntie in the states. The perfect replica of Buddy's guitar.

Baron shrugged. "Who can explain the ways of the heart?"

And he wanted to look eastward then, toward the front of the shop, where he could hear Eddie pounding his hands against the keys of one of the pianos. Chatting with the salesman. Charming him.

But he wouldn't.

"How's she sound?" asked Liam. Baron shrugged again. And then he reached up, his leather creaking. Took the guitar down off the wall. Plugged her into one of the amplifiers. Another necessary component the band were lacking. Wired now, Baron sat at one of the piano benches. Started to play.

The neck, bizarrely small, narrow all the way through, like a banjo neck. It felt like - it reminded him - of his Mum, and Baron winced to think about it. Stupid dead Mum, teaching him those banjo chords at the start of it all. Sometimes he still had to resist the urge to tune up his little plywood acoustic and play on four strings only. Was so much easier, even if Ed told him not to, that the sound was hollow and shallow and poor. Anyway, still, this guitar, its curvy body, felt easy too, and a certain kind of tender familiar.

He'd gotten better in these two years. Oh, oh, loads better. He was no Liam still, of course. Had no interest in flashy fiddly bits, besides, but now he knew how to *swing*. His hand moving, jerking, strumming out a rhythm. He understood now something he hadn't before, which was how music was like wanking. Had to pull it right, fit in the natural rhythm and strokes. Don't be self conscious. Don't rush it along. Linger and build. Find the pattern inherent inside you. *Blow.* He felt Liam watching him, nodding his approval, felt the piano go silent near the mouth of the store, felt the others watching. Charlie and the salesman. Ed.

"You! Boy!" the salesman rumbled, standing straight, his eyes boring straight into Baron. "What do you thing you're doin'?"

The man was in his fifties or sixties, a gray kind of oldish, and his voice was filmly and fleshy and gross, thickly accented. Thick with phlegm. Baron didn't stop playing. Let Liam turn, answering for him.

"He's just trying it!" Liam answered in his whine.

"You have money?" the salesman asked. Baron stopped then, flexing his fingers over the pick-ups.

"Haven't decided if I like it yet," he replied. Charlie, behind the salesman, snickered. But Ed, who sat there still on the piano bench beside him, wasn't snickering. Was watching Baron. Waiting for something. A crash. A kick. A punch. Ed knew, better than anyone, how hot Baron's temper could run. Knew well enough to be - well, not afraid, exactly. But to anticipate.

"No money?" the man said. He was stepping closer. Baron could see now that he was a big, burly guy in a well-fitted suit, someone who cared about his appearance, his comportment. What was Baron in comparison to him? A stain. Brown and greasy. Small. This guy had muscles, had probably fought a war or two.

A Nazi like the rest of them, thought Baron, and he thought, in a moment, in a flash, of how the man had jovially sat *Eddie* down at that piano bench, lifting up the fall board for him. Pretty perfect Aryan Eddie. Just as unwashed. But somehow cleaner, worth more - in the German's eyes.

(In Baron's own eyes too, of course. Just as biased as the rest of them. Against himself, and for Ed. Even on the days he hated him most, he couldn't deny Ed's blond, stupid beauty. His worth.)

"No money?" the man said again, and he put his hand around the cord that was plugged into the amplifier, wrapped his thick glove of hand around it, and, in one smooth movement, yanked it out.

The guitar strap was already over Baron's shoulder, so when he stood, fists flexing, the guitar came with him. Cord trailing like a tail.

"Oi," was all Baron said, and he wished he were taller, not for the first time. Only came up to about the man's nose. But Liam - Liam was tall. He stood, too. Two of them. Against one.

Two yearlings, strapping and wild and spoiling for a fight. But the man wasn't shaken. He held out a hand.

"You give me the guitar," said the man. Standing dangerously close to Baron. Baron could see the small flecks of green in brown eyes, and beneath that, there were hints of something. A love of music, maybe, or at least beautiful girls. A spark. Some greater depths. But Baron pushed that thought away. This was a Nazi pig. And truly, all that Baron had wanted - had ever wanted - was to play a few bars of music. Ed was allowed that much. Why shouldn't Baron be? Where was the harm in that?

Baron forced a snort through his flared nostrils. Wound up his fist. That's when there was a crash. At the front of the store, by the percussion, Baron looked over the salesman's thick shoulder just in time to see Charlie go flying into a display of music stands and toward a row of drums, and to see Ed, standing in front of him, his arms extended. He'd *pushed* Charlie, and now, falling, Charlie yelped out. Charlie Peck was older than they were, dignified, wasn't yet used to anticipating their antics, maybe never would be. And now he tumbled in what seemed like endless, almost comedic freefall. Trying to get his footing from the metal stands, failing, flailing, falling into a set of drums. Endless rattle. Everlasting crash. The salesman rushed over to break up the fight or *whatever* it was, to help, and that's when Baron felt Liam's hand on his shoulder.

"*Lauf*," he whispered, one of the few German words that they'd already learned. *Run.*

Baron didn't even think about it. There was a door at the back, behind the counter. He'd noted it without noticing it. And now it opened for them, and Baron and Liam raced into the alleyway, the cord of the guitar skipping over the pavement behind them, and Baron wasn't sure, but he thought he heard, above a din of cymbals and snares, Ed saying to the salesman in his sweetest voice, like a bleeding Boy Scout, "Thought he was stealing something. Must have been wrong."

Couldn't stop to listen or confirm. Couldn't stop to see if Charlie was alright, or Ed. Baron had that pink guitar over his black leathered shoulder as he climbed up a chain link fence, his pants squeaking their objections, as Liam pulled him over and down and they ran together out into the streets in their cowboy boots, which weren't made for running. The street, slick with rain, and not enough traction, the two of them almost tumbling around the corner, and then slip sliding across the street, through a soggy park. Past mongrel dogs and smoking prostitutes and a pair of sailors, sharing a bottle, past a rain-pounded fountain and across the street where Liam pointed toward some sort of ancient tenement building. There was an old woman there, holding a door open for her husband. *Nazi*, Baron thought, as he shoved past the man and almost knocked him over. At last, stopping to pant, he tucked himself in the back of the old dingy lobby, back behind a stairwell, as Liam goofily goosestepped around the old folks, then saluted as they drifted out together into the rainy day. The gesture Liam made was not quite a sieg heil, but not *not* a sieg heil. Baron laughed.

Funny, back in Liddypool, how he couldn't stand Liam. Nowadays it felt like they were mates, if not best, then good enough for a time. They shared a room over the seedy little theater where they performed. It had been a whim, picking Liam as his roommate, a split second decision meant to irritate Ed, because he'd been irritated by Ed on the trip over, because Ed'd been more concerned about writing letters to his *girlfriend*, Genie Waller, than paying attention to the adventure at hand. Of course, later Baron realized his mistake, randy and stuck in a bunk beneath Liam, all alone. But really, not so bad. Liam was a bit of a pig, like he was, and now neither of them had to cope with Ed's henpecking.

"You forgot your tail," Liam said, as the door closed behind them, and, reaching down, yanked the trailing cord out of that beautiful guitar. Grinning.

"Guess she's all yours, mate," Liam said, giving a nod toward the guitar as he pressed the cord into Baron's hand. Baron took it. Stuffed it down into the pocket of his leather jacket.

"Yeah, if the gestapo doesn't find me," Baron said. He fumbled around for a half-crushed pack of ciggies. Found a soggy little stub of something half-smoked. Didn't have a lighter. Liam had to light it for him, from a book of half-damp matches from his trouser pocket. They shared the fag there, in the bright yellow lobby, peeled paint and the gray of the day outside. Grinning at each other as the cherry got longer and the fag got shorter. *Two electric guitars now*, they were thinking in unison. *Three quarters of the way to a real, proper band.*

"You think they locked up Charlie and Ed?" Liam asked. He went to the doorway with the tiny stub of a cigarette, looking out the warped, ancient glass. Watching for their band mates in the street beyond.

"Probably stripped them down naked and whipped 'em," Baron said, almost without thinking. Grasping that skinny neck in his hand. Gripping it. Thinking of pinkness.

Liam whipped his head up. His dark eyes, narrowing into pointed chasms.

"Wot?" asked Baron. Liam stubbed the cigarette out under the sharp toe of his boot.

"Sometimes I convince myself I'm wrong about you," he said. "And then you go and say things like that."

Baron wondered what Liam expected him to say to that. It wasn't a joke. To either of them.

"Perverts in glass houses shouldn't fuck fat stones," Baron said at last. Just as pointed. Just as sharp.

Liam made a scoffing noise. Shaking his head, his high, greased hair, he turned away.

* * *

Should have slept. But didn't bother sleeping. On the stairs on the way up to their room, they'd run into Gretel, just about to go on her first shift. She pressed skinny Liam behind her soft fullness, kissing him against a brick wall, and Baron felt that old familiar throb of horniness at the sight of it, and so stood back, just watching. As a parting gift, Gretel passed a scattered handful of prellies into Liam's hand, and the boys split them between themselves on the stairwell, grinning.

"She's the one you're achin' for, Liam?" Baron asked, swallowing the dry pills down whole, though at least they were small enough, and Liam blushed and rearranged his pants a bit, trying half-heartedly to hide his arousal.

"At least I got a bird," Liam said as they headed up the stairwell.

Baron just grunted. Been awhile since Sue Grasso had got herself knocked up by some other bloke and become married and domesticated. He's sunk it into a few birds since coming to the continent, but the practice cost him too much in either his pride or his once-scant foreign money, now all ran out.

"I don't need one," Baron said. "I've got you."

And he reached out and pinched Liam's non-existent arse through his leather pants, and Liam made a noise between a yelp and a growl.

"Fairy," Liam muttered, throwing their bedroom door open. Baron did not bother denying it.

The concrete walls of the room seemed to be sweating. *Like the inside of a snail's shell,* Baron thought, finally taking the guitar off of him, setting it against the cracked window glass, and sitting down on his bottom bunk to look at it. Their room was damp, the clothes that they left strewn about always stank of mildew, and sometimes it seemed that the open, half-eaten cans of beans and half-drunk beer bottles they left about were about to evolve sentience and walk away. No matter. This was the first place Baron lived that was anything approaching his own, and he loved it. Now, the guitar shone like a jewel behind that window, the centerpiece of it all. His magic carpet to fame.

Liam peeled his coat off. Stood with his spine against the bed. Contemplating it, too.

"Now we have a fighting chance," he said, with entirely too much gravity for Baron, although at least half of what bothered him about what Liam had said was that it was *true.* They'd never be able to compete with the other Hamburg bands - Derry or Rory or the Silver Beatles - living in an entirely acoustic world. They were rock 'n' rollers. Rough. Hard. Electric. And they needed instruments that reflected that.

A moment's pause, both of them looking at the Ricky. And then, Liam:

"You and Ed planned it, right?"

"Wot?" asked Baron, his head snapping up. There was something in Liam's gaze he couldn't describe. A hard fierceness. A probing.

"The two of you planned it, yeh? So you could steal the guitar?" Another pause, longer, while Baron chewed. "The two of you queers, together, planned it?"

The prellies had kicked in, maybe. Maybe that's why Baron's tongue felt like a dry washcloth in his mouth, why the swing beat of his heart pounded behind his back teeth. Maybe. He knew he couldn't respond the way he wanted to respond, a laughing, uneasy, "Eddie's not *queer*," because it was one thing to joke about it himself, to sow uncertainty, but to let even a friend say such a thing about Eddie was *dangerous*, for all of them. But Baron knew he couldn't say that. Would be just as good as admitting it.

"Didn't plan it," was all Baron said, neither confirming nor denying, still feeling his heartbeat beat beat beat as Liam stared at him, inhaling, exhaling, but barely moving, besides.

Nothing to say, for either of them, conversation going nowhere so they were trapped there in their mutual trapped unmoving until there were heavy footsteps on the stairwell outside the door, shouts, and it came flying open and in walked Charlie, his jacket torn, his nose bloodied, pointing a finger up close and personal to Baron.

"You *prick*!" he seethed. "You 'orrible *prick*!"

Baron blinked, twitched. Before an answer came, there was Eddie, wrenching Charlie back. Charlie Peck, who had seven years and four stone on Baron, less that on Ed, but not much, but Ed being brave about it, being unphased.

"Lay off, Peck!" Eddie said, not a shout, but firm, and Baron saw now how Eddie's hair was disheveled too, like he'd been in a scuffle, and Baron felt a stabbity stab of worry. Ed. Ed hurt? But the blood smeared against white flesh seemed to be only Charlie's, not Ed's. "He didn't do anything!"

"Oh, yeh?" Charlie asked. "Well, what's that?"

He pointed a finger at the pink, pink guitar. Baron fought an urge to throw himself in front of it, to use his body as a shield.

"What was he s'pose to do?" piped up Liam, "Leave it on the side of the road?"

Charlie wheeled around, looking at all three of them. His eyes like the crazy eyes of a crazy cat in heat.

"You," he said, pointing at Liam, "You're not even old enough to have work papers. You're all going to get us killed! I didn't leave—"

"Dylan Miranda and the Tempests," Baron said in a sing-song tone just as Charlie's voice hit the same words, and he glowered, like he was ready to *hit* Baron.

"Oh, come off it," Liam said coolly, "We're a better band than they ever were and you know it."

"Haven't gotten paid," muttered Charlie, like it didn't matter, "Get my arse kicked by some bleeding Nazi in a piano store while this one—" He jerked a thumb at Ed. "—just stands there laughing about it."

"I pulled him off," Ed said. Charlie stabbed at his own wrist with an index finger, pointing at some imaginary watch.

"Only took you an *hour*."

"Oh, it wasn't any more than three or four minutes," Ed replied, and for a minute, Charlie said nothing, the blood dripping down his face onto the piles of dirty pants that blanketed the concrete floor.

"It's over," Peck said at last. "I quit."

He turned and stormed out.

Silence, for a moment. All of them looking at each other. At last, sighing, Liam shook his head.

"I'll go get him," he said. "Can't have a band without a drummer now, can we?"

"Good luck," said Ed. "You may need it." And he aimed a playful punch at Liam, who ducked and dodged as he walked out through the door, as well.

The hinges creaked. The metal slammed shut. And Baron and Eddie were alone for the first time in ages.

No speaking at first. No breathing. Or entirely too much breathing, on Baron's side, loud enough that they both could hear it.

"He'll be back," Baron said at last. "Can't get back to Liddypool without cash, right? And we know *he* doesn't have any."

Ed, standing there, sloped his body against the wall. "Yeh," he said. "Yeh. He's right mad, though, Baron."

"Well, Edmund," said Baron, "Isn't really *my* fault, is it?"

"Dunno," Ed said. He nodded toward that pink guitar in the window. "You did steal it." A pause, cricketing out between them. "You plan it, Barry?"

Baron frowned. Was one thing for Liam to accuse him of some sort of plot. Was another thing entirely for it to come from Ed. He didn't answer. Maybe didn't hafta, as Ed just shook his beautiful towhead.

"No, I suppose not," he said. "Would have been a crap plan. Not like stealing a mouth organ. Couldn't have put it in your pocket, besides."

Baron's own words surprised him. Squeaking out, loud and bright and there were too many of them, and they didn't stop. "Wasn't planning nothing at all. Was just trying it out. Thought maybe I'd pay for it, when we finally get paid, whenever that will be. Why is it, *Hammy…*" He paused only long enough for the name to sink in. "Why is it a boy who looks like you will be shown around a shop like that like you're king of the Goddamned world while I go in there and get berated for just *touching* a precious guitar? And then everyone goes around acting like I intended it. Me own friends. Supposed friends. Supposed-" And then he stopped, because what was there to call what Ed was to him, what he was to Ed? They loved one another, but they hadn't snogged in months.

Ed just watched him. Face a mask. Not saying nothing, which he never did when things like this came up. Their essential differences. That Ed was straight and pale and beautiful, that women wilted when he walked by, that he oozed easy charm like he'd been born in it, which he had. Whereas Baron was queer and small, uncertain of origin, and other people seemed to sense it on him, the queerness. In all senses. And were disgusted by it and afraid of it, maybe both.

"Dunno, Barry," Ed said, and his voice was small, as if he really didn't. "Anyway." Swallowing, casting his eyes down for a moment, into the drifts of clothing piled up on the floor. And then he looked up again, not at Baron, but at the Rickenbacker.

"She is a beautiful guitar."

Wasn't sure why, but Baron found himself laughing. Cruel, sharp laughter. He flopped down on his bunk, putting his arms up over his head, looking at the guitar, too. Not looking at Eddie.

"He," he corrected him. "But whatever."

Silence silence silence. Baron counted out nine or ten beats before Ed's voice came back to him, even smaller than before. Daft little girl's voice, timid and unsexy.

"D'you want me to leave, then?"

Baron reached down, started trying to take off his boots. Regretted putting them on, as always, when he couldn't get them off.

"What's that then?" he asked, irritably. He pried the first one off and it hit the wall behind him, revealing a half-fallen, sweaty sock and the brown heel of Baron's foot.

"Well," said Ed, more soft, more timid. "I thought maybe you didn't want to anymore. Since you said Liam was your roommate."

"Want to *what?*" Baron snapped, tugging now at the second boot, but it wasn't budging. In truth, he thought he might have known to what Ed was alluding. In truth, he knew it was a bit mean, to play dumb. Felt good, anyway, today, now, to be a little mean.

"*Baron,*" Ed said, smaller still, and mortified, maybe. Baron could have pressed. Could have made Ed cry fat, embarrassed tears, made him *say* it, that he *wanted* Baron, that he wanted to *fuck* Baron. Would have been satisfying, wouldn't it? To finally have Ed admit to it. That he wanted Baron - needed Baron - just as much as Baron ever need/wanted him.

But Baron turned, a hand on the still-stuck leather of his boot, and saw Ed's face. It wasn't just his cheeks that were blushing. It was maybe all of him, bright red, like the lights the whores kept up in windows, a red that seemed to go right up into his pale hairline and down, too, below the collar of his jacket. Hmm, Baron thought. Lower maybe, even. Perhaps.

"Cor," Baron said. "*Ed.* Don't be a bird. I asked Liam to be my roommate because we're a couple of pigs, and you're not. Would you really want to live in *this?*"

Ed looked around, at the decomposing food, the sweaty clothes. Started to laugh a little, dry. Then his gaze fell on Baron, and he stopped. Gave Baron a look that nearly *killed* him. A wanting. A *yearn*.

"Wot," Baron said, because it was almost embarrassing, to be looked at like that. He was supposed to be the shitty weak one, not Ed.

"When we started talking about going to Hamburg," Ed began, in a shaking tone, "I thought somehow, in my head, it would be - it would be our chance. Because we haven't… I mean, you at your auntie's house, Barry, and me with me dad and brothers everywhere, when have we… "

"Done the twist with our Chubby Checkers?" Baron asked, his smile small, wry, wanting to duck the question with a joke, because they hadn't much, really, since that first time, nearly two years ago. Oh, they'd stole a few illicit kisses before they'd be inevitably interrupted by said brothers or auntie, their bodies thrust apart by the sound of an opening door.

Well, there was that once. Scotland. When it all had finally boiled over in the back of Lord Jessamine's rusted van on that night when the roads had frozen over, slick with black ice, when the snow had blotted out the darkness in the headlight's circle. Then, they'd been not a yard away from Liam, scared for their lives, their breath low and ragged but suddenly, on some level, not caring if Liam or Charlie, asleep in the front seat, or Jessamine, driving the van beside him, heard, and Baron always wondered if any of them *had* heard, thought that maybe they *must* have, when Baron at long last let himself blow into Ed's trousers and Ed let out a small, strangled cry, but, well - nobody had ever said nothing about it.

Ed didn't say anything for a moment, definitely didn't smile, didn't laugh. Blinked once, hard, and there was too much hurt and anger there for Baron to bear when finally Ed said, harshly, "When have we *fucked*, Baron. I can say it. Why can't you?"

"Oh," said Baron, looking studiously away. "That. Well. Why didn't you say so?"

"Just did," Ed said, and Baron thought of a puppy then, one that's caught the end of a bone, and even though you're trying to pull it away from him, he will not let it go.

"Dunno if I'd call what we've done *foocking*, anyway," said Baron. "It's more frottage, innit?"

"Baron…"

"The way I seen it," said Baron, "If you want *foocking*, you've got Eugenia Waller for that."

Ah, there it was, the knife. The hypocritical, ugly knife. Because it wasn't as if Baron hadn't stuck it to Sue Grasso two or three dozen times since his own deflowering, the day he turned eighteen. A wonder, in a way, that he hadn't been the one to put a baby in her. But in his mind, somehow, a difference between what *he* did *to* Sue and what *Ed* did *with* Genie. Yes, Baron liked it. His prick liked it. Throbbed at the thought of it even now. Christ, it had been too long. But neither he nor Sue was ever laboring under any general impression that they *loved* one another. He treated her rotten, in fact, and knew it, but she didn't seem to mind his using her, and he certainly didn't pretend to be doing anything but using. Had never written her a God damned *love letter*, much less the dozens of them that Ed had penned to Genie. Up all night in the next room. Mooning…

Ed, blue eyes big a'blinking. "You're jealous," he said, and the words were almost gasped. Baron grunted.

"You are!" said Ed. "Jealous, like a little *baby*. Like a *bird*."

"Oh, come off it," Baron said. He finally gave his boot one last angry tug and flung it across the floor. The foot it revealed was revolting. There was an oozing blister on the heel, and he picked at it and pretended it was interesting. Pretended it wasn't true, that his jealousy wasn't a searing ball in his chest.

"Jealous," Ed said one final time. "Baby," he repeated.

"And if I am," Baron finally said. Not a question. Because he was. He looked up at Ed, was surprised to find that in the time he'd been studying his dirty, sweaty foot, that Ed had come closer. Standing beside the bed now, one hand up against the rusted metal frame.

"Could have said something," Ed told him.

"Couldn't," said Baron. He swallowed, hard, found his throat dry and painful and the tears close. Was horrified by it. All these feelings. "No use.

No use in any of this. Me and you. Never going anywhere. Not like we could…"

We could what? Baron found himself asking himself. In truth, he didn't even know what he wanted from Ed. To put him in a dress, make him his bride? A funny enough temptation, the image so absurd it was almost soothing. Ed, his flat, fair body in a *dress*. Flowers in his dumb curls. Amusing, sure. But not necessary.

No, he didn't want that. But something else, yes. To write love letters. To… to hold hands, even though he always tried to avoid holding hands with Sue. To cuddle on a bus late at night after a long show, both of them stinking of cigarettes and their throats all raw when they kissed. To be queer, the way that the queers that had become friends with Liam were queer, the German pseudo-intellectuals, fay and proud about it even if the sailors were always beating them senseless and robbing them for every cent they had. He knew it was a danger, the greatest danger. And yet. Well.

Ed standing there, looking at him. His lush mouth gone tight, holding in his feelings, but only barely.

"Tch," said Ed, sadly clicking his tongue. "Barry."

"Do you love her?" Baron asked suddenly, not knowing he was going to ask it before it was asked.

"I don't," Ed replied. "No. But I need her."

Baron winced.

"I do!" said Ed. He sat down on the bed beside Baron's legs, and the mattress springs squeaked. "But it's not like—"

"Oh, come off, Ed," Baron said, and he started to turn, staring at the wall and all the naked drawings he'd done there in pencil, right on the thick lead paint. Boys and girls fucking, and boys and boys fucking. Men wanking their enormous cocks. Bodies arched and aching and exploding over, too. Spilling their ecstasy in the creases between the bricks.. Made him sick to see it now.

"It's *not*," Ed said. And he put his hand on Baron's hip and pulled, just a little, as though to turn Baron back toward him, but Baron resisted. Feeling the pressure of that hand against his hip. The growing irrepressible pressure of his own body, already, just from that one little touch. Ed sighed. Let his hand rest there. A heavy, heavy weight.

"Baron, I'm already half-sick over you most days. Over *wanting* you. Up there every day on stage, shaking your tail right in front of me in that leather. Looking like a… " Ed trailed off, considering. "Like a darker shade of James Dean."

"Cor," Baron said, glad the shade *was* darker for how ruddy he felt himself going. "Nothing like James Dean."

"You are!" protested Edmund. "It's the jaw. An' the cheekbones. Christ, I must have seen *East of Eden* nineteen times when it came out. Never understood, really, why I was so drawn to it. Not until I saw you, and I realized what it was. It was wanting."

Baron bit his lip, still not looking at Ed. He knew what it was like, to be that way, so full of desire, and never be able to really say why.

"When we're sitting together in your room back home," said Ed, "Writing a song with your auntie down the hall and her cats staring at us, when we're looking at each other and I'm just… falling into your eyes, Baron, I'm wanting you so hard that it *hurts*. I try to tuck those thoughts away until the nighttime, when I'm alone and no one can see it. But then I wake up so hard I can barely walk. Wank and wank and hope my brothers don't hear me and it's no use. I float around all day, whistling the songs you show me. And I'm somewhere else. Not there. Not *here*. They all know, Baron, that I'm lovesick over someone. Me brothers and me dad and Charlie and Liam and every goddamn whore on the street of Hamburg. They don't even try me for a shag. They know I don't want it. It's obvious to them that I'm a fool. And they're right. But they don't know all of it. They don't all know over *who*."

"You want them to think it's Genie," Baron said, feeling disembodied as he said it. Half his brain, still stuck on the image of Ed, wanking and wanking. The other half hearing what Ed was saying, feeling the tenderness of it. The pain. Of having to pretend.

"I *need* them to *know* it's Genie. We can't risk it, Baron. If they all knew the truth? What would that mean for us?"

Baron didn't answer. Didn't have to. They both knew what it meant. Jail. And no more band. And the clink. And no more band. And the slammer. And no more band. For either of them.

"I sometimes dream about running off with you," Ed said. His hand was still there, on Baron's hip, but he began to move it slowly over, toward Baron's belly. "But where would want us? Can't run off to China or Australia or Paris. No place for us to go."

"I always thought," said Baron, turning toward him at last. Showing him how hard he was, straining away at his leather trousers. His black eyes boring into Ed's blue, "We'd get a farm somewhere no one could find us." A pause, for just a moment. "Scotland. Some little town where no one would care that two blokes were shacking up together. We could grow something. Maybe sheep—"

And Baron's words ended then, because Ed's mouth was on his mouth, Ed's tongue on his tongue, and Ed's hands, cupped around either side of Baron's face, like what he was saying was precious (which it was), like Baron was precious to him (which he was, too).

Ed's mouth on his mouth. Ed's cock swelling up, right near his cock, grinding their bodies together. *Frotting*, and the two of them kissing and kissing, and Baron grabbing at Ed's soft arse through his pants, pushing him closer, like they could almost become one body if they just eliminated every whisper of air between them, if they could just eliminate the entire outside world.

But what had Ed said he wanted to do? Not just rubbing up together. Baron gripped Ed's arse harder, and harder, both hands, his cock so full and grinding into Ed's soft belly, and Ed was moaning through kisses and gasping between them, close to the edge already, so Baron pulled his mouth away, and grunted, right into Ed's ear: "I want to put it inside of you."

Ed's blue eyes bolted open, and Baron wondered for a moment if he'd said the wrong thing, asking for that. That thing he'd never done with a boy, and certainly not Ed - that thing he'd only had done to him. But, oh, he wanted it. Had never wanted anything more.

Ed, his own cock still pressed to Baron's belly for a moment, looked down at him—and hesitant, uncertain, nodded. He peeled his body away from Baron's, and Baron was cold electricity in Ed's momentary absence as he stood up, at long last taking his coat off, hanging it off the frame of the top bunk, and then, carefully, slowly, began to undress. Taking off his boots. His sweaty t-shirt. Then, reaching down, unzipping his trousers. Revealing himself.

Baron was frozen for a moment, his breath hitched in his chest. He realized he'd never seen this before. Ed. Full naked. He'd seen birds, and fat old blokes in the art college, posing for the sake of art. But he hadn't seen *Ed*. Ed's alabaster skin, like a china doll, blemishless. His pink nipples, sharp against the cold. His belly, just a bit soft, and his hips, and how the bones jutted in a way that led one's eyes naturally to, well… to obvious conclusions. The glistening head. And the blue vein that wrapped around it. The balls high up and tight and scattered with pale hair. Baron took it all in.

And then hastily he scrambled to remove his own shirt, his trousers. Casting them off into the center of the ocean of clothes that occupied his room. *Caution*, he thought to himself, *here be dragons*, and he reached down and squeezed the head of his own cock, just once, but hard, hoping it would help stem the tide that was already building in him. He sat back on one end of the bed and waited to see what Ed would do next.

Ed seemed to be moving very slowly. Lying down on his back in Baron's bed, pulling his legs up with both hands. Like a bird might. Offering himself. His deep cleft, his pinkness, his balls, his cock, pointed straight up and hard as it could be, resting against Ed's soft belly.

"I don't want to hurt you," Baron said, because he knew it could hurt. Always had, for him. Ed didn't say anything. His eyes two blue pools. Vulnerable-like. Baron realized that Ed was scared Baron would hurt him, too.

And so even though he wanted nothing more than to just plunge himself into Ed's waiting tightness, instead he brought his head down, between Ed's legs. Kissed him there, in the place he'd never been kissed before, not by Baron and certainly not by Eugenia Waller. Kissed him, and then kissed deeper, pushing his tongue into him. Tasting the musky darkness, feeling

Ed grow looser, more open, like an eye might open, like a camera lens, like a fanny. Ed, moaning then, reaching his hands down to pull at Baron's greasy hair, as Baron opened him up, like a flower opens up. A crocus. On the first day of spring.

His tongue, deep inside Ed, feeling all the soft tissue and then - something else there, a strange tucked-away firmness, and Baron felt Ed's legs tighten suddenly around his ears, and his body throbbed, all of it, and Ed's hands wrenched Baron away abruptly, squirming, gasping.

"Too close," he said, his voice strangled. "I'm too close."

Baron nodded. Waited, for a moment, for Ed's throbbing to subside, feeling his own throbbing, too, as he watched it, his eyes on Ed's eyes, until Ed nodded that yes, he, too, was ready.

He licked his hand. Rubbed his slobber all up and down his own cock. Feeling his pulse in it, his heart. Worried, for a moment, that he might be *too* excited, that he might be sloppy, that he might stab it into him too fast. Felt himself move into position anyway. The head of him right up against Ed's pinkness. Then slowly, slowly, the head of him, and his length, blissful, beautiful, moving inside.

It felt like nothing Baron had ever done before, or ever felt. Ed's body, throbbing, all around him, just the same way as his own body throbbed, so tight it almost hurt. And he worried, again, that he was hurting Ed, and so somehow, against all odds, he managed to ask.

"It doesn't hurt?"

Ed, whose eyes had been closed in careful concentration, slitted them open, and managed to whisper, "Only a little. Feels good, Baron. Go slow."

So Baron did. Sliding in, as far as Ed could take him, which was all the way. Noticing how Ed groaned when he did. Staying there for a moment, both of them throbbing. Then slowly, slowly pulling out. Pausing, to rearrange himself, hooking his own arms beneath Ed's legs so he could dive in even deeper. All of Ed's softness all around him, and himself so hard.

"Nnf," Ed said, biting down on his lip, twitching, and his eyes were closed again and his cheeks were starting to blot up red and he looked like an angel, like a cherub from a painting, so beautiful, and it felt so good, and Baron felt his rhythm build, the way it would build when they were playing a song together, Baron finding the pace, the style, and Eddie plucking out the bass line. Eddie, tightening around Baron's rod as he started fucking him faster, and he didn't want to hurt him, but he couldn't stop, and it felt like Ed's body, like Ed, didn't want him to—getting tighter and tighter as Baron went in deep and went in fast, hearing the drumbeat of his hips hitting Ed's ass, and Ed's garbled cry, and suddenly all was tightness, and he was locked in there, held tight as a vise against Ed, and Baron couldn't tell if he was seeing or feeling a ripple move through Ed, from the inside out. Ed's arsehole tightened and his balls tightened and a wave moving up his cock as he began to come across his stomach, coming against his own chest, against his face, and then suddenly it felt like he was pushing Baron out, and Baron, already, incredibly close, incredibly hard, and he started plowing into Ed, faster, harder, faster, until he sank down inside him deep and lost it. Coming and coming inside of Ed. Filling him and filling him and filling him. In some vague way, aware that Ed was touching his stomach, his chest, his face as he came, that Ed was watching him come. Enjoying it. But not really feeling anything but the ecstasy of it. The moment of creation. Coming inside Ed. Ed twitching once, twice more.

It felt like a long time that they were stuck together like that. Still, except for their blood in their parts. At last, a lifetime later, slowly, Baron pulled out, leaving a stick trail against Ed's inner thigh.

"Christ, Hammy," he said, and laughed a little. Opened his eyes in time to see Ed's eyes open a bit, too, and hear his sweet, tender laugh.

"Christ," Ed agreed.

God, Baron thought. *I love him.* And he bent down and pressed the longest, warmest kiss to Ed's lips, and then, pulling away, moved his mouth to the trail that had been left against Ed's jaw and neck and belly. Baron kissed that, too. Drinking him clean. Until he his put his ear to Ed's heart and let himself relax against him, at last. Both of them tired and soft. Both of them tender and good.

* * *

It could have been an hour later. Could have been a minute or four. The sky darkening past the windows, and Ed, beneath him, stirring, and waking Baron.

"Hmm?" Baron asked, yawning. Ed was stretching, a full body stretch, from his fingers right down to his toes. Reached up, scratched at his own head. Waking up more. Glancing sidelong, at Baron's new guitar. Baron glanced, too.

"You'll have to paint her," Ed said sadly. "Otherwise someone is bound to tell the music shop. Can't be very many Rickenbacker Combo 800s in pink pearl in Hamburg. You'll have to paint her another color."

Baron looked at the guitar, silhouetted dark now in a darkening window. Hated to admit, because he loved the pink, but Ed was right. Wasn't Ed always right about these things?

"I'll paint him green," Baron said, grunting.

"Him?" Ed asked, lifting one pale eyebrow. Baron laughed.

"I've already named him," he said. "In my head."

He waited a beat, a long beat.

"Well?" Ed asked.

"His name's Eddie," Baron said. Ed didn't say anything for a moment, though Baron could tell by his expression that he was pleased.

"Christ, Barry," Ed said, blushing. And they kissed again and blushed together. The two of them. Together.

* * *

Not too long after that, but altogether too soon, that they both realized that the others would be back soon, that it would be time for them to go on stage. Baron peeled himself away from the warm bed that was Ed's body, fished about for clothes on the floor, found only filthy things, put them on anyway. Ed, too, began to dress. Pants and trousers first. And then, still shirtless, found his socks, and began to pull on his cowboy boots.

That's when Baron remembered that he had meant to tell Ed something. Something important.

"Hammy?" he said, his stomach aching a bit at having to break the news, because when Ed looked up, his expression was sweet, open, innocent.

"Yeh?"

"I think Liam knows," said Baron. And then he added, though he didn't have to. "About the two of us."

First Night

Liam told him not to go.

Maybe that was the greatest insult. Not hearing the vows, or sittin' around at the reception after, watching all of Ed's brothers getting entirely too drunk. Not the speech that Ed's dad gave, too mean, really, for sweet old Ed, who sat handsome in his suit, a lovely deep burgundy with a blue paisley tie, forcing laughter - Baron could see - as his dad mocked his music, his wealth, his songs.

Baron had been asked to give a speech, but Baron declined. When the time came, he only stood briefly, lifting his glass. "To the bride," he'd said, and some brothers pounded the table and howled like he'd meant something dirty by it. Ed's expression was unreadable as he, too, lifted cup. No, that wasn't the most awful part. It had to be this. After the music and the food, after bride and groom left on the back of Ed's moped, after all of it, how Baron went to leave, and suddenly found himself faced with Liam Waller, who put a hand on his shoulder, steadying him.

"Where you off to, Barry?" Liam asked, grinning wide enough to show his back teeth. Baron curled his lip.

"What's it to you?"

Liam had a ciggie dangling from his lips. Took a puff. "Hope you're not off to the Hammond abode," he said, and Baron looked past Liam, to the doorway.

"Why do you care?" said Baron.

Liam laughed a little. Said, in a low voice, "Albert sent me to do it. But we all agreed."

Baron fixed his hands on the lapels of his own suit, which was deep blue velvet. Not far from the color in Ed's scarf. Almost a secret thread, linking them. Albert was their manager. Unimportant. Outside of them. "Why?" he asked.

Liam took one last puff at his cigarette, then stomped it out on the ground. "Baron," he chided, low. "All these years, I've always told meself that it didn't matter *wot* those fairies did together, so long as it didn't get in the way of me career. Me band."

Baron glanced at Liam. Waller was drunk, for certain. It was only when he got drunk like this that he ever addressed the situation of Baron and Eddie at all head on.

"Well," Baron said, not bothering trying to deny it. Not tonight. "It didn't. The band is fine. You're loaded, Wally, aren't ye?" *Loaded.* He meant it in both ways. Stinking rich. Stinking drunk. Baron reached out and gave Liam's cheek a gentle pat. Liam reached up, caught Baron's wrist.

"She's my *sister*, Barry. I won't see you breaking her heart."

Did Baron feel any sympathy for Liam, for his sister? Oh, of course he did. He had a little sister, too. Fat sweet Bess, who hadn't been fat in years. They barely ever saw one another, but she wrote him letters sometimes. Sweet, moony things that sounded like they were written by a fan. *I thought we could go on a trip this summer. I'd like to see America with you. Francis, the boy at university I told you about, gave me a joint last week and I think he wanted to smoke it together but I saved it for your visit at Christmas...*

Baron understood Liam's feelings. But in truth? He did not care.

"It seems," Baron said, wrenching his hand away, "On account of the vows tonight that her *heart* is Ed's concern now. No one else's."

He stalked forward past Liam Waller.

"Wait!" called Liam, but Baron did not wait. He was off into the night. London. November. 1967. A sort of cold that reminded him of something, but he didn't stop to reckon precisely what it might be.

* * *

The new missus had turned in early. No wedded bliss for Ed that night. Anyway, she was nearly six months pregnant and it had been a hard slog for the last one or two, new stretch marks appearing on the daily beneath her popped-out belly button, and sick most mornings, still. Tonight's dancing had made her ankles go all swollen, all the way up to her knees, and he'd tried to tell her she shouldn't have worn those shoes but she hadn't listened, was determined to look fashionable for the papers before her belly had really started to show (thank Jesus, Mary, and Joseph for empire waistlines, because otherwise, that would have been beyond hope.) Ed wouldn't have minded, actually, a roll in the hay that night, swollen ankles or no. He and his brother Tom and Charlie Peck had shared a joint in the men's room just before leaving, a fat spliff to iron off the edges that had started to appear after his damned drunk of a father's speech, and somehow all that anger had turned to horny. But Genie didn't want to do it, didn't want him to even go down on her.

"Get off me," she said, "I feel disgusting. We have the whole honeymoon to do that."

So he left her up in the third floor master, closing the door behind her, and padded downstairs on his bare feet to make himself a cheese butty.

Some stars had cooks. Ed, who only employed an occasional housekeeper, couldn't stand strangers in his space. Sure, sometimes when they toured - back when they still had toured - it meant the cat boxes got all rank and smelly and the cats pissed in the closets upstairs, but he relished his solitude, still. Would be hard, actually, he thought, as he got out the expensive sprouted hippy bread that he had Albert's assistant get for him down at the farmer's market on weekends, to share his space with Genie now, and full time, to boot. He'd had just six years of his life to live without *family*. And though the nights of solitary living were hard sometimes - though he sometimes had dreamed, even plotted, to bring in *other* companions - it still didn't feel like it was enough.

But was his bride s'posed to move somewhere else? With a *baby*? No, that would never do. He was determined to be a right kind of father, the sort who gave out piggyback rides on the daily and taught his kittens to play the piano, like his Mum had taught him, and who might be stoned sometimes but drunk less, at least, than dear ol' Dad. Co-habitating was the only way to do it. Marriage, the only right way. A baby needed a mummy and a daddy, right there. Hadn't it been when his own mum had died that the whole family had fallen apart? He sliced up the bread, got out a brick of cheese and sliced that up, too. Smeared the bread with butter, mushed it all together the way he liked it, ate it in huge sticky mouthfuls. Needed something, he thought. Tea. He left his sandwich on the Formica and went to put the kettle on.

Ed put a teabag in a cup. His Mum's China. No one else had wanted it when he'd moved the family out to London, anyway. Ed waited. The water was just beginning to boil when there was a yowl in the front parlor. He sighed.

"Alonzo Coricopat," he chided. Knowing, but not really wanting to know, what musta set him off. He went over to the door. Alonzo circled his feet, leaving his long white hair on the legs of his wedding trousers. Alonzo - the name hadn't been his decision, but someone else's, when, beaming, this someone else had beamish brought him a kitten as a housewarming gift just after Ed had bought this place - always acted this way when certain parties arrived at the door. But, no. Couldn't have been. Not on Ed's wedding night, and well past midnight, besides. No one had rung the bell. But... Ed pressed his ear to the door. Heard shuffling. A thump. Sighed. He opened the door up, and Alonzo went skipping out, entangling the legs of the man who waited on the other side. He was stooped over, a bottle of champagne in one hand, a bouquet of soggy-looking white flowers in the other.

"Oh, 'allo, puss," Baron said brightly, and then, looking up at Ed, in the doorway, his smile fell.

"Well, then," Baron said. Ed didn't answer at first, just let the look of confusion answer for him. Surely, Baron would have known better than to show up *tonight*. Surely, he had *some* compassion.

"Realized I forgot to get you a wedding gift. So I thought-"

Baron pulled himself up to his feet. Swaying, slightly. Ed, standing in the door, was looking down on him, but still he could smell him, still he knew that sway.

"You're drunk," he said. Baron bit his lip. Grinned a little.

"Stayed sober through the whole wedding," he said. "But then Liam was on me about coming over here and I thought it was only right if I brought something and so I had a little nip myself. No harm." Baron stood there, still grinning, but his gaze was piercing its way into Ed's eyes.

"Besides," he added, "You're stoned."

No use in denying it. Ed only stared at him.

"Well, I brought me tribute for the missus," said Baron. "Aren't you gonna let me in, or do me and Alonzo have to stay out here like a coupla alley cats?"

He held out the flowers and wine. Ed didn't take them. Just kept staring. Oh, to be Baron Templeton. To just do whatever the hell it was that you wanted to do, at all and any times, and to take no punishment for it.

"Unless you're too busy screwing," Baron added sharply. He looked Ed up and down. Reading him, like an open book. "But no. Your cheeks are usually all pink after that."

"Christ," Ed said lowly. He didn't take the so-called gifts from Baron, just turned and stalked off on his bare feet. He went back toward the kitchen but left the door open. Left Baron to follow.

Baron took his God damned time. Scolding the cat.

"Come, come, Alonzo, or else no supper for you. Naughty boy."

Naughty. What even a word like that could do to Ed, especially at a time like now. He stuffed the feelings down. Went into the kitchen, picked up his sandwich, chewed. Pretending like bread and cheese were enough for him. The kettle was screaming now, but he only turned it off and did not pour. No use now. There would be no hope for a peaceful night. After a moment, he heard the door close. Watched Baron come dancing down the hall and into the kitchen, followed by all three cats, mewling and calling. They always acted like fools around Baron. Like he was their God damned pied piper.

Baron set the champagne and flowers down on the counter.

"Sorry they're in a state," Baron said. "Hard to find a shop open this late."

Ed looked down at them. They *were* sorry. Half-wilted white roses. They reminded Ed of funeral flowers.

Ed only grunted.

Baron was watching Ed for a moment, watching him as he chewed.

"Christ," Baron said. "I'm starving."

He went to the cupboard, got out some eggs. Set them on the counter in front of Ed. Ed looked at them a moment, still chewing. Then sighed and put down his sandwich. He started getting out a pan, without really knowing *why* he was getting out a pan, except it was something he'd done for Baron dozens and dozens of times before. Late night, frying an egg for him, just the way he knew Baron liked it, easy, because his Auntie had always scrambled them halfway to rubber growing up. On most nights, Ed hadn't minded it. Had felt good, to nurture Baron - who, in his life, had enjoyed so little nurturing.

Not tonight.

Killed him, though. Had to admit it killed him. When the pan was warm and he cracked the egg on the side of it and heard Baron's voice come up, small and uncertain.

"Thank you, Ed," he said softly. Ed winced.

Nothing worse than gratitude. Because that's what told him things had truly changed.

* * *

They ate in silence at the counter, but it wasn't a comfortable silence. Both of them sotted, both of them afraid to speak of what had just come to pass. At last, clearing the plate, pressing his mouth to a cloth napkin, Baron looked at Ed.

"The missus turn in then?" he asked. Ed was careful not to let himself wince, which in truth he wanted to do, at hearing her called that. By Baron.

"Yeh," Ed said. "You don't have to worry. She sleeps like the dead."

Baron's gaze flickered. Fair, Ed supposed. They'd developed certain rules over the years, never sharing details of their times with other lovers. This revelation held new depths. Ed hadn't meant it to, but he knew it must hurt.

Baron put his plate on the floor, and Alonzo and the other two rushed over to lick it.

"You shouldn't be here right now-" Ed said, at the same time Baron said, "You should have said something to me sooner."

Both of them stopped. Baron was the first one to look down. Guilty. Terrible, Ed thought, to see him looking like that. When he was *right*. He should have told Baron sooner, in private. Not at the studio with the rest of them, like he was just a lad like the others were lads.

"Yeh," Ed said. "Well." There was no good answer. He'd been a coward. As simple as that.

"Sorry," Ed added at last, which hurt to say, because Ed Hammond, as a general rule, did not apologize. Baron said nothing for a moment, and then, when he did speak, his voice was throaty and drunk and sad.

"Scotland?" he asked, the word sinking into Ed like a bullet. Like a harpoon. Meant to spear him, and oh, it did. Ed Hammond, as a general rule, did not cry. Not even when his Mum died. But now. Tears, fucking tears, burning his eyes. He snorted them back, rubbed his eyes on the heel of his hand.

"I'll sell it," he said. "She'll never have to know."

Baron looked at him, hesitant. Nodded. Not happy at this news, not exactly. Why should he be? To have what had happened between them forever stay a secret?

"Yeah," Baron said. "Right. I'll go-"

"Barry-" Ed said, and he knew it was the wrong thing to do. The cruelest thing to do. But he couldn't just let Baron walk out like that. From his kitchen, from his life. Baron, standing there, about to leave, maybe, so Ed did the worst thing. He put his hand on top of Baron's hand.

Baron, frozen, the words caught in his throat, looked down at it. And then slowly, very slowly, he turned his own hand over. Squeezed Ed's hand.

The only sound was the sound of the cats licking the plate clean. The sound of ceramic, gently tapping against the tiled floor.

"We'll go to the den," Ed said. His heart was pounding when he said it, a certain kind of illicit franticness he hadn't felt for years. Not since they both lived in their parents' homes, not since those days, not since they knew they could really be interrupted - ruined - at any moment. Baron was still looking at Ed's hand in his hand. Silently, wordlessly, he nodded.

They went downstairs to the den together. Holding hands. Silent, except for the cats calling out after them. Alonzo Coricopat, crying after Baron, wondering where his favorite human was going.

* * *

Down in the den, the door closed. Baron sat down stiffly on the sofa. Under ordinary circumstances, he would have sprawled out there, made himself look - feel - bigger than he actually was. But these were no ordinary circumstances. For one thing, he wasn't really *that* drunk. Had only had about three pints and the eggy Ed had made him had sopped some of it up. For another. Well.

Ed was moving slowly across the plush shag carpet, barefooted, but moving as though he might at any moment step on some sliver of glass. The walls were all cabinets he'd had built for his records. Thousands and thousands of records, clean dark wood. And he got out one and dropped it on the turntable. Baron perked his ear. Listened. Hmm. Petula Clark. Bit fay, not what Baron would have chosen, had he been asked. But he hadn't been asked. Instead, all he could do was listen to old Petula, tellin' him not to sleep in the subway. As the music swelled, Ed came and sat on the sofa, too. Three or four feet between them.

Funny, for them to both be so stiff. So hesitant. Like they'd been back when they was boys and they didn't know how to start it. Wasn't as though it were even the first marriage between them - Baron had shacked up with that American Jewish shampoo heiress for a year or two. But she'd been different. Queerer than Baron, even, and though she'd never been told, she had seemed to intuit that there was something untouchable about his "friendship" with Ed. Though she and Barry had tried to screw once or twice, as an experiment (Christ it was awful, with her just lying there like a corpse, and laughing at his cock when he pulled it out. Telling him it looked like a turtle), she'd allowed him to hide away with Ed sometimes in the attic. Eating acid. Working on songs. Fucking, if either of them could manage to get it up, which they couldn't, always, on account of the acid. Anyway she'd left, eventually, bored with the cameras chasing them everywhere, the lie.

Somehow, anyway, Baron sensed that things would be different with Genie Waller. Genie Hammond, he meant.

"Christ, Ed," Baron said finally, breaking the silence. Looking at Ed with a laugh on his lips. "A *baby*."

"What d'ya mean by that?" Ed asked, wounded. Baron bit his lip, holding in a smile.

"Nothing!" he said. "It's just hard to imagine it. A second little Ed running around. Getting into scraps, smashing up his daddy's guitar."

"Might not be a boy," said Ed, shrugging. "No way to know."

"I hope it is," said Baron. Looking at Ed, more serious now. His heart achin' now, as he looked at Ed. "I hope he looks just like you."

Ed flashed his pale eyelashes down. Not smiling. And Baron knew he shouldn't go on, but he had to, for some reason. Beer always made him stupid.

"Beautiful," he said. "Like you. Clever, like you. Precious -"

"Baron," Ed was saying, wincing. But then he looked at Baron, and Ed's eyes were two wounded, achin', randy pools, and even though the next word he said was, "Stop," Baron could tell that he didn't *really* want him to stop at all.

"Like you." Baron said simply. And it's funny, how much it reminded him of the old days, a decade before. The two of them dancing, denying it and then and then - Ed had sprung forward, smothering Baron's mouth with his mouth, his longer legs wrapping around Baron's slender waist, Ed hard already, and Baron feeling it up against his belly, not hard yet himself, but he knew he'd be soon, as Ed's hands frantic, frantic, shoved back Baron's velvet sport coat, tugged off his tie, unbuttoned the buttons on Baron's shirt, exposing the cotton vest beneath, and the skin just a shade more brown beneath that. His nails raking over Baron's back, his mouth hot and starving.

"I need to be in you," Ed said, which made Baron laugh a little, because they'd hardly even gotten started, but Ed just shook his blond curls.

"Not a joke," he said. "I *need* it."

Baron, his hands on Ed's thighs, squeezed, and he looked up at Ed, and a thought crossed through him, and he should have stopped it, but he didn't.

"Is this about what your Dad said in his speech?" he asked softly, "About you taking it up the arse from the record company?"

Ed was peeling off Baron's vest, touching his chest, his nipples, the black hair between them, trying to make it look like he didn't hear what Baron was saying - but Baron knew he did. Because after a moment Ed just said, "Shut up," and Baron did. Didn't need any more confirmation than that, in any case. Half of what Ed Hammond did at any time - like marrying Genie or buying those houses for his brothers or amassing piles and piles of cash while the rest of them spent most of it - was trying to prove to his daddy that he was good. The other half of it - his cock grinding against Baron's now-hardening cock and moaning already, and scratchin' at Baron's skin with his fingernails, and pulling his hair - was Ed trying to show to the rest of the world that really, deep down, he was very, very bad.

"I want you in me," Baron said, moving his hands around, to Ed's back, squeezing the two of their bodies close together. He said it both because Ed wanted him to say it, and because it was true. He always wanted Ed in him, or to be inside Ed. Wasn't a moment he was conscious that it wasn't true on some level, and these opportunities didn't come up often. Fastidious Ed, usually wanting to be the one on the bottom, because he thought it was dirty, on some level, and was usually too in his head not to think of it. But now, on top of him, Ed was all body, very little conscious thought. And he needed to be inside Baron, and Baron wanted Ed to be inside him.

Ed moaned at their bodies pressed up together like that. The compass points of their bodies pressed up together like that, and then slid his body off Baron and hastily, stumbling, with less grace than he normally possessed, undressed himself, and Baron pulled his own trousers down, watching him. Watching Ed's pink cock stabbing at the empty air. Baron turned himself over onto his knees on the sofa and waited. Throbbing. And there was a stumbling sound as Ed went into some drawer and slammed it shut and then, almost too sudden, almost too forceful, there was fingers inside him, buttering him up. Ed's mouth on his back and shoulders, kissing him as his fingers worked him open and everything was hot and bright and he could feel himself dripping down onto the sofa already as Ed's hands worked him, and it was almost enough to make him forget why he'd come there that night. Ed's nuptials. How Ed should have been fucking some bird that night, but was, instead kissing the back of Baron's neck, wrapping his arms around him, pushing himself into him. Without much preamble at all, sinking in deep. Staying there, still for a moment. Their two bodies one resonant throb.

"You nearly there already?" Baron asked, surprised. Ed let out a noise that started a whimper and somehow, before the end, became a growl.

"Shut up," he said.

So Baron did. Just let himself feel Ed's full, deep heaviness inside of him, and how his own body liked it. Eddie's prick, all the way in him, and now pulling out slowly, in a way that made Baron involuntarily cry out, and that was when Ed plowed it back inside, hard now, and fast, and Ed's hands worked their way downward, wrapping themselves tight around Baron's shaft, so that with each stroke of Ed's body, Baron was stroked, inside, and out, and it happened again, and again, and he felt his own cock swelling, the pressure in his balls growing greater, and it was so feral, so rough, that Baron was almost surprised, as Ed pounded into him, at Ed's words whispered husky into his ear.

"I love your tight little hole," Ed was saying, and then tightening his hand around Baron's prick like a vise grip. "I love your long, hard cock." Baron let out a strangled cry as Ed pumped into him again. "I fucking love you, Baron. And no one else. I only fucking love you."

Somehow, then, Ed plunged into him, deeper than deep, and Baron felt a wave that began behind him, somewhere in Ed's body, and move all the way through. In that moment, the two of them both cried out, and Baron felt Ed twitching in him, and felt himself twitching onto Ed's hand, all over it, coming. The two of them both coming then. An endless moment. And then, somehow, for some reason, the waves of it didn't even stop after Ed stopped coming. Baron's body trembling on and on and on. Almost painful, and Ed holding him tight to him, and feeling every twitch, every beat of it, like he could feel Baron's pleasure himself in every cell from cock to fingertip to toe.

Ed held him, kissing him, until their bodies had both stilled and began to go soft. And Baron was just turning and starting to kiss him back when there was a voice down the hallway.

"Edmund?"

"Bollocks," Ed said, and wrenched himself out and away from Baron's body, leaving him cold, confused, as Ed scrambled to put on something resembling clothes. His own pants, but Baron's shirt, buttoned off-kilter.

"Wait," Baron said, as, moving as though in slow motion, he went to pull on his own shorts. But Ed didn't wait. He was down the hall and up the stairs before Baron could say anything else, the door closed between them, and over the skipping, silent record, Baron could hear the faint sound of voices, but not what was being said.

He sat on the sofa, cold. Felt the pain and the loneliness searing inside him. Tried not to cry. After all, the *words* that Ed had just said. The *feelings* he'd shared with him. About his body, about his heart. Baron sat there and told himself that Ed would be back, soon. That Ed would make it right.

Soon enough, Ed slipped back into the den, quietly shutting the door behind him.

"Thank God," he said, going to the bar in the corner and starting to pour both of them some whiskey. "I told her she must have just been hearing me records, and she believed it. Here, mate."

He held out the drink to Baron. Baron looked at it. And finally, somehow, despite all his toughness, his hard skin, grown over all these years, Baron burst into silent tears.

"Barry," Ed said. He put down the drinks and rushed over. "Baron, it's all right."

Ed held him, and kissed his face, his tears.

"You don't have to worry," Ed said, not realizing he was saying the wrongest thing, the worst thing. "She doesn't know. No one knows. I told her she'll have to get used to me staying up late. Always was an owl, eh?"

Baron laughed a little, despite himself, found his mouth pressed up against Ed's mouth, kissing him, for some reason, despite crying and laughing unfunny laughter. The terribleness of the moment. Laughing and kissing and crying, all at once, and his mouth tender and hungry for Ed's mouth, still. Wanting to deny it. What he knew was happening, what had already happened. What had always been happening between the two of them. Something impossible.

Baron kissed him deeply, with tongue. Holding onto something that he now realized had never been his to hold. And Ed kissed him back, stupid and unknowing, and Baron felt Ed pressed up against him, grown somehow impossibly hard again. And. Christ, if Baron didn't love him. Didn't want to show him that he was still loved. One last time. One final time.

Baron's head dipping downward, between Ed's legs, nuzzling and licking what he found there. Tasting the muskiness of what had already happened. Sucking him tenderly, and Ed's hands tangling up in Baron's hair.

"Oh, I love you, I love you," Ed was saying as he came again, stupid and oblivious, and Baron knew that he did, that it was true, and that more, worse, truer, that it didn't matter at all. Did he love Ed? Of course he did. But part of loving Ed was *knowing* him, wasn't it? The things that Ed wouldn't never stop hiding. Not from Baron, but from the world.

Baron swallowed, and then he kissed a trail up Ed's stupid, stupid belly, and he kissed his mouth just once, just one last time, and set his head on Ed's shoulder, and they slept there for a moment or maybe an hour together, holding each other. And sometimes, in the years subsequent, as he drifted off to sleep, Baron would pretend that he was still there, on that last night, caught between sleep and waking, and that he was still Ed's, and that Ed - in his stupid, insufficient way - was still his.

Was near dawn when Baron pulled his body away from Ed's and began in silence to dress. At first he thought Ed was still sleeping, but then Ed slitted his eyes open, and they shone like two knife-sharp flints of aquamarine, stomach-turning and beautiful. Ed, yawning, sleeping, scratching his head.

"I'll see you next month, then?" Ed asked. "Albert says the record company expects us to get started on the album."

Baron grimaced. Grunted. Had forgotten about that. There would be no clean breaks, then.

"I know," Ed said, misunderstanding, "But the songs always come once we get working, right, pet?"

Baron hesitated. Nodded. "Right," he said at last. "Goodbye, love."

He bent over and kissed Ed on the cheek. A gentleman's kiss. And was gone.

* * *

Would take Baron two days to work up the nerve to do it. Driving around London in circles like a loon, while Ed was off to Aruba with his fat fertile wife. He *knew* rationally that it had to be done. It *had* to be done. Because Ed would never end things properly, would never have the heart to, would always say he wanted one thing, but really want another. And Baron was nothing if not wanting. Driving around. Telling himself he could be brave enough. The brick on the passenger's seat of his Rolls while he swerved through the city streets.

At last, on the second night, between one pub and another, he found himself there, outside the townhouse where he and Ed had written so many songs together, had fucked once or twice or half a dozen times, for a laugh. It wasn't very late. The streets were still crowded with pedestrians, and the fans who hung around outside Ed's gate on most nights were there, like always, and they saw Baron in his long velvet coat with the fur on the collar and one of them asked him for an autograph, but he didn't answer, feeling the weight of the brick on his hand.

Someone had a camera. The flash went off. Baron had a key to the gate. Of course he did. But he wasn't going to use it. Was going to do something better.

"You," he said, indiscriminately, to one of the girls, "Bird. You look like a strong one. Help me up that tree."

She was a husky lass and she giggled to be looked at like that by him and he could have murdered her in that moment but he didn't.

"I'm light as a feather," he said, flirting with her, and she giggled more and called her girlfriends over and they helped him up the tree, that brick weighing down his pocket, and someone took another picture as he climbed the tree swiftly, like he once climbed boyhood trees, and in a moment he was over the gate, and then dropped down into the silence on the other side.

Hesitated only a minute, thinking with a small streak of guilt of Alonzo. Well, hopefully the brick wouldn't hit him. And besides, if the cats got out through the hole in the window, through the broken glass, then they'd be better off than he was now, pissing in Ed's closets, yeah? Deciding he was right, that this was somehow noble, Baron took the brick and hurled it right through the living room window.

Then he turned. Got out his key. Opened the gate, just like that, and left it open, so that the fans could descend. They were shouting questions at him as he left, taking pictures. He didn't answer them. It was a grim thing he'd just done, he knew. A euthanasia, of sorts. His own heart breaking breaking breaking as he got back into his Rolls and drove away.

* * *

By the time they got back to London, it was old news. All over the papers. *Saffron Singer Hurls Brick Through Hammond's Windows - Songwriting Dispute or Spurned Lover?* Ed had done a good show, laughing with Genie about it, stuffing his feelings down.

Still, it was something else to see it. The brick, red and ancient - where'd Baron get it, anyway? - sitting there in the middle of the front parlor, and the mess the fans had made of the place when they'd gotten in. Pillaging his records, his food. It's a wonder the cats had survived. They circled his feet now, mewling, pitiful. They knew, Ed thought, that this was *Baron's* brick. They missed him, even now.

"Why would he *do* this?" Genie asked as she stepped over the broken glass. Ed could have almost murdered her for being so stupid. For not seeing what she had never been meant to see. For not seeing *him*.

"We had a fight over the next album," Ed said, which wasn't a lie. They were always fighting over the next album.

No, not fighting. Flirting.

"He wanted more than a split?" Genie said, and Ed looked at her, raising one eyebrow. She'd been listening, then. Sort of.

"Yeah," Ed said.

"Well, pet," Genie went on, wrapping her arms around his shoulders. "What you do with your career is up to you, but I don't know if I'd feel safe in your position, working with a man like that."

She'd known Baron for over a decade, but she talked about him like he was a stranger.

"Thanks, love," Eddie said and kissed her and felt nothing, which is what he usually felt.

"Honestly," she said, pulling away. She went to look out the front window, gazing thoughtfully. "I'm not half as angry at Baron as the fans. Thought they were better than this. Don't know what we're going to do when the baby comes. What if one of them kidnaps him?"

Ed looked at her for a long time. Thinking.

"Well," he said. "This was meant to be a surprise, for after the baby came…"

Genie turned, a bright look of questioning crossing her brow.

"I bought us a little farm," he said, and the words felt like acid on his tongue. "Scotland. Our children can be feral out there. No one will care. Our own private hideaway. What do you think about that?"

She went over to him. She kissed him. Ed kissed back, feeling nothing, still.

Lord Arran

etween his legs, Ed's moped purred as he gassed it up from London
and toward St. Albans. It was a rare rainless July day, the sky
blue and endless and Ed thought at any moment the moped might
sprout wings and fly.

But it wasn't because of the weather.

The square of newspaper felt like it was a shining gem in his back pocket, something incalculably precious, something a pirate might spend a lifetime digging through the sand to find. This morning, when he'd woken up, he'd had no idea what waited for him that day. Thought maybe a walk to Liam's, to work on the solo bits for the new songs. Thought maybe a picnic, in the park, with Genie. Fucking, maybe, up in his room, as they always fucked after a date. Dry, ruthless fucking. It wasn't that he didn't enjoy it, on some level. But it was more a box that wanted ticking, most days, and until now he'd told himself he would pay his dues with Genie to get himself what he wanted, what he needed in life. Security. Babies. His father's begrudging respect. That whole bit.

But then came a knock on the door. One of his damned fans - Dolores, he thought her name was - had gotten in past the gate again and stood there beaming with the paper.

Can I come in? she'd chirped, giggling. Because getting inside was always the ultimate goal of the fans. She'd looked back to her friends, who gave her thumbs up and peace signs and waved. Not jealous at all, just happy that one of them got to stand ever so close to *him*. And he in his pajamas and dressing gown, at that.

"No, thank you," he replied politely, because they'd all learned it was better to always be polite with them. They'd make your life hell if they felt spurned. Her face began to fall, and so he grabbed the paper before her face could collapse. Brought it in. Grabbed his tea and went up to his tidy third floor bedroom, setting his weight in his Eames chair, putting his feet up. Sipped tea. Opened paper.

Saw it.

Sat forward reading, stroking his scruff, a few days unshaved. Was sure he was mistaken. Drank more tea. Read it again.

After that, all plans were off. He dressed quickly, in his favorite blue jeans and a white undershirt. Stuffed his feet into his old cowboy boots, the ones he'd loved once, harder than hard, in Hamburg. Cheap then, and last year one of the toes had started to split, and he'd had it sent to a cobbler to have fixed but then it had only split again. Not the best for riding, maybe, but it made him feel good to wear them, and it was a day to feel good, Ed had decided. The best day.

He tore the page from the paper, stuffed it down into his back pocket.

No need to ring up Baron. What would be the point? Probably asleep, still, and he wouldn't answer his phone, anyway, even if he wasn't. He went and got the white helmet that Genie insisted he wear even for a buzz down the road, fixed it over his skull. Took a quick glance in the mirror. He looked handsome, yes, he knew. One curl down in front of his big, blue eyes. Iconic. There were times he understood it plainly, how handsome he was. Days where he felt his own worth like a song inside. All the right chords falling into all the right places. Making him feel *incredible.* Today, today was one of those days. A good day. A blessed day, his mum would say, were she alive to say it (*Would she? Well, felt good to imagine she would*). Leaving an open tin of food for the cats, not bothering with breakfast for himself, he grabbed his keys and headed out. Whistling.

A good day indeed.

* * *

Was watching the road, but not his speed. His mind was elsewhere.

Wasn't the first time. Wouldn't be the last. When the police car's sirens lit up behind him he sighed, because this always seemed to happen on this stretch of road, three or four times already, and he eased the moped into the grassy space at the edge. The air streaming by him had kept him cool before, but almost as soon as he stopped he started sweating. Thick drops down his neck and back.

Had always hated coppers. Not as much as Baron did, what with him Mum being killed by one and all. But hated them enough.

It was on account of how little respect they showed him, maybe because he was so good looking. Normal people liked him. Mums and his dad's friends and men in shops. But coppers treated him like he was a little *baby*, every time. Before he could even dismount his bike, they started shouting at him in thick East End accents and he knew he was in for it, because it was a hot day - his armpits starting to soak through already - and a beautiful day, the kind where tempers boil over if you're not cool beneath the shade. There was two of them, one that was lanky and taller than Ed was. The other small and round. The small round one was chewing on a fat slobbery piece of chewing gum, glaring as he approached. Tall Lanky, on the other hand, was jovial.

"'Ey, you, boy, d'ya know how fast you was goin'?"

Didn't. Eddie knew he should have *sirred* and all of that, but Christ, he hated coppers. Only shrugged.

"No," he said.

Tall Lanky looked at Small Round. They both laughed.

"'No,' he says!" Tall lanky said. "Too fast, that's f'certain. D'you have your papers?"

Eddie stood there, torn. They hadn't realized who he was yet. If he showed them his driving documents, he knew what would come next. One of two options. What came next would be better.

Or else it would be worse.

But they were standing there waiting. Small Round, still angry-eyed, chewing his gum. And Tall Lanky, smiling, sort of, one long hand out.

Wriggling his fingers. Eager.

Ed reached into his pocket. Pulled out his wallet. Didn't see the slip of newspaper fly out at first. None of them did. Mind elsewhere, he handed his driving license over. The Bobby opened up the little book, and his eyes went wide, and he started howling.

"Oi, Georgie, look who we've pulled over."

He showed Small Round his book. Small round snorted once, looked up at Ed, snorted again.

"Real celebrity here!" Tall lanky called out to the road behind them. "Oi, will you give me an autograph for the missus?"

Ed sighed. But really, knowing that this was the best of all possible outcomes, gave his head a nod.

"Course," he said.

"All right," said Tall Lanky. He felt around his uniform pockets, then elbowed Small Round. Georgie. Georgie took a pen from behind his ear and gave it to Tall Round, who pulled out a pad of driving tickets and handed it all back to Ed.

"What's her name?" asked Ed dully.

"Rosie," said Tall Lanky.

Dear Rosie, Ed thought, as he wrote out "Best wishes, Love Eddie Hammond" in his nicest cursive. *Go fuck yourself.*

He shoved the paper and pen back to Tall Lanky.

"Can I leave now?" he asked, squinting into the sunlight. The sweat was dripping down into his eyes, burning him. He ignored it. It didn't matter. Just needed to get out of there, before they remembered that he was rich in addition to being famous. Before the shakedown started.

"Yeh," said Tall Lanky. He was gazing at the autograph, beaming. Satisfied. For now.

Eddie stuffed his hands in the pockets of his jeans, turned on his boot heels, hustled off toward his bike.

He'd just thrown his leg over it when he heard heavy footsteps on gravel. Not Tall Lanky's. Short Round's. The sound of something being picked up, light as a leaf. Ed started up his bike, but still heard over the sound of the engine a voice thick as diesel.

"Wot's this?"

Ed could have gunned it, but instead Ed glanced over. It was a miscalculation. Small Round was looking at a square of newspaper. Squinting at it. Eyes dark and uncomprehending.

"Wait a minute, you," Small Round said to Ed. It felt like the blood had gone to sludge in his veins, despite the heat of the day. Ed killed the engine. Set fisted hands on his knees. Waited.

"Look at this, Louis," he said. He handed the paper scrap to Tall Lanky, who took it. Squinting, too. Like he didn't understand, either.

"Ey," said Louis, looking up at Ed. His lip curled. Not angry. Confused, mostly. For now. "Are you a fairy or something'?"

Ed felt his stomach squeeze. It was the question he'd been waiting for. Somehow, the question he'd never in his life been so directly asked. His hands tensed. He glanced down at his knuckles. At the grass beneath his boot soles.

"No," he muttered. Bracing himself.

"What's that, boy?" asked Georgie. Ed pressed his lips together. He was sweating, but it's like his whole body had turned to ice.

"No, sir," he said.

But the coppers were coming closer, anyway, taking out their billy clubs.

* * *

Ed knew he was lucky, really.

Lucky to have survived it. Lucky to be left in the ditch on the side of the road, with his bike still sitting there, waiting for him, and the keys and his driving license tossed into the dirt beside him. Any cash he'd had had been pilfered, but, well, that was only money, and he'd expected that from the start.

He hadn't expected the mouthful of blood and dirt, really. Though in another way, he'd been bracing himself his whole life for it.

He pulled himself painfully to his feet, spitting out gravel. Looked around for his helmet. Dented, now. It had somehow nested itself against a fence post, and looked something like a cracked-out egg. Ed moved toward it, was surprised to find out how much it hurt when he moved. His ribs, maybe broken, or at least bruised. He bent low to pick up the helmet and found himself wheezing out a wheezy cough.

Lucky, really, though, he thought to himself as he fixed the helmet back down over his aching head. Because they could have taken him in for some imagined charge, gotten the press all over it. They could have killed him, left him dead in the ditch. Could have raped him. Could have done all manner of things, terrible and imagined and all-too impossibly possible.

He sucked on his bleeding lip as he went and fetched his documents from the road. As, dizzy, he bent low, something flashed in the corner of his vision, something gray. He went and picked it up. It was the newspaper clipping, wadded up into a ball and tossed away. Very carefully, Ed unfolded it. Very carefully, he tucked it back into his pocket, where it belonged.

He got back on his moped and proceeded on his journey.

* * *

Baron had slept in. But then, Baron hadn't seen the brighter side of a morning in years. Unless the band were touring - and they didn't, anymore, not after the nonsense that had happened on their last trip to America, nearly a year ago now - he stayed in bed until ten or eleven, at the earliest. Since Cassandra Ruth had moved out, he had no reason not to, anyway. No need to look proper anymore. Could embrace the general state of sloth.

Most days, even after he woke, he'd get himself a ciggy and a tea and head back to bed, turn on the BBC, grab a guitar, write a little, maybe. Later he'd get the paper from the front walk, if he could be bothered to fetch it. If he was really feeling saucy then he'd have a wank or eat a tab of acid and lie there, staring at the ceiling tiles, trying to feel something new. Watched more tele in the evenings. Or else read a book. It's funny, how the papers had always painted him as some sort of bad boy, the worst of the bunch. On account of his skin color, he supposed, though Albert had managed to hide the truth of his origins from the press so far. Still, certain things were apparent. Apparently.

But really, at heart, he was a boring, boring man. Loved an afternoon kip in the sunroom. Loved his cats. Most days, alone out in suburbia, staring at the ceiling until the sun went down. The others were still out in the city, had girlfriends, had friends. Baron mostly kept to himself, relishing the quiet, the peace. Smoking a fag, grunting a hello to the gardener, going for a walk.

Lonesome? Sure, on some days. When he was horny, especially, yeh. Sometimes he'd call up a prostitute. Male or female, it didn't really matter to Baron. Sometimes he'd call Ed, which was better, always, when Ed came, but Ed was so often busy with Genie, and Baron always felt so wounded to be rejected when Ed said he had plans. Better sometimes not to risk it. To keep your heart to yourself.

Anyway, they'd be getting rolling on the new album soon, which meant Ed would come calling anyway, and maybe they wouldn't fuck most days, because *We have work to do, Barry, songs to write, what's the record company going to do if we're late again?* Or *I'm supposed to go to the Waller's tonight for dinner, can't risk going over there stinking of you,* and it would sting, but less than Baron would ever admit to him, because anyway, he'd be able to spend the afternoon down by the pool with Ed, strumming away together, the sunlight glinting in those sea glass eyes and Baron's gaze falling in so deep he might as well have been drowning. Ed biting his lip, trying to pick out a melody. Looking sun-burnt and beautiful.

In his sleep, Baron stirred. Pressed his hard cock to the too-big lonely mattress. Funny, how thinking about writing songs with Ed was always almost as good as thinking about fucking Ed. Wasn't far off, anyway. The rhythm of it. The dance. Waking more, Baron wrapped his hand around his cock, started thrusting into his palm. Was just getting going good when he heard the doorbell chime.

"Christ," he muttered. He lifted his head. There was pretty Peggy Jones, his blue tabby, a longhair like he was getting to be, staring away at him, one blue eye, one green.

"Can't you get it, Lady Bo?" he whined at her. She looked at him. Licked her lips. Baron sighed and let go his cock, gave the mattress one last thrust, for good measure, then rose. As the doorbell rang again, he grabbed his dressing gown, rearranged himself *justso*, and tied it tight around him. Hrm. Would have to do.

Peggy Jones padded down the hall after him, begging for breakfast. The doorbell rang again. Baron sighed. Seemed like everybody wanted something.

"I'm coming," he called.

He cracked open the door, expecting to find a delivery man or some dopey fan or six standing there.

Instead, it was Ed.

Only something had happened to him. His white shirt was dirty, one sleeve torn. His face looked dirty, too. And his skin had a weird, puffy quality that Baron had never seen before in all the years that he'd known Ed. Sometimes else was wrong, too. Baron studied him. It wasn't just the dented helmet. No, Baron realized. Ed's *lip* was split. It made Baron suck in a breath to see him like that. So... tenderized.

"Cor, what happened to you, love?" Baron asked, throwing the door open wide. Peggy Jones went running out into the day, to join rangy tomcat Waylon and sleek black Shakaboom and the rest of them. Usually he tried to keep her in - she was just a bit more delicate than the others - but today, he let her go. No tinned breakfast. She'd have to content herself on songbirds, then. His attention was on Ed.

His sometimes-lover licked his lips, then winced. Must have hurt, the way it was bleeding.

"I - I spun out on some gravel," Ed said, and Baron knew at once it was a lie, though he couldn't tell yet what the truth was. But he'd learned over the years that it was best to let Ed lie if Ed wanted to lie. Safest for all of them.

Baron leaned his face against the door for a moment, looking at Ed. Then he spun on his bare heels and headed inside.

"Well," he said, after a minute, letting his voice echo back to him. "Come in. We'll get you cleaned up."

Without waiting to hear if Ed did as he was told - mostly because he knew that Ed would - Baron went to the downstairs bathroom, the one off the kitchen, and got out the medicine kit that his uncle had gotten him as a housewarming gift when they'd bought this monster of a castle.

In case you get into any scraps, he'd said. It was a sweet gift, really. Not that Baron needed gifts, not from them. But though he had the money for it, when was he ever going to spend it on plasters and antiseptic and needles and thread? He brought the little tin box into the kitchen, where Ed was standing near the enormous center island, holding his dented helmet in hand, looking awkward.

"Sit down, pet," Baron said. Ed did as he was told, wincing as he sat on one of the breakfast stools. *Must've been some fight,* thought Baron, though it was strange. He'd never known Ed to be one for fighting. Liam, maybe. Charlie, once or twice, when he was pissed. Not Ed.

Baron washed his hands good. Splattered alcohol on a cotton ball. Came close to Ed, smelling sweat and dirt and blood on him, and dabbed it on. Ed winced as he felt the bite of it.

"That's how you know it's working," Baron said wryly, what his auntie used to say when he skinned his knee. Was strange, in a way, to be fussing over Ed like this. Nearly mothering him. Usually it was the other way around entirely. Baron looked very seriously at the way Ed's lower lip was split. The blood was bright red, still faintly pulsing with Ed's heartbeat. He could see white bits of flesh beneath. Meaty parts that weren't supposed to show.

"That might need stitches," Baron said. Ed drew back away from Baron, his eyes wide and indignant.

"I'm not letting *you* sew me up," he said. Baron laughed.

"I wouldn't dream of it. Wouldn't want to ruin your pretty face."

Ed's expression softened. It was all Baron could do not to kiss him tenderly on the mouth, just then. Would have hurt too much, he knew. Instead, Baron just lifted up a hand, cupped Ed's cheek into it. Ed sighed, leaned into the touch.

"If it still looks ugly in a few hours, you can drive me to the hospital," Ed told him. "Promise."

"Good," said Baron. He pulled back, satisfied, turned, started putting the medical kit away. Was surprised, a little, when he felt Ed's hand edge up the hem of his dressing gown. Touching the back of Baron's thigh and the seam of his Y-fronts. Baron was hard again, but then, he'd never really gone soft.

"Oh," said Baron, wryly, "Is that why you came, then?"

He heard Ed rise up from the stool, grunting a bit as he did, as though every centimeter of movement hurt. It probably did. Ed had really made a mess of himself. But not all of himself. He pressed himself against Baron's back, and Baron could feel Ed's hardness right through his jeans.

"I came to see you," Ed murmured coarsely into Baron's ear. Baron leaned back into him. Didn't say anything, not yet.

"Make love to me," Ed said gruffly, and Baron was struck by the contrast between Ed's words - tenderly phrased - and his general appearance. Bruised. Disheveled. Busted. Baron reached back, took Ed's hand in his.

"Not here," he said. "Too many sharp corners. Wouldn't want to hurt you any more'n you've hurt yourself."

"I wouldn't mind a few sharp corners," Ed said, and reached out to grab at Baron, but Baron dodged it. Ducking. Weaving. Instead, he gave Ed's hand a tug, and led him up the back staircase - the servant's staircase, the Realtor had called it - and all the way up to his room. His bed.

That grand king bed was the center of Baron's universe, even if the covers were unmade and half trailing onto the floor. It was his sacred space. His sanctuary. The tangled sheets were littered with magazines and books, and he'd left his favorite acoustic tucked up next to the pillow as if it were a wife. Now, seeing it all through Ed's eyes, he wondered if Ed found it pitiful compared to the life Ed lived.

"I don't know how you live like this," Ed said, as though he could read Baron's mind as Baron moved the guitar, set a few scattered plates on the floor. Baron hastily pulled the covers up. If Ed weren't so obviously injured, he would have just thrown him down roughly at the tease, right into that unmade bed, crumbs and plates and all. Would have stabbed his cock right into him for being so rude. But couldn't, with Ed looking the way he was, sucking the new fresh blood off his lip again. Wouldn't seem right. Felt he needed to treat him like a piece of delicate china.

Like a beloved instrument.

"I don't judge you for your choices," Baron said softly, which wasn't true but at least he never outright raised his objections. He sat Ed down on the edge of the bed and began undressing him. Peeling off his white t-shirt, unbuttoning his jeans. He could see now that Ed's whole body was reddened in splotches. He'd be black and downright blue later, but for now his pale skin looked nearly sunburned. Ed winced at every movement.

"*What* did you do to yourself?" Baron asked again. Ed just shook his head. Still lying. Still wanting to lie.

"I told you. I spun out on some gravel."

"Yeh," Baron said, pressing a hand to Ed's collarbone. "Gravel."

He could see that Ed *wanted* to wince. Probably hurt just as much as anything. But instead, defiant, Ed's blue eyes stayed steady and wide open.

"Are you going to fuck me or not?" Ed said, like a brat. Christ, Baron wanted to *slap* him. But he wouldn't. Couldn't.

"Yeh, fine," Baron said. "If you want to call that foreplay. Turn yourself over."

Ed stood up, shimmying all the way out of his jeans. He wasn't wearing pants, and his cock was rock hard already. So was Baron's. He watched Ed get onto his hands and knees. Baron felt himself throb at the sight. Ed, on all fours, open and waiting for him. His arsehole was a tight puckered knot. Baron opened up his dressing gown, getting up on the bed behind him. Pulled his cock over the waistband of his pants. Paused. He started to open Ed up with his spit-slick fingers, warming him up.

"Please, Barry," Ed said, in a voice that was more desperate than anything Baron had ever heard from Edmund Hammond *ever* before. "Just stick it in me."

Surprised, Baron stilled his hand.

"Are you sure you're alright, Hammy?" Baron asked. "I don't want to hurt -"

"Christ, just fuck me already," Ed said, and though part of Baron's heart and belly and chest were squeezed right now, doubtful, his cock was ready enough. So he withdrew his fingers, and did it. Plunged right into Ed, and Ed whimpered and twitched around him and Baron half expected Ed to stop him anyway, for the pain of it. But if anything he just drove Baron in further. Baron felt the tightness of Ed's body around him, his skin broiling hot, smelled the scent of asphalt like a perfume between them, felt his own balls tighten, his own stomach warm. He found himself taking another stroke, and another. Fucking fast, right from the start, and Ed's head cast back as he was fucked, and moaning, hot, wild moans. A cat in heat.

"Fuck," Ed said. "Fuck."

Baron said nothing, breathless, his cock moving in and out. So close already. Close enough that he was surprised when Ed came first, right down onto the covers, his knees going weak, his arms failing. Pressing himself into Baron's bed as he writhed. Making strangled, animal noises

Baron just pressed into him. Harder. Harder. Finally, at last he felt his body shake. The orgasm that came was seismic, and he felt Ed start to twitch again, his arsehole squeezing Baron, tighter than tight.

Usually now was the time for laughing, the time for kissing. Lazy and sweet and stupid, but there was no laughter, this time. They were still for a moment, neither speaking, and after another, second moment Baron realized something else was going on entirely.

Ed was *crying*.

Baron had known Ed for a decade now, and he'd seen Ed sniffle a few times when they were boys, but never once had seen Ed spill *real* tears. Ed had seen Baron cry, of course. More than once. He'd seen all seasons of Baron Templeton's tempestuous moods. But even though Ed had a reputation in the press for being soft-hearted, the most tender of the four, they all knew it wasn't true. Ed was slick - controlled. A real conniver when he wanted to be. And never, ever vulnerable. But here he was, Baron's cock still buried deep inside of him, letting out an animal bray of tears into the crook of his arm, his pillow.

"Eddie," Baron said, hearing the worry in his own voice. "Ed, you alright?"

But he was crying so hard he couldn't speak.

So Baron did the only thing he could think of. He held him, tight against his chest, until the tears were done. Until Ed's voice sobbed out to nothing, and then, shaking, he stilled. They were like that, still together, sticky with their bodies' emanations, for what felt like a long time. Until Ed was breathing normally again, his eyes open and gazing somewhere, toward some middle distance out the window.

"Hammy," Baron asked again, gentler than gentle, *What happened?*"

He knew when he asked that Ed wasn't going to answer, and he didn't. Instead, Ed just slid away from his grasp. Their bodies had already mutually softened, and though the hard mask that Ed had worn earlier was gone, now he seemed to move with a studied sort of nothingness all about his body, his face. He scooted over to the nightstand, found the pack of Baron's expensive French fags. Took one, sitting up against the headboard. Lit it. Ed wasn't much for smoking cigarettes usually, but Baron had to admit that he loved it on the rare occasions when he did. Looking so cool and handsome, split lip or no. A blond Elvis, or maybe a Brando. Baron sat beside him, and Ed passed him the Gauloise, and they passed it back and forth between them, smoking together.

"I'm not going to tell you," Ed said, his eyes not touching Baron's eyes. "Ever."

"All right," Baron said softly.

"But I came to show you something," Ed said. He took the cigarette back, took a drag. Gestured with it toward the pile of clothes on the floor as he exhaled, a short burst of foggy breath.

"It's in me trousers. Get it for me?"

Baron glanced at him. Wanted to kill this strange, still mood between them. The miasma of hurt and violence, barely contained by the brick wall that was Ed Hammond.

"There's no harm in saying please," he said, his tone coy and teasing but the teasing didn't go anywhere. Ed didn't smile or laugh. So Baron climbed down from the bed and went in Ed's pockets. Pulled out his wallet, his driving license, put both back. Checked the other one. Ah, there. A wrinkled slip of paper.

"At 5:50 am BST after a night of dubious jokes and personal clashes, a social revolution begins," Baron read, frowning. Ed exhaled the last of his cigarette smoke, then stamped the Gauloises out in the overflowing ashtray on the nightstand.

"What is this?" asked Baron. Ed's smile was wry, a bit grim.

"They're calling it 'A Charter for the Outsiders,'" he said. "They passed it, Barry. Labour."

"Passed *wot*?" Baron demanded, his eyes flashing, almost annoyed, to Ed. He was tired of hinting, dancing, secrets.

"It's not a crime anymore," Ed said, shrugging. Like it was nothing. Nothing at all. "What we do."

Baron's brow furrowed. He'd heard the rumors, of course. The scandalized newspaper stories. But he had never actually considered the possibility that Labour might *do* it.

"How?" Baron asked, and he had to sit, suddenly. Sank onto the edge of the bed. Hand rubbing at his three days unshaved jaw. Contemplating.

"Over 100 MPs stayed overnight," Ed said, then, when Baron glanced at him, he flashed an apologetic look. "I read it three times. I wanted to be sure I was understanding. Lord Abse fought for us. Worked with Lord Arran. Did you see what he said?"

Baron looked back down at the article, skimming it. Found it. Laughed a little, dryly.

"'I ask those, who have, as it were, been in bondage,'" began Baron, in a grand tone, "'And for whom the prison doors are now open to comport themselves quietly and with dignity. This is no occasion for jubilation and certainly not for celebration.' Oh, feck off." Baron gave the paper a rude gesture. Ed snorted a little.

"Keep reading," he said.

"'Any form of ostentatious behaviour now or in the future or any form of public flaunting would be utterly distasteful and would, I believe, make the sponsors of this Bill regret that they had done what they had done,'" said Baron. He raised a jagged eyebrow at Ed. "Well, then, Pet, do you have any ideas how we might propose to make them regret it?"

Ed looked at him for a long time, and Baron wondered what he might be contemplating. Some sort of rude cover for their next record, maybe. Two homos in a pornographic state, perhaps. Probably with some elaborate explanation as to why the image was art, and publicly allowable in the bedroom of every libidinous teenager in Britain. For as conventional as Ed could often be sometimes, he also had a stubborn, bratty streak. Wanted to make trouble. Wanted to do the opposite of what he was told.

He broke his gaze with Baron's, then. Went blankish, staring out the window. Bit his lip, then winced, having forgotten that he was hurt.

When he spoke it was in a small, soft voice.

"Scotland," he said simply. Baron frowned. Sat down on the edge of the bed, looking at Eddie.

"Wot?" he asked. Ed looked at him. Eyes searing like a pair of lasers, nostrils faintly flaring.

"It's time, Barry," he said. "I don't want to be away from you anymore. No more driving back and forth between London and fuck-all suburbia. I'm tired of hiding it."

Baron's belly felt squeezed. He almost couldn't believe what he was hearing. It felt so improbable. No, impossible.

"What about Genie?" he asked.

"Fuck Genie," Ed said. "Genie can fuck right off."

Somehow, Baron knew, even in that moment, that it wouldn't be so simple. But still, to *hear* Ed say it. He half felt like he was going to be sick.

"Scotland. You mean you want to find a place… for you and me?" Baron asked carefully. Ed nodded stoutly.

"You and me and the cats and three dozen sheep you can screw if I'm not enough for you." Ed said fiercely. Baron blinked. Laughed.

"No, no, I think that'll do," he said. He moved up to the head of the bed, so that he was sitting, naked, next to Eddie. Their legs stretched out in front of them, toes touching. Questions, Baron had questions. Like what this would mean for the band, for the press. For Ed's father. For Baron's auntie. For the fans. For the world.

But those, Baron decided, could wait. Right now, his toes played with Ed's toes, and silently, one arm folded over his own bare belly, he contemplated a future where it might all come together. Alonzo and Peggy Jones snoozing in front of a fire together. Ed up early every morning, making him eggs. Sitting at breakfast with their guitars and their cigarettes, forgetting to eat, almost not needing to. Surviving only on one another. Not needing anyone else.

"Hey," Ed said, "Can you hand me your guitar? I was working on something last night. Wanted to see what you think."

Baron got the guitar for Ed. Tucked in next to him. Not speaking, barely even *thinking*. Just listening to Ed.

Beautiful, bruised Ed.

Rip It Up

The problem wasn't that Baron hated to tour.

The problem was that Ed loved it.

Wasn't he always the one who lingered in the dressing room long after the shows were over, his make-up somehow, improbably, not entirely sweated off? Sitting surrounded by birds, Ed would insist on staying just a bit longer and just a bit longer still, offering extra autographs to give to mums or mum's friends or hairdressers or the cleaning woman. Whomever. He'd grab up whatever guitar was closest, not necessarily his own, offering them private songs, and how could they resist it? Looking up at him with adoring eyes, knickers all soaked through. He'd last long after the other lads had begged off to bar or bed with some floozy or another, eager to close the deal. But Ed was all foreplay with the fans, or mostly foreplay, basking in their adoration. Ed was the one who wanted the show to go on and on and on. Always did. Always would.

Always the charmer. Kissing the ring of some portly mayor's wife. Laying hands on children in wheelchairs like he thought he could actually heal them. And when the rest of them let out giggles, stoned half out of their gourds, Ed would shoot them dagger-eyes. Angry at them for breaking character.

Truth be told, Baron and Liam and Charlie, when they were on tour together, could have survived without speaking to anyone else. Sure, they participated in the general Satyricon of the thing. Sticking it indiscriminately into a bird or three or four. But they didn't ever really want to *talk* to them. They had learned quickly enough that not their roadies nor the road hogs nor the management nor the opening acts understood what it was to *be* Saffron. How could they? The four lads from Liverpool were no longer considered really human. Untouchable - or else existing only to be touched. Everyone wanted something from them. Money. A lock of hair. An autograph. A fuck. A song. Money again. In a way, it was like they'd become, in fame, public property, incapable of normal human interaction. Except with each other.

Why, then, did Ed insist on chatting with the birds before fucking them? With sharing their drugs with the openers, giving them advice on their next albums?

"I don't see the harm in it," he'd say. "They're nice blokes. I'm just helping them."

The kind of argument that was useless to have, because it was, on its surface, so perfectly reasonable. When they'd found themselves in a world without much reason at all, without sense.

By '65 it no longer mattered what they sounded like, what they sang. No way to make the music sound like it did on the albums anymore, and besides, no one was listening any more neither. They were all looking at them with eyes wet with yearning, and screaming for them with mouths full of teeth. Baron couldn't tell you where or when his own feelings had shifted. Once upon a time it had been pleasant to be up there with Ed. The two of them harmonizing, sharing *their* songs - their love, their art - with the world. But then things had changed. Gotten bigger, more beastly. Somewhere between Hamburg and their second tour of America, Baron's feelings had shifted too. He decided he hated it worse than the others, but then, they all knew that. Wasn't easy to hide, when he spent the day before almost every show either shitting or puking his brains out with nerves.

But it was a box he had to check. For the money. For the band. For Ed.

At some point, though, Baron realized he wasn't alone.

Winter, '66. January, when the suits got them into their offices to discuss their next tour.

"I just don't see why we have to do it anymore," Liam had protested, after it had already mostly been decided for them. *Liam*, for chrissake, who may have whined a bit but never raised real problems with anybody. Their manager Al had given a glance to the man behind him, but it had been Ed who answered.

"C'mon, son," Ed had said gently, "Don't you think we owe it to the fans? They've grown up with us, right? They want to see how our music has changed. How we've changed, too."

"They can see us on tele!" Liam insisted, but Ed just shook his head.

"You know we sell more records this way."

That had settled it for Liam, the money bit. As if they didn't have enough money already. Baron had watched this all in the meeting, saying nothing, one foot rudely up on the meeting table, his hands folded in front of his belly. Nobody had said nothing about neither foot nor silence. Baron had realized, sometime in the last few years, that he could be as rude as he wanted, as silent as he wanted, as drunk as he wanted, if he wanted to be drunk. Hell, he could spit on their carpet and wipe his boogers on his chair if he felt like it. The suited men had come to accept whatever version of Baron he chose to give them. Because of the money, you see. The money he had (somewhere, supposedly, never felt like he got enough of it before the taxman came), the money he was making for them.

Money, money, money. It was all money to all of them. But Baron watched Ed, contemplated Ed. Ed cared about money, Baron knew. But he could tell that there was something else here besides the cash of it.

Couldn't have just been the cash of it. Had to be love.

Nobody asked Baron how he felt about touring at that meeting. Nobody had to. They all knew. It had been enough at first to grin and bear it. Or to do it for the rest of them, who always seemed to be having fun. And oh, there would be bits of joy to steal here and there. Flirting with Ed at a press conference, seeing who wouldn't notice. Mucking up the lyrics to their songs intentionally, singing them dirty. Seeing who wouldn't notice. The drugs and the dancing sometimes. After. And then, of course, there was being with Ed. On stage, and backstage, and on the tarmac. Not holding hands or kissing. But *being* there. Seeing how Ed shined.

But he never really got over the terror. Something about the hunger of all those eyes and hands, the stench of teenage girl bodies hanging like a cloud over them, and the *screamin'*. The rushing from place to place in disguise or with decoys, keeping their heads down, trying to outrun the hands. Sounds fun until you live it. Then you realize it's its own kind of hell. Sometimes a blade would appear out of nowhere and snip off a lock of hair or a square of fabric. Somewhere deep down in his belly Baron always feared a worser kind of blade would appear. Or, when they were in America, a gun, perhaps. He was jumpy, ill at ease on tour. He hardly ever stopped smoking. His jokes with the press were terse and sometimes nonsensical. But nobody noticed. And if they noticed, nobody cared.

In January, the suits plotted out their summer for them. The continent first, again, then Japan, then over to America via California. They'd do a roundabout loop, finally landing in New York City, then back home to wrap it all up. 8 weeks of hell, the whole summer, thereabouts. But then they'd have a lovely autumn free to work on the new album and whatever was going to come next.

Rinse. Repeat.

Baron was bored of it by the time they reached Japan. By California, he was halfway dead. He was losing weight already, from the shitting, and the muscle relaxers Al's assistant had given him made him feel like a zombie. Sometimes he'd be up there in some stadium meant for American football players to murder each other, squinting into the stage lights and he'd feel certain that his soul had left his body. Hearing the roar of it, watching the flashbulbs, in the distance, explode. Once in Texas he just stopped playing mid-song, staring out in dumb confusion. Until Ed went over to him, put a hand on his shoulder, squeezed, hard. Not a friendly squeeze.

"It seems our Barry forgot the words again," he offered into the microphone, a tease, or a warning, hard to tell which. "Let's see if you darlings can help him."

Backstage that night, Ed was *pissed*. Practically threw his bass guitar at their road manager, loosening his tie. Baron slumped down in the makeup chair, pretending not to notice. Didn't matter. Didn't help.

"Christ, what's *wrong* with you, Barry?" Ed asked. Baron signaled to Al's assistant Sheila Jean to get him a drink. Didn't say anything, not at first.

"Leave him alone, Ed," Liam said, wiping off his makeup. "It's not like anybody noticed."

"*I* noticed," Ed said. The fans had come streaming in then in their customary fashion, waving their tits and their autograph books, cutting the argument short. Baron signed his name on a few slips of paper, sucked his bourbon down. Looked at Ed, who sat like a king surrounded by his subjects. Got up without another word to anyone else and walked off to the bathrooms. Didn't come out of the stalls until Charlie knocked on the stall door to let him know that the limousines had arrived to take them back to their hotel.

* * *

He thought about how to tell him. Wanted to. Sat on the bus, contemplating it. Watching Ed play his acoustic, quietly to himself, lovingly.

Can't do this anymore. It's killin' me soul, Ed. The problem isn't the music. Or you. The problem is I can't do this. I'll die.

Ed looked up and toward him like he could read Baron's thoughts. But Baron only looked away.

* * *

They were still in the middle bits of America moving toward Chicago when the mood began to shift. Darkening. Worsening. Baron read about it in the papers first. The riots on the west side, where the police had nearly killed a boy. Well, not a boy. A young man. Only 21. But Baron was 26 now and felt a certain kind of tenderness toward him, protective, when he read. Somehow, the youth of the city had heard about it, taken up the cause. Surrounding the coppers, demanding that they let the boy go free. But then they all went wild. Feral, like dogs, the papers said. Looting and smashing, the papers said. Throwing stones. Firing shots.

It was a press conference in Memphis when they were asked about it. Usually their press interviews were puff pieces, all about *when will the bubble burst* and *what made you decide to quit wearing leather?* But for some reason on that day a bird-boned woman with the *Star* looked right at Baron, and asked him if he'd heard of the riots.

"Of course I read about it," Baron said. "I'm not some kind of ignorant swine."

"Of course not," the woman said, her smile small - but pointed. "But I wondered, given your race, if you have any thoughts to share on the situation?"

My race? Baron frowned, licking his lips. Wasn't the first time a reporter had said something like that here in America. Never knew what to think of it. "As a member of the human race," Baron said, leaning into the microphone, "I hope that police officers learn in whatever country they serve to leave innocent Black boys alone."

There were murmurs from the reporters, flash bulbs. Somehow, Baron knew as soon as he had said it that it was the wrong thing to say. But. Well. It was true, wasn't it? He smoked on his cigarette, looking dead ahead. Not turning sidelong to where Ed sat, staring at him. Stunned.

"Good thing you're already the controversial one," Albert told him after.

"Wot?" said Baron, "Was I supposed to lie? Call those boys 'animals,' scold them, tell them to behave themselves, just because they're Negros?"

"Baron, darling," Albert said, and patted him on the cheek. "I never expect you to be anything but yourself."

Baron winced. Noticed how Ed was standing there, in the corner of his vision, watching him. Like he wanted to say something. But he didn't.

* * *

At the show that night, the usual mob scene. But a difference. Halfway through the set someone started throwing eggs. They didn't know where they was coming from at first until security could catch them - a pair of little shitty teenage boys, being teenage boys - and haul them off. None of the eggs hit the band except one, which landed on Ed's favorite shoes.

"They was right to be offended," Baron told him, between songs. "They really *are* hideous shoes."

* * *

By the time they reached Indianapolis it was all over the national papers, Baron's comment. Everywhere. At the press conference it was all anybody wanted to talk about.

"Mr. Templeton, what did you mean by that?"

"Meant what I said. I'm not sorry I said it. It's true."

"You know," Ed added, in a mumbly voice, "His mother was killed by a police officer. Hit and run. Terrible tragedy."

Baron shot him a look. What right was it of Ed's, to air Baron's sad, soggy life story *here*?

"Yes, but surely you could have acted in some consideration of those officers' families who-"

"Look, all I said was that innocent men - "

"'Innocent Black boys,'" the reporter interjected again. "Those were your words."

"Yes, right. Well, they need to be allowed to live their lives in peace."

"As a Negro, do you find it easier in England than you do here?"

Baron looked up, squinting into the crowd of reporters through his sunglasses. Who had said that? What were they *talkin'* about, anyway?

"England's my home," he said, a muddled response. As muddled as he felt. He saw Ed take his mic, leaning his mouth right up against it.

"I can answer that," Ed said. "We've never been treated as anything but gentlemen, all of us, in any country we've visited."

"Thank you, no more questions," shouted Albert. The other three were getting up, heading off toward the backstage area where they would get ready for the show that night, only a few hours away. But Baron's motions felt slow, exaggerated. *As a Negro?* Sure, folks had commented on the color of his skin before, but he'd never been called a *Negro*.

"Barry," Ed called out to him, just as he stepped through the door, but Baron was thinking about the show ahead. His stomach hurt.

"I need to take a shit," he responded dryly, crassly, and he walked off without hearing what Ed had to say.

***

Most nights on tour Ed Hammond took a bird or three to bed. And sure, the fucking was fun. He couldn't say that wasn't part of it. But it was mostly because of the sleeping. Ed *hated* to sleep alone. Had never known the quiet of an empty room in childhood. At his flat now, he got through it thanks to the cats. Fancy puss Alonzo, his secret favorite, a gift from Barry given expressly for the purpose of giving him someone to snuggle at night. And then Hoagy and Jelly Roll, who joined last year. They'd tuck in with him at night, or else tussle, yowling, on the floor beneath his bed, and wake him up drooling in his face asking to be let out or fed, and that was the only way he managed, really, to sleep, with the lively noise of it. Before cats he tossed and turned all night, the emptiness of his bedroom feeling to Ed more like a tomb more than a place of real respite.

But on tour, no cats. Nothing worse than an empty hotel room, an empty bed, nothing inside it but the sound of his own heart beating in his ears. Thinking about dying, because he always thought about dying when he was alone at night. How someday, that heart would go still, and his field of vision would narrow - and then what? The world would march on? And he'd never know? It made his chest feel tight. So he didn't think about it. He distracted himself with girls, with screwing.

But not that night. Indianapolis. In Ed's honest opinion, they'd been playing like crap all tour. The other three weren't even bothering to fake it anymore. Baron dropping songs mid-verse, just standing there like some kind of zombie. Liam chewing gum on stage, sometimes spitting it out on the floor for one of the others to step in. Charlie dragging the beat left and right. And in a way, Ed couldn't blame them. It's not like anyone could even hear if the songs were going wrong. But Christ, they could have tried. They could have *pretended* to care. He'd been gearing up to say something to them about it, to give them a real rouser of a speech. But then came Baron's comments in Memphis, and the eggs, and then the thing that reporter said to him before the show. Calling Baron a Negro. And Baron's befuddled look in response, like he couldn't quite make 2 and 2 make 4.

Who could blame Baron *that* night when he sounded like crap? His Ricky went out of tune halfway into the second song and he didn't bother tuning it, even, and Ed didn't bother telling him that night, because he had other things on his mind.

How to tell Baron the truth.

That night, Ed cut things short*er*, at least, with the fans backstage. He could see that the others were surprised when he tucked it in earlyish, when he didn't drag a bird into the limo like he normally did, whatever choice cut he wanted, a dark-eyed beauty, usually. No, no, tonight, Ed was alone.

"Alright, Ed?" Liam had asked and Ed laughed.

"Yeh, felt like I needed my beauty rest tonight."

He looked at Baron, pointedly, he thought, but Baron was instead just staring out the window, watching the city stream past.

Maybe he should have followed Baron right up. But Baron was closed to him and Ed didn't feel brave enough yet. He went to the hotel bar, drank a Scotch, resisted the urge to flirt with some socialites who were whispering to one another about how *he* was sitting there. Would have been so easy to distract himself. No. Not tonight. He ordered another. A double. Ate some pretzels out of a little bowl. Pretended not to be himself for a moment, pretending to be an ordinary, lonely schlub.

At last an hour or so later he went upstairs. Ignoring the whispering family in the elevator, he went up to the penthouse suites, which were only for them, their party. Went to his own room first, to wash off his make-up and get out of his wide-lapeled suit and paisley tie and don instead a white t-shirt and a pair of jeans. No shoes or socks. Ed hated shoes. Needed to be comfortable. To say what he had to say.

At last he went across the hallway. Knocked on the hotel room door, once, twice. After a pause, a rustle, a muffled voice came back.

"'Minute."

Ed waited.

The door opened up. There was Baron in a dressing gown, smoking a fag. Christ, Ed loved to watch him smoke, how his neck went long and his eyes foggy.

"Wot," Baron asked, his voice flat and miserable. Ed sighed. He could feel already that this wouldn't be an easy conversation.

"Can I come in?" he asked. But Baron just stood there for a moment, and that's when Ed heard a voice rise up from the darkness of the room behind him.

"Oh, does your friend want to join us?"

Ed frowned. He leaned past Baron, peeking. There was someone in Baron's bed. Not a bird. A man. Or a boy, really, almost. A teenager of some stripe. Sitting in a pile of blankets. Shirtless and handsome.

A boy in Baron's bed. Not a bird. A boy, who wasn't Ed.

"No," Baron said flatly, and Ed wasn't sure who he was answering. The bloke or Baron.

Ed exhaled hard, rubbed his hands against his face. He should have known that this sort of thing happened. Probably. With boys, not birds, too. But he hadn't - well, he hadn't ever *thought* about it, and hadn't ever *asked*, and Baron had never brought it up and and and there was a boy in Baron's bed, on tour. A boy that wasn't him.

No, no, *focus*, Ed, he told himself. He was here to *talk* to Baron. To tell him something important.

"I need to tell you something. Something about what happened tonight."

"If you're here to harangue me about me playing, I don't care, and I don't want to hear it," Baron said. "They wanted a show. We gave them a show. What's it matter if the strings are tuned? They don't give a fuck."

Ed knew then that Baron had let his Ricky go flat *on purpose*. Not just forgetting. But deliberate. He felt a flash of anger at that, but stuffed it down. Christ. This wasn't what he'd come for, either.

(A boy. A boy in Baron's bed. A boy that wasn't him.)

"No, damn it," Ed said. Why did Baron have to make this so hard? "That's *not* why I've come to talk to you."

"Why then?" Baron asked, taking another drag.

Ed wished he was more of a smoker, wished he had a cigarette, or maybe a joint right now - which he did, in his room, half a dozen of them left unsmoked. The alcohol hadn't helped, really. Had somehow made him feel only sloppier, more on edge.

"It's - it's what they've been sayin' to you, Barry," Ed said finally. "The reporters. What they've been *callin'* you."

Baron stopped smoking for a moment, resting his hand on the door jam. Narrowing his eyes at Ed.

"Negro. The reporter tonight called me a Negro," he said.

Ed's anxiety was all piling up. Worser and worser, higher and higher. "Yeh," he said. He was starting to talk too fast, too much. He could feel it. "And all these years, I thought, *He* has *to know. They must have told him.* But I realized today - they must not have, Barry, and *I* know, and I've been a coward, in not telling you. They're cowards too, but I - I should have told you. All these years, and me knowing."

"What're you going on about?" Baron asked. His eyes going even narrower. Careful. He was being careful. Right now, they could both walk a line, one they were used to walking about other things. Plausible deniability. But someone had to come out and say it. Right?

Still, Ed's mouth and mind weren't going to make it easy for him. Talking and talking. Entirely too much.

"Your Auntie told me. Years and years ago - it was right after your mum died. She's known, they all *know*, and no one *told you*, including me. Christ, Barry, I'm sorry. You deserved to be told sooner. Not now, by me, like this."

"Damn it, Ed," Baron said, raising his voice enough that Eddie jumped at the sound of it. When he did, Baron glanced back to the man in his room. Flashed teeth. Said, "Sorry." Then turned back to Eddie. "Just spit it out."

"You're Black, Baron," Ed said. What a ridiculous thing to find oneself saying, to find oneself telling someone else. "Or at least Mixed. Your dad - your Auntie told me. His mom was from one of the island colonies. Trinidad or Jamaica. One of them. I don't know about his dad, or anything like that. Maybe your father was half. I suppose that would make you a quarter. But your Auntie told me. She said she thought you knew. *I* thought you must have known. Never giving a straight answer to anyone about it. But - "

Baron wrapped an arm around himself, taking one last long drag of his cigarette. Put it out on the door jam. Hugged himself.

"No," he said softly. "Didn't know. Suspected. Didn't know."

"Oh, Baron," Ed said, softly, too, back, "I'm so sorry -"

But Baron flashed a hand at him. Dismissive. Waving it away.

"Right," he said. "Thanks, Ed."

Then he let the door slam shut right in Eddie's face.

Ed stood there for a moment longer, not saying anything. At last, he dragged his bare feet back to his room. Got on the phone. Dialed Sheila Jean.

"Hello, Sheila?" he asked. She wasn't asleep yet. Her voice came purring back to him, flirty and familiar. They always flirted, but it was more like flirting with one of our kid's girlfriends than a real flirt.

"Edmund?" she asked.

"Yeah. I'd like you to get me someone tonight." A long pause. And then her surprised voice. It had been awhile, actually, since he'd needed her help at that.

"A bird?" she asked. "The usual sort?"

A long pause. Longer than long. Ed sighed.

"No," he said. "A bloke. You know," as if she didn't, "A man."

There was a very, very long pause now. It felt like it stretched on forever. Ed had never, ever asked for that. Not once.

"Oh," she said. "Do you - I mean, dark hair and eyes, olive skin? Small, like - like with the birds?"

Now it was obvious what he'd always been asking for. If it hadn't been before. Someone who looked like Baron.

"Yeah," he said, as if he didn't really care. Like he was ordering room service and had just been offered cream and sugar with his tea. "Sure. That'd be great."

"Okay," Sheila Jean said, and hung up fast.

Didn't take long for the bloke to get there. Twenty minutes, maybe. And, oh, it was *fine*. Like having a bird or three was fine. Was nice, in a way, the novelty, of being fucked instead of fucking. Had been too long on that count, because he and Baron almost never fucked on tour. Too dangerous. Too many eyes all around. This, though, a bit different. Discreet. Private. Uncomplicated though of course that was a lie. Of course it was complicated, too. But.

Well, it was fine. He enjoyed it. But when the man fell asleep in the bed beside him, Ed listened to him breathing, and even *he* couldn't fool himself into thinking it was Baron. Because it wasn't. It was someone else.

* * *

Chicago. Ed was worried on the bus over because of what he'd told Baron that it would all go wrong. And on the bus over they didn't speak to each other, but if anything, Baron actually seemed *lighter* than he had for months now. Cracking jokes. Teasing Liam, Wrestling with Charlie in a rest stop parking lot when he'd stopped to take a piss at the side of the road.

Baron didn't talk to Ed, though. Would barely even look at him. And Ed, well… somewhere, deep down inside, it felt like he'd broken a promise between them inviting that stranger into his bed. Not Baron. He'd expected it from Baron. But he hadn't ever expected it from himself. He wasn't *queer* like Baron was queer, and it was one thing to fuck Genie or a fan but it was another to *be* fucked by somebody else.

Christ. Fuck. The guilt on his Catholic heart. Heavy at breaking a promise he didn't know he'd even made.

But Baron. Well, he seemed alright, all things considered. Looser. In the customary press conference before the show, he dodged any questions about the riots. About himself. Was cutting and charming, maybe smiling just a little *too* much, what Ed knew, in other circumstances, might have been a dangerous mood. But he'd take it, really. Could have used a decent show.

And at first it seemed it was. Better than it had been in ages. Christ, when Barry was on he was *on*. Shaking his tail feathers, letting his jangle hand go jangle jangle jang, hitting every note perfect. And when Barry was on, he was infectious, too, like the best kind of disease. Dancing in front of the drum kit to keep dear ol' Chuckie darling on beat. Kneeling in front of Liam during his solo. Faux-fellating him, an old joke from Hamburg. Had been years since he'd pulled that one out. Liam, blushing, but not flubbing a single note. Rocking it. *Yeh.* Ed could have gotten used to that.

"Alright, chickadees," Baron said into the microphone, sweating like a maniac between songs. "This next song is by my good brother Little Richard. An old one, from the vaults. But I know me mate Eddie can 'Rip It Up.'"

Baron looked at Ed, quickly, directly, for the first time in two days. And Ed? Well, surprised at this, sure. Had been years since they played any covers. From the vaults, indeed. But Baron was bringing it. Ed, Ed, he needed to bring it then, too.

Ed glanced at Liam, at Charlie, who nodded, both, turned back to the microphone. Started them off.

"Well it's Saturday night…" He began, and Christ, if it wasn't *working*. The crowd, going bananas, just absolutely batty, and Ed's voice louder and rawer than it had been on stage in years and getting into the groove of it, the four of them, Ed's voice and bass notes and Liam and the drum beat and Baron Baron Baron banging away on his guitar and Ed was just getting to his favorite part of the song, the part about being a *happy soul* when suddenly there was a noise, louder than loud, and it somehow blotted out even the drums, even the crowd, even the four of them, and what Ed first thought was *gunshot* and they all looked instinctively at Baron, who was looking around as confused as the rest of them, but playing somehow, still, and Ed heard someone scream something distinct through the ringing in his ears, faint and yet somehow percussive.

"Nigger-lover!"

And he saw something strike the ground by his feet. Bright red, like a fat candle, with a flame on one end.

"Crap!" Ed screamed, and kicked it forward with his shoe, and the firecracker went off as it was spinning halfway off the stage, and there was another boom and his ears went screaming again, but somehow, against all rationality, he realized they were still *playing*, the four of them, that he was counting off his missed beat in his head. And somehow he managed to join in on the next bar, because it's what they *did*, Saffron, the band, no matter what they were feeling or how fucked up they were. They just. Played. On.

No jokes between songs, though. Baron, shaking beside the microphone as he stiffly introduced the next, and the next, until by some silent agreement Ed took over. Somehow, though, they did it. They got through the set. Bowed, all four of them, quickly.

No encores.

They rushed from the stage. As soon as Baron spotted Albert, he shouted to him.

"'Ey, no fans tonight!"

Albert nodded at that, went off to secure the doors.

They all put down their instruments one by one, standing scattered about, not talking, no one knowing what to do or say until at last, Baron put his hands over his face, shouting into them.

"Fuck! *Fuck!*"

Liam and Charlie went over to him, patting his shoulder, there-thereing Baron. But Ed just stood there in the dressing room, shaking, watching.

✳ ✳ ✳

Another night, another limousine ride to another hotel. But this time, no birds. And this time, Eddie didn't hesitate. Didn't go down to the hotel bar for courage. Didn't set himself apart from the rest of them. From Baron. Instead, the four took a silent ride up the silent elevator together, and while Charlie and Liam went directly to their own suites, Ed just followed Baron, like he was supposed to, right up to his door.

"What're you doing?" Baron asked as he stood fumbling with his keys.

"Comforting you," Ed said in a low voice. Baron said not a single word. Got the door open, finally. Opened it for both of them.

"Shut it," he told Ed, as he stepped inside and started immediately stripping off his clothes. Ed did. Locked it. Began to take off his own shoes, his socks, then loosen his tie.

"I don't want to talk until we're done fucking," Baron said. Ed's hands hesitated on his tie knot for a moment. But only a moment. In truth, part of him knew that the two of them could use quite a bit more fucking, and a bit less talking, too.

"Alright," he said. Ed's tie loose now and breathing a little better, he looked across the room at Baron. Baron, shirtless, his trousers undone, and as he stepped closer to Ed it was so bleedin' *obvious* the differences. Baron's lean, muscular chest. Brown. The coarseness of the black hair on his chest, his belly, the trail leading down. Stepping closer and closer to Eddie. Still moving slow as he reached out, unbuttoned Ed's shirt. Revealed Ed's soft, pale belly, his pink nipples, his own soft hairs, so pale as to almost be invisible. Baron, sliding the shirt off Ed and onto the floor, sliding warm, strong hands around Ed's back, kissing him. Softly at first, all lips, on the mouth. And then, all at once, with fierceness, and Ed kissing fiercely back, as Baron's small, lithe body shoved Ed's softer, larger body up against the hotel door. Kisses turning into *bites*, teeth against Ed's neck and throat, and fierce hands forceful, grasping at Ed's love handles, his belly, scratching a line downward to Ed's hardening cock. Getting them both out. Holding them against each other, their skin mutually broiling hot and hard as hell and and and

"Foock, Baron," Ed breathed, his knees feeling weak and wobbly already and when he slitted open his eyes he could see the heads of their cocks, pressed up against each other, and Baron's smile, jagged, wicked, teasing.

"What's that?" he purred. "You want me to fuck you?"

Ed started to nod. Frantically nodding.

"Say it," Baron hissed out, squeezing their cocks harder.

"F-fuck me, Baron," Ed barely managed to stutter out. When Baron started to turn him around, Ed let out a ragged laugh.

"I thought you didn't want me to talk-" Ed said, but the last word got cut short as Baron dropped Ed's trousers and ran his cock along the seam of Ed's body.

"Shut it," Baron said. So Eddie did.

He was too dry, and it hurt when Baron shoved it into him, and though he heard himself let out a whimper, that only seemed to make Baron harder, and it made him harder too at first, and at first Ed thought that the adrenaline would carry them both, but then Baron kept plowing and plowing into him, and the pain started to eclipse everything else.

"Stop," he finally let out a coarse whisper. "Baron, stop."

Baron, to his credit, did.

"Sorry, Ed," he said softly, pulling out. Ed shivered, let Baron take his hand and lead him to the bed then. Let him lie him down on his belly. Apologizin', over and over.

"Sorry, love," he was saying, kissing a line down Ed's back. "Sorry."

And Ed was going to tell him to stop apologizing, but then Baron's mouth was kissing in between his cheeks, and Baron's mouth was kissing his arsehole, gently now, and Baron's tongue began weaving in and out, erasing every memory of pain, and Ed was moaning again, long, mumbly, endless moans, and he was ready now and Baron knew it, and Barry got on top of him, and this time, when he slipped it inside, he went slow. More making love than fucking, for the first time in a long time. Slow, slow, tender, both of them shuddering together with every thrust, their bodies sweetly throbbing, and Ed was just thinking that he could have done it all night when Baron came, surprising him, lying twitching on top of him, moaning and moaning, and after a moment, pulling out of him, kissing his shoulder.

"You didn't come yet?" he asked Ed. Ed, right on the edge still, shook his head. Baron sat back for a moment, stroking Ed's lower back, feeling the slope of his body. Then gestured for him to turn over. Went down on him, slowly, slowly, taking him all in. Ed sat back, feeling Baron's mouth envelop him. Only took a few strokes before his balls went tight and legs began trembling and he lost it in Baron's mouth. Baron, sucking it down deeper still. Swallowing him.

After, Baron laid half on top of Ed. Pulled the covers up over them both. In the dark under the blankets, there was no difference between their bodies. Only the same sweet softness possessed by both sets of skin. Ed kissed the crown of Baron's head, hugging him. Snuggling him. Oh, what a sap he was.

But it's all he ever wanted to do. To have a bleedin' *snuggle*.

"You were a nutter out there tonight," Ed said at last. "On stage. Before…" He trailed off, not wanting to say it. Not needing to. "Well, a real nutter."

Baron gave a small, quiet laugh. "Y'know why?"

"No?"

Barry sat up a little, looking at Ed. "I called me Auntie Deedz up yesterday," he said. Ed's eyes widened.

"You didn't."

"Yeh. Really tore her a new one. Screamed at her until she hung up on me. I know in a way I was losing doing it. Confirming everything she thinks about me. About men like me. Black men, you know? But, *fuck*, if it didn't feel good."

Ed laughed soft little laugh as Baron laid back down against him.

"Christ," Baron said. "What a thing to keep from a boy."

Ed pressed his lips together. Feeling a tug of guilt.

"Sorry," he said.

"Yeh?" asked Baron wryly. "Well, you too. Could have told me sometime back in bleedin' '58 if you wanted to. Probably looked like a fool to you."

"Sorry," he said again. "No, not like a fool. You didn't."

"Yeah, well," Baron said. "Still, should've told me. Before we found ourselves *here*."

Ed squeezed him a little. Baron was right, of course. But he couldn't change time.

A pause, both of their hearts beating together. Then Baron softly asked, "Did it bother you, what they shouted at you? At the concert tonight? When they threw that firecracker?"

Ed didn't even have to think about it. "No," he said. "It didn't bother me. Bothered me that they *said* it to you like that. But *it's* never bothered me."

Baron grunted. But it was a pleased sort of grunt. "Right," he said. "Well then."

Ed kissed his head again, enjoying the smell of Baron, the musk of him. But then remembered something. Bit his lip.

"Barry?"

"Mmm?"

"I probably shouldn't ask this," Ed said, but then did, before he could regret it. "The man you had in your room the other night. Was he - was he better'n me?"

Now, a less happy grunt. "No, you shouldn't arsk," Baron said. "Have I asked you about any of your orgies? About how it is to stick it in Genie? Have I ever arsked you about that?"

"No," Ed said lowly.

"Well, you shouldn't arsk either. He's a whore. How d'ya think he was? He fucked me senseless and then I fucked him. Got my money's worth. It were fine, as fucking goes. Wasn't the same as what you and me do, Ed. But then I don't think any two people ever do it the same way. Isn't that the magic of it? Like music?"

"Mm," Ed said. Regretting asking, even though he knew Baron was right. Was his fault, really, for wondering. For wanting to be puffed up, in a way that Baron was incapable of puffing.

"Anyway," Baron said, glancing up, and Ed could see in Baron's eyes the hint of a wicked smile. "What about the man that *you* had in *your* bed the other night?"

Even as he held Baron against him, Ed's hands went cold.

"You knew about that?"

"Sheila Jean couldn't wait to tell me," he said. "Our kid Ed, a fruit."

Ed winced to hear it put that way. To imagine it being said. Maybe not just to Baron, if she told Baron. Maybe to Charlie or Albert or the roadies or anyone who would have listened.

"Oh, don't look like that," Baron said, rolling his eyes. "She only told me because she thought maybe I could *help* you, somehow. To come to love yourself or some fresh crap like that. Y'know. The way I love myself."

Ed snorted a bit of laughter. They both knew how Baron felt about most parts of himself. Squeamish. Full of loathing. Still, it wasn't the queerness, really, that bothered Baron, and maybe in some universe where Ed's proclivities were news to him, Baron would have been able to help. Y'know, had Baron not been the precise source of the *problem*, as it were.

"Well?" said Baron after a moment.

"Well, what?" said Ed. Baron laughed.

"Well, c'mon, how was he?"

He sensed Baron's excitement to hear about it. Not the cloying neediness Ed knew underlaid *his* questions but a libidinous sort of curiosity. Wanting to know. Wanting to imagine. Ed felt himself turning redder than red. Wanted to die there in Baron's hotel bed, right alongside the bedbugs and the pubic lice.

"Yeah, he was alright," Ed admitted, not being able to fully lie and say he *didn't* like it.

"Alright," Baron said, grinning. "Good. You know, I only ever want you to be happy, Edmund. It's all I ever want for you."

"But he wasn't you," Ed added quickly, ignoring the sappiness of what Baron had just said. "None of them ever are, you know."

"Well, I wouldn't expect them to be." A pause. Baron glanced at Ed, frowning. "Do you?"

Ed wasn't sure what to say to that. He didn't *expect* it, of course. He knew, more than anyone, that Baron was one-of-a-kind. But somehow, in his deepest, most secret and locked away heart, he kept hoping that someday, sticking it in someone else - or being stuck - would make him feel the way it felt when him and Baron screwed around. That someone would grab onto his heart like Baron had, way back in 1957. That someone else would distract him from it. Make it easier. Somehow.

"No, of course not, Barry," Ed began. "Me and you, I mean, us - "

He didn't know how to finish that sentence. But he didn't hafta.

"Yeah," said Baron, cutting him off. And they both laid there in that bed, feeling the same way.

Together.

* * *

Didn't fuck again that night. But kissed, on and off, between sleeping. Sweet, spitty kisses, warm and gentle after the violence of what had happened that night - the implied violence of what *could* have happened, what they'd all feared. To not sleep alone, that's all that Ed ever wanted, he'd told himself, had lied to himself, but in truth, what he wanted, truly, was to sleep like this. With Baron. Next to Baron. Kissing Baron, because Baron was right there, and why not kiss him when he was so very, very close at hand?

* * *

Ed woke very early. Not yet five according to the hotel clock, and for a moment the bed felt excruciatingly cold and he thought Baron had left him there alone and gone elsewhere, until he turned over and saw the lean rectangle of Baron's bare back, as Baron sat perched on the other side of the bed and smoked away at a cigarette.

"You're up," Ed said. Baron sighed, ashing on the carpet. Exhaled. Didn't look at Ed.

"Couldn't sleep anymore," he said. "Know I need to tell ya something, Edmund. Don't know how to do it."

Eddie sat up. What could there be left to be said that hadn't been said already? But then Eddie realized that there *was* something. Something obvious. Something that had hung between them for a long time, like a bad moon, an ominous portent.

"You don't want to tour anymore," Ed said. Baron was still for a moment. Took a drag. Exhaled again. Nodded.

"It's not a matter of wanting or not wanting," Baron said. "Until yesterday, if I could have forced myself to want it, I would have. Christ, I tried, Ed."

Baron squeezed his eyes shut, inhaling. Holding the smoke in.

"I know you did," Ed said. Put his hand on Baron's arm, but Baron didn't soften at all into his touch. Ed pulled his hand away.

"Makes me want to die up there," Baron said. "Makes me think I'm dying. Maybe both. Sometimes I go to sing and I know the sound isn't even coming out. It's not just the screaming, Hammy, why they can't hear us. It's because I lose me voice up there."

"Stage fright's understandable in our-"

"Stage fright." Baron blew smoke out his nose. "Never had stage fright when I was a kid, you know. Used to love acting. Played a lost boy once at school. Should have been Peter Pan. But now it's like I stand there and I see *them* and no matter how I try to convince myself otherwise, that they're just fans, I think *They're going to murder me.* It's always on my mind, how they want to eat all of us alive."

"They don't-" Eddie started, because he really didn't think of the fans like that. There was no harm in them that Ed had ever seen, ever experienced. Maybe they want to touch greatness, get a little glitter in their hair. Hadn't they felt like that as kids, too? Over Elvis and Buddy and Eddie Cochran and all of them?

But Baron cut him off again. "They do. And I convince myself it's normal, that my stupid foocking life is normal, but then we go back on tour and I have to make myself do it over and over again, even though I know how I'll feel when I get up there. Ignoring every cell in my body screamin' *don't do it. You're going to regret it. They're going to hurt you.* Do you know what it does to a man to ignore a voice like that? To put yourself in danger every single day, for hours at a stretch?"

Ed didn't say anything, because Ed didn't. It wasn't like that for Ed.

"Do you think I want to be puking me brains out before a show every night? Christ, Ed, I'm thin enough already. Do you remember what I looked like back when we was kids?"

Eddie glanced at him. He did. And the truth was, even when he looked at Baron now, he saw more the kid of 1957 than the man beside him. *That* Baron had been a little skinny, in that gawky teenaged kind of way. But his cheeks had been full, and there had been a little softness to his belly. He'd gotten taller in nine years time, and that was part of it. But it wasn't all of it. How narrow Baron was now. Rangy, like a tomcat.

"Every time we go home, I put on a stone or two, and then it's back to the buses and the planes and there I am in the WC, shitting it all off again. 'Snot normal."

Ed let his eyes rest on Baron's spine. Baron's knobby spine, and the shoulder blades that jutted out just a little too much. He sighed.

"No, Baron. It's not. Our lives aren't normal. They're not. You won't hear me argue that they are."

"Not to put too fine a point on it," Baron said, taking one last drag before putting the cigarette out in the ashtray. "But yesterday you all thought I'd gotten *shot at*, Ed."

"Well," Ed said. He couldn't deny it, could he? That had been his very first thought. That they'd finally gotten him, whoever *they* was. Not Liam or Charlie or Ed himself. But Baron. They all knew, if it was going to be one of them, it was going to be Baron. Because he wagged his tongue. Because of the color of his skin. Because he was queer, and as prickly as he was, he was delicate, too. More rock candy than an actual rock.

"*Well,*" Baron said, sourly. Ed flinched.

"What do you want me to say, Barry?"

Baron shook his head. Laughed a little, but painfully. Got up. Walked to the dresser. Stared into the mirror there.

"I keep waiting and waiting for you to notice what it's doing to me. But there's the thing, innit? You do notice. You know. You've known for a long time. But you love it, don't you? And so you're just going to keep pushing it away. You're going to ask more and more of me. You don't care."

"I do care -"

"Not enough!" Baron said, and he slammed his fist on the dresser. "Not enough to make up for the fact that you love it more than you love me."

"But I don't -"

"Ed." Baron's black eyes bored into him from his mirrored reflection. His voice was firm, flat, letting no argument in. And how could Ed argue? He did love it. More than Baron? No. Not more. But different. Equal. When he was up there with every eye on him it was better than any screw, any drug. He knew how to shake and twist and move and give the people - all the people - precisely what they wanted, and at exactly the right time. To know how to satisfy, not just one man, but *millions*. If you could make magic, *real*, palpable magic - well, why wouldn't you?

"I'm not tryin' to hurt you," Ed said, feeling the tightness in his throat. "I never wanted to hurt you."

"Yeah," Baron said. "I know. But I can't do it. It'll kill me, one way or another. If it's not a gunshot and it's not a mob and it's not shittin' myself until I'm a ghost then it'll come some other way. Pills or somethin'. That's not a threat, Ed. I just can't do it no more."

Ed looked at Baron, at the grim way he regarded himself in the mirror. At the way that he really was a shadow of himself. Gaunt and lean, but, more. How the spark inside of him had somehow almost, almost burnt out.

"Okay," said Ed at last. "That's fine, then. It's over. This part of it, I mean. Not… "

And he trailed off, because he wasn't really sure, then, what came next. Baron went over to the edge of the bed again, but this time, when he sat down, he faced Eddie. Looked him straight in the eye.

And if Ed had thought that Baron might have *thanked* him for the sacrifice - and it was one, they both knew, and considerable - then he would have been deluding himself. Baron had moved on already. Was turnin' the pages of their book ahead.

"I was thinkin' about what we can do to end this tour with a bang," he said. "Something to set up the next album. Something to make it up to you."

Ed frowned. Sat up a little against the headboard, cocking his head to one side.

"What're you talking about?" he asked.

"D'you remember that song I wrote for you years and years ago? The one I told you you could have. To make you famous, someday."

The corner of Ed's mouth quirked up. Of course, Ed remembered. "Cymbeline." The first song Baron ever wrote for him, beautiful like a poem. He hadn't believed, then, that such beauty could really come from so rough a boy. Had wondered at times where Baron had stolen it from. Had searched a little, here and there. Through Baron's auntie's records and old music books. Finding nothing. It had been years before he realized that the initial story had been true. Yes, Baron Templeton was, indeed, capable of such searing beauty. Complexity. Depth. He'd been a fool to ever doubt it, but then, he'd been a child then, filled with a child's petty emotions, jealousy among them.

"Course I remember, you old fool," he said, and Baron smiled a little bit, wryly. Then Ed added, "But it seems we never needed it to become famous, right?"

Baron laughed. Lifted one eyebrow. Ed sighed. It was true in a way. But even now, Ed knew somehow that their fame was ephemeral. Right now, touring America, playing their pop standards, love songs, rockers, still, they were just a *band*. They weren't immortal, not yet.

"It's time, Ed," Baron said gently. "It's time to play it. New York, I think. Close out the set. Send 'em all home. Write down your name in the book."

"What book?" Ed asked. Baron shrugged.

"The book of wizards, poets, and kings."

* * *

Charlie and Liam took the news that morning at breakfast in stride. Seemed like it was a relief to them, really, when Baron hooked his hands in his suit pockets and announced that the show in New York City would be their last. No more touring. Albums, fine. But he wasn't going to kill himself to sell a few more discs of hot wax anymore. Baron noticed Albert looking past him when he spoke, right to Ed, searching for approval, confirmation, some little bit of hope to hold onto that the gravy train hadn't yet derailed. But Ed didn't say anything. Wouldn't. Couldn't. Because in the end it was more or less a joint decision.

"Can't say I'm not glad, really," Liam said, later, before their Toledo show, coming over to straighten Baron's tie. "But can't say I'm not surprised, neither. Didn't think Ed would ever let you off that leash."

Baron frowned, pulling away. "What're you going on about? It was me own decision."

At the next make-up chair over, Charlie snorted. "Come, now, Barry," he said. The older man - only a few years older, wasn't he? But he always seemed like he was ages and ages older than the rest. "Don't play us for a fool. The two of us is just glad he set you free before you got yourself *murdered*."

Liam nodded. Clapped Baron on the shoulder, twice.

"Yeh, mate," he agreed. "We are. Scary stuff, this America."

Baron grunted. Well, he couldn't disagree.

Down to just three shows. And wasn't it funny? Now that the end was near, it had become manageable. No more shitting, no more puking. Maybe their performances were different, now. A bit more sedate. But they did their work and kept their heads down and were charming enough at the press conferences before - polite, uncomplicated.

That last night in New York, Baron and Ed didn't warn the others. In fact, they let them walk right off the stage at the end, until Liam realized that Baron wasn't following, and stopped, frowning into the darkness. The crowd was deafening, trying to squeeze an encore out of them.

"Barry?" Liam called. Baron flashed a smile at him. Went back to the microphone. Spoke into it.

"We'll need a spotlight, lads," he said, and after a moment, whoever it was up in the lighting booth obliged. More screams. Baron stood still, waited. Until somehow, that enormous crowd approached something resembling quiet.

"A final treat," Baron said. "For all the little boys and girls. Our kid Ed has something special for you tonight. This is a genuine Hammond original."

He felt Ed's hand on his shoulder, turned, as the crowd started up again. Could have kissed Ed then, in his suit, looking so handsome, the acoustic over one shoulder. Could have, but couldn't. So he gave Ed's hand a shake instead, like they were brothers. Mates. And nothing else.

He tried to make his eyes say what he was feeling, though. All that love.

"Alright, Barry?" Ed asked, his pale eyebrows knitted up. Just making sure. Baron nodded. And then he let go of Ed's hand, and jogged off to the wings with the rest of them to watch.

Ed, looking almost like a ghost in that spotlight, his voice silky and so, so beautiful as he played that song just like they'd been up all night rehearsing. There was something so dead gorgeous about it, so simple. Just a pretty boy, and a pretty song, and thousands of people moved to silence. Baron stood there, arms crossed over himself, watching Ed. Feeling proud, feeling lonely. As Ed played his song.

"Wow," Liam said, leaning in toward Baron, "I've known Hammy since I was twelve years old. Didn't know he had it in 'im."

Baron watched Ed's fingers move up and down the fretboard, watched Ed's eyelashes tremble in the light of the artificial moon.

"I did," was what he said.

Reunion I

For all his nerves, the introduction went smoothly, and without a hitch. The audience laughed at all of Matthew's jokes - scripted, sure, but delivery counts for something, right? - and murmured their appreciation when he mentioned "Dad's body of work, which becomes a history, of sorts, of the 20th, and now the 21st, century." When he finally called his father out on stage to hand him that brass gramophone, the crowd went wild. Not for him, he knew. Only for his father. But Ed Hammond gave Matthew's shoulder a warm clap, let those somehow still-youthful eyes sink into his own somehow, still-youthful eyes, and told him, "Nice work, son."

And Matthew knew from the tone of his voice that he meant it.

As his father gave his speech - the audience laughing already to jokes that Matthew couldn't hear - some assistant brought him back to the green room. "The Legends Room," it was officially called. Matthew had been there once or twice before on the last tour - a decade ago now - and at least once years before that. The place had always reminded him of an airport VIP room, somehow anonymous. Deliberate, probably, to give the hoi polloi some illusion of being ordinary, which Matthew knew from experience many of them craved. But not *too* ordinary. Someone sat him down at one of the tables in view of his father giving that speech on a large corner television, called him "Mr. Hammond," and took his drink order. He ordered up a Scotch in honor of his dad and sat sipping it. Watching his father wink and charm the camera. Not really listening.

Old Ed made some reference to his family, and the cameras flashed to them waiting at their seats. His sisters, with their husbands, and their kids. The empty chair where he'd sat, earlier. And Five. Matthew sat forward, frowning. Five wasn't supposed to be seen on camera. The producers had agreed. Inevitably, there would be questions later, from the fans online. Speculation. He'd catch hell from Kara. But then, wasn't he always catching hell? Five spotted himself on the jumbotron, blushed bright pink, gave a tiny wave. And up there on stage, as he clutched his lifetime achievement award, Ed chuckled.

"Atta boy," he said, and then kept on talking about his songs, his adventures, his long-absent friends. Matthew sipped his drink, ignoring the phone that was buzzing frantically in his pocket. It was bound to be Kara. No need to let her drag him down, now. What happened had already happened. Couldn't put the toothpaste back in the tube. Besides, Five hadn't looked *traumatized*, like she always insisted he would. Shy, a little, maybe. But what eleven year old wasn't shy when faced with the spotlight? And he'd have to get used to it someday, being a Hammond. Whether now or at eighteen, Matthew didn't really understand the diff-

"Matt?" A voice, soft, earnest, pulled him out of his musings. He turned away from the oversized image of his father and saw there, standing over him, a familiar face. High cheekbones, dusky brown skin, heavily lidded eyes. She had barely aged in a decade, though she'd *changed*. Of course she had. She was wearing one of her suits, the kind he'd caught her modeling in *Rolling Stone*, a three piece one in a checkered pattern. The shirt underneath was a mustard color, which brought out the warm undertones of her skin. Her hair was a bit longer now, bleached blonde and combed rakishly over one eye. She shifted from one foot to another, regarding him, the smile on her lipsticked mouth tentative.

"Matt? I thought that was you."

"Naomi," he said, choking out the name.

His heart had risen instantly to his throat. Hastily, he put down his drink, stood. Moved to - what? Hug her? He wasn't even sure *what* he was doing. She stood there, a bit stiffly, not reciprocating, and so he settled on putting one hand on her shoulder and leaning forward, kissing her cheek. She took the kiss. But didn't quite reciprocate that, either. He stepped back, gesturing just a little too wildly as he spoke. Christ, she made him feel like a kid. He'd forgotten that.

"It's been awhile," he said. She was nodding slowly, frowning.

"Ten years..." she said, and with an awkward, unnecessary laugh he added, "Eleven."

"Sure," she said. "I saw your introduction. For your Dad." She gestured to the screen. He seemed to be wrapping it up now, but Matthew knew from holiday dinners and other assorted family events that Ed Hammond often took his time, wrapping up. "It was sweet."

"Oh," he said. "Thank you. I - well, it was mostly scripted for me."

"Well," she folded her hands in front of her body, smiling sweetly. Teasing. "You did a very good job reading the cue cards."

He grinned at that. Too big of a grin, too dopey and genuine. He could feel it, how terrible it was. *Well,* he told himself. *Might as well speed along my demise.*

"Would you like to join me?" he asked. "Have a drink?" He gave his tumbler a shake, rattling his ice cubes. Her smile - sweet enough that he knew it was at least half-fake - was frozen on her lips.

"Thank you," she said. "But I'm going on soon. I try not to drink before a performance."

"Oh," he said. He could feel himself blushing terribly. Why? He had no idea. "Of course. I remember those days." Of course, back in those days he *always* drank before a performance. Helped settle his nerves.

"Buuuut..." she said slowly, half-ignoring what he'd just said. "I could sit down, maybe have a soda water with lemon? Kill some time with you before..."

"Oh!" Blushing worse and worse. Christ, was he fifteen or something? Rather than fifty something? Sure felt it. "Sit down. I'll go..."

He didn't wait for her to respond, just rushed off toward the bar. Asked for a soda water and a second bourbon. Glanced back over toward her, and when he saw that she'd sat down and was intensely watching the broadcast, rather than paying any attention to him, he buried his face in his hands.

Hadn't he fantasized about this moment a thousand times? They lived within three hundred miles of each other, worked in the same industry - shared a *manager* (though Matthew couldn't claim he possessed a particularly sizable share of Sid Edelman these days). Of course their paths were going to cross. Once it had been a painful possibility. After their long weekend together - just three measly nights - she'd ghosted him. He'd gone back to Kara. Had wondered if that would be it for them, for months. Until nearly two years later, when she put out that album. That frigging triple platinum album, composed almost entirely of songs they'd written together. Well, he'd wanted her to do it. He'd *told* her to do it. But it's not like it it didn't hurt, being home with a rambunctious toddler while songs - *his* songs (their songs) - were always blasting through to him on satellite radio and on commercials during football games and when her image was mailed right to him courtesy of the friendly folks at *Rolling Stone*.

It wasn't jealousy, not exactly. Matthew had had his own successes of course. In the past, distant, as well as recent. The album with his dad, released just weeks before the baby was born, had been a critical darling, and his dad had used his distinctive Hammond skill at strategy to make sure it charted, crucially timing different colored disc pressings to various independent record stores. His fans were collectors, you see. Completionists. They would spend their way right up the charts for Ed Hammonds III and IV.

"Consider it Everleigh's nest egg," his dad had said, and he appreciated it, appreciated *him*. So damned supportive. But. Those sweet lullabies and nostalgic rockers that he and his dad had made weren't art, not like his music with *Naomi* had been art, and now, with his art (their art), she had been launched into a different stratosphere of success.

(The big reveal in that first *RS* article that she was Templeton's long-lost daughter hadn't hurt. Hard to compete with a story like that, with an image of Naomi Templeton, dressed in leather and looking just like her dad in the early '60s, holding her father's worn out little parlor guitar.)

"Whistlepig up and a soda water with lemon," the bartender said. "Are you alright, Mr. Hammond?"

"Yeah, I'm fine," he said, took his drink, half-drained it, before heading back to Naomi.

"There you go," he said, too brightly. She took her soda, nodded. Stared at him.

"You can sit, you know," she said. He cringed. Sat.

"Sorry, I…" he started. Stopped. Shook his head. "I didn't expect to see you here. It's been a long time."

"Yeah," she said carefully. "Ten years."

"Eleven," he corrected her again. "Almost twelve." When he noticed her looking at him oddly, he shrugged.

"Kara was pregnant when we-"

"Oh," Naomi said. Stiffly. Suddenly, just as awkward as he was. "Yes. How are Kara and your daughter?"

Matthew sighed. This never got any easier, though his therapist liked to remind him that *he* wasn't the person it was hard for. "My, uh, *son* is wonderful. He goes by Eddie now. Or Five." Matthew rolled his eyes at that. This was a script, one he could rattle off in his sleep. Meant to deflect questions, mostly. To elide the listener into other subjects. "He plays guitar, you know. Following in the family tradition."

Naomi frowned for a moment. Then her mouth formed an O. "Five," she said at last. "That's quite a choice in name."

"Well," Matthew said, and flashed a grin. "Because he's the fifth. You know, I'm Edmund Matthew IV, Dad's three. Eddie's-"

"Five," Naomi said, finishing his sentence. Sipping her seltzer. Nodding. Understanding. "I'm surprised I haven't heard anything in the press about… that. Not that…" She trailed off. Matthew wondered what she was going to say - not that she was looking for news about him? Not that the press would be interested in Ed Hammond's trans grandson? What? Well. No matter. Matthew shrugged.

"His mother likes to be careful about it, since he's so young. Protect him. He was sitting with the family tonight, actually. But she didn't even want him there, much less on camera. They promised to keep him off air. Didn't keep it. Guess she was right - I'm sure the Saffron boards are lighting up as we speak."

"Oh!" Naomi said, her eyes widening as Ed rambled. "That boy, you mean? God, he looks just like-"

"My dad?" Matthew asked. Naomi shook her head.

"I was going to say he looks like you."

Matthew felt himself blush a little. He looked down at his drink. Sipped it.

"And Kara?" Naomi was saying. Carefully.

"Oh, she's great," Matthew said. "She and her new husband are very happy together."

A pause. And then Naomi snorted laughter.

"What?" Matthew said. He glanced up. She was smiling at him. Looking at him. *Really* looking at him. He remembered now, how it felt to be looked at by her. Like she was really truly studying the person in front of her. Not the son of Saffron bassist Ed Hammond. But him. Matt.

"That's funny," she said. Reached out. Knocked her fingers against his knees. He watched that narrow space where her skin, the boundaries of her body, trespassed on his. "You're funny."

"Yeah," he said, trying to ignore the fact that she'd just touched him. Like it was normal. Like it was nothing. "I guess I am. Anyway." Sipped his bourbon. Looking owl-eyed over it. "How is your… love life… treating you."

Cringed at himself. The alcohol wasn't helping. He wasn't even bothering to hint around it. What he wanted to know. What he really wanted to know. Because he knew, from reading everything he could about her, that she'd been with an actress for a few years. Had even been engaged. But then that fizzled. Hadn't heard anything about any entanglements since, not through six albums and as many press tours.

"Oh… " she said, and he sensed she was trying to sound smooth, because she always did sound pretty smooth these days in her interviews, her Instagram lives. Nothing like the raw live wire he'd known a dozen years ago. "You know how it goes. I'm so busy with my career."

He nodded slowly. He didn't know how it went, actually, not anymore.

He'd quit the business mostly after Kara dumped him seven years ago. Wanted something more stable, then, for the child who had been known at the time as Everleigh. Had gone back to school, gotten a job teaching music at a local middle school. Time passed differently now. Quicker and slower all at the same time. Plodding through semesters, his life broken down into digestible problems. What the band was going to play at the winter concert? Whether he'd be able to get any of the trumpets to switch to French horn? Who was going to sign up for marching band next year, and how he was going to get his son to do his homework, and whether they were going to go on puberty blockers (he said yes, and soon, but Kara had "concerns")? Sometimes he would go months without picking up his guitar. He cleared his throat.

"So," he said. He was looking at her. Deeply. At *her*. Not the designer suit in front of him, or the make-up, or the flash. But her. Naomi. "It seems we've both found ourselves unencumbered."

She stared back at him. Laughed a little. Wistfully, she reached out a hand. Put it on his leg, just above his knee. His thigh, almost. Touching his thigh.

"Matt," she said, "I don't think there's ever been a moment in our lives when you and me were unencumbered."

He didn't answer. Just felt her, touching him.

"Naomi Templeton?" some gopher called from across the room. Naomi removed her hand. Too abruptly for his liking. Like it had never been there. Like, if it had, it meant far less to her than it did to him.

"That's my cue," she said, standing.

"Yes," Matt said. He stood, too, dusting off his suit. Not that he needed to. Just needed something to do with his hands. "I should get back to the family, anyway."

But she hadn't gone yet. She was watching him.

"Will I see you at Sid's after party, later?" she asked. And when he didn't answer, she added, "He said he invited you. I asked, when I saw that you were going to be introducing your dad."

Matt pressed his lips together, didn't answer, yet. Took in this information - that she'd been asking about him.

"You should come," she said softly. "He said you don't answer his calls."

What was there to answer, really? Matthew thought. He wasn't really a musician anymore. His debts to the record company were done. It wasn't like he'd *buried* his talents. He'd just passed them on to someone more worthy.

He'd given them to her.

"I'm supposed to get dinner with the family after," he began. "My dad…"

"You can bring them," she said. Paused. Smiled a slightly wicked smile. "You know, I've always wanted to meet a member of Saffron."

Matthew stood there, frowning at her. It hadn't ever occurred to him that she hadn't.

"Okay," he found himself saying. It felt like someone else was saying it, but, no. It was his own voice. "I'll see you there."

"Good," she said. "Wish me luck." And then she kissed his cheek, so quickly that he almost wasn't sure it had *happened.*

"Break a leg," he told her, and then he watched her take those long strides away from the Legends bar.

* * *

He went back to the audience to watch her. Squeezing through the aisles, apologizing. Sitting down in his seat, right between Five and his dad.

"Hey, Matt," his father whispered. Leaned in toward him as though to whisper something else, pulled back. "Christ, you smell like booze."

"What?" Matthew said. He grinned at his dad. Talking to him used to be hard, but things had changed since he'd become a father. He knew, now, that they were more alike than he'd realized at thirteen or eighteen or thirty-seven. "I needed a little liquid courage after introducing a living legend."

"Cor," his dad said, and rolled his eyes. Matthew grinned at him. It felt good, to tease.

The lights went low then. The announcer announced her by only one name, which is how she went for albums and interviews. *Naomi.* Matt realized that somehow his father hadn't known about this performance. Maybe hadn't remembered. At 85, details like these sometimes slipped through. But when the lights came up, on Naomi, at a white baby grand piano, Ed III's expression shifted. Changed. He sat forward in his seat.

"Is that Baron's girl?" he asked softly. Matt was stroking his rough chin, his face. Looked at his dad, realized his father was doing the exact same thing.

"Yeah," Matthew whispered. "Naomi Templeton."

His sister Shelagh shushed him. Matthew ignored it. Ignored, too, how he saw Five flash his aunt a middle finger in the darkness. He grinned a little at it, too.

But then she started playing, and he didn't *want* to talk. Just wanted to watch her. Her serious face. Those fingers on the keys.

Suddenly it was twelve years ago. Wintertime, before Five even existed, before his heart had been torn from his chest in a thousand savage, tender ways. Walking down a long hallway in a mid-century house to the sound of her fingers on the keys. Sloppy and intuitive and and and like a *heartbeat*, completely vital. And in a way, in more than a decade, her playing hadn't changed at all. Her voice, rich, full, raw, hadn't changed, really, either. And yet it had. In a way. A bit more polish. A little less warble. More practiced. Confident. Sure. But but but.

He expected her to play something off one of her new albums. There was that ballad, "The Bird King's Palace." Beautiful song, a charter. He'd expected that. Not this.

"Heavy boots made light again," she sang into the microphone, and the crowd went wild at that. Because it was a hit. Her first big hit. From years and years ago. "He'll write you a song again. While he's working in the muddy yard, he'll keep you in mind."

Matthew's throat felt squeezed. His chest. His belly. He hadn't expected this. This ancient song. The one she'd pulled out of *him* twelve years ago now, when he'd been young(er) and whole and careless. The one he'd given to her, made up of his most precious and most private memories.

And maybe he should have felt angry, as she eased herself into the chorus

- *his* chorus. Maybe he should have felt jealous that she was up there, all eyes on her.

But he didn't. Instead, Matthew just sat there, feeling quietly moved. Because what would he have *done* with the song, anyway? Nothing nearly as good as this. She hadn't stolen it. It had been gifted to her. And it was clear, from the tender way her fingers played the keys, that she'd done nothing but kept it safe.

When the last note ended, when the crowd exploded, when the house lights came up, Matt glanced over to his father. He saw that his face was wet. Tears? Matthew had hardly ever seen his father cry.

"You alright, dad?" he asked, putting a hand on the old man's wrists. He wiped his eyes, laughed, just a little bit.

"She's great," Ed admitted. "She's doing her daddy proud."

Matt put an arm around his father's shoulders, gave him a gentle squeeze.

"You should tell her," Matt said. "Y'know, she invited us to an after party, when this is all over." Matt paused a minute, licked his lips. "Well, I was already invited. Sid Edelman's place. Would you mind checking it out after?"

Ed's eyes shone as he looked at his son.

"No, Matt, I wouldn't mind that at all."

The Next Best Thing

He'd been deep, deep in dreams when the call came. Deep, deep in memory. Sitting in the corner of the back garden at home, at the house that his father had recently, finally, consented to sell, but it looked different in the dream. The hedges had grown, or else he'd shrunk, and when he squatted down in the dirt there in his short pants he realized that the hands he raked through the hard soil were not the hands of a grown man, callused from bass strings, but the hands of a tiny boy. Dirty fingernails. Fat fingers. There were brothers somewhere, and they were calling for him - *Ed! Ed!* - and so he had to work fast to hide his treasure. Raking his hands painfully through the dirt.

Their voices were warm, but Ed knew it was a trick. If they found it, they'd take it from him, and worse, they'd hurt him for having hidden it at all. The tin can cradled between his feet looked like nothing. Label peeled off and going all rusty. He dug and dug and it felt like his fingers were about to come off but at last, he decided, deep enough. Just as his brothers came flying out the back door, racing toward him, he poured his treasures in. Gold coins. Dozens of golden coins. More coins than could rationally fit inside a tin can but they came pouring and pouring and Ed was patting the dirt down on top of it when he felt Tom's hand on his shoulder, wrenching him away, and the scream of a voice becoming the scream of a bell becoming the scream of a telephone and, gasping, he jerked himself awake.

Heart pounding in the darkness. Ed cast his wild eyes about. There, beside him, barely stirring, was little Matthew, tucked under Genie's arm. She had one breast out, pale against the tangled covers. Neither of them moved, even when the telephone rang again. How late was it, anyway? Maybe an emergency, maybe something with his dad again. Last time, he'd fallen down the stairs, drunk, and called up Ed to drive all the way to London to take him to the hospital. Ed contemplated not answering it at all. But then it rang again, and he did.

"Yeh?" he asked, his voice rough in the receiver. There was a long, crackly pause, and Ed sighed.

"Da-" he began, but before the syllable could fall, full, from his lips, a different voice came rumbling velvet back at him.

"I've called to speak to Alonzo Kittycat," that old, familiar voice said. Ed sat up.

"Baron?" he whispered, glancing again to Mattie and Genie, who slept like a pair of dead, dead logs. When there was no immediate answer, he cleared his throat. "Yes. I'll, er, get him. Will ring you in five."

Carefully, he set the phone back in its cradle and pulled himself from bed. It was autumn, the air turning cool already, getting too cold to sleep in just cotton pants and no shirt, as Ed usually did. He grabbed a dressing gown and headed downstairs to the kitchen. Sighing to himself, put a kettle on for tea. The clock said it was almost 4 am. A reasonable hour in New York City, maybe, but when had Baron ever been reasonable? He went to the shelf of cookbooks, pulled out the overstuffed planner where he kept the numbers of his old lovers and even older ghosts. Went to the phone. Dialed Baron's endless, American number. Sat down at the counter and waited for him to pick up.

This time there wasn't silence on the other end, but rather wailing. The sound of a *baby*, Ed realized. Must've been Baron's little girl. Naomi.

"Barry?" Ed asked, squinting, and Baron's voice came panicked back.

"Moment," he said, and he had a sense of juggling, shuffling, on the other end. The crying hiccuped, softened, but didn't stop.

"She won't stop crying, Ed," he said. "Had to go out to the fire escape to call you before. She won't stop-"

"Where's Alana?" Ed asked. The kettle was screaming. He went and poured himself his tea.

"Got cross with me yesterday. Went to a friend's. Dunno. The baby won't take the bottle, Ed. She's - I think she's *starvin'*."

The child's cries intensified as though she agreed.

"I have no idea what I'm doing, Hammy. She wont stop!" Baron's voice had a hysterical, frantic edge. Ed found himself smiling, almost, to imagine it. Baron Templeton. Undone by a *baby*.

The first thing, Ed thought, was to calm Barry down.

"It's alright, pet," Ed said gently into the phone. "Haven't you survived worse than this? Fans? The press?"

"They've got nothin' on her," Baron said. And sounded near tears himself, like he believed it. Ed chuckled. Not cruelly. But there was some humor in it, in the entire imagined scene.

"Okay, okay, Barry," Ed said. "D'you have a bottle ready? A warm one?"

There was a pause. "I'll get one," he said.

"Okay. Good. Go get one. I'm not goin' anywhere."

More shuffling around. The cries grew muffled, more distant. Ed sat there. Waited. One of the cats scratched at the back door, and Ed went and opened it. Old Alonzo Coricopat himself, streaking into the kitchen, white as a ghost. By the time he sat back down, Baron had returned. His voice close and jittery, jumpin' into his ear.

"Okay," he demanded. "Now what?"

"Now you're going to take off your shirt," Ed said, and Baron let out a hard laugh at *that*.

"I didn't call you to get sexy," he said. Ed laughed, too.

"I didn't say you did. It'll help, Baron. Promise. Take off her clothes, too, except her nappy. They like to be up skin to skin. Makes 'em feel safer."

"Christ. This hippy shite. Alright, Ed." A rustle. "An' this works?"

"It works. Barry, don't be stubborn. Take off your shirt and pick her up. Put her right up against you."

The crying came close again. Ed added, "Now you can give her the bottle. Hold it right next to your skin. Like you're, you know. Her mum."

The crying went on for a moment later, hiccuped, jagged. And for a moment Ed was worried it hadn't worked. But then he heard the noises slow to gurgles. Heard Baron exhale.

"It worked, Hammy," he said. Sounded right on the edge of tears. Like he hadn't believed for a moment it would. "Oh, I could kiss you right now."

Ed smiled wistfully. "Hard to do across an ocean, love," he said. Baron laughed softly at that.

"Right," he agreed. And then he made a cooing noise into the receiver. It took Ed a moment to realize it was directed toward Naomi. Not to him.

"That's my girl. That's my darlin'. My sweet Naomi."

Ed felt his mouth curl, imagining it. Baron Templeton, shirtless and domesticated. Still, in a way, didn't really feel like it was any of his business. Baron and his child, his daughter. His child, which a woman had born for him, made out of their two bodies - so different from the whole lotta nothing Ed and Baron had built between them.

"I should let you go," Ed said. "Get some sleep."

"No, 'salright," Baron returned, quickly, before Ed could dare to hang up. So Ed hung on. Sitting at his stool. Drinking tea. "It's easier with someone else here. Christ, how'd you get through three of 'em, Ed? This is awful."

"It gets easier," Ed told him. Then chuckled to himself. "Harder, too."

"What's that?" Baron asked. Ed sighed.

"Shelagh's been teasin' a girl at school. Or she's been teasin' her. Can't tell."

"Maybe they're in love," Baron offered. "How old's she, now?"

"Nine."

"Could be a lesbian," Baron said. Ed rolled his eyes.

"Barry…"

"Wot? It's true. 'Sgenetic, innit? Apple might not have fallen far from the tree."

Ed snorted. "Wouldn't call myself a lesbian."

"What would you call y'rself, then?"

Ed sipped at his tea, blinking in surprise. Strange, to hear the sudden aggressive edge in Baron's voice.

"You know, Baron. I'm just me. What about you, then? What do you call *your* self?"

"Well," his voice came back low and gravelly, "If you ask th'missus, I'm a useless old faggot"

Ed winced. "Ouch."

"She's not wrong," Baron said. "But she thinks I fucked Peter X."

"The radical?"

"Yeh. Didn't, though. Well, did, once, but that was years ago and she was there for it. Told me to do it. This, now, it's nonsense. I wouldn't even be in touch with him anymore if it weren't for… Well, no use getting into it."

Ed tucked the receiver under his ear. He wouldn't have minded, entirely, hearing Baron get into it. Hearing what his life was like now, off in New York City, with the radicals, with Alana. He *missed* him, often, on such a fundamental level that it seemed to rattle in his bones. Most nights, he wasn't able to admit, even to himself, what it was precisely that he missed. But he knew he missed *talking* to Baron. Laughing with him.

"Well," Ed said softly. "Sorry you're fighting."

"'Sfine," Baron grunted. "Don't know why I thought it was worth trying for all this domestic bliss."

"We're at the age for it. Nearly forty."

"Speak for y'rself," Baron told him. "I'm not a day past twenty-two. But despite my youthful demeanor I think I'm just not built for women. Not the way that you are. They ask too many questions. Push too much."

"Like I didn't push you?"

"You didn't," Baron said. "Too much."

Ed snorted at that. He was old enough now to know himself. That he was a right dick when he felt he needed to be. He had often been the one nudging the other three along, shaping things to the best of his ability. Pushing them to tour. To America. To release two albums a year, not just one. He hadn't always gotten his way, but that was to be expected, with Baron who he was. But he couldn't pretend like he hadn't *tried* to always get his way.

"Is she asleep now?" he asked, changing the subject. There was a moment's pause. In his mind's eye, he could imagine Baron there, shirtless, the wrinkled little peanut of a girl cuddled against him. Sweet, the image. Just unbearably sweet, so sweet it made his teeth ache.

"Yeah," Baron said. "At last. Going to put her down. Hold on, Hammy."

"Holding on," Ed said, and waited. There was a cricket chirping some-where. He'd have to go send Aisling to catch it in the morning with her little bug jar.

"She's alright, though," Baron said, when his baritone voice returned.

"Who? 'Lana?"

"No. Naomi. She's the only gal for me."

"Yeah," Ed said faintly. "Kids are great." But it sounded unconvincing in that moment, and maybe Ed himself wasn't convinced. In that moment, at least. Small and private. Wasn't often he admitted to himself this, how *hard* he found it most days. With Shelagh spatting with her friends and leaving out Aisling and with Mattie only halfway toilet trained and still stuck like glue to his mother. Didn't matter how many songs he wrote that child. Never seemed like the boy wanted to spend even a moment with his old man. Screamed until he was blue when Ed tried. Lately Ed spent most of his time with the sheep. Sheep were easier than three children and a tired wife in a ramshackle farmhouse.

"Regrets, Hammond?" Baron asked. Ed sighed.

"No. But I do sometimes wonder what it would have been like if…" he trailed off. This wasn't something he often admitted to, either, even to himself. But he could see it right now, *feel* it. How different their lives would have been if sperm had never met egg. Resulting in Shelagh. Resulting in matrimonial bliss. If it had never happened, perhaps then this place would have been for *Baron* and Ed, like they'd planned. Ed allowed himself to wonder, for a moment, what his life might look like if *Templeton* was the one waiting upstairs in that farmhouse bed for him. Better? Maybe?

No, no, he told himself. It would never have worked. Maybe it would have been fine for a spell, at first. But eventually the glow would have faded. They would have fought about things, just like Baron and Alana. Just like him and Genie. But perhaps worse, since Baron's temper always ran so hot. Ed could believe it might have been okay for a year or two - but a decade? Impossible. Before long, their days would have given way to broken bottles and screaming, some kind of mutual destruction.

"Yeah," Baron said, his mind clearly elsewhere. Faraway, in other places, with other thoughts. "Wish we'd had our moment."

"We did, in a way," Ed protested, but it was a weak one. He knew what Baron really meant, but didn't want to admit it. "You remember that first night in America? Bandstand? Felt like we was meteoric that night."

"We were," Baron said. His voice was wry, tired. "Y'know, that's when I knew I wanted to live here, someday. The way the Americans loved us. Felt like I'd never been loved like that before or since."

Ed wasn't sure what to say. Of course the Americans had loved them - had loved Baron. He had been young and beautiful and funny and unbelievably *cool*. All that black leather. The mean green guitar named Ed. But Ed, the real Ed, had never doubted that the Americans would love Baron Templeton, because *Ed* had loved Baron Templeton, too.

"Not true," Ed said softly. "You know that's not true."

He heard Baron let out a long sigh. "Are you saying Scotland loved me more?"

It hurt, in a way, to admit it. The sticky pain that formed a ball in the bottom of his belly. Ever-present. A low ache. He ignored it most days. But now, with the sky turning gray past his big kitchen window, with Baron's silence snapping and hissing on the other side of the line, on the other side of the sea? He couldn't. Not for one minute longer.

"Still does," he said.

Baron didn't answer for a long moment, until he did.

"Well," he said. "Maybe in our next lifetime we'll get it right." Then his voice shifted, changed. Or maybe Baron did, across the ocean, dropping his head against the pillow, sinking lower into his bed. "Christ, Hammy, I've never been so tired."

"Close your eyes, love," Ed said. And then added, because it felt important to say, "I'm not going anywhere."

Baron didn't answer, just let out a sleepy grunt. After a moment, his breathing had deepened, thickened. Ed stayed on the line for quite a bit longer. Didn't care about the long distance charges, or the sleep lost. All he wanted to do was listen to Baron sleep, as he watched the sun crackle on the eastward horizon, sending fiery bolts out, like souls, through the gray, sleepless sky.

Bandstand

America. Fucking finally. America.

It was on the flight over, as the others played cards across their economy seats, that Baron decided it was here, now, that the band would make it. Looking out at the sun dogs dancing over the ocean, he knew that the moment was finally right. That at last, five years after he first heard Little Richard womping and bambooming over the radio, that he, too, would know just what to do. Because they'd paid their dues, in Germany and Paris and some shitty, damp Scottish dance halls, because they'd accrued a fan or ten, even a fan club, at the Casbah, a pair of teenage girls who would draw pictures of them and ask if they could have their chewed up gum to save for posterity. Because they'd been growing, musically, the four of them, and in infamy, slowly and steadily, but Baron knew it was worth nothing if it was just old mother England that loved them best. America. They needed it. Needed to break through in the birthplace of it all. *Rock 'n' Roll, brothers.* And fast.

While the others played cards, while Albert and Eddie argued about the set list for their first week of shows - they weren't even the opener, Albert didn't understand why Ed thought the audience would want to hear any originals at all - Baron plotted it all out. The outfit he'd wear and the grease in his hair and the jokes that he'd tell to shiny-faced Dick Clark and the energy he'd have to bring, most of all, to that performance. The Bandstand show would be recorded only a few hours after they de-planed in Philadelphia, no time for a sleep, a shower only if they were quick about it, Al had said, and it would air on Monday, and their first show in New York opening for the Shirelles was on Wednesday night and Baron had a suspicion, sinking and heavy, that if they didn't rustle up some American enthusiasm in New York, then it would be back to Merry Olde England with them and that would be it, more or less, for his plans of world domination.

Couldn't let that happen.

Baron ordered himself a Scotch up double from the stewardess, gulped down a handful of prellies with his first sip. Watched the winter lights dance over the runway. Felt himself waking up at last.

* * *

Ed should have known something was going on with Barry that afternoon. As soon as they stepped off the aircraft, Baron started acting all hyperactive. Dancing. Kissing the ground. Crying out, "America! At last!" and bellowing "My Country 'Tis of Thee," as he sashayed across the airport. Yes, it was good to see Baron excited. Was always better to catch him in one of his bright moods instead of one of his dark ones. But it made Ed uneasy. A kinetic Baron could be unpredictable.

Like when they got to the hotel, at the front desk, Al went to hand them their room keys in the usual configuration: Templeton and Waller in one room, Hammond and Peck in the other. But Templeton gave his head a shake, tossed the key ring over to Waller.

"This time I want to shack up with Hammy," he said, as Liam caught it. When Waller looked at him, arching an eyebrow, Baron smacked his bubblegum between his teeth and rolled his eyes.

"What? Been meaning to finish up a song we've been working on. Unless *you* know how to fix the middle eight, William."

Liam blushed a little at that. They all knew that Waller's songs were rubbish.

"I told you," Al said sternly. "They only want covers for *Bandstand*."

"That's fine, Allie," Baron told him. Reaching up, he wrapped an arm around his manager's burly shoulders. The man often looked more to him like a bouncer than a suit. But wasn't his fault, that he was built like a top-heavy potato. "Covers for *Bandstand*. This is for Wednesday night."

"Templeton -" Albert warned, but Baron just hefted his guitar case in hand and sauntered off toward the elevator. Hammond looked at them all, shrugging. Couldn't say he minded having Baron on his side. Even if it meant that their sleeping arrangements held a certain degree of... danger.

They only had about thirty to shower and get back on the road for their taping. Ed opened up their room door, put his suitcase down on the first of two double beds. He wanted to ask Baron what he was plotting, but sometimes it was hard to break that seal. Acknowledge it. Point to it plainly.

"Go ahead, Hammy," Baron said, as he pried off his boots and peeled off his dirty blue jeans, leaving them in a heap on the floor. "Ask what you mean to be asking."

"Are you sure it's a good idea?" Ed asked softly. Trying not to look at Baron as he undressed. He was so used to wearing a mask of propriety with him on trips like these. Ed took off his overcoat, loosened his tie. "Liam seemed suspicious."

"What? All I told them was the truth," he said. "I have a song I'm needing you to finish for me. Before Wednesday. Tonight's as good a night as any. It'll be a real cracker when we're done."

"What's it called?" Ed asked. Glancing up. Seeing Baron standing there in his Y-fronts. Glancing away.

"It's 'riding Ed Hammond like a bleedin' pony all night long in Philadelphia PA while Liam Waller watches,'" Baron said. His grin was wicked as Ed felt his cheeks light up bright red. "Oh, don't be so uptight, Ed. It'll be fine. I'm off to shower. T'ra."

And with that, Baron dropped trou and skipped off toward the bathroom.

Ed sat on the edge of the bed. Sighed. He was *exhausted*, if he was honest with himself. But exhausted would have to do. They had a show to put on, anyway.

* * *

Perhaps he shouldn't have been worried.

Because Christ, if Baron wasn't *on* that afternoon.

He'd teased his hair into the perfect quiff. The clothes he'd chosen - a new white t-shirt without a spot on it, his tightest leather pants, those old boots, polished to their highest shine - all looked impeccable. Some nights, Baron managed to look like he didn't care a whit, probably because he didn't. Wore stained clothes, a five o'clock shadow. Yet tonight, there was a sharpness to him that couldn't be underestimated. When the TV people showed them their marks, made pleasant small talk with them about their flight over, Baron managed to be both warm and funny. Ed could see how the stagehand girls giggled and blushed, glad to be in the presence of this thick accented, foreign charmer. Ed couldn't say he blamed them. Hadn't he felt like that before, when Baron was his best self?

On days like these, it was clear that Baron was their leader. People turned naturally to him, looking for his affirmation, his approval. Of course, Saffron had been *his* band first, back when it was known as the Bartlebys. But there were some days when Ed had felt it shifting, mostly when Baron was bored with it. There were three lads with guitars, of course, and while no one would ever mistake zitty, gawky Liam for the band's principle, occasionally, Ed had noticed, people would turn to him. Because he was beautiful, probably, and in a way Baron wasn't. Still, was nice, to not have to worry about answering questions, polishing his smile, performing like a circus pony just hours after they'd been dangling in a tin can over the Atlantic ocean. Today, he thought, he'd settle for letting Baron handle it.

And handle it he did.

The tracks were pre-recorded. Off their EP, which they'd released three months ago in England and which had hardly made a splash on this side of the pond. Yet. And yet, as Baron lip synced behind his shiny green guitar, Ed couldn't help but watch him. And found himself shaking his leather-clad tail right along Baron, found himself mock-screeching into the microphone right next to Baron, too. The kids in the audience didn't care that they weren't really performing. They were up on that dance floor, dancin'. Doing the Peppermint Twist, just like they were supposed to.

In between songs, sweating and bright under the stage lights, Baron answered questions for Clark. How they were finding America - with a map, Baron said, and the audience giggled - and why their band chose to wear leather instead of suits - because, Baron said, their dry cleaning got lost. More laughter. Clark asked them about their tour with the Shirelles, and Baron told him he couldn't wait to meet Shirley Owens, and made his hands into the shape of a woman's body, then turned directly into the camera. Lifted an eyebrow. Winked. Coming from anyone else, it may have looked corny. Awkward. But Christ, Baron was *good looking* that day. He got away with it. And then came the surprise.

Because Clark asked them what the Shirelles' audiences could look forward to when they saw Saffron play. More Peppermint Twist, perhaps? Baron set his hands on his hips, nodded. Yes, songs like this one, from their last album. But they were planning on playing another one, too. Something new. Something just written by himself and his songwriting partner - and here, Baron grabbed Ed by the shoulders, pulled him closer so the camera could see them both.

"This here's Eddie Hammond," he said. "Our bassist, and your next teen heartthrob. And on Wednesday, in New York, at the Palladium, we'll be playing 'I stole her away from here,' our next hit record."

This was news to Ed. He'd never heard the name of this song before, and to his knowledge there was no new album in the works. Hell, they'd hardly sold any of their first. Dick Clark was just smiling his very white, shiny smile.

"And you say you're partners?" he asked. "Like Goffin and King?"

"Sure," Baron said. He'd hooked his leather-bound arm casually over Ed's shoulder, holding him close. Real genial. Almost brotherly. "Goffin and King. Rogers and Hammerstein. Hammond and Templeton. He's the sugar. I'm the spice."

The teenaged audience laughed at that. Well, more than laughed. One of the girls made a sound, a strange one. A sort of giddy, high-pitched squeal.

When they launched into the pantomime of their next song, a cover of Little Richard's "Rip it Up," the temperature in the room had changed. Had gotten a little hotter, it seemed. A little stickier. The girls were dancing more wildly. At one point, Ed realized, a few of them had broken off from the dance floor, where they were supposed to be courting the watchful eye of the camera. Instead, they stood at the foot of the stage, watching the four of them with wet, shining eyes. Screaming a little. Laughing at themselves. Funny, that the four of them weren't even *singing*, not really. But the crowd? Really, truly going wild.

* * *

More birds. That's what Ed noticed, right away. How more birds stuck around their dressing room after, pressing forward their autograph books, touching them, asking them questions. Stupid questions, mostly, like *have you met the queen?* And *is it true they drink their beer* warm *there?* Ed noticed, as he cleaned off his make-up, how the biggest crowd was clustered around Baron. Seven or eight of them, pushing their way closer, trying to touch his hair. But when Ed turned, he realized he wasn't doing so poorly either. Three pretty birds were standing there, waiting for him to pay attention.

"Hullo, ladies," he said. "What do we have here?"

He put his name in their books. *Ed Hammond III* in his bubbly script. One of them, a little brunette, asked in a sweet little voice if he was really a songwriter.

"I guess I am," he said humbly, and of course it was true. They'd written dozens of songs by then. Hadn't gotten much of a chance to play them, but he knew that most of them were at least halfway good.

"I can't wait to buy your record," she said. "Will you come back to Philadelphia when it comes out?"

"Well," said Ed warmly. "I think we can manage that."

He looked over their heads at Baron, who caught his eye back, and gave him a wink.

* * *

Al was annoyed at them all through the limo ride home. Ed could feel it almost radiating off of him like a stinky cologne. It was one thing for Ed to beg and wheedle to be allowed to have a few of their songs on albums or to play them at shows. Was expected, really. He'd been lobbying for that for *years*. But all this time, Baron had sat in wait, acting obedient, mostly, acquiescing to Albert's grand plans for their career. Al's line was that they were a guitar group, not a bunch of songwriters. It didn't make any sense to have songwriters wearing *leather* and shaking their arses. Besides, he'd argued, the songwriting thing hadn't worked out that well for Buddy Holly and there was no reason to think it would work out for *them*, who were just a bunch of wild scruffs, not nerds like Holly was. But now, Baron had sailed right in above Al's helmet, taking away whatever illusion of choice he had, whatever illusion of control.

But angry or not, Al couldn't *say* anything now. Because their limo was packed with birds and the boys were all jubilant, hooting and howling, even Ed. It really had been a smashing success. Better than they thought it would be. The kind of thing needed to drum up excitement for their tour, for their songs, for their albums, for their futures. So no chance for Al to say a word, not that night, not on the long ride back to the hotel. Couldn't embarrass the birds. Couldn't embarrass himself.

After, the four of them all squeezed into Baron's room, the four of them and six or seven birds, all who were not ready for the party to stop, all except Al, who turned in, glowering, but would come around and forgive them in the morning, probably. Ed wasn't worried. They ordered up room service and one of the girls had a handheld radio she put on the dresser and cranked it up and Liam got out Ed's acoustic and started strumming it along with whatever was on and Charlie sat with the guitar case between his knees banging on it and the girls all started dancing. And Ed loved to dance, so when a bird offered him her hands he took them and started dancing too, and it wasn't long before food and booze arrived but Ed wasn't interested in eating, anyhow, just wanted to dance.

Famous, he was thinking. *Gonna be famous*. It would happen as soon as this aired. He could *feel* it. He'd always wanted fame, of course, but never expected to get it without a fight, without clawing and scraping for it, maybe for years. And wasn't as if they hadn't struggled, but they were young, still, handsome still, and he had an inkling, just a drop, that what was about to happen was going to be stratospheric. These birds - high schoolers, really, too young for them but cute enough, entertaining enough - already saw them as celebrities. Wicked, clever songwriters, bad boys from across the pond. And Ed wasn't about to disappoint them.

And so he danced.

At first, it was just Ed and the girls dancing, with their cups of white wine in hand, while Liam and Charlie thunked out music in the corner and Baron stood, thoughtfully off to one side, eating a heaping plate of chips and ketchup. Baron watched them all dance, staying outside of it, at first. But then, after a few songs, he put down his plate and joined in. And Ed, buzzed from the wine and the excitement, was glad to have him there. His partner, his *partner*, the spice to his sugar, who was going to make it all happen, for them. For Ed.

He'd forgotten, really, how dangerous it could be to have Baron on your side.

Baron was dancing with a bird, a lanky lean one. Spinning her around and around while she laughed and laughed. And then the songs switched over and there was a shifting of partners, of moods, and Ed heard Baron's jokey voice joking, having a laugh.

"Mind if I cut in?"

And the bird Ed had been dancing with, the dark one with the stars in her eyes, giggled and let go of Eddie's hands and suddenly Ed found himself *dancing* with Baron. A jokey little waltz. Silly enough, right? Plausible enough to deny? And Ed laughed like it was just a laugh, fluttering his eyelashes at the girls who laughed, too. Laughing laughing laughing. All a joke.

And then. Maybe not. The song ended. Ed dropped Baron's hands, refilled his cup. Drank it, panting. While Ed just watched him, and saw the look on Baron's face: prowly, possessive. The birds didn't notice. They were laughing, pouring themselves more wine. The radio announcer read off the name of the next song. Carl Perkins' "Sure to Fall."

"Oh, I love this," Liam said, and he walked bouncily over top one of the beds to the radio and turned the music way way up and then stayed on the bed, bouncing, dancing. While Ed put his cup back down on the drink cart. Empty, now. Felt the buzz of alcohol in him and Baron's eyes on him again, though really, they hadn't left. Not for a minute.

"Another dance?" Baron asked. This song was slower than the last. Ed did maths in his brain, trying to figure if it would be odder, more obvious, to turn Baron down. Because Baron had a way, if he wanted something. Push just right and he could make it obvious, somehow, that Ed saying *no* was just as queer as his saying *yes*. Because Baron knew how to *trap* you. To get you to do exactly what he wanted.

And what did Baron want tonight? For some reason, right now, what he wanted to do was dance with Ed. This song was slower than the last. Soppier, too. A bit queer, Ed had always thought. Embarrassingly queer. The two blokes singing to each other about their love being natural and right, about holding each other, all of that. Baron was waiting, and Ed had waited too long. Some of the girls were getting quiet, watching them.

"Oh, you nutter," Ed settled on at last, grinning. But his tone was fake, somehow wrong. Almost like a parent scolding a naughty child. He stepped out and offered Baron his hands and together they danced for a moment, a little stiffly, because Ed was being careful not to let the music worm its way inside of him, what with the way they all watched him. Watched both of them. Baron was leading, and they were grasping hand to hand, dancing. But then, Baron gave Ed's body a spin, and Ed laughed, and just as Perkins sang, "Hold me tight. Tonight's the night. Darling... " he pulled Ed closer, so that their bodies were pressed together at the hips. Swaying together.

"Barry... " Ed said softly, as the guitar solo blared. Blushing as he looked away from Baron's gaze.

"It's the natural thing to do," Baron said, his eyes twinkling. Naughty. Ed could feel himself start to burn, over cheeks and neck and throat. That's when he caught sight of Liam's expression. Waller had stopped dancing on top of the bed, and was watching them. No one else was paying attention.

But Liam was.

Quiet, for a moment, as the entire world orbited those two boys, dancing in the middle of a room full of people. As they teetered on the edge of stardom. And Ed found himself unable to stop it, even if he wanted to stop it. He was stuck there, really, dancing with Baron. Wanting it, but afraid of it, too. Ed heard Liam clear his throat.

"Right, girls," he was saying, speaking just a little too fast. "Let's go off to me and Peck's room. These two have songs to write. I've got some whiskey in me bag if you want it. Coming, Charlie?"

Charlie's drum beat stopped. He looked at Liam for a moment, narrowing his eyes. Charlie was a serious sort, rarely caused problems unless they all caused it for him. He shrugged.

"Yeah," he said. "Later gents."

"Goodnight, Chuck," Ed said softly as the door closed, and he noticed how one of the girls left her radio there. Carl Perkins, still crooning. And the two of them, Baron and Eddie, swaying together. Their hips pressed together. Their bodies close. And somehow, growing closer still.

Harder.

Now, without an audience, Ed dropped Baron's hands. Tore his body away from Baron's body, the leather, briefly, sticking, making a *snnnnckt* sound as it became unstuck. Ed went to the dresser. Picked up the radio.

"She forgot this," he said, holding it up. He switched off the dial. Turned to Baron, who stood watching him. Half-hard in his pants, arms folded over his chest.

"What?" Ed said.

"Hammy," said Baron sternly. "I did it for you, you know. Today. I'm given' you what you want. The songs. The fame. The birds."

Ed looked down at the radio in his hands, studied it like it was important or interesting. "You want those things too, don't you?"

"Not in the same way that you do," Baron said. "I never expected I had any right to *be* anybody, anyway, Would have been content to settle for the scraps we've been getting. It's better than drunk or dead in a ditch somewhere, innit? But I know you won't settle. I know what you want."

"If you want me to say thank you," Ed said. He put the radio down on the dresser. Rested his hands against it. Keeping his distance from Baron, for now. "Then thank you. Really, Barry."

"It's not enough to say it," Baron said. "When you say it like that, it sounds like *you* don't even believe it. If you're grateful, why not show it? Give us a kiss."

Ed glanced at the door, his brow knit with worry. Where were the others? he wondered. Would the bird come back soon for her radio?

"Ed," Baron said.

"Look," Ed said, cringing, "I'm just worried. Liam seems to kn-"

"Liam's not here right now, Edmund," Baron said, and Ed could see how his patience was at the edge of wearing out completely. Ed sighed. Pinched the bridge of his nose with his fingers, rubbed his eyes.

"But he could come back. Christ, Barry, this isn't Hamburg. We can't just sneak around like this. There might be *consequences*."

"What, they won't have us on Ed Sullivan if they know we're queers? For fuck's sake, Ed-"

"I'm not a queer!" Ed snapped, not knowing he was going to say it until he did. Immediately regretting it. But soldiering on, anyway. "I never even thought about kissing a bloke before you. If you hadn't have come along-"

"Then what? You'd be working in a factory somewhere, handing all your cash to your old drunk dad?"

"Oh, fuck you," Ed said spat. "And what would *you* be doing without me, then? Dead in a ditch somewhere, like you said? Or maybe still taking it in the arse from Dick Ashby?"

A mistake. A mistake and Ed knew it, from the way that Baron's expression seemed to collapse inward, imploding. He waited for Baron to fight him, to tell him it was different. But to his surprise, Baron didn't. He just stood there, blinking. Then shook his head.

"Got to piss," he said abruptly, and stomped off toward the bathroom, slamming the door behind him. Ed jumped at the sound. Stared across the empty hotel room at the closed door. Thought about following. Didn't. There was no use. Instead - angry, still, his movements jerky and almost violent - he undressed himself, mostly. Took off shoes, leather jacket, trousers. Dropped them in a heap on the floor, messier than he'd usually be. Messier than Baron. And just laid down in silence on one of the beds. Waited.

Apparently it was the world's longest piss. Felt like nearly twenty minutes passed before the door opened again. Baron had shed his coat, and now he came out dressed in only his t-shirt, untucked, the leather pants unbuttoned at the waist. A cigarette was dangling from his lips.

"You fall in?" Ed asked, but it wasn't a friendly tease. Angry, still, Ed was. Baron only grunted at him. He went over to the other bed, where Liam had left Ed's acoustic. Picked it up. Went casting around the case for a plectrum. Found one. Sat down on the edge of the bed. Not too far from Ed. Tuned up.

"This is the song I've been working on," he said, the cigarette bobbing in between his lips as he spoke. "Goin' too dark in the middle eight. Needs some hope in it. You're always good for that, yeh?"

Ed didn't sit up, and he didn't say anything. Just laid there on his back, listening to Baron as he played.

And *foock*, the song was good. But then, of course it was. Ed was never sure precisely why, but Baron had a way of finding patterns, chords, that always surprised him. Not the next logical or rational step, but to take him someplace new, in every single song. This one, really, on its surface wasn't much more than a simple rock ballad. About taking some bird away from there, wherever there was. Home, Ed supposed. With her parents. The place where her soul was bound to die, though Baron didn't use those words. None-the-less, obvious. Funny, how that was all in there, the story just beneath the surface, even as Baron was bumbling and stumbling, still, through the structure. Too dark, yes. Not enough hope.

Ed sat up. Put out a hand. Baron stopped playing. Handed him the guitar.

"Try this," Ed said. Shifted the chords, a bit, at that tricky middle bit. No, no, not a B minor. Move into major key tonality. Crack open the song, let in a little light. Baron listened, smoking away at his cigarette. Put it out on the hotel ashtray. Nodded.

"Yeh," he said. "That's better. What about the lyrics?"

Ed looked down at his hands. "Dunno. Something about how the rest of it doesn't matter, I guess. Whatever is waiting for them back home. Mummy and daddy or whoever would stop them. Something like that. A *commitment*, of sorts. Like a vow. Y'know?"

"And yet we're not too young to know," Baron quoted, his mouth still set in a grim line, though there was some lightness - just a peek - there. "This love will last though years may go."

"Exactly," Ed said. He played through the middle 8 again, making up some words as he went. Baron was watching him very closely as he moved toward the verses, already written. Playing them perfectly, the first time through.

"It's about you," Baron said gruffly, at last, "You know that, right? Hard for me to see the light in *us* sometimes. Hard to see anything but a sorry end."

Ed looked up from the guitar. Baron's expression was careful, guarded. Very guarded. But underneath it all, Ed knew, there was pain. He felt it, too.

"Sorry," Ed said softly. He set the guitar next to the nightstand. Sat looking at Baron. "I don't mean to be a prick to you. I don't. I'm just scared."

Baron looked down his nose at him. "Look, love. It's only me. Nothing to be scared of." He sighed. Cringed. Went on. "If you don't want to fuck, we don't have to fuck. If you're not a queer, or whatever. I don't need it, if you don't want it. I only want to please you."

Hurt, to hear Baron like this. Because Ed knew, on some level, what a lie it was. About needing it. But knew, too, how true it was. That Baron fundamentally just wanted to *please* Eddie. At times like these, Baron was like a sad, hopefully puppy - one that kept getting itself kicked. Ed cupped his hands around his face. Spoke into his palms.

"Christ, Barry," he said. Dropped his hands between his bare knees. Looked at Baron. Earnestly. Openly. "Of course I want it. Haven't I told you enough times that I do? It's just. Well. You know. *The world.*"

"Yeh," Baron said. There was something tight, painful about his voice. He drew up his legs onto the bed, sitting criss-cross. Rocking a little. "The bleedin' world," he said, squeezing eyes shut. *Crying*, Ed realized. Fuck.

"Fuck," he said, and went over to Baron, and sat next to him. Hand over his shoulder. Drawing him close. Hooking his index finger beneath Baron's chin. Kissing his lips, the salty tears.

"Baron Templeton," he said softly. Saying corny things. True things. "You don't even see the magic you make. Those cameras loved you today, pet. The birds loved you. Dick fucking Clark loved you."

Baron laughed a little bit through the tears. "Don't care a whit about Dick fucking Clark," he said. Ed kissed him again.

"If you're asking me again if *I* love you," he said, "Then of course I love you."

They kissed again, sticky, snotty tears. Baron pulled his mouth away for a breath, speaking his words on Ed's lips.

"Queer," he teased. Eddie laughed a little.

"Maybe," he said. "Doesn't feel queer to me. Feels natural."

And then they kissed fully, open mouth, tongues and hearts and hands. Baron was still crying. Had never really stopped crying, as they laid back in the bed together, all tangled up. Ed's legs around Baron's waist and Baron's hands holding Ed against him and kissing and kissing and hard now, rubbing against each other, Baron moving his mouth from Ed's lips to his throat to the soft parts of his neck and down, kissing the base of his throat where his heart was beating hard and in that moment there *was* no outside world, just Baron and Eddie. Heartbeats and hands moving up inside cotton. Skin and shoulder blades. Warm and sticky and soft and hard, and Baron's mouth was moving down, and Ed knew where things would go next, but tonight, this night, he needed something else. To show Baron how very much *he* was wanted.

So he stopped, momentarily, even though it hurt to stop, even momentarily, gently pushing back Baron's body onto the bed, and knelt over him, and got out Baron's cock, and looked at it. Momentarily. The truth was, he had never done this before. Had had it done to him, by Baron, by a few birds, but never... Still, he wanted to do it. Wanted to show Baron that he wanted it, that he could. Held him for a moment, felt how hard he was, smelled the scent of his body, sweaty and acidic, a bit, from performing but also some other smell, a sort of nutty, clean, sweetness. Kissed the head of it, the bead of wetness, and then brought his mouth down all around Baron, sucking. The way Baron sometimes did to him. The way he knew would feel good to him. Not really *sure* it was right, still, doubting himself, until Baron let out a gurgled moan and buried his hands in Ed's pale, curly hair, holding him there, and Ed felt him throbbing, close, so close, but pulled himself back anyway, sucking him, finding a rhythm. And he felt Baron try to pull his head back, to stop him.

"I'm going to cum," he breathed, but Eddie didn't care. *Wanted* him to cum. And so kept going, and Baron sucked in a great breath, and pushed Ed's head down now, all around him, and in a great *whoosh* and with a strangled cry, he came, his whole body twitching and twitching and twitching. And Ed swallowed him. It wasn't bad, the taste, not so different from the way his own tasted, which he'd tried once, when he was younger. Curious.

Baron's hands stayed in Ed's hair for what felt like a long moment after, playing with his curls. Then finally, finally, when his body stopped twitching, well and good done, he let Baron lift him off his cock. Let Baron pull him up, kissing his mouth.

"I love you," Baron whispered between kisses, his hand down and rubbing at the heaviness in Ed's y-front. "You fruit."

Ed laughed. Didn't protest or argue. Couldn't, really, in that moment. Soon enough, the laughter turned to moaning, as Baron rubbed and rubbed at Ed, vague circles at first, then up and down his shaft through the fabric of his shorts. Ed's body arcing into Barons, stabbing at him, desperate to go, and Baron reached down and pulled Ed's cock out, and held it against the soft part of his thin belly, and Ed was so hot, so hard, rubbing it indiscriminately against Baron's body, his softening cock, his balls, his thighs, thrusting and thrusting into whatever bit of skin he could find and Baron holding their bodies together, and then his hands went to Ed's lower back and pulled him even closer, and Ed felt Baron's hands reach down into the back of his underpants, grabbing him, stretching him. Pushing fingers into him as Ed thrusted more, and faster, and Baron's fingers dipping into him, finding places that were nothing but electricity and Ed thrust and thrust, while Baron's fingers thrust, and finally, abruptly, Ed came against Baron's body and lie there throbbing against him, his whole existence a series of ones and zeroes, of darkness and light.

Funny, but not really surprising, how fast Ed fell asleep after. Because it felt like it had been days since last he slept. Head against Baron, Baron's finger still inside him, their bodies glued together, their hearts and lungs slowing. Ed drifted off to the darkness. Cor. He'd never been so tired.

* * *

He woke early, the sun coming gray and feeble through the gaps in the curtain. At some point in the night, he must have rolled away from Baron, and they'd slept half-dressed, side by side, sticky and cold. Ed watched Baron sleep for a long moment more. He was frowning as he did, occasionally opening his mouth, smacking his lips. Sighing. A restless sleep, for a restless body. Brown and spent.

Ed got up and went into the bathroom. Christ, he looked a mess. His pale skin, faintly shadowed beneath the eyes in purple from lack of sleep. His curls all tangled and frizzed. His lips bee stung and almost swollen. Needed a shave, but knew he was too tired to bother. Glad there was no show today. Only some radio interview, later, and then hitting the road to New York City. Felt a bit unlikely, like going to Xanadu. But, apparently, real enough. Ed got in the shower, turned it on hot. Scrubbed hard. Washing all remnants of the night away.

He combed out his hair. Dressed in the quiet. Not leather. Really, for Ed, that was just a pretense. Just for the stage. Today, pale, bright January, he donned a pair of wide-wale trousers, a plaid button-down, a scrubby sweater. A pair of dress shoes. His overcoat. The others liked to look scruffy. He never felt like his true self dressed like that. Truth be told, if it were up to him they would have worn suits on stage. But the other three would have rioted.

He stood for a moment longer, watching Baron as he slept, feeling something warm and spiky in his belly at the sight. Finally, grabbed a blanket from the empty bed, and pulled it over. Tucking Baron in. Gave him a kiss, a quick one, on the lips. Baron smiled a little, vaguely, like he knew who was kissing him, but didn't wake. So Ed headed out of the room and down into the lobby.

There was an area there with tables and chairs and the continental breakfast all laid out. Ed went over, searched for a cup of tea. Didn't find one. Had to get himself a coffee instead. Picked up a pastry, a waxy looking orange. Turned to find himself a seat. Saw Liam sitting there alone, reading a paper, eating a bowl of cereal. He waved Ed over, so Ed went and sat down beside him.

"The best to you each morning," Liam said. Ed smiled vaguely, digging his thumb nail into the skin of the orange. Starting to peel.

"Good morning to you," Ed returned. "Can't believe they don't have any tea."

"The coffee tastes like rubbish," Liam agreed. "But I'll take it. I hardly slept." The corner of his mouth lifted, just a touch. "Two birds in my bed last night, you know."

"Two?" Ed asked, blinking. "Good show."

"Yes," Liam said. There was something strange, curated about the tone of his voice. "The little one was looking for you. But I didn't want to interrupt whatever it was that you and Baron were up to."

Ed put the orange peel down on the table, avoiding Liam's gaze. Being a bit curated about it, himself.

"Yeah? Thanks. We got the song finished. It'll be a real smasher."

Liam was staring at Ed.

"What?" Ed said, peeling away a slice of the orange. Playing innocent. Even though he wasn't.

"Hammy," said Liam.

"What?" Ed said again. Liam shook his head.

"Christ. How old were we, Hammy, when we met?"

"Dunno," Ed said. He shrugged. "Twelve, thirteen, something like that?"

"And do you really think I don't *know*?"

Ed was chewing on his orange slice, but he stopped chewing then, leaving it tucked against his teeth. Swallowed it. Sighed.

"No," he said, his voice, for once, sounding raw. Honest. "Baron told me he thought you did. Years ago. Hamburg."

"Hamburg," Liam said. Snorted. "It was years before that. I had an inkling back around the time that you quit the band. After Baron's birthday in, what, '57?"

"58," said Ed.

"Yeah. You were both such a mess without each other. Thought you might off yourself."

Ed peeled another orange slice away, ate it fast. Unsure of what to say. Nodded. It was true. They had been a mess.

"But I *knew* it in Scotland. Christ, I was right there, Ed." Liam's face was screwed up in a sour expression. Ed felt guilty, a bit. He'd known that night that they were being indiscreet. But somehow had been unable to stop it. After all, they'd nearly died that night. He'd been so, so scared.

"Sorry," Ed said. Liam rolled his eyes.

"D'you think I care? You know you're not the only queers I've known. Tried to bring those blokes by in Hamburg, to show you it was alright. You never did seem to get the joke."

"I'm not… " Ed said softly. Stuffed another slice of orange in his mouth, spoke with his mouth full, like it somehow made it better. "I'm not like your friends. Not really. Baron… well, he's different. Maybe he is. In some ways. But. It's not like… "

"Not like you're a *fruit*?" Liam snapped. "Like the rest of them fruits? You act like a bunch of lovesick birds over each other half the time, Ed. The way he looks at you. Christ."

That was enough to make Ed blush, finally. His eyes darted around, taking stock of who might be listening. "Lower your voice, Wally."

It looked for a moment like Waller wasn't going to, like he was going to just keep arguing with Ed, right then and there in the hotel lobby. But instead, he stuck a spoonful of cornflakes in his mouth, chewed suddenly. Swallowed.

"Look, I don't care," he said, in a lower voice this time. "I don't care which one of you sticks it in the other and which one of you sucks it and I don't care if the two of you want to dance around with each other like a couple of birds. I don't. But I don't understand what you're doing with my sister, then, too. Maybe it's none of my business. Seems she's going to get her heart broken, though."

"I care about Genie," Ed said softly. "Don't intend to hurt her. Liam, I want *babies*. A family. The whole bit. She does, too. Baron can't give me that."

Liam looked at him, scowling. "No," he said at last. "I suppose not. Imagine Barry, with a pram. Christ."

Ed did imagine it for a moment. Smiled, for a moment. Then, Liam added, "But I mean, do you even like doing it with her? The way the two of you were dancing last night…" He shook his head, as if he couldn't even speak of what he'd seen. Baron and Ed, shoved up against each other. Desperate for each other. Ed sighed.

"I *do* like it. You know, Baron likes birds, too. I told you. It's not like your queer friends in Hamburg. Not entirely, at least. She's sweet, and I like when we're together, and she'll make a good mum someday."

"But?" prodded Liam. Ed sighed.

"But. You know. When you were with a bird, did you ever feel like she didn't really like it? Sex, I mean. Like maybe she thought kissing was nice enough, or listening to records, but when it came down to your *body*, no matter how much she told her friends she thinks you're cute, it's like she's doing you some sort of *favor* touching it?"

Liam shrugged. "Yeh," he said. "Sure, but that's just birds, innit? They're not supposed to enjoy it, right, as much as we do?"

Ed lifted his eyebrows, as if that was the point, and it was. "He loves it, Wally. My body. Like I'm some kind of priceless artifact, and he can't stop touching it."

Liam wrinkled his nose. "Queer," he said at last. Ed laughed a little. Ate the last piece of the orange.

"Yeah," he agreed. They sat in silence for a minute, drinking that terrible hotel coffee.

"One last question," Liam said at last. Ed shrugged.

"Go on."

"Back years ago, you remember when we used to have a wank together, you and me? Before Baron and the band and all of that."

Ed made a laughing noise. Remembering. "Yeah, what of it?"

"Was that because you… you know. Because you fancied me?"

Ed looked at Liam. Lifting one eyebrow. Trying to tell what Liam *wanted* the answer to be. Finally decided to just tell him the truth.

"Sorry to disappoint, pet," he said, "But we're just friends. You and me."

Liam sighed, relieved. And Ed felt relieved to see that, too. He shrugged to admit it. "Truth be told, when it comes to blokes, it's only Baron for me."

* * *

And it was. Christ. They didn't share a room for the rest of the tour, but on the road, and on stage, Ed was just like everybody else. He couldn't take his eyes off Baron. As the audience, with each passing night, seemed to swell and throb, as the media got more *interested*, as they started to be asked more about their new album, the one they hadn't written yet, he felt glad just to be in Baron's orbit, whether they were fucking or not, sleeping next to each other or not.

Didn't matter. Christ, Christ, Ed thought one day as they sat next to one another on the tour bus, strumming their guitars, making up nonsense lyrics. Pulling faces at each other. There was no better place to be than besides Barry, on the verge of breaking out big.

Reach Out and Touch Someone

It must have been a dream, because his Mum was there. Had been such a long time since he'd seen her. The auburn hair, set in impeccable curls the way she liked it. The coral lipstick that she'd taken to wearing in the last year of her life. She sat there, at Ed's farmhouse kitchen table, the one he'd brought back to life himself, with his own hands, pressing her knees together beneath a gingham dress. Waiting for her tea.

He slowly filled the two little tea cups, which had been his mother's first and before that, his grandmother's, which he'd pass on to the kids someday. The girls, probably, because they were always fighting about his things, talking about what would be done with them when he died. It made him want to say the hell with it, to toss them all out. But Genie said it was normal for them to have a more ruthless view of his mortality than he did. Meant that the kids were well-adjusted, that they accepted death as an ordinary part of their lives.

Was it, though? Was it really?

He brought both of the cups and saucers to the table, handed one to his Mum. He knew she wouldn't drink it. Couldn't. On account of being dead and everything. But he had to go through the pantomime, didn't he? If he let on that he knew she was dead - if he let *her* know that she was dead - then she would vanish, or maybe rot away to nothing. He wasn't sure how he knew the rules of the game, but he did. He sat down with her, drinking his own tea. Studying the lines on her face. She was, he realized, just about the same age as him now, and looked older than she did in his ordinary memories. Some tucked away corner of his mind had memorized the crow's feet, the mole under her jawline, the tooth up front that had a stain on it. These weren't flaws, mind you. Only particular details.

"Where's Billy?" she asked. "I thought he might be here."

Ed faked a smile. "Couldn't make it today," he said. "Sends his regards."

"Oh, I do miss him," she said vaguely. Her eyes darted around like she thought she might find him in some corner somewhere. Ed just drank, didn't say anything. The truth was, Billy had been in and out of hospital for the last three years, and though Ed had tried to help him here and there when he could, buying him a flat, a car, getting him a job on the road with him, he'd took to the bottle the same way their old man had, had dark moods, talked about offing himself. Often. Still. His Mum didn't need to know that.

She made a *hmm* noise. Reached out her hand, and almost, but not quite, touched his. He knew she wanted to. Knew she couldn't. Because, y'know, she was dead.

"Poor sweet Ed," she said softly. He looked at her, lifting his eyebrows.

"You mean Billy?" he asked. His mom blinked at him, addled, maybe.

"My poor sweet Ed," she said again, in exactly the same sort of tone. "You won't have an easy time of it soon."

He looked at her. Frowning. Put down his tea cup.

"What do you mean?" he asked. She sighed. Tucked that pretty hand under her chin. He noticed the silver bracelet on her wrist. Wondered what had become of it. Whether she'd been buried with it, or if his Dad had sold it with the rest of her jewelry. Probably the latter. Money was so tight then.

"Don't fret, darling. I'll watch over him. And he won't be gone long."

"Billy?" he asked again. But then there was a screaming. It seemed to come from somewhere *inside* his Mum's body. Shrill and tearing. Ed put his hands over his ears.

And then found himself upstairs in his bed, in the dark, the phone ringing. He bolted upright. As always, Genie slept right through it. The Wallers used to joke that she slept through the bombings, too. Even Matthew, in his little pile of blankets on the floor, barely stirred. Ed's heart was beating wildly. The telephone rang again. He picked it up. Was barely able to choke out, "Hullo?"

"I'd like to speak to Alonzo Kittycat," a familiar voice purred in return. Ed swallowed, hard. Laughed roughly.

"Yeah, okay," he said. Putting the receiver back in its cradle. Getting up. Heading downstairs.

Baron. It was only Baron.

He didn't go want to go to the kitchen this time. Too many ghosts. Instead, he thought, he'd go to the basement, which was also a den and a recording studio and an office - whatever he needed it to be, really. Dressed only in his shorts and a worn out t-shirt from the last tour. It was July, and too hot upstairs, without air conditioning, but cool down in the bowels of the farmhouse, down below. On his way, he stopped and fished a pack of ciggies and some matches out of the decorative shell by the front door where Genie hid them, thinking he didn't know. Shook out a fag, lit it, brought it downstairs with him. Didn't smoke often, but needed one tonight. Christ. After that dream, of course he did.

When he reached the basement, he closed the door behind him. Stood smoking at the top of the stairs for a moment, then headed down. Smelled mossy down there, as it always did. Bad for the instruments, the memorabilia, but not much could be done about that, the workers had said, unless they tore down the walls and "mediated the water infiltration problem," whatever that meant. So he was stuck with it. Not that it mattered to him, not really. For the most part, they were only things. He went to the sound board. Sat down behind it. Got out the phone and dialed Baron, surprising himself that he'd managed to memorize the number since last time. Not that they'd spoken. But he'd looked at it a few times, contemplating calling him. Funny, how certain things, sometimes, get lodged in one's brain.

It rang twice. Someone picked it up.

"Alonzo here," Ed said, sitting back in his chair. Smoking. There was a small, wry chuckle on the other end.

"Atta puss," Baron said. "I was dreaming about you, you know. Were you dreaming about me?"

Ed sucked at the fag. "Don't think so," he said, trying to ignore how the very mention of *dreaming* made him feel a bit queasy and miserable. Didn't want to think about that dream. Willed it away. "What were we doing?"

"Each other," Baron said, and Ed had to laugh at that. There was no beating around the bush with him, was there?

"Ah," Ed said. No ash tray down here. He rolled his chair over to the wet bar in the corner, grabbed himself a tumbler, ashed into that instead. "Thought you might be calling for more babycare advice."

"Well, Mr. Spock-"

"I think you mean Dr. Spock."

"The wife and offspring are away right now. Left me all by my lonesome. And so I'm feeling lonesome."

"Nobody in New York you could call?" Ed asked carefully. Not really sure *why* he was asking. Except there was a part of him that wanted to know, always, what Baron was up to.

Who he was up to. And all that.

"Oh, sure, there are friends. A lad named David I've been spending time with. British. A musician, actually. A blond. Like you."

Ed sucked at that cigarette, taking a long draw. Rolling his eyes a little. Wasn't that just like Baron, to hint he was screwing Bowie? Maybe trying to make him jealous, a bit. Ed felt too old for that sort of game.

"If you mean who I'm thinking," Ed told him. He snubbed out the cigarette in the glass. "Then he's got a cute arse at least."

"Bit small, actually," said Baron. "Yours is sweeter."

Christ. He was all alone down there. Blushing like a child.

"Christ," said Ed. "You know I'm payin' for this phone call."

"Might as well get your money's worth, then," Baron told him. "What are you wearin'?"

Ed glanced down at himself. Contemplated lying. Decided against it. "T-shirt. Shorts."

"Gorgeous," Baron said, then there was a pause, long and sticky, and he added, "You should take 'em off."

Ed let out a puff of laughter. But Baron's voice was dry, stern in response. "Not a suggestion, Ed," he said. "I'll know if you haven't."

"Um," Ed said. He glanced at the closed door at the top of the stairs. Then he set the phone down on the sound board, stood, and peeled off his clothes. Dumped them in a pile on the floor, like some kind of slob. Sat back down. When he picked up the phone again, Baron's breathing was heavy on the other side.

"Are you hard?" Baron asked. Ed looked down again, even though he didn't really have to.

"Yes," Ed said, his own voice coming out husky and muddled. "Hard."

"Good," Baron said. "I am, too."

"What are *you* wearing?" Ed asked. His hand drifting down. He began, idly, to stroke himself.

"Just a robe, as they call them here in the states," said Baron, his voice wry. "Ed, are you bein' naughty? Are you touching yourself?"

He was. Stroking slowly, his voice smaller now. "Yes," he said.

"Didn't tell you to do that, yet," said Baron. "It's not time yet, love."

Ed didn't want to listen, but he let himself go. Letting out a strangled little gasp when he did. His balls were almost aching. Hadn't even realized that he was so randy. Though if he thought about it, it had been a long, long while. Genie wasn't in the mood lately. Didn't want another baby, hated using rubbers or the pill. And Ed had never wanked much. Usually didn't need to. But maybe he should have been making a more regular habit of it. Fuck, it ached.

"Okay, Barry," Ed said in a quivering voice. Feeling himself, balls and cock and all of him, throb uselessly for a second. Christ, almost felt like he could come without touching himself at all.

"If I were there…" Baron said slowly. There was a smile in his voice. Ed heard a crackly sort of sound. Baron moving his hand down his own chest, maybe. Lower.

"You'd what?" Ed demanded. Desperate to know. Among other things.

"Oh, you know…" Baron began, the smile in his voice turning into a full-on wicked grin. "I think I'd take that delicious cock of yours and suck it nearly dry. Then right before you blew your load, I'd let you fuck me. As hard and as long as you wanted."

"Wouldn't take long, actually," Ed said. He was really throbbing. Wanting to touch himself *so* badly. Refusing to allow himself yet. Though on the other end, he heard Baron's breath getting faster, heavier. The rhythmic sound of him stroking himself, too.

"How's it sound?" Baron asked. Ed chewed on his lip.

"Yeah, it's alright," Ed said coarsely. Laughing a bit. "Wouldn't mind that."

"No, no," Baron said. "Of course you wouldn't. Always loved my arse, didn't you?"

What was the use in denying it? He had. Sometimes made him feel funny, sometimes he'd worried it wasn't quite clean, but... well, if he had regrets in this world among them were the number of times he *hadn't* stuck it in Baron. Should have done it more. You only live once, after all.

"Yeh," Ed said, squeaking a bit. Gasping.

"Say it," Baron said.

"I love your arse, Barry."

"More," Baron said. Ed swallowed. Throbbed.

"I love your tight little arse," he said. "An' I love putting my cock inside it." Baron let out a long, low moan.

"I'm touchin' it, Ed," he panted into the phone. "My arsehole. Can you tell?"

"Yes..." Ed said, almost gurgling. Still not touching himself, though his cock was bobbing in the empty air, threatening to resolve the problem without any touching at all.

"Do you want to touch yourself, Ed?" Baron asked. Ed moaned.

"Yes, yes," he said. Desperately.

"Then I want you to beg me for it."

Ed winced. "Please, Baron, let me touch myself."

"More," Baron commanded, his own words coming shorter now, more grunted.

"Please, Baron," Ed whined. "Oh God, please let me. My balls are achin'. Please let me cum. *Please.*"

"That's better," Baron said. "Go ahead, love. Touch yourself for me. Let me hear you cum."

And so Ed did. Stroking it fast, furiously, and it took almost no time at all before he was writhing in that chair, semen spilling over his own belly and hand and cock and balls. His toes curling, his back arched, and he let out a long, strangled moan and on the other end, he heard Baron cry out too. Cumming at the same time, in different time zones, across a vast, vast sea.

It took a moment for Ed to unarch his back, for his toes to stop twitching. Laughing and laughing to himself when, at last, he returned to his body.

On the other end, Baron was chuckling, too. "Fuck, Hammy," he said. "I made a mess. Think I hit the ceiling with that. An' they're high ceilings."

Ed looked at his own sticky hand and body, laughing even more. "Same. Christ. Where are the tissues? Hold on a minute, love."

He put down the phone. Went into the basement bathroom, tucked away in the corner, to clean himself off. Rinsing himself with a little hand soap and warm water, drying himself out. Using a piece of toilet paper to squeeze out one last drop, moaning a little at the sensation. Fuck, he hadn't expected that. To cum so hard.

He picked up his shorts from the ground, pulled them on. Sat back down, tucking the phone beneath his chin.

"I miss you," is what he said, by way of greeting, not even stopping to think about whether it was a good idea. "You old fruit. When are you coming back home?"

"New York is home now," Baron said. Ed could hear how he was smoking a cigarette on the other end, exhaling. "But it's bound to happen eventually. Not soon, though. Taking me trip to Trinidad first. Next week, actually."

"Oh?" Ed said, sitting forward in his seat. Trying not to sound concerned. Baron had been talking about this trip for awhile in his letters, writing about how he was going out to find his dad. Ed thought it sounded like a terrible idea, but when has he ever been able to convince Barry of anything?

"Yeah, that's why Alana and Naomi are away. Staying with friends, the two of them. While I'm out of town."

"They didn't want to come with you?"

"No," Baron said. "Alana's done with Peter X."

Ed wasn't sure what to say about that. Wanted to say, *Well, maybe you should be done, too.* But didn't. Knew it would have made no difference. How long had Baron kept Dickie Ashby around, even inviting him to visit them on tour in the states? No one could convince Baron Templeton to make a wise choice. Certainly not Ed.

"Anyway, will only be out there a few weeks. But I wanted to tell you. I sent you a package."

"Yeah?"

"Me guitar, the Ricky. For safekeeping. In case something happens. Alana can have the rest of them. But I want you to have that one."

"What's gonna happen, Barry?" Ed asked, frowning. There seemed to be something grim to him in the idea of Baron without that old guitar, his very first electric.

"Nothing, probably. I'll be fine. I'll be home in a few weeks. Then you can mail it back. I'll pay, if you're too cheap for it."

"No, it's fine," Ed said. Chuckling to himself, noiselessly. They were both loaded. What a thing to worry about.

"Maybe you can take a look at it while you have it. One of the pick-ups is dead. Tried to fix it but I'm crap with a soldering iron. Just burned me'self."

"You need to be careful, love," Ed said. "Or at least hire a professional. Got me old bass appraised a few years ago. You know what that's worth? Good lot more than a car or even a house. You forget we're famous, Barry."

Baron sucked at his cigarette.

"Don't care," he said. "Don't want anyone besides me or you messing around with it. Alright? It's special. Good ol' Ed."

Ed smiled a little, toward the darkness of the room beyond the glass.

"Still can't believe you told the press you called it that."

"No harm. They thought it was a joke."

"Wasn't, though."

"No," Baron agreed. Ed sighed. Squinting into the darkness. His own instruments were there, hung up on the walls.

"Y'know, it's funny. There's something I never told you."

"What's that?"

"Y'know the Supro? The first one, not the second one that the company sent. The one I bought in Hamburg."

"Yeah," Baron said. "What of it? Always thought you should have stolen something a little cooler. A Framus, maybe."

"I was a Boy Scout, Barry. Framus was too rich for me, and I didn't want to nick my instrument. Saved up for the Supro fair and square."

"Sure, sure," Baron said. "Well, what of it?"

"Well," Ed drew in a breath. He'd never admitted this to Baron before, had carried it around in his pocket like a secret for all of these years. "In my head, I always thought of it as Baron. Y'know, after you."

A pause. Long and full. Finally, Baron let out a pleased little sound. "Edmund," he said. "How very queer of you."

"Yeh, well," Eddie said, shrugging. "Guess it is. But I figured, you had a guitar named after me. So. I thought I'd return the favor."

"You sweet, sweet boy," Baron said. Ed smiled a bit. Sighing.

"I was, wasn't I?"

"Yeh," said Baron. "Still are."

Ed sat back in his chair for a moment, pleased. But then his gaze fell on the digital clock on the shelf in the corner. Square red numbers saying it was nearly six. Not long, now, before the kids were up, before the animals would need feeding.

"It's late here, Baron. Or early. I should go."

There was a pause. When Baron answered, his tone sounded a little sour. "Sorry to keep you, love, from your real life."

"Oh, no…" Ed said. He sat forward. "Baron, you've got to know. What happens between you and me? That's the real stuff. The rest of my days are just static."

"Hmm," Baron said.

"What?" Ed asked.

"Sounds like a song. You should put it in one."

Ed smiled. Chewed on his lip. "Right. Think I will. Been awhile since we wrote one together."

"You'll play it for me when you're all done?" Baron asked.

"Course."

"Good. I'd like to hear it. G'night, love. Or morning, I suppose."

"Night, Barry," Ed said. "Sleep tight."

Hard, to hang up. But had to be done. So Ed did it fast.

Was only later, when he was making the kids breakfast, that he realized he'd forgotten to tell Baron he loved him, in those exact words. Well, no matter, he told himself, flipping over the eggs. He'd talk to him again soon enough.

Reunion II

T h
   i
   s
 s
 s
headache was
  n o o o o
g
o
o
o
d
  t h i r d
  this
  week
  t w o
  the
  w
  e
  e
  k
before and the week before
  that

n

o

n

e

.

So

Cymbeline

t h o u g h t

maybe

the

t

w

o

before that

had just been

dehydration

or

something

because they'd told her

no more headaches after the surgery

And it was

t

r

u

e

so far

more than 20 years no headaches

though hardly any

m

u

s

i

c

  either
they hadn't told her that
  before
maybe they hadn't known
maybe they knew if she knew she
n
  e
v
  e
r
  would have done it.
  So pretty bad,
  y
  e
  a
  h,
that the searing old pain
  behind the left
  (
always the left
)
  eye
  back and not much b e t t t e r
  that she'd sat down at her piano
  that morning
  and began
to
  p
  l
  a
  y
  .

Well, sweet Sidney -

no Edmund -
no, *no*
    Sid
    said
    "

We need to cancel the party,
    "

Don't be daft, Ed
    she said
I'll go to the doctor's first thing Monday
    not much we can do *now.*
h
e
didn't correct her
    about
    the name
    t
    h
    i
    n
    g
    but said
    "

    Okay
well
    I'm not leaving you here
alone,
    "

    didn't go to the
    a
    w
    a
    r

d

s

as the caterers came

and went

the two of them snuggled

u

p

under

the blankets watching

Ed

Hammond's

dad

(

he'd gotten hair plugs?

)

get that lifetime achievement

t

h

i

n

g

and his beautiful

stunning

beyond perfect

baby

Naomi

sing her beautiful

stunning

beyond perfect

song

and he sang it to himself *her*self

while getting dressed a little

black dress

Ed
  had picked
  (
no, *Sid*
)
  and when he looked in at her he said
  "

You look pretty, how's your head?
"

  Fine
  F
  i
  n
  e
  she lied
and kissed him
  and he was
  mollified

* * *

she got confused sometimes and the crowds of people who had come streaming into her house hadn't helped because there were a lot of faces and names to remember and sometimes those left her when she was having a headache which she wasn't supposed to be having but she was and at some point she was standing beside her husband (what was his name again?) nodding and chattering with someone and she realized halfway through that it was *Lady Gaga* ridiculous to forget a name like that a face like that which no one was ever supposed to forget Sid kept squeezing her elbow and asking if she was okay so she knew she wasn't hiding it as well as she should have but she finally shook him off and said *stop henpecking me, Ed* and he drew in a breath and she winced and said *oh I did it again I'm sorry* and he said *well it's okay you know I'm not offended by it I'm just worried* and she said *there's nothing to worry about I'll go take one of my pills*

* * *

had to wait in line for her own bathroom the party was so crowded *ridiculous* and someone finally noticed her and said *oh! Cymbeline!* and let her cut and she wondered who it was and if they were just being polite because she was the hostess or if they were someone who knew about her stupid swiss cheese brain and it was always so hard to tell anyway she went into the bathroom and closed the door and opened the medicine cabinet wondering if any of their guests had snooped and found her pills the ones she didn't often have to take but sometimes did when she saw an aura they hadn't been working this past month but it was worth a shot because the aspirin and tylenol she'd taken hadn't cut it and she filled up a paper bathroom cup with water and drank it and stared at her own face and saw a stranger there but was fine with that because she was used to being confused sometimes it happened

* * *

she was used to being confused sometimes and she walked downstairs and into her crowded dining room where people were milling around the long tables the caterers had set out for food and she heard music and she drifted toward it to the cluster of sofas in the corner and there was a boy sitting there at a guitar his curls glossy golden even in the dim light and there was a crowd gathered around him and it was a familiar thing this boy and this crowd she'd seen it before how he bent over the guitar bending the strings and *oh* he was *good* and she came around and watched him for a moment too and she was right it was Ed her Ed returned to her a boy again delicate and young she hadn't seen him this way in so long that day he eventually realized Ed did not remember at the newspaper stand and they'd never even talked about it but he'd carried the memory with him all this time his Ed talented and beautiful and sweet and funny even then walking off with his heart in his pocket stealing it and not even knowing he was stealing and when he met him again three or four years later he had a guitar and thought they were strangers and he let him believe it and now here was Ed her Ed playing gentle music bending strings for her beautiful beautiful and it was confusing because wasn't Ed an old man now and wasn't she dead?

* * *

the song broke off and everyone applauded Cymbeline included and she saw then the old man that sat beside Ed on the sofa Ed's dad no it was Ed another Ed *old* and she thought maybe she was going to vomit in the middle of the party so she let herself drift away downstairs to the music room where nobody was yet and sat down at the piano trying to catch her breath and found herself playing instead

* * *

It was a lovely party, the kind that made Ed feel young again - not a feeling he often felt these days. Sure, he'd had the hair plugs and the personal trainer and the face lifts, but age catches up with one eventually, inside, and on many days he simply wanted to set his old bones in a chair in front of the fire and doze. Still, he knew, his body possessed a certain spark, a magic. He had been famous once, had written songs that folks had sung to their babies and danced to at their weddings and fucked by, and that wasn't something everyone could claim. He knew, still, that when he was in a crowd, people wanted to speak to him, to touch him, like he was an elder guru. Even famous birds and blokes. Lady Gaga, he'd seen, had been hanging in the wings of the party, waiting to catch his eye, and when he went over to shake her hand she giggled like a little girl and told him how her mother's Saffron records had gotten her through hard times as a kid. He was generous, polite. Thanked her for sharing. Wasn't much to say after that - sometimes these conversations would go down the rabbit hole of *what can we do together? Do you want to collaborate?* But Ed had let it be known at

80 that he was retiring from recording (though not really, he still recorded sometimes himself, alone in his basement, but that didn't *count* to those in the industry) and so the chatter fizzled with our Lady, Gaga.

Luckily, he'd noticed that the youngest Ed had taken a guitar down off the wall and was tuning it up. Didn't even ask whether he could, the rascal, and the biggest Ed went over and sat down and listened. He was good, our kid. Matt said he played *constantly*. Couldn't be arsed to do homework, but this, he could do. Made Ed proud to hear it. Once, he'd been that child too. He watched the boy move swiftly between chord changes, admiring how fleetly his fingers already worked. Ed almost didn't notice the crowd that was gathering around them until he started clapping at the end of it and they all were clapping together. The boy cringed. Blushed. Christ, he was so timid. That mother of his, keeping him out of the limelight. When he was born to be something so much more. Was in his blood, after all.

"Can I show you something?" Ed asked. Little Ed - Five, he went by, most of the time - nodded and handed old granddad the guitar and Ed took it, sensing how hungry the crowd was for him to play one of his old standards, and he ran through the Byzantine scale and Little Ed watched, wide eyed, soaking it up.

"You learn that one and you'll be able to add in solos on surf songs like that." He handed the guitar back to the child, who played it through once, flawlessly.

"Good show, man," Big Ed said, clapped him on the shoulder, and the boy beamed bright. Big Ed knew he was always craving it, to be treated like one of the lads. Well, why shouldn't he? They had always been more alike than any of the other grandkids, two peas shearing sheep together or banging on pots and pans or sneaking ice cream from behind his mum's back and when Matt had called up and said Little Ed was going to name himself that, was going to be a boy now, from then on, Big Ed had only laughed.

"Of course he is, Mattie," Big Ed had said. "You didn't know?"

And Matt had protested and grumbled that of course he did, but Kara thought he'd been faking it or making up a story, something about TikTok which Big Ed didn't understand and Big Ed had only sighed.

"Look, Matt, I was raised in a time when we had to hide ourselves most of all," he said, in a firm pointed sort of way. He hoped Matthew caught his drift. They'd only spoken of it once, that thing that Matt knew, which few others did. The thing about Ed and his old band mate. "The child - your son - is *lucky* to live in different times. Let's not spoil that for him, right?"

And Matt had agreed, and it was clear, from then on out, that Little Ed had an ally in his granddad even if old Mummy sometimes proposed to muck it all up for them.

He watched Little Ed begin a new song. Well, an old one. A Saffron tune, actually. "I stole her away from here." Early composition, one of Barry's, though Ed had helped a little on the middle eight. The boy's voice was high, but clear. Not a man's voice, though it would be, someday, Big Ed would see to that. Still, gorgeous. Gorgeous kid, singing that, and Ed could feel how the audience shifted as he sang, transforming. Was used to feeling that when *he* sang, didn't often encounter it in other performers, even. The spark. Was good, to see it passed down. Mattie had a bit of it, but it wasn't what he wanted, really, from life and Big Ed had always known it. But this kid, the newest Ed. Yes. He leaned into the crowd's response, singing louder, moving his hands with more flourish. Eating it up.

Big Ed smiled. He got up, then, moving out of the way. This wasn't his moment, not now. This was for the boy.

He went to the caterer's table, got himself a Scotch. Felt something in the floor, then. Vibrations. Hmm. No, not only that. *Music.* Different music from what Little Ed was playing, and not the music that was piped in, neither. Music down below. Incessant and pounding and somehow calling out to him. He gave one last glance toward Five, who was lost up in the crowd. Then he found a door in the corner and went downstairs.

Nice place, this one. Wide, smooth wood floors, a floating staircase. Guitars hung up on the walls, and then bookcases, a big picture window, the curtains open just enough to show the dark of New York City. And the room, though dimly lit, warmed up with the sound of music playing. It made his chest feel tighter, with how familiar it was. He couldn't entirely tell you what it was. But he knew he loved it already. He came to the bottom of the stairs. There was a woman there, about Mattie's age, playing on a baby grand piano. She wore a simple black dress. Was familiar. Hmm. Ed was usually good with names, though sometimes they escaped him more, lately. But he watched her playing, and thought about it, and remembered.

Cymbeline. Like the song. His song. A singer. And the hostess. The wife of Matt's agent. Famous, once, briefly. Not anymore.

He came closer. She really was playing beautifully, the third time that night he'd been moved by a song. Or maybe he was just getting sappy in his old age. Her face was drawn and thoughtful as she played it, a little frown creasing the space between her eyebrows. But then the chords seemed to suddenly crash together - not a-musical, but as if she could not help where they were going anymore. Then they piddled out to nothing. She looked up, pale eyes boring into his. He smiled.

"Lovely," he said. Clapping one hand against his arm, still holding his Scotch. She just kept right on staring at him.

"You're Cymbeline, aren't you? Sid's wife."

The stare went on. "Um," she said. "Yes." She looked down. Put a finger on the keys. Struck a high note. Once. Twice. Three times. Was really a bit strange, what she was doing.

"Is that an original composition? I remember your album, you know. Had a copy. My daughter Aisling bought it for me. I think because of your name, and that cover you did of my song. 'Cymbeline'?"

She was still striking that key. "My song," she echoed quietly. "Yes."

"It had something that most covers didn't, always thought. Was always surprised we didn't hear much more from you after that second album. I know the critics didn't love it, but they're always hard on a second album. Even mine."

He smiled a little at her, but she wasn't even looking at him. She finally stopped pressing and de-pressing that key.

"Couldn't do another one," she said. "After the surgery. They took it away from me. Music."

Ed frowned. Wasn't really sure what she was going on about. "Well, doesn't look like it went anywhere to me. Do you mind if I sit down with you?"

She looked up at him. Shook her head. Scooched over on the piano bench, making room for him. He sat. Let his fingers move over the keys, warming up. Started playing the opening chords of "Cymbeline," which he could play in his sleep. She watched him for a moment. Lifted up her hands, started playing too.

But the notes were different this time. Just a little different, just a little *more*. A bit like she'd played it on her album, but not even that. Little unexpected corners that he'd never noticed in the song before - suddenly lighting up.

He looked at her and laughed a little, but she wasn't watching him. Just playing, playing, playing. Until the song was over, and her hands did that same strange thing again. Almost crashing into each other.

"Wow," he said. "You are *fantastic*."

"Yeah," she said. She wasn't looking at him, had her head turned away and was staring off into the middle distance. "My song."

"Well," Ed said, chuckling softly, "The publishing company might disagree with you there. I wrote it in '66."

She blinked as though trying to shake a dream from her mind. Winced. "I wrote it. '58."

And then she was silent. They both were.

He was about to say something, to excuse himself, to go back upstairs to the party and to get away from this crazy woman, when she opened her mouth instead.

"I'm calling for Alonzo Kittycat," she said. Ed, silent still, longer, laughed once, a dry laugh. Then took his Scotch and took a gulp of it.

"Been decades since I heard that name," he said. "You must be a fan. Read about all my cats and dogs in a biography, yeah?"

"Oh," she said softly. "Alonzo. What happened to him?"

"Lived to a ripe old age. Nearly twenty. Started having seizures. It was really dreadful. We were going to take him to the vet. Even made the appointment. Woke up that morning and saw him sitting there in a beam of sunlight and thought, *oh, maybe one more day*. But then when I went to pet him he was gone."

Funny, Ed thought, how it still hurt to talk about the old dead cat.

"Left this world on his terms," the woman beside him said. "That's our Alonzo."

Ed finished his drink. Put the glass on the piano. Looked at her. "I'm sorry. Do I *know* you?"

She wasn't looking at him, not directly. Talking in a different sort of voice, one that didn't seem like it was coming from her. "Sorry, Ed," she said, wincing. "It's hard for me here, in this life. They lobotomized me. Basically. Didn't know they were doing it, thought they were going to help. Didn't help. Didn't have any more headaches for awhile and I don't think about you no more, don't get lost no more, but I also don't have music. And here we are and I don't even know what to say to you. Don't even know how to make it make sense."

His heart was pounding hard. *She's troubled*, he told himself. *Very troubled.* That is, if what she was saying about being *lobotomized* (was that even done anymore?) was even true. But he didn't want to be cruel to her. Didn't want to hurt her.

"How about this, love?" he said. "We'll play together. Seems like it helps you, yeah? And you say what you have to say and you don't worry about it making sense."

She still wasn't looking at him. But she nodded. Still didn't move for a second, so he reached over, and took up her hand - small, cold - and put it on the keys.

And just like that, she started playing again. Not "Cymbeline." Something he'd never heard before, her fingers making wide, sweeping gestures. Ed listened for a moment, then picked up his own hands and joined in. Adding a counter melody. Lovely, lovely stuff.

"I should never have thrown that brick through that window," she said suddenly, over the music in a stubborn, resolute kind of voice. "Should never have gone off to America. Should have listened more when you were hurting that day, when you came to me all bleeding and tender. Should have arsked you what happened."

Ed was frowning, listening, playing. Hearing what she was saying. Hearing the meaning *behind* what she was saying. But skeptical, still. A fan, a fan. She had to be a fan.

"It's alright," he said carefully. "It wasn't your fault. You were doing your best."

"It's the world that fucked us," she said, laughing hard. "Making it impossible for us. It's better now, I think. For the kids. They don't understand it. How tortured we were."

"Speak for yourself…" he said gently. She looked at him, surprised, though her hands still moved. He smiled, but it was a grim sort of smile. "Well, yes. Tortured plenty. But we got some beautiful music out of it, didn't we?"

"Not enough," she said. Her teeth were gritted. "Not enough." And her hands seemed to pound out the words: *not enough not enough*, hard and ragged, but the countermelody he was building behind them was gentle, sweet, beautiful. Because it was true, it hadn't been enough. But most of the life he'd had? Had been gentle, sweet, beautiful.

"Well," and the pounding stopped and she went back to sweeping notes, tinkling melodies, and just kept right on talking, "I have this husband now, you know? And he's sweet and he's fine and he loves my cunny and he'd do anything for me, Ed. But it's not the same as what me and you had. It's not like meeting your soulmate at fifteen and deciding you'd give it all away for him. All your best music, wrapped up with a bow, and handed off to him. Christ, how could he ever compare to that? We had a love that could burn up the sun. Still might, I sometimes think. When I'm alone at night remembering you and telling myself it's just a fantasy. Feels like I'm being burned alive."

Ed didn't know what to say to that. So for a moment he didn't say anything. Just played, and let her keep talking.

"The worst part was I *knew*. All along I knew Genie was going to get knocked up and you'd be taken away from me, and I knew that the wise thing, the best thing, was to let it end. But. How could I let such a thing ever end? I got myself hacked into pieces and I still came back for you."

Ed winced, deeply. Stopped playing. She did too. Looked down at the silent keys.

"Sorry," she said. "I know it hurts to think about. You should know I didn't suffer long. I really don't remember being scared much, even. Once it started, I just closed my eyes and I remembered you. Went somewhere else. Maybe that's why our souls are so tied up together. Or something."

"Look, I don't - " he started to say. He needed to end this. It was too much, too God damned much. But she made a sharp gesture with her hand. Cutting him off.

"I think I've figured it out," she said. "This body was just a... a waystation. A rest stop. Nearing the end of it now. Time for us to move on soon, both of us. Hence the headaches. But it's okay. Maybe we'll come back. Have one last go at it."

"And then nirvana?" Ed asked, surprised to find he was asking anything at all. The woman beside him laughed a little.

"Maybe. If we get it right, this time. Maybe. Maybe we'll both be birds next go around. It's not bad, you know. Easier in some ways. Harder in others."

"Don't think we get much of a say," Ed mused. Surprised again that he was saying it. Any of it.

"No," she said. "Maybe you're right. Besides, you always did like cock."

He turned sharply to her. She was wearing an innocent expression, and laughed at him. And he felt himself blush. Laughed a little too.

"You are one strange bird," he said. She bit her lip. Nodded.

"Always was. Haunted, my mother used to say. Not me mum, the one you knew. The other mother. But it's okay. A waystation, Ed. A rest stop."

"Okay," he told her. Started to play piano again. Softer, this time.

"A shame, though, that this is the end of the Templeton line. Well, there's the sister's kids, but they don't count. Had hoped that boy of yours and Naomi would make beautiful music together. But."

"Naomi..." Ed said. Stopped playing. Sighed. "Well, the kids are old for babies, but not too old for music, I think. And Matt's kid... I think he could use a friend. Not a mum. But a friend."

"Are you proposing a great union between our two families?"

Ed laughed softly, dryly. *Where* was she getting this stuff?

"Sure," Ed said. "Why not?"

"Good. Consider them betrothed," said Cymbeline. "Though I've been trying to make *that* happen for, what? A decade now? Longer? Those two are as stubborn and stupid as we were."

"They wouldn't be ours if they weren't," said Ed.

"Yeah," said the woman. She, too, started playing. Adding to Ed's melody, this time. "Cor, you were beautiful when you were young."

You, too, Barry, Ed wanted to say, but somehow couldn't bring himself to.

Her notes crashed abruptly. "Oh!" she said, in a bright voice. "Been meanin' to arsk you. Did you ever fix up the Ricky? You know, the one called Ed? Did you get that pick-up fixed?"

Ed's notes crashed now, too. His stomach felt tight. How could she have *possibly* known about that? He'd never told a soul about the box that had arrived two weeks after Baron Templeton's death, all wrapped up with packing tape. Baron's Rickenbacker Combo 800. Precious, precious. Ed had taken one look at that box and shoved the whole thing back into a closet. Had never told the press, or the fans, or the biographers where it went. Sometimes someone would ask about it. Baron Templeton's long lost guitar. And he would lie and shrug and tell them that their guess was as good as his.

Sometimes he took it out on days when he was lonely. Didn't play it. Just laid hands on it, feeling close to Baron. But then, always, he'd put it back away.

"No," he said stiffly, "I never had it fixed."

"Oh," she said. She puffed out her lower lip a little bit, disappointed. "I'd hoped you'd gotten the hint. Left something for you there. You've got to take off the pickguard to see it."

Ed drew in a breath. Shook his head. "I can't believe this," he said softly. "I just can't."

She looked wistful. "I know. It's not your nature, is it? Always liked things orderly. But here. Try this."

"What?" he asked, and he turned toward her, and that's when she reached up, and took his old face between her hands, and kissed him, full on the mouth. And for a moment, his eyes were open and he was surprised, shocked, even, but then something happened. Shifted. And his eyes slid shut and he was no longer 85 years old and the woman on the piano bench wasn't a stranger. Instead, he was young and his body was a livewire, and the lips that pressed into him, the hungry tongue, the body against him was *Barry's* body, a kiss that seemed to go on and on, breathless, endless, and he could hear his old heart pounding in his throat and worried for a minute that he might give himself a heart attack, and so he pulled away, wide eyed, and she was smiling at him, her strange, serene smile.

That's when he realized that there was someone on the stairs watching them. A boy, watching them. Little Ed. Five. His grandson.

"Um," Five said, in a bored, pre-teenage kind of way, that suggested that he didn't care, really, who his grandfather had just been kissing, or why. "Have you seen my dad?"

Ed looked at Cymbeline, and frowned. Pulled away, sighing.

"No, son," he said. "But let's go find him."

He left her there, sitting on the piano bench alone, in the dark.

One Last Night, Alonzo

In a fit of rage, and after the long divorce had been all finished in '71, Baron had torn the address of the Scotland house from his phone book. After Ed squeezed him for everything he could, dragging his name through the courts *for his protection, for the safety and the sanctity of his family*, Baron had thought he'd never wanted to see him again. Charlie and Liam had tried to warn him that Ed was only doing what his lawyers said, preserving the nest egg for the next little litter of Hammonds, but Baron hadn't altogether believed it. He knew that Ed had a vicious streak, driven and calculating and that, when it came down to it, Hammond had never cared about anything as much as he cared about money. Wasn't that his first worry when his dear old mummy died? What they were going to do without her cash? Well, he hadn't changed one bit in fifteen years, if you asked Baron. Was all money to Ed.

Certainly Ed hadn't seemed to care about Baron Templeton's *feelings*. Even after everything that had happened.

So Baron tore it out. Burned it. He kept the photos, the letters, the lyrics sheets, the scrap of newspaper from the day buggery had been made legal-*ish*. He was, after all, a sentimental sort. But burned the addresses, the phone numbers in a metal trash bin out back while Peggy Jones and Shakaboom both watched, wondering what their nutter of an owner was up to.

"You see, love," he told Peggy, crouching on the ground, "If I'm going to make a fresh start I need to be sure I'm without temptation. This will keep me from getting pissed and ringing him." Or, worse, showing up at his home in the middle of the night. It was the nights that were hardest, always, in part because he knew how poorly Ed slept, knew that he was probably up somewhere, thinking of *him.*

Fuck, no more of this, he told himself. *Let it burn.*

Embarrassing, then, just a few years later, to ring up Liam and ask him if he could have Ed's address. Again.

"What're you plotting, Barry?" Liam asked. They had a different sort of ease with one another these days. No longer bandmates, though they'd played on each others' last albums. Liam's loopy avant garde crap, if you could call it playing. Baron's protest flops. Hammy's star meanwhile had of course been rising again, the stadium tours and all that, but that was just fine with Baron, and he suspected Waller felt the same. What good was money if it was all going to go to the lawyers, anyhow? Besides, they'd always hated touring.

"I'm off to find work in the New World, Wally," Baron told him. "Need to be able to say a proper goodbye to me old friends."

"Are you sure he *wants* to say goodbye to you?" Liam asked. "It's a different sort of life he leads out there, mate. Peaceful, like, with the sheep and kids."

"What do I care that he's fucking goats?" Baron asked. There was a long pause. Then Liam barked laughter.

"Look," Baron said. "I'll behave. Just want to send him a letter, give him me new number when I have it. That's all."

"Alright," Liam said, "If you promise me not to rile up Genie. Christmas holidays are already awkward enough."

"Scout's honor," Baron said, not mentioning to Liam that he had never even contemplated being a Boy Scout.

But. He had *intended* to keep his promise, as life on this side of the pond began folding up for him. He arranged for the cats to go to his Auntie and Uncle. He got ready to sell the palace grounds. He put his life into boxes, eating takeaway with Alana on the carpet after he'd sold the dining room furniture, all that crap he'd never needed and always hated, anyway. Began writing Ed that letter.

I thought you might like to know what I've been up to...

You've had my number all this time but you haven't called. Well. Fuck you, too. But here's where you can reach me now, if you want to, though I'm sure you won't...

How do you know you love a woman? I can never be sure...

Dozens of false starts. None of them good.

* * *

What happened was that he had a fight with his Auntie. Of all things. He suspected he should have asked someone from the record company to bring the cats out to Liverpool, but when it came time for it, it just didn't seem right. They were *his* cats and he'd loved them and they would have been confused, he thought, if he didn't tell them a proper goodbye. So he put them in their cages and drove them up himself in his Rolls, while Waylon pooped and shitted in the carrier and Peggy Jones wailed the entire way. He'd always been a fair crap driver, and the tension didn't help, the pervasive cloud of feline misery, and it started raining hard before he got back into his old haunt and by the time he reached his Auntie's house he was white knuckling it. Miserable.

At first she was all happy-to-see-him acting. "Oh, you came *early*," and warm hugs and he carried in the cages and let out Lady Bo and Shaka.

"This one made a mess," he said about Waylon, as Deedz buzzed around the kitchen, tut-tutting, and he told her he was going to bring the cage up into the bathroom to clean it all up. Lord knows, he thought, he'd be in trouble if any of *his* cats made a mess on *her* carpet. So he lugged the thing up into the bath and closed the door and opened up the cage, flushed the turds, started running water to wet a towel and clean him. The cat threw his body down onto the tile in obvious pleasure, and Baron smiled and called him sweet stinky puss, and marveled about how everything felt just the same in that bathroom, same as it did in the '50s. He'd offered his Auntie a new place, more'n once, but she'd said no. She wasn't a house proud woman, she said. And this place was her home.

Home. Well, weren't Baron's home anymore. Funny, how small it seemed now. He finished drying the puss, threw the dirty towel over his shoulder, rinsed off the cage in the old claw foot. Then he opened the door and wandered down the hall. Gazed into his old teeny bedroom, where Deedz had taken to storing her sewing machine. It was like a closet. He opened the door, peeked to see if the cigarette burns and initials he'd put in along the jam, where she couldn't see them with the door open when he was young, were still there. Smiled to see that they were.

"Baron, you didn't use my *good towels* for that?"

He jumped, hearing her voice sharp right behind him.

"Christ, you scared me, Deedz. Well, what towels were I supposed to use?"

"Not those! Those are Turkish cotton!"

He squinted at the thing on his shoulder, which did not look at all special to him.

"Well, we can wash it. And if that's not enough for you, then I'll buy you a new towel."

"Wasteful," his Auntie said. "Just like you to think you can go throwing away money because you're a big rock star."

That's how it started, you know? Thirty-five bleeding years old, richer than he would have ever been able to imagine himself as a kid, getting hollered at for using the wrong towel. Before he knew it, hollering back.

Christ, Christ, Christ. He'd wanted to take his Auntie and Uncle out for tea when his Uncle got home from work. To say a proper goodbye to them, and his cats, too. Well, no use, now. Within fifteen minutes they were screeching at each other, and she picked up a glass jar of buttons as if to throw at his head, and when he went to stop her she started screaming like she was being violated, and he ended up rushing out into the rain and slamming the door behind him. A fine farewell.

His Uncle was pulling up the drive, actually, just as Baron stumbled out onto the walk. He waited there while it poured down on him, panting mad.

"Barry! You off already?" asked old Fred. Baron shrugged.

"Got into a tiff," he said.

"Oh, the old bat," said Fred. "Too bad. I bought you a going away present."

Baron crossed his arms over his chest, feeling embarrassed. Was embarrassing, really, how good Fred was to him.

"You don't need to buy me things - " He protested, but Fred *shushed* him and went into the backseat and handed Baron a massive bottle of Beefeater's.

"Gin?" Baron asked. He was a Scotch drinker, mostly. Had become a habit for all of the Saffron lads back in the touring days. Fred laughed.

"Just like you used to steal from me when you was young."

Baron hugged his uncle to his chest, feeling the rain pound down on him. "Thanks, Fred."

"Alright," Fred said. "Alright. Now you best go before you get me into the doghouse."

Baron watched his old uncle doddle up the walk. Pulled at his heart a little, that old man. Not that Fred had been perfect. Had never been able to do much to stop the hurricane that was his wife, especially when she was bearing down on Baron. But. Well, it meant something, that bottle. Baron looked down at it, started peeling the seal away. Uncorked it. Took a long chug.

Alright, he decided, seemed his afternoon was free. Why not go for a drive?

* * *

The address was on the envelopes he'd tossed in the front seat, the letters he'd never sent. Chugging at stop lights, and in the parking lot of the petrol station where he went to get himself a map. Six hours away, the attendant said. But what was six hours, really? Not like the cats were waiting for him back home, begging to be fed. He drove through lunchtime and as the sky darkened and only around eight did he pull off and slump his way into a pub, where the bartender recognized him as famous and bought him a fish supper and a cider on the house, and Baron stuffed himself and sat down at the piano for a song or six and they were all rushing around him singing and he thought *This could have been home,* but pushed that thought away, bought everybody a round and paid several hundred pounds too much for it, eager to be loved by them, and then slumped back out again, hazy with drink, before anyone could ask where he was headed or if it had anything to do with the ex-bandmate (ex-everythingmate) who lived just another hour north. Almost eleven o'clock when he got back on the road, and it was still pouring, so he took another slosh of gin and he'd always hated gin but it wasn't so bad today and he was truly properly slosh-ed. *Drunk drunk drunk,* he thought, as the wipers pounded, and as the road weaved in and out of his headlights he remembered another night, black as pitch and twice as dangerous, when the road - maybe this same road? - had nearly killed him and despite the way his heart was pounding he knuckled the wheel harder, drove slower, because maybe this road was ready to catch up with him now. Take the flesh that was promised to it long, long ago.

He got turned around. He pulled over. Squinting at the map. Drinking more. Heading out again. It was nearly midnight when he realized he'd found it. Thefuckingfarm, the one the old sap had written *songs* about like it was a *wonderland* like Baron wasn't *listening* like it didn't *hurt* him. A rotting wood barn and a splintered paddock that seemed to go on and on for miles and the sheep huddled up under it like *muppets* and Baron found himself turning up a drive, of sorts, unpaved, the Rolls dipping and bobbing and dancing and he saw the farmhouse and his chest felt a stab. He'd seen it, of course. On the album covers. Ed and Genie and their *babies* and the stinking sheep. How very *pastoral.* He pulled the car up behind some *stupid* bleedin' truck and got himself out into the rain, that bottle in one hand, a fistful of stupid *awful* letters which weren't even *finished* in the other and took another long slug. Courage. Courage. Marched up to the farmhouse door. And started slamming his fists on it.

"Edmund!" he screamed. "Edmund, you bastard! Open up!"

There was silence, and then there were footsteps on creaking stairs somewhere, and Baron was frozen there, ear cocked to the door, listening, and he contemplated for the first time what would have happened had someone else opened the door. Stupid bloody Genie, who was supposed to be with child now. Again. The cunt. Or one of the kids. Baron waited. Barely breathing.

"This is a private home," a bellowing, familiar voice called out, "You can't just come here - "

The door thrown open then, and Ed, Ed there in the darkness in his pajamas and dressing gown, warm and dry and sober, and Barry, soggy and sloshed and slump-shouldered on the other side.

"Baron? What on Earth - " Ed started, standing there, dumb. Baron wiped at his face with the back of a hand which still held a bottle. And he just kept screaming.

"I'm leavin', Ed! I'm leavin' you and I'm leavin' England and you don't even care, you 'orrible *fuck*! Goin' to the states with *Alana* who likes *books* and we're going to have fat black babies, a whole litter of them! An' we're going to be *radicals* in *America* and you can stay here and screw your fucking stupid *sheep*!"

Ed. Ed staring at him, not saying anything, with something almost resembling a smile in those stinking blue eyes. And Baron opened his mouth to start yelling again, but that's when Ed held a finger to his mouth, went "Shh, shhh, shh, it's alright, Barry. No need to shout. Do you want to come in?"

Baron looked at him for a moment, feeling something inside his chest collapsing inward. Sucked in a braying wheeze of air. Fell against Ed's shoulder, crying. Ed was frozen for a moment, but then lifted up his hands and patted the back of Baron's sweater.

"Alright, love," he said. "Alright."

* * *

At Ed's kitchen counter, Baron sat, slumped, his arms on the table and his head tucked beneath an arm. Feeling the world spin, and the pain stabbing into him. Ed's house. Smelled warm and weedy and familiar somehow. But different than he expected. Not tidy. Cobwebs and dust in the corners, a massive pile of dirty dishes in the sink, cat food bowls on the floor, the food all stuck and dried to them and some ants crawling in. And *Baron* was supposed to be the slob. Still. Ed. Ed's house. After all these years.

"You still take two sugars?" Ed was asking as the kettle started to scream and Baron nodded, his head still down on the counter.

Ed bustled about, fixing them tea. Set a tea cup in front of Baron, who didn't move. Ed was standing there, leaning against the sink, sipping.

"Ach," Ed said. "Too hot." He put his saucer back down. Went to some cabinet, got out a wooden box. Sat down across from Baron while he waited for his tea to cool and started rolling himself a joint.

Baron finally pulled his head up. Sat looking, squinty, at Ed. Hadn't changed much. Same stupid curls. Hairline receding a bit, *maybe*, but hard to tell with how he wore it, which was probably on purpose. A few more crow's feet, maybe. Not so baby faced. He was licking the rolling paper, his pink tongue darting out. Made Baron feel something terrible. He had to resist the urge to let his head crash back down on the counter.

"Fuck," Baron said sourly. Ed looked at him. Laughed.

"I'd offer you some," Ed said, "But I think you've had enough tonight."

Baron curled his lip. Didn't like it, Ed's smug tone. Ed touched Baron's teacup with his fingers, testing it.

"Go on, love," he said, sliding the saucer closer. "Safe to drink now."

Baron looked at the teacup, scowling. Some ancient, floral thing. Picked it up, slurped loudly, rudely. Ed was ignoring him. Lighting the joint. Taking in a long draw. Letting out little puffs.

"So Alana?" Ed asked. Baron took another loud, rude slurp again. Scowled again. Sitting straighter.

"Yeah, *Alana*. She's brilliant, Ed. A great thinker." He waited a beat, a long, mean beat. "Smarter'n *you*."

Baron saw Ed startle a little to be told this, a little wince that was almost hidden, almost invisible, except he knew Ed so very, very well. But if he wanted Ed to admit he was hurt by it, then he was disappointed. "Good," he said. Took another draw of his joint. "You deserve to be with someone who can match you."

So bloody reasonable. It made Baron want to puke.

"Oh, yeah?" he said, scowling more. Ed laughed.

"Yeah, Baron," he said. He looked at him for a long moment, smoke clouding his eyes. "Christ, how much did you drink?"

Baron put his teacup down. Looked at the bottle of Beefeater's, which he'd put on the counter beside him. Slid it toward Ed. Was more than half empty.

"This. Plus three pints on the way up. Cider."

Ed lifted his eyebrows. Exhaled through his nose. "That's a lot."

"Yeh?" Baron said. "Well, how much did you *smoke* today?"

Ed glanced at his joint. Shrugged. "Too much," he admitted. "Yeah. But I'm not showin' up at anyone's house *screamin'.*"

"Sometimes ye gotta scream," Baron said. Then he narrowed his eyes. "But that's not your style. You would *never* let on to how you really feel. Not without your lawyers to protect you."

Ed looked at him. Rubbed his hand over his eyes, wincing. "Liam told me how sore you were about that."

"Oh, *Liam,*" Baron said. "Is he your best mate now?"

"Jealous?" Ed asked, lifting his eyebrows. "He's my kids' uncle, Barry. Besides, it's not like I had him on my album playing songs about *you.*"

"Weren't about you," Baron said, folding his arms over his chest. "Who said they was about you?"

"Oh, come on, Baron. *You sucked me dry like a dog's old bone/Now you fuck your sheep and stay home stoned?*"

Baron sat a little bit straighter, looking - feeling - pleased with himself. Ed had been *listening.*

"You memorized the words," Baron said.

"Not exactly hard," Ed said. Shrugged. Took the last draw on his joint, then stubbed it out. "Had a good tune. Too bad you had to be so crass about it."

"Well," Baron said. He lifted his hands, gesturing to the dank, messy kitchen that surrounded them, "We can't all be as posh as you."

Ed's gaze had started to go sleepy and stoned. He looked around. And then laughed. Really laughed.

"Yeh," he said. "Well. Drink your tea, Barry."

Somehow, that did it. The anger that had been building and building inside of Baron - all ran out.

"Fine," he said, more a tease than before, "But I'm not going to like it."

"Wouldn't expect you to," Ed said, and went to put his box of weed away.

* * *

They sat for awhile in the mostly-quiet. Not long after the tea was done, there was a yowling at the window. Ed went and propped it open, and a white, soggy shadow came streaking in.

"Alonzo Coricopat!" Baron cried, rising from his seat. The cat walked over the counters and right to Baron, rubbing his rain-wet body against him. Purring instantly, arching his back, eating Baron's presence up.

"My love," Baron said, "My true love!"

Kissing his cheeks and whiskers, knuckling his ears. Purring and purring and purring, both of them. Ed watched as Baron peeled off his sweater, revealing a worn-out tie dyed t-shirt beneath. Ed noted that Baron was less skinny than he was years ago. More finely muscled. Chiseled, almost. Ed noted it, tried, was unable to push the thought away. Baron took the old wool jumper, used it to dry off the cat.

"What are they feeding you, pussy puss?" he asked. "Oh, you're all skin and bones. My sweet sconner. My love."

"He eats better'n the rest of them," Ed said. "Turned out to be our best mouser, you know."

Baron looked straight at Ed for a moment. Glowering. "Alonzo should be feeding on nothing but the fattest rats in the empire. None of these scrawny Scottish mice."

Christ, Ed thought. Rubbing his eyes. Was he feeling jealous of a cat?

"I thought you were an anarchist," he said. Only a little pointedly. "Seems a very colonial thing to say."

"With kings like Alonzo," Baron said, "We should all be monarchists." He bent over, putting his forehead against the cat's forehead. Both of them purring to each other. Ed bit his lip. Hated himself for what he was feeling, then. For what he always inevitably felt in the presence of Baron. Reached down, rearranged himself, hoping Baron didn't notice. He didn't seem to. Baron was too drunk, and too smitten by Alonzo, beside.

* * *

Sittin' there, still a bit sloshed, but less of an edge now, with Alonzo on his lap, in Ed's kitchen, drinking his second cup of tea, Baron started to feel… well, *right*. At home, too.

"Do you have a fag, love?" he asked Ed, surprised to hear himself call Ed that. Or not surprised, precisely. Because Ed *was* a love. But surprised that the word came so easy still. Ed got up from where he was leaning on the counter.

"No," he said, "But the missus does. Keeps saying she's quit. Right pain in the ass. I'll get you one."

He walked off toward the front hall for a moment, into the darkness. Went riffling for something. Baron listened to him, pretending not to. That's when he heard a little voice come from above, and Ed said something in a low tone, then sighed. When he returned - pack of Albany's and a matchbook in his hand - he was followed this time. By a little girl, her towhead all tangled, wearing a flannel nightgown.

"Daddy, who's this?" she was asking. Standing barefoot in the kitchen, rubbing her eye, staring at Baron.

Baron shook out a cigarette, lit it.

"Allo, Angel," he said, in a just-too-loud voice. He never did quite know what to do with children. She chewed on her nail. Stared at him. "I'm your daddy's old friend from his days in the war."

"You were in a war?" she asked, looking at Ed, her pale brow all knitted up. He chuckled at that, running his fingers through her tangly hair.

"No, pet. He's joking. I'll get you that warm milk."

Baron watched as the girl, this Hammond-Waller spawn, pulled up a stool and sat down across from him. Looking at her own feet, at the ground. Anywhere but Baron. He smoked a bit more. Stroked Alonzo.

"What's your name, beautiful?" he asked. Wasn't just saying it, neither. She was a very pretty little girl. Ed, in miniature, bit more delicate, maybe. A china doll.

"Aisling," she said.

"Pretty name," Baron said. "For a pretty bird. You want to know what my name is?"

She looked at him, very seriously, eyes sort of trembly-like. Nodding.

"Klerkie Von Bleppington," he said. At the stove, Ed let out a coughing noise. The little girl was wrinkling her nose. Not knowing what to believe.

"Isn't?" she asked. Baron nodded very seriously.

"It is. I was named after the prime minister, Klerkie Von White. Haven't you 'eard of him? Don't you know your 'istory?"

Her whole face seemed to erupt in sunshine at that. She let out a squeal of laughter.

"No! That's a silly name!"

"I think it's quite beautiful, actually," Baron said. Took a draw of his fag. Fluttered his eyelashes.

"Daddy, that's not his name, is it?" she asked, squealing more. Ed chuckled, pouring the milk into a cup.

"No, love. Your dad's friend is a kidder."

She was giggling still. Sipping her milk. Looking at him, with eyes shining and bright. He fluttered eyelashes more. She rewarded him with still-more laughter.

Ed leaned his elbow on the counter, propped his face on his hand, looking between them. "This is Barry, love. Or Baron, you could say. Remember I told ye I used to be in a different band than the one I'm in now?"

She started to nod a bit. Then piped up, hopefully, "The Sapphires?"

"No-" Ed started, but Baron barked out laughter over him.

"Yes! The Sapphires!" And he started singing "Who do you love? I wanna know! I wanna know!" to Alonzo. Scritchin' him on the haunches.

He saw Ed roll his eyes. "No, love. Saffron."

"The Sapphires would have been a better band name, Ed. Shame you didn't think of it."

Ed sat up a bit. "Well, I'm sorry. They can't all be the Bartlebys."

"Prefer they not," Baron said, sucking away at his fag. He wanted another one, really. Wondered if the missus would be mad to find her cigarettes all gone.

"That's the one with the Cinderella song, right, daddy?" Aisling asked, pulling on her father's sleeve. Redirecting his attention back to her. Pretty little pet. A queen.

"Yes, that's right, love," he said.

"Shelagh said the Sapphires were *really famous*. More famous than your band now."

Baron snorted laughter at that. Ed looked at him, chiding.

"Well," he said to her, "It was different then. We were young and beautiful then."

"You're still beautiful," she protested, and threw her arms over his shoulders. Baron watched for a moment. Put out his cigarette. Rolled his eyes.

"Thanks, love," Ed said. "Now, it is *very* late. Would you like me to tuck you in?"

"Okay," she said. She hopped down off the stool. Took her dad's hand. Baron sat there, ready to wait, maybe smoke another fag, when she looked over her shoulder at him.

"Klerkie, are you coming, too?"

He snorted. "Me?"

She nodded. He glanced at Ed, who only shrugged.

"Not bad practice," he said, "For those fat Black babies you'll be making soon."

Baron sighed. Didn't want to go up there, not really. But they didn't leave him much of a choice.

"Fine," he said, sighing again. "'Scuse us, Alonzo Kittycat." He extricated the feline from his lap. Aisling laughed.

"*That's* not his name," she said.

"Says you," Baron groused, following them up the stairs. "I'm the one who named him."

* * *

Weird. Bein' in Ed's house. In Ed's other life. The floorboards creakin' under his boots, while Aisling and Ed walked barefoot, quiet as church mice. He was drunk, and the stairs seemed very long, and it felt like his feet fell too heavy on them, and when they got to the top he stood there dizzy a moment, peeping in the half-open doors. Another girl sleeping in another room in the yellow circle of a nightlight. A woman's head, tawny-colored, peeking out from rumpled covers in an old four poster. Ed walked his youngest down to the end of the hall where her bed was waiting for her. Wrought iron frame, Victorian-like. Horsie wallpaper. A fantasy bedroom. The kind he would have dreamed about as a boy when he shared *his* bed with his mummy, or else squeezed himself to sleep in that room in Deedz' house, the one that never quite felt like home.

Ed was tuckin' the girl in. Sitting on the bed's edge.

"Night, love," he said, and started to put the light out but her hand darted out and she told him to wait.

"Will you and Klerkie sing me the Cinderella song?" she asked. Christ. Ed looked at Baron, and Baron looked back, the cringe just barely invisible behind their gazes, and Ed was waiting for Baron to say something, maybe no. But instead, Baron just shrugged.

"Sure," he said. "No harm in it. The royalties all go to you, anyhow."

Ed rolled his eyes at him, and Baron felt a little mean - they didn't *all* go to Hammond, just, in his opinion, a disproportionate amount - but, well, given the circumstances...

"Alright," Ed said, and snapped his fingers a few times, and Baron stood up a little straighter. And despite the gin still oozing its way through him, the two of them sang. Ed first, then Baron. Just like they had on their album.

"A feller (a feller) says Cinderella can't keep up with sister Stella. She keeps that glass shoe somewhere new, inside her mummy's knapsack... "

And oh, *God*, it was magic. Of course it was. It always was. Not just in the way their voices mushed together, harmonizing easily, Ed's sweetness with Baron's sardonic *whatever*. But also. In how Baron. Was transported. This one had been off the last album, their masterpiece. Written one sunny afternoon right before Ed had found this place in Scotland, supposedly for the two of them, when they ate mushrooms at Ed's flat and went out walking in the park together, barefoot hippies, and found themselves talking about the songs they both loved on the playground when they were young, the crass ones, the gross ones. But. Also. The double Dutch songs the girls sang, which had always been denied them, and the day had pulsated and warbled and in the grass they laid out together and touched their bare toes together, singing rhymes together, magic, and walked back together to Ed's place, tryin' to resist holding hands because this was London and there were eyes around here. Sometimes just their knuckles touching. And when they'd come home they'd sat down at the piano together and their hands had melted together and they wrote something that sounded like it could have existed when they were kids, but it was theirs, it was theirs, and Ed got his tape recorder and they made a demo, right there. Piano, for Ed, and Baron slithering his way over to his guitar, and it was jangling and crackling and beautiful and later their producer Bruce had added in all that mellotron and the backwards tape *perfect*. Some folks called it hippy nonsense, but it wasn't nonsense. Had been vital, Baron thought. Necessary. He'd been thinking that even as the sun had come up that day and he and Ed made love and it hadn't been *foocking* that time, it had been *making love*, truly. Sweet, tender beauty.

They sang *that* song to Ed's daughter, and Baron's heart hurt as he remembered all of that. The song ended. Edmund kissed his child. Baron just sort of smiled vaguely, trying to cover up the pain, said, "G'night, sweetheart," and strolled outta there with his hands in his pockets. The little girl called out, "G'night, Klerkie!" back and he smiled even more, grimly. She was a funny kid, that one.

Ed followed him. Closed the door. While Baron pawed at the back of his neck, took slow steps toward the stairs.

"Should be off," he said. "Long drive home."

And he stepped down the stairs but swayed a little and his shoulder went hitting the wall and he winced, because he knew what was going to come next.

"Don't be daft," Ed said. "You're still drunk off your rocks. Can't let you drive home like that, and in this rain, too. I'll get sheets for you."

Didn't even bother objecting to it. Baron stood there at the top of the stairs, waiting. Hurting. As Ed went to the linen closet and fetched a sheet set and a pillow.

* * *

The flannel sheets. Those would do best on a wet cold night like tonight. And the Afghan his auntie had made them for the wedding, and a pillow. Ed busied himself looking for sheets. Trying not to think about how absurd this was. Drunk, drunk Baron, singing his daughter bedtime songs. *Their* songs. The ones they'd written together during those brief, bright weeks in summer, 1967, between the time when Ed had resolved to end it with Genie and when he'd learned that Shelagh was already a small live thing, swimming inside of her. That summer when they made the best music of their lives and he spent his weekends driving up to different farmhouses in Scotland, searching for the perfect place for them, someplace out of the way, hidden from the fans and the press and the prying eyes, someplace where they could have room for a studio and a piano and friends could come visit and they could learn about each other, could learn what it was like to *be* with each other day in, day out. Not just in secret.

Well. Fat lot of good that had done. Those few weeks. The best music of their lives, the best record, the best sex. The best house, this house, *their* house, and he'd just put the down payment on it and they were going to go up to see it together that weekend when Genie rang him up, mad that he'd been avoiding her calls, and told him what the doctor had told her. A *baby*. And then and then and then.

The damage, as it were, already done, and what was he going to do, *leave* her? Asked his old man for advice, and his old man had given it. Time to put away childish things, Ed. Time to put away your music, and I've never liked that mate of yours, that dark bloke, and isn't it best if et cetera et cetera.

He'd hated the old fuck then. Hated him now, too. But he didn't know what else to do. He listened.

Fuck. *Fuck.* His stomach hurt to even think of all of this. That summer.

Which he usually avoided thinking about at all. He grabbed the sheets and the pillows and the Afghan and started stomping away down the steps. Mad. At Baron for coming here tonight. At himself. At his own damned, stupid sperm and the two, soon to be three, beautiful babies it had made him. Barry was standing there, kind of slumped on the stairwell, and as Ed started to pass him, Barry put out a hand, touched his arm.

"You alright?" Baron asked, sensing, maybe, how angry Ed had grown in the time between closing Aisling's bedroom door and now. Ed gritted teeth. Didn't answer him. Breathed heavy. They both stared at each other for a moment. Stoned Ed. Drunk Baron. Glowering into each other's eyes.

And then *foock foock*. Kissing.

Foock.

And it was Ed, Ed doin' most of it, even though he knew he should not have been doing any of it. The bedrooms so close upstairs and the doors open, and the blankets between their bodies and Ed just plain dropped 'em, put his hands against the wall, pressed himself to Baron, kissed him hungry, hungry, hungry, sloppy kisses that meant that their teeth knocked once, percussive. Ouch. But didn't stop, just kept kissing, standing up, squashed up together. Beautiful Baron, here, in his house. Feelin' those muscles up against him, that chiseled chest up against him, hands working on the hem of his t-shirt, his abdominal muscles, and he hadn't known Baron to look like this before or feel like this, neither, and Ed was so, so hard against him already. Baron felt nothing like Genie, and Christ it had been so *long* and he wanted him so, so bad.

He came up for air for just one second, panting hard, holding Baron's soft, worn out t-shirt between his fists. Baron, breathing hard too.

"We'll go downstairs," Ed said, whispering now. Baron nodded slowly. Yes. And Ed bent down and hastily picked up the blankets and the pillow he'd dropped, and Baron took the Afghan, and they walked down into the kitchen and then Ed led him through a door off the side of it. Could have been a pantry, but instead, there was a stairwell going down, dimly let. Ed raced down those stairs, hearing Baron close behind.

It was his basement-turned-den-turned soon (he planned) into a proper recording studio, though right now all he had was the sound board propped up on some cinder blocks and the glass wall dividing it. He opened the door to the booth. Inside were a few chairs, a folding table, some hung up guitars, a bookshelf, a futon. Ed was moving sloppily, hastily, still breathing hard enough he trembled. He pulled open the futon and started making up the bed. Could feel Baron watch him as he stood in the door to the booth. But then heard him close the door behind him.

Ed was smoothing down the corners of the fitted sheet and then spreading out the top sheet and blanket. Out of the corner of his eye, he could see Baron stumbling out of his boots, then unbuttoning his pants to drop them on the floor. That slob Baron, he thought, shaking his head, but he didn't *really* mind. Because Baron was *here*, and they were going to fuck, and he was looking at the leanly muscled shape of Baron's thighs under his y-fronts as Ed smoothed down the blanket, tossed the pillow down on one end.

"You look good, Barry," he told him, plainly, wanting to say it. Wanting Baron to know. The last time they'd seen each other had been at a low point for both. Ed had put on a good 2 stones after the baby was born, grown a scraggly beard, had been ill dressed and sullen in court. Baron had been so thin then that he was practically skeletal. But Ed knew that they both reacted to stress in different ways. Ed ate. Baron didn't. And often took to the shitter at times of stress, too. And, well, there had been rumors that Baron had developed a drug problem after the break-up. Maybe it was true. Ed knew Baron had tried snorting heroin a few times in the '60s, but it had made Ed nervous, so Baron had stopped. Now, though, probably none of that. Baron's arms were unmarred and strong, he had some extra meat on his arse, looked healthier - more alive - than Ed had ever known him to look.

Baron glanced down at himself. Shrugged. Reached down and squeezed the erection that was straining his pants. But just sort of stood there, not coming close. Ed sat down on the edge of the futon, gesturing.

"C'mere, love," he said. Baron hesitated a moment longer. Then walked closer to him. Standing over him. Ed just about at eye level with Baron's t-shirted belly, his cock, and he could *smell* him. Alcohol, yes. A hint of sweat.

Sweet patchouli or something, a woody smell. His skin, the mustiness of his skin. Ed reached out, put his arms around Baron's lower back, hugged him close to him. One more beat of hesitation. Then Baron put his hands in Ed's hair.

"This is why I couldn't come see you, Hammy. All these years," Baron said. "Knew what would happen. The same thing that always happened. How could we move on if we're always tangled up with each other?"

"Dunno," Ed said. He lifted up Baron's shirt, felt his skin broiling against him. Kissed those stomach muscles, so new and fascinating. "Didn't see why we *had* to move on."

"You sued me," Baron said, his hands playing in Ed's hair as Ed's mouth moved lower. Laughing a little.

"You threw a brick through my window."

"You married someone else."

"Didn't think it would cause that much trouble. You tried it first."

"Yeah, but she knew about you. More or less. I didn't want to be a secret no more." Baron's prick was hard against Ed's shoulder. Ed turned his face, nuzzled it against him. Baron moaned.

"The best secret, though," Ed said. "The best part of it all."

"Yeah," Baron said. "'Strue. But it wasn't *enough*."

"No," Ed said. Pulling away from Baron for a moment. His own voice sounded faraway, like it belonged to someone else. "It wasn't."

Kissing Baron's belly again, moving lower. Pulling down his pants, so his cock sprung out. Burying his face in Baron's bush, inhaling his nutty, woody scent, and wrapping his hand around Baron's length, and Baron's head casting back, and moaning, and Ed kissing along the length of Baron, and then the damp, salty tip, and then sucking down the length of him, hard, and Baron letting out an animal noise, his knees going wobbly, and Ed's arms around him, bolstering him, as he took him in deep. Withdrew. Then took him in deep again.

"God," Baron whispered, spouting nonsense. "Your pretty little mouth. God, God."

Ed knew it never took Baron very long, even after drinking, but he could tell that he was especially close tonight. He sucked him for a stroke longer, maybe two, then sat back a bit on the bed, his hand squeezing Baron's wet length. Keeping him close. Holding him there.

"How do you want me tonight, Barry?" Ed asked him. Knowing what *he* wanted, not wanting, for some reason, to be the one who said it. Wanting to know they both wanted it. Equally. Mutually. Baron laughed. His eyes were closed.

"Want you up me arse," he said coarsely. Then cracked one eye just-open. "If that's what *you* want?"

Ed reached down, felt himself hard in his pajamas. "Sure," he said, because he *did* want that. Too. Wanted all of it. "If you'll return the favor after?"

Baron laughed at that. Bit his lip. Nodded. Stepped back for a minute to peel off his t-shirt and pull his y-fronts down and step out of them, so Ed started unbuttoning his pajamas, too. Feeling self-conscious for a moment at the softness of his belly compared to the lovely sharpness of Baron's body, but if it bothered Baron, he showed no sign. Just knelt on hands and knees on the futon, waiting for Ed. God, he was gorgeous. Ed slid his pants down, knelt behind Baron, both of them fully naked now. Ed so hard and ready. Moving his hands all along Baron's sides, touching all of him. His rib cage. His hips. His flanks. The soft hair on his legs. And he leaned against Baron, so that Baron's arse was on his belly, and he kissed a line down his muscular back and lower. Pausing. Because he didn't have any lube down here, why would he? He and Genie only ever fucked in bed, and didn't need it, anyway. And there were certain things he'd never done with Baron, but Baron was waiting for him, as Ed paused, stroking Baron's balls, his shaft, and finally, letting out a sort of a sigh, he bent over and started licking him. Not thinking about it at first, or else pushing out thoughts of *dirty* and *wrong*, but then he didn't have to anymore, realizing that flesh is flesh, and it wasn't that different from licking a fanny, though it wasn't as wet and the taste was different, and it was *Baron* anyway, and he loved him, and worked his tongue and fingers in deeper and Baron's knees were wobbling again and Ed was even harder, so he sat up and pressed the head of his cock against Baron's wet, waiting arse and then pushed into it. Slid in easy, though he was so, so tight. Ed rested there, in up to his pelvis, feeling Baron's whole body, taking him in. The sight of that muscular, beautiful back. His sculpted shoulders. Feeling both of them throb.

"God, oh, Christ," Baron said, cloudy at first, then turned back to glance toward him. "Take it slow, Ed. If I'm going to top you after, I don't want to come yet."

"Okay," Ed said, nodding a little as he throbbed again. Surprised a little, at the language Baron had used, the certain clinical casualness. He wondered who Baron had been fucking these past four years, who talked like that, not their usual Scouser grunting of *fuck me* and *touch my arsehole* and *stick it in*. While he'd been fucking just Genie, or mostly just Genie - a few fans, too, here or there - but women all of them, and mostly women who laid flat on their backs and just waited for him to pound into them, indiscriminately, though Genie had gotten better lately. Liked being on top sometimes at least, now. Let him eat her out now and then.

"You alright, Hammy?" Baron asked, and Ed realized he'd gone elsewhere for a minute. Brought himself back to where he was. *Here*, with Baron's dusky body laid out in front of him, and Ed started fucking him slowly.

"Nnnf," he grunted. "Yeah. I'm alright." Building a slow rhythm. *Lento*. 4/4 time. Easy. Easy. Baron's body tightening, rippling around him, and Ed felt his own body go tight, and the pressure down below, and he didn't want to come yet, wanted to be in deep forever, but it was too much for him, Baron's body like a vise around him, and him moving in and out, in and out, and *fuck -*

"Coming," Ed managed to grunt, as his back arched and he throbbed and throbbed, filling Baron up, and Baron leaned back against him, his smooth body against Ed's sweaty body, tight and close and perfect and Ed came into him, saw stars, going nowhere and everywhere, all at once. And before he was even done, Baron was reaching back and kissing him, stroking himself. Kissing and stroking. Ed threw his arms around Baron, hugging him to him. Kissing his neck, his shoulders.

"I love you," he said, almost, not quite, crying as he said it, and Baron, still stroking himself, holding Ed's arms to him, made a murmuring sound.

"I know you do, pet," he said. And then added, "Here." He pulled his body away from Ed's, slowly, slowly, and then laid down on the made-up bed. Got down under the flannel sheet and Afghan, holding it open, waiting for Eddie to join him. Ed did, with one hand around his sticky, softening cock. Not wanting to muck the blankets up. Baron chuckled. Held Ed against him, and Baron was still hard, and kissing him, and Baron was still hard, and Ed was half-hard too, still, not minding it, though now everything had a haze of sleepiness over it. Cloudy and warm. Barry, Barry, safe, in Barry's arms, being kissed and touched and pressed up into.

"Still want me inside you, love?" Baron asked. Ed nodded. Yes, yes. He did. Holding Ed close, Baron took his own hand, working it up and down Ed's half-hearted erection, and Ed realized he wasn't wanking him, really, but taking the stickiness, and then he moved his fingers to the other side, using Ed's own fluids to open him up. There was a sort of shifting there, fingers, cock, arsehole, and then Baron stuffed himself up into Ed, holding him closer and closer, his legs doing a sort of scissoring motion beneath him, working him sideways and up and big and hard and warm and everything, and Baron was kissing him at first, soft, stickysleepy, and then harder, then small bites on his shoulder and then crying out as he was coming, an unbelievable orgasm, animal sounds against Ed's back, and Ed was surprised, because he found his own body ticking ticking ticking against Baron's body, everything going blotto. Another orgasm, which had never happened to him before, and them both twitching together, throbbing together, not humans anymore but some kind of conjoined meat machine, animal noises and shaking and a sort of pain mixed with pleasure which he thought - which he hoped - might never, ever stop.

Sleep, almost immediately, for both of 'em.

* * *

Woke up a few hours later, still wrapped up in Baron's arms, both of them soft together, and sleeping. Dreamin' of the same thing. Nuthin'.

Ed got up and went to the bathroom on the other side of the half-wall, which was only half-built A sink, a toilet, and walls with holes through them. He'd finish it soon enough, if Genie would stop nagging him about other things. Cleaned the cum off his belly. Checked the clock outside the door. Not yet 4:00 a.m. Hadn't taken them very long then. The foreplay and the fucking. Well, good. Still time before the family got up. He went back into the other room, put his pajama pants on, laid down next to Baron, whose eyes were closed, still, but he reached out an arm for Ed, anyway.

"C'mere, Hammy," he told him. Hammy snuggled close.

"So America," Ed said, blinking up at the track lights, which were half-dimmed but still felt too bright.

"Mmm," Baron said. "Birthplace of rock 'n' roll."

"It's still illegal there, innit?" said Ed. "What we do?"

"Not planning on being queer there," Baron replied. "But there might be temptations. New York City's the place where they say et cetera."

"Maybe you'll get yourself a handsome glam rocker."

"Mmm," Baron said again, grunting. "No. No more musicians for me. Too much drama."

"You!" Ed said, and tickled Baron, who opened his eyes, grabbed Ed's hands, tickled back. Like a coupla kids together, tickling in bed and sniggering, then Baron held Ed's hands down and got on top of him and kissed him and they were kissing. Both too tired to fuck, but a long kiss, and then Baron laying on top of him, pretending to doze again.

"Don't want it to end, Barry," Ed said softly. "Tonight."

"Never really does for me," Baron said. "In me head. Figured out something a few years ago. If I lie there, before I go to sleep, telling myself that whoever is there beside me is actually you, even if the only person beside me is me own loneliness, then it's like it's almost true, innit? Can't really tell the difference."

"It's not the same," Ed said, feeling both touched and sad to think about it. This long pantomime that Baron had been engaged in. That Baron had been thinking of him, holding him close, all this time.

"Mmm, no. But I figure it's the closest I'll get for now. Until you're done playing house. Someday, maybe, when the kids are grown and your daddy is dead and the world don't care anymore, we'll be a couple of old faggots together. Sharin' a bed together properly. Then we won't have to pretend."

"I'd like that."

"I know you would," Baron told him. "Ye fruit."

They both smiled at one another. But then were interrupted by a mewling on the floor. Baron lifted his head, looking past Ed's line of vision.

"Alonzo!" he cried. "Come snuggle, puss-puss."

He rolled off Ed. Bent over, and picked up the cat, plopping him in bed between them. Alonzo did not seem to mind.

"Cor," Ed said, sitting up to watch them. How Baron tucked his body around Alonzo, making a proper bed for him. "You two."

"He's my true husband," Baron said, pulling the blanket over the cat. Ed snorted a bit. Laughed a bit.

"Yeah," he said.

"Now Alonzo," Baron was saying, scritching his ear, "I'm going to be goin' on holiday. America. But when I'm gone I want you to remember that I always loved you best."

The cat purred and purred. Ed sat back in the bed, his hands tucked behind his head, listening. Grinning. Remembering the day that Baron had brought him the kitten, right after he'd bought the house in London. A tiny mewling thing, almost too tiny to have left his mum.

I've never had a pet before, Ed had said. *What do I do with it?*

Him. Alonzo Coricopat's his name. After Eliot. You just love on him. Give him kitten food and let him keep you warm at night when I can't do it proper.

Their love had been new then, inconstant and hesitant. Ed had blushed then at the implication. Had taken the creature into his hands, felt his tiny death claws, his soft, warm belly. Had felt grateful, then, to be loved by Baron, though they barely ever talked about it. But he knew. He knew.

Felt grateful, now, to be loved by Baron, too.

The three of them snuggled up together under the Afghan, drifted off to thin, distant sleep.

* * *

Morning. The sound of plates and water running upstairs. Ed sat up, saw Baron, barely waking there. Alonzo, still tucked into the crook of Baron's arm, mewed up at him. But didn't budge. Happy there, next to his favorite human. Next to Ed's favorite human.

Ed bent down and kissed him.

"I'll go warn the girls you're here," he said. "There's a bathroom. You go get decent."

"Impossible," Baron said, winked. Kissed Ed back, long and warm. The last kiss. The best kiss.

Ed went upstairs into the kitchen in his pajamas. Genie was there, makin' the girls eggs.

"You slept in the studio?" she asked, and it wasn't an unusual question and it wasn't an unusual thing for him, when he couldn't sleep. Ed sighed. Putting the kettle on for tea. Putting bread in the toaster.

"Yes," he said. 'Sort of. Barry stopped by last night."

Genie dropped the spatula. Turned, one hand on her hip, frowning at him. "Baron *Templeton?*"

Ed laughed. "That's the one."

"Well," she said. "That explains the gin."

Ed glanced at the counter where the girls sat. The bottle of gin there. The envelopes.

"Yeah," Ed admitted. "He was drunk off his rocker at first. Dunno how he managed to get here in the rain. Couldn't let him drive home. We stayed up late. Talked."

He knew, vaguely, that he was giving too much information. But somehow couldn't stop himself.

"And it was… okay?" she asked carefully. Ed reached out, took the envelopes. Tryin' to look subtle. Who knows what was written in them.

"Yeah, okay," Ed said. That's when Aisling piped up.

"I met Daddy's friend. Klerkie Von Bleppington. He sang me the Cinderella song."

Genie glanced at her daughter, lifting one eyebrow. "Well, that's something."

"Really, it was fine," Ed said, laughing. "He was sweet with her. He's moving to America soon. Wanted to see me before he headed off. Thought maybe I'd take him around the farm today. Show him everything. Fishing, maybe, if the weather clears."

"His name isn't *Klerkie*," Shelagh was saying. "You're *ridiculous*."

"*He* told me his name is Klerkie. *He* said he and Daddy were in a war together."

"Don't be *stupid*. Daddy wasn't in a *war*. He was in a *band*."

"Girls," Genie warned. "Well, that sounds fine, Ed. The rain's stopped."

"Good," Ed said. The toast popped up, and he went and put it all on a tray. The letters. The toast. The tea. Kissed Genie on the temple as he passed her. Grateful that she wasn't pushing, that she wasn't asking anymore questions.

"'Ey," Ed called as he walked down the stairs. Hadn't even noticed how the door was open. Must have missed it opening up when the girls were fighting. "Barry!"

But when he got downstairs, Baron was gone.

* * *

He laid there and cuddled with Alonzo for one moment longer. Kissed him on the scruff. Got up, stretching himself out fully. The cat followed him, stretching, too.

"No, love," he said. "You stay here. Keep our kid company."

The cat looked at him, head cocked in confusion. But then laid back down on the bed, as if he understood.

Baron didn't bother washing up, as Ed had told him. Wanted to keep Ed's smell on him a little longer, and besides, no one would know. He pulled on his dirty jeans, his t-shirt, his boots. His sweater was upstairs somewhere. Guess it was Ed's now.

He passed through the door to the glass room. Stopped next to the staircase, hearing Ed talking to his family upstairs. Felt a sticky pain in his belly. Told himself it was alright. This was the way it had been for a long time now, and it was time to find his own rhythm. America. Land of Chuck Berry. Little Richard. Bo. Sister Fucking Rosetta Tharpe. Maybe there, then, he'd feel like he was belonging. Like he wasn't such a stranger. That's what Alana had told him, at least. That's what he hoped.

Listened to Ed's voice one moment longer. Would miss it, though. Would miss Ed.

He glanced to one side, where there was a bookshelf, a clock, reading just past nine. Saw that it was full of mementos. Grammy's, and a photo of the band on the night they met Elvis (fat old drunk), and some of those 'orrible dolls one of the American companies had made of them. Was supposed to be him and Ed and Liam, but they looked nearly demonic. Gave him the creeps. He shuddered.

Then he glanced up.

On the top shelf. Just two things. A fat chunk of brick, red and dusty. And a handheld radio. Baron touched it, remembering. Smiling wistfully. Oh, that Ed. Sentimental old sod. Baron wondered what Ed would take away from this night. His letters? A half-drunk bottle of Beefeater's? His sweater? Well, no matter, he told himself. As long as he was taking away *something*.

Baron didn't wait to go any longer. Couldn't. Because if he waited, well, he'd have to stay. And they couldn't have that. He swallowed down whatever it was he was feeling, putting the handheld back in its place on the shelf, and hustled up the stairs. Opened the door quietly, quickly, and headed out the front door while Ed's girls were still arguing, before anybody could notice. Into the mud and the cool Scottish morning. Started up the Rolls. And drove away.

Reunion III

Sid had been nagging her to talk to this record producer, an old friend of his, for months now, and it wasn't that Naomi was necessarily *opposed*. He'd produced his wife's second album - which Naomi frankly preferred to the first, critics be damned - plus a slew of quirky indie artists after that, but she wasn't sure that she was really a quirky indie artist anymore, anyhow, and she liked the rhythm she had going with Mirrortone on the last two albums and disliked change, as a rule. So she'd been ignoring his advice.

Plus, it pissed him off when she ignored him, and she enjoyed that.

But it seemed that Sid had decided that it was time to force the issue, because almost as soon as she arrived at his house, after dumping her checkered jacket in the guest room in an enormous pile of coats, Sid ushered her off to the kitchen for a drink and as he mixed her a Brandy Alexander, saying *They're amazing, like milkshakes*, she found herself trapped in a corner with him and this guy, Rick Ashby was his name, and he was maybe a decade older than she was, in an expensive suit, with an expensive shave, and was the type of man in this business she usually *hated*, except when he spoke he sounded kind of like this rough little kid, and within a sentence or two had launched into this ridiculous story about meeting her father at the Plaza Hotel in the '70s. About meeting *her*. As a *baby*.

"Man, and he just adored you," he was saying, sucking on a vape pen, exhaling. "You were this fat little butterball and he looked ready to eat you *up*. I'd never seen anything like it. You read about Baron Templeton - and I mean, I did, as a kid, constantly, magazines and shit - and you expect one thing, like some kind of snotty rock and roller, and instead he's like five feet tall, this tiny fag, cooing over his kid."

Naomi couldn't help it. Her eyes went saucer-wide over to Sid, who was just standing there, grinning, the fuck. Like he'd planned this whole thing.

"Your mom was hot as hell, too," Rick said, and now Naomi's wide-eyed look went half maniacal.

What the fuck? she mouthed at Sid, but Sid wasn't saying anything, just standing there, shit-eating grin on his face. Like he'd fucking planned this whole thing just to fuck with her.

Maybe he had. It never paid to try and one-up Sid Edelman. That's what she liked about him, of course. When it came down to her career, he was *ruthless*. But it also had its drawbacks. She sucked down more of the Brandy Alexander.

"You should tell her the story of the night we met," Sid said, elbowing him. "Only time I ever lost a bet."

Rick laughed.

"Oh yeah. Man. Has Sid ever told you my theory about that song 'Cymbeline'?"

"Um, no," Naomi said. Screaming inside.

"Yeah, I'm pretty sure your dad wrote it. So, you see-"

Luckily, Naomi didn't get to hear Rick's theory, which she was sure was probably exhaustive and came with charts. They were a special breed, Saffron fans, she'd learned. But at that moment, someone she didn't know, some narrow woman in a slinky dress, came into the kitchen and whispered to the three of them, "*Ed Hammond* is here!"

"Oh, God," Rick said, taking another draw of his vape pen, "That old fuck."

But Sid had glanced very seriously toward Naomi. "Must mean Matthew's here," he said, *sotto voce*, and Naomi shrugged, trying to look nonchalant, herself.

"Yeah, I saw him in the green room tonight. Told him he should try and make it. That okay?" She arched an eyebrow, feeling a little bit like a teenager who had been caught sneaking out in that moment. Or maybe a teenager who had invited her boyfriend to Thanksgiving when she knew she shouldn't. But Sid touched his hand to Rick's arm.

"Of course it is. Excuse me for a moment, Rick."

Naomi watched the square of her manager's back walk away, hating him, for a hot minute, for leaving him there in his kitchen, sucking on that disgusting drink with this guy, whose gray hair was pulled back into a ponytail (of course it was). He gestured to the drink.

"You should be careful with that," he told her. "Those things'll knock you on your ass."

"Thanks," she said tersely, taking another sip. Glancing toward the door of the kitchen, hoping Sid would return soon. Knowing he probably wouldn't. He'd told her recently that he'd been chasing Matthew Hammond around for *years* trying to get him to return to the studio. Failing. Hard to compete with that. When it came down to it, her manager was so damned needy.

"Y'know I was supposed to work with Hammond's kid at one point. Matthew."

This got Naomi's attention. She glanced up. "Yeah?"

"Yeah. You know him? I bet all you Saffron kids know each other." She didn't answer him, so he went on. "It was like a decade ago. More, maybe. Kept getting delayed, and then he decided to do that schmaltz with his dad instead. Recorded it in the UK, and anyway, I didn't have the right sound. They wanted something more 'commercial.'"

Rick moved his fingers in air quotes.

"Ah," Naomi said. "Well, you know. I wouldn't take it personally. The whole Hammond machine seems pretty slick."

"Yeah, I don't," Rick said. He shrugged. "Shame, though. Kid's a great songwriter, nice set of pipes. Found their collaboration flat. Could have done something better."

Naomi wasn't sure what to say. She'd finished her drink. Left the glass on the counter. Rick was staring at her now, really, truly staring.

"You know who else has a nice set of pipes?"

When she didn't answer, he pointed a finger at her.

"Aw," she said, rolling her eyes. "C'mon."

"You do! Your song tonight was great." He paused. Vaped again.

"Emotionally, I don't think your music has done much for me since that first album. But I think I'd be able to get you there again."

Her brow furrowed. "What are you talking about?"

He reached into his pocket, pulled out his card. "I'm just telling you to think about it," he said. "No hard sell. You decide there's something to what I'm saying, that you want to do something more, then you call me."

She stared at his hand for a moment. Reluctantly took the card. Shoved it down her trouser pocket. Looked around, desperate for an escape.

Luckily that was just when Matthew Hammond wandered into the room.

"Matt!" she called. Didn't even give Rick a backwards glance.

"Sorry," she said. "I've got to run."

"Sure, sure," he told her. "Nice talking with you." He took one last draw on his vape pen as she rushed over to Matt.

* * *

On the elevator up, Matthew realized how absurd it was that he was even *there* that night. He wasn't a musician anymore, not really. A freaking middle school music teacher. *That's* what he was. His sisters had decided to turn in early, and Matthew knew that he should have, too. He had a kid to worry about, didn't he? Theirs were grown. His still needed his beauty rest. Though Five didn't look particularly tired as he stood there next to his grandfather, hands in his pockets. The two of them looking like time-delayed clones.

"Will there be other kids at this party?" Five asked, talking more to his grandfather than to Matthew. The oldest Ed shook his head.

"Probably not, son." Stood waiting for a moment, hands in his pockets still, then glanced at the boy. "But I'd hazard a guess that there will be a guitar up there. Somewhere."

Five grinned at that, the sort of grin that split his whole face in two. Matthew felt a pull in his belly at the sight of it. Big, full love for the kid, the kind he had never contemplated before becoming a father. But something else, too. Jealousy. Maybe. A little bit. Matthew had *liked* music. Had been talented at it as a boy. Enough to garnish some attention. But it hadn't kept him going the way it had seemed to keep Five going. Necessary, he knew, for the child to have that in his life - the same way some of his students needed to spend all of their lunch periods in the band room, talking to him about their favorite songs. But still, a certain sort of tender loss there. It was something Edmund Matthew Hammond III possessed, and Edmund Matthew Hammond V, but that brilliant, addictive spark had somehow skipped a generation. Not that he could *complain*. But he knew that he stood outside of it. That he was disappointing, in a way, to all of them.

The elevator dinged and they arrived at the Edelman flat. It was already thronged with people, and Matthew noted how everything went quiet a bit when his father walked in. The hush. He was used to it. The way people interrupted their conversations to look at each other, eyes widening, and then look away. The phones that were brought out and which hovered surreptitiously at the edge of their visions. Sneaking photographs, as if they didn't know. His Dad took it all in stride, clapping Five on the back.

"C'mon, son. Let's find where we can put our coats. Matt?"

Matthew shrugged his off, handed it to his father.

"Thanks," he said. Hearing the nerves in his own voice. "I'll find us a Scotch."

"Yessss," said Five, pumping his arm. "Scotch!" His Dad ruffled Five's hair, laughing.

"Shirley temple for this one, yeh?"

"C'mon…"

"Don't worry, Five," Matthew said. "I'm sure the maraschino cherries are a fine vintage."

He walked through the well-dressed crowd, finding the caterer's bar. Ordered their drinks. Waited. Looked around, feeling pretty outside of himself. Wondered where Naomi was. If she was even there. Wouldn't be unlike her, he thought, almost hopefully, to invite him and then bail. To toss him into the belly of the beast and then leave him. She'd done it before - hadn't she?

He was thinking about it, feeling sorry for himself, when he spotted a familiar face coming toward him. Waving at him. Calling, "Matty-baby! Matt! Matt!"

Edelman.

Fuck. The panic in his chest was real then, staccato. He tried to look away, to pretend like he hadn't seen him. But Edelman was shouldering through the crowd straight for him. Fuck. In his panic, Matt did the only thing he could think of doing.

He walked off in the other direction, shoving through some chattering record execs, even as the bartender called out, "Excuse me? Sir?" and Sid started waving his arms wildly. "Matty, hold on a second!"

He did not hold on. Would not. Could not. Instead, he took off toward the back of the apartment, heading for the kitchen. The most crowded place at a party, right? Every time.

He was surprised, then, when he found the kitchen practically empty. There was a narrow woman in a slinky dress in the corner, trying to dab a stain out of the front of her dress in the kitchen sink. A man - familiar, a bit - with his gray hair pulled back in a ponytail. And Naomi. Rushing toward him. Her eyes wide, like she was relieved to see him, waving, calling his name.

"Matt!" she said, then hooked her small hands in the crook of his arm, pulling him in the other direction. Dropped her voice to a whisper.

"Play along," she said, "And there's a joint in it for you."

Matt bent down a little to put his mouth close to her ear. "Only if you help me escape Edelman," he said. She looked at him, her smile sparkling like steel on flint.

"It's a deal," she said.

* * *

Up a long stairwell to the top of the house. Presumably off-limits to the rest of the party, but didn't they both enjoy a special relationship with their manager? Well, Naomi told herself, she was sure that Sid and Cymbeline would understand. When they arrived in the master bedroom, empty of everyone who would make demands on them, she closed the door behind her. Locked it, even. Stood there, still grinning for a moment, looking at Matt.

He'd cut his thinning hair short, let it all go gray. It didn't look altogether bad. Silver fucking fox. Something different about him now, she thought. Once he'd taken up more space than he should have, sucking most of the air - his, hers - from the room. Seemed more comfortable in his skin now, in his low key suit, no tie. But somehow sadder, too. And wasn't it funny? Despite her general preference for women, sad men had always been her favorite kind. The ones who wanted to make art together and stay up late talking about feelings. Processing, like she used to with her mother. Tender. Vulnerable. Familiar.

"Got that joint?" he asked. She reached into her pocket and pulled out a baggie and some papers. Held it up. Shook it a little. He rubbed his hands together.

"Fantastic," he said. "I could use it."

"Here," she told him, and tossed it his way. He caught it in the air. "I suck at rolling."

He went over and sat on the edge of the bed, his dress shoes flat on the floor, and started to roll it. She watched him from the other end of the room - the quick, careful way his hands worked. Considering the flash of pink when his tongue darted out. Feeling something. Denying it.

"So. Avoiding Sidney."

"So," he answered. "Avoiding Rick Ashby."

Touche. She came over to the bed, stepping out of her shoes, and climbed up into the middle. Sitting cross-legged at the center.

"You know him, right? He mentioned you were supposed to record together."

"Years ago. I wanted to. He's an amazing producer. His sound's like nothing else. But Dad didn't want to travel and what Hammond III says, goes." He dipped the entire joint into his mouth. Saliva as glue. Gross. Sexy. Sort of. Both.

"Mmm," Naomi said carefully as Matt passed her the joint and the lighter.

She lit it. Took a long draw. Took another. Held in the smoke. Passed it back while she coughed a little. Strong, dry stuff. "He wants to do my next album. Sid thinks I should."

"Sid's right. If he's interested in you, you should do it. He doesn't work with just anyone." Matt held the joint between thumb and forefinger. Took short puffs.

"Dunno. Feel like I'm at a point in my career where I should be firming up my style. Not experimenting with it."

"Don't think it would be like that," Matt said, passing the joint back. His hand looked kind of splotchy out in front of him. This was strong stuff. She took it. Kept smoking. "He likes to strip an artist down to their fundamentals. They've seen you polished. Now it's time to remind them what they loved about you in the first place."

She looked at him, feeling an eyebrow arch.

"What?"

"Is that your advice as a music teacher?"

He laughed, which turned to a giggle. A little too much for the joke, which was a little too mean, she knew, but, well.

"Fair," he said. "What do I know? You're doing a hell of a lot better than I ever did with this shit."

He let his body flop back in bed. Sat staring at the ceiling. She watched the way his flooded eyes traced the high-up molding, the light fixture.

"Do you miss it?" she asked finally, giving him the joint. He was smoking more slowly now, contemplatively.

"Nah. It never felt natural to me to be up there in front of everyone. You know, I was thinking tonight, for someone with stage fright, you do okay."

She laughed. Stage fright. "Xanax and a metric fuck ton of EMDR, baby," she told him. "Sid insisted after seeing my first show. I almost can't feel it anymore. Most of the time. Sometimes I remember what I'm doing and it all goes wrong."

He gave her the joint. Looking at her now, truly looking. His blue eyes shot with gray were thoughtful. She edged closer. Kept smoking.

"Sometimes I think that's the worst thing someone can do." A long pause.

The joint was a little stub now, almost burning her fingers.

"What?" she said.

"You know. Thinking. I mean. It doesn't matter what we think, anyway, right? That's what I think, at least."

"You think?" she asked. Wrinkling her nose. They both snickered.

"Yeah," he said. "I think - I think I don't believe in free will."

"Getting cerebral, Matt."

"Well, then call me cerebral."

"Nerd."

"Poser." They grinned at each other like a couple of kids. Time was moving so slow. She looked around for somewhere to put out the joint. Finally found a tiny plate on one of the nightstands, probably meant to hold jewelry, wedding rings. Smooshed it out.

"Well," Matt said, "Do you want to hear my grand sweeping theory of the universe or not?"

"I have a feeling I'm gonna," she told him, sitting back against the pillows. He hadn't moved from where he was laying, from where he was still staring up at the ceiling. Arms stretched out over his shoulders. His left arm almost touching her outstretched leg, though she wasn't sure he noticed.

(She noticed.)

"I think time is an illusion."

"Oh boy," she said.

"Hear me out. It's just a trick of our perception, that we're moving through it. Everything happens because of the physical laws of the universe, right? And so there's only one way anything could ever end. Or begin. Those beginnings created their endings. In a way, those endings create their beginnings. So really, all of time exists all at once."

"So what about free will?" she said.

"We only think we have it. What we really do, I think, really, is look for validation for choices that we would have made anyway. And that includes believing we're choosing things, when we only would have ever done one thing from the beginning."

"You don't find that depressing?"

He frowned. A funny, grimacey frown. Kind of cute, the way he was thinking about this, like some college kid.

"Used to. Don't anymore. It's kind of liberating. No need to get all worried about what's going to happen. That worrying is just a performance. Like, a social performance. Not rooted in who I am, here, right now, with you."

He looked at her. A pointed kind of look. A softly smiling kind of look. Whatever it was he was thinking, it was too close to the surface for her. She glanced away.

"Like," he went on, "You'll either record with Rick Ashby, or you won't. I'll either go back to songwriting, or I won't. Whatever we do will be okay, because it's all okay. Right now we're here, in this illusion of the present, together, but we're also already dead. We're also not even born yet. There's a big bang, and there's a big freeze, and -"

"Matt," she said softly. She wasn't sure why, but this was all upsetting her, to hear him talking like this. Filling the room up with particles and quarks.

"Sorry," he said. Laughed a little. "I'm really fucking stoned."

After a second, she let herself laugh, too. "I can see that," she said. A long pause. It seemed to take eons for her to find words again and when she did, they were the wrong words. But she said them anyway. Maybe she had no choice. "You really fucked me up, you know."

Now he frowned for real. Sat up, looking at her. His silvery hair was a hot mess.

"I mean," he said, and there was pain behind his eyebrows. "The feeling is mutual. Was mutual. Is." Frowned. She frowned back. Her emotions were a sticky ball of masking tape at the base of her throat. She cleared it. It didn't do any good.

"But you had a kid," Naomi said. "A wife or girlfriend or whatever. A successful career. What did I have?"

"I gave you our songs," Matt said. She saw him swallow, pretty hard, too. "*My* song. You know. The one you played tonight."

Naomi grimaced. Maybe it had been a mistake, playing that one. It wasn't something she had planned. Hadn't been what she'd rehearsed. But when she was sitting up there on stage, in front of those keys, knowing he was out there in the audience somewhere, watching her - it had just seemed right. To send up a signal flare. Like, *hey, Matt, I see you, too.*

"Sorry," she said. "I should have considered… " She trailed off, shook her head, not really sure how to go on.

"It's fine. I *gave* it to you. But that's just the point. I gave it to you. And for good reason. I didn't leave you with nothing, and you didn't have nothing to start with, either. You're talented, Naomi. We both know it."

He stared down at his folded hands as he spoke. "Besides, it's not like what I had was all that great. Or even stable. I knew my relationship with Kara was over the minute I came home to her. I loved Five from the very beginning. I *appreciated* her for carrying him. But I didn't… "

He trailed off, not quite able to say whatever it was that he wanted to say. She had a clue, maybe. But she knew it wasn't up to her to say it.

"I thought you two had an open thing," she said finally. He laughed a little, mostly to himself.

"Yeah, fucking. But we weren't supposed to… " He trailed off again, shaking his head. Geeze. He really *couldn't* say it. She sighed, chewing the edge of her nail. Reached out and gave his leg a shove.

"Anyway," she began, "You're talented, too, Matt. It's not like you aren't talented."

"Maybe," he said, "But writing wasn't the same after that weekend, either. I could *do* it. But it didn't have the same kind of magic."

He looked at her. Hopefully. Hesitantly. It made her uncomfortable, mostly. Her brain felt soupy, heavy, stoned.

"It's like masturbating," she muttered at last.

"What?"

"Like rubbing one out," she finally said, a little sharply. "Which is fine, in its own way. But it's not the same as getting laid."

Their eyes locked. They were thinking, perhaps, of the exact same thing.

"That weekend ruined me," he said. "The best sex of my life, before or since."

"Yeah," she said softly. "Well."

Crap, now she was doing it too. Holding *her* cards close to her chest. If he noticed her hesitancy, if he could see how her cheeks had gone all ruddy, then he didn't acknowledge it.

"Going back to Kara after that was hard. I'd kiss her, and she'd know I was somewhere else. With someone else. I didn't hide what happened from her. Told her it was over, anyway, between you and me. Figured it was. But she didn't believe me. She thought I was still seeing you, for months after. Years. Any time I traveled, or seemed distracted, she'd ask me if I'd been talking to you. *That Naomi.*"

Naomi pinched the bridge of her nose. Closed her eyes. "Look, I'm sorry, Matt, that I wrecked your perfect fucking life -"

"God," he said. She couldn't see him, but she could imagine how he looked. Dopey. Sad. Hopeful. "You didn't wreck my life."

He put his hand on top of hers. After a moment, she squeezed his fingers. He squeezed back. *Hands,* she thought. *They were holding hands.* After all this time.

"I didn't say it back then," he said, in a low, fierce tone, "And I've regretted it every single day."

"Say what?" she asked. Her eyes were still squeezed shut. She almost couldn't stand to look at him, to take in whatever he was feeling, thinking. Her own thoughts were jumbled enough.

"That I love you."

She pulled her hand away. Veiling her face with both of them, seeing blotches of light and dark through her closed eyes. Christ. Christ christ christ. She was just too stoned for this. Too...

"Are you okay?" he asked her.

No. No. Not okay. Panic, thick in her chest, like she used to get before a show. She forced her eyes left and right, thinking of the safe spaces she'd built in her therapist's office. There hadn't been many. The music room at her elementary school. Up there in the risers, among the musical stands and chair legs. A safe, fuzzy space.

Or else Sid Edelman's house upstate on a snowy afternoon. In bed with him. Just before it all ended.

"We had our moment, Matt," she said. "Ten years ago. Eleven. Twelve.

Whatever. Wasn't that enough?" Eyes still closed, still covered. He didn't respond, and the silence made her want to tear her own body in two.

"Oh," he said softly. "I see."

"I mean, if our dads could never make it work, I don't see how we can."

"I don't really see what our dads have to do with this... "

She dropped her hands finally. Quit trying to conjure *music room, music room*. She was too stoned for any of those therapeutic methods to do any good, anyway.

"Everything. If we're together, how do you think the world will look at us? What will they expect from us?"

He laughed. It wasn't a kind laugh, but a broad, exasperated one.

"Christ, Naomi," he said. "I don't care anymore. I spent the first forty whatever years of my life living in my father's shadow. Either trying to reject who he was or trying to live up to it. Not going to spend the next forty doing the same thing. I told you. I don't worry about what's going to happen anymore. All I know is that I know who I am. Turns out I'm a relatively simple guy. I want to go work, help the trumpets with their embouchure, help the kids figure out their jazz solos, come home, nag my kid about his homework. And maybe you could come over sometimes for dinner, and we can make pasta and drink too much wine and embarrass him, and maybe we could write a song or two together after he goes to bed, and maybe we can fuck sometimes, or make love, or whatever you want to call it. Maybe we could even wake up next to each other once or twice and I could bring you coffee and when you go on tour I could make you playlists of songs you can't stand that make me think of you. Domestic. That's what I am. And if it's not what you want, or if I'm not what you want, that's okay. We don't need to fucking torture ourselves with it."

She cringed. Didn't answer at first. Couldn't. Her chest felt squeezed. The weed had been too strong and this was a lot. Sitting here, in the Edelman's marital bed. With Matt. He saw her silence. Sighed, slowly. Put his hands on his thighs and stood up, smoothing down his suit jacket.

"Okay," he said, at the same time she said, "Wait."

Both of them frozen, staring at one another. Not speaking yet. Not knowing what to say. Finally, her words thudded out.

"It was the best sex of my life, too, you know."

He looked at her. Laughed - a wry, sweet laugh. Raked his fingers through his hair.

"What do you want me to do, Naomi?" he said. She closed her eyes for a moment, still feeling a tender sliver of that same old panic. But at the same time, she felt the simple truth of what he'd said. Thought about who she was. Who he was. Considered the only inevitable ending. And then she opened her eyes. Sat, waiting, looking at him.

"Come over here," she said. "Wouldja?"

He could have just come over and sat beside her. He didn't. Instead, he seemed to be moving very slowly. Deliberately. Taking his time. He was taking off his suit jacket, laying it on the edge of the bed. Loosening his tie, unbuttoning the top of his shirt and his shirt cuffs. He stepped out of his shoes, then, too, and then, in a pair of dorky fucking socks with hot peppers on them, he knelt on the bed, and walked closer and closer to her, on his knees. Letting his fingertips drag against her leg on his way. She watched the spaces where their bodies intersected already. Felt them. Studied them. He knelt down beside her. Grinning at her. Beaming, actually, like a little boy.

And isn't it funny? Maybe it was just the weed, because in that moment, she saw who he'd *been* as a little boy. Sweet and breathless and ruddy-cheeked and sensitive, blond curls misted with rain. Dragging his wellies around the mud in fucking Scotland. Feeling the fur of moss as he hefted his body through the trees. And she felt in herself her own girlhood, the one she'd lost. Her brown arms, stronger than his, as she raced up after him, past him. How if things had been different, for their fathers, for themselves, they might have been children together. The smell of wet wool and rainwater would have been all around them as they might have kissed then, close lipped, like children kiss, and she felt a loss so profound in that narrow moment that it made her stomach ache. But then of course she knew - if their lives hadn't played out exactly the way they had, they never would have been there, in that bedroom, looking at each other. Both of them waiting for the other to make the first move.

"Well," he asked. Waiting. Waiting. "Are you going to kiss me or not?"

And in that moment, before she sat up, putting a hand against his rough cheek, she beamed back at him. And then their mouths met, and they were grown now, and so their kisses were wet and hungry and heavy, and their hands were soon undressing one another, and their bodies were tumbling together, matching heat to heat, and reader, I'm sure you can imagine the way - the only way - their evening might have proceeded next.

* * *

It was after two a.m. when, disheveled, they finally left Sid and Cymbeline's room. Matt had lost track of time. Had lost himself inside of her, the velvety folds of her body, her sweet tits, her ass, her hands. It had been a long time since he'd gotten laid, but more, it had been a long time since he'd felt this young. Stealing time with someone else at a party when you should be schmoozing, and just for the joy of it.

The joy their two bodies felt as they knocked them together, setting off sparks.

Holding hands, squashing down laughter, they slipped through the bedroom door. The party had gone quiet now, though there was the muffed sound of water running, of conversation. They went down into the living room. Empty. Except for a pale-haired boy sleeping on the sofa, both arms wrapped around a guitar. Matt stopped for a moment there, his hand still tangled up in Naomi's, feeling that same profound sense of silence and enormity he always felt when he looked at his child.

"All tuckered out," Matt said in a whisper.

"Cutie," Naomi added. He laughed softly at that.

"Don't let him hear you say that."

He gave her hand a tug, and together they headed into the kitchen.

There were Sid and Cymbeline, drying dishes. Whatever tension Matt had felt earlier at confronting his manager, it had somehow dissipated when he'd shuddered into Naomi's body that night. He realized now how long it had been, actually, since he'd seen either of them, and he'd missed them. Sid was looking well.

Cymbeline? Well enough. Thinner, maybe, and there was something a little lost about her expression, but then, that had always happened, on occasion. Getting turned around at dinner in the middle of a conversation. Forgetting his name. She was lost now in drying a plate, though Sid, at least, glanced up when Matt and Naomi walked in. Naomi still held his hand, and hid now behind his shoulder. Embarrassed, maybe. And fair enough. The look Sid was giving both of them was pointed.

"There you guys are," he said. "Couldn't get into my room earlier, you know."

Naomi let out a small snicker, still hiding behind Matt. He arched his eyebrow.

"Sorry about that, Sid. We were… working on some songs."

"Is that what the kids are calling it these days?"

Matt grinned. Naomi snickered again. He tugged at her hand.

"Someone's got the giggles," he said. Then glanced back at Sid, sighing apologetically. "Sorry I tried to give you the slip earlier."

Sid waved his hand. 'That's alright. Wasn't the best time to talk business, anyway. I can see you had other things on your mind."

Abruptly, Cymbeline stopped polishing the plate in her hands. Looked up, like she only just noticed that they were there.

"My Angel!" she said. She went over and kissed Naomi on the cheek. Naomi gave her a peck back. "I watched you on TV tonight. You were stunning."

"Thanks, Mom," she said, without a hint of irony. Matt glanced between the two of them, wondering about their relationship. Sid and Cymbeline were around the same age as them. Not like parents, not really. But Naomi and Cymbeline apparently shared an easy familiarity. Funny. In truth, she always seemed a bit spooky to him. Disconnected from the world in front of them.

"You know that song is one of my favorites," Cymbeline told her. "You should write more like them."

Naomi glanced at Matt. "Maybe," she said, then pressed her lips shut before she could say anything else.

"Naomi," Sid asked, looking at her, "Would you mind helping the missus upstairs to bed? Want to talk to Matt here for just a minute."

"Sure," she said, and the two of them drifted out of the kitchen. Matt sighed, crossed his arms over his chest.

"You're not going to convince me to record again," he said. "I'm *happy* as a music teacher."

"Mazel," Sid said. "No, of course it's not that."

He closed the dishwasher. Rested his weight against the counter. Folded his arms over his chest, and regarded Matt sternly.

"Not sure what you have in mind with Naomi," he said, "But she's special to us. If we find out that you hurt her -"

"Oh, God, no," Matt said. "Trust me. She's special to me, too."

"Good. And don't make her *too* happy, either. We need her a little bruised. You know, for the art."

Matt scoffed. "For the art?"

"Yeah, for the art," Sid said, but before he could say anything else, Matt's dad came into the kitchen.

"Ah, there you are, son," he said. "We were looking for you all night."

"Sorry," Matt said. Funny, to see his dad looking so tired, so worn out. Even at 2:30 a.m., his father was usually rearing to go. Life of the party. "Naomi Templeton and I got to talking and we lost track of time… "

Sid coughed. A cough that sounded just a little bit like "bullshit," but Ed Hammond didn't acknowledge it, so Matt didn't, either.

"Barry's girl?" he asked. "I'd love to say hello to her before we leave."

A clear alto voice sounded from the doorway, "I think that can be arranged."

They all turned. There was Naomi, her plaid jacket draped over her shoulders, her hair shoved thoughtlessly back, showing her eyes. She looked beautiful, and tired, and a little nervous, too, from the way her smile trembled. And for a second, Matt saw her as his father must have seen her. The heavy lids. The high cheekbones. The dusky skin. The slight frame. Baron's daughter, older now than Baron would ever be. But *here*. Alive. In front of him.

"Cor," Matt's dad said softly, sounding like more of a Scouser than he normally did. "Look at you."

"Um," Naomi said, and she grimaced briefly. An embarrassed sort of look he recognized from years of meeting fans with his father. People would get instantly flustered just to be in his presence. And then mad at themselves, for not knowing what to say, how to act. "Hi. Ed. Ed Hammond. From Saffron. Hi."

Matt's dad chuckled. Stroked the scruff on his chin. Matt was watching the space between them. Thinking about it. Wondering. He grew up knowing that Baron and Ed had been bandmates. Best friends for a decade, before their friendship reached its violent, but inevitable, end. Matt could remember asking his father about the brick on the shelf in the farmhouse studio, next to his dad's old radio, one of the only times his father was ever at a loss for words. It would be his mother, much later, drunk after his sister's wedding, who told the tale. *That maniac Baron Templeton chucked a brick through our window when we went on our honeymoon. Never trusted him.*

He knew now that they hadn't been *only* friends. But what *had* they been to each other? Teenage jerk-off buddies, like Matt and some of his pals? No, that didn't seem like his dad's style. He was too fastidious, too uptight. Mostly unconsummated lovers for all those years? It's what those letters had suggested, the ones that Naomi had given Matt to give to her father. But no, no, that wasn't right, either. From the way that Ed Hammond III was looking at Naomi, it was like she was pure magic, standing there, mostly speechless in Sid Edelman's kitchen.

(Not that Matt would have argued against her being magic. He thought she was pretty magical, too.)

If Matt knew anything about his father, it's that he possessed a capacity for a fathomless love. Whether you were one of his old farm cats, or his grandson, or an old mate from back home - when he loved you, he loved you like nobody else ever could. Once it had felt stifling to Matt. He'd longed to escape it. Now he understood what a gift it was to be born into the circle of Edmund Matthew Hammond III's undying affection. Watching him watching Naomi, his sea glass eyes glistening faintly, Matt had no doubt that his father had loved Baron Templeton. That he'd been gutted when he died, but that his love had shined on and on and on. And now, watching the two of them, Matt had no less doubt that his father loved Baron's daughter too, now, really, truly, already.

His old man went over to her, as if it were the most natural thing in the world. Opened his arms to her.

"C'mere, love," he said. Naomi's eyes were wide with disbelief, confusion, as he folded his arms around her. She was stiff for a moment, uncomfortable, as he began to rock her. Stroking her shoulders, the back of her neck, her hair.

"Christ, did your father love you," he told her, smooshing a kiss against her head. "He would be so proud of what you've become."

Naomi was stiff for just a moment longer, but then she seemed to kind of melt into him, her forehead hitting his shoulder. Squeezing her eyes shut. Crying. Shaking. Ugly tears.

"There, there," his father said. "It's such an honor to finally meet you."

* * *

It turned out that Naomi didn't live far from him, over in Sugar Hill, not far off from where he was in Morningside Heights. Had for years, actually, which Matt found shocking, because how was it that they'd never run into each other? But they hadn't, somehow. Still, made it easy to plot a route home. Dad's driver would drop her off. No problem

In the back of the limo, Matt sat between Naomi and Five. The boy had fallen back to sleep almost immediately, his head in his father's lap. Matt stroked his hair, his soft, smooth face - untouched, still, by acne. Naomi was on the other side of him, and after a few minutes, she let her head hit his shoulder, too. Snoozing. Matt in between both of them, feeling the strange rightness, the *peace* of this moment. Sitting across from his father, who sat alone.

At first, he thought it was only the street lights that shone in Ed Hammond III's face. But no. He realized after a moment that it wasn't that at all. Crying. His father was crying. Sitting there, staring at them, hands folded, silent. Face streaked with tears. It was a rare occasion that he'd seen his father cry. At the deaths of animals, mostly. When Mom was sick, in private, something only heard, not seen, and behind closed doors. When he gave a eulogy at Charlie Peck's funeral a few years ago. But all of them had sobbed at that, even Uncle Liam.

"You alright, dad?" Matt asked softly, his hand pausing in his son's smooth curls. Ed drew in a great, stuttering breath of snot. Wiped it against the back of his age-spotted hand.

"Yeh," he said. "Sorry."

Matt frowned. His father had no reason to apologize.

"It's just been a strange night," Ed said. "Not my first. Won't be my last."

Matt smiled vaguely. Nodded. Tried to ignore the uneasy feeling in his belly that they really couldn't *know* that now, at this point. Knowing, as the moments ticked on, that his father was barreling closer and closer to the end.

The Road to Kingcausie

The trip to Scotland was doomed from the start.

Everyone told them not to go. Ed's father, for one, who wanted to see the sort of contracts Jessamine had prepared for them. Not accepting that there *were* no contracts, that he was just doin' the lot of them a *favor*, really, because he had a van and so a way to get Peck's kit out there for the show in Aberdeen, which a cousin of Waller's had set up, and if Jessamine had said he wouldn't mind settin' up a few more shows on the drive up through Scotland, for just the smallest cut, why *wouldn't* they have taken it, really? Ed's dad didn't like that.

"You should get it in writing," he said. "That man might be a grifter."

"Christ," Ed said. "Known him for years. Just because he's Black doesn't mean he's a grifter."

That had shut up his dad. Didn't like the implication, that he was prejudiced and all of that.

But also Genie had been needling him. Wasn't it time for the two of them to look to settling down soon? Wasn't it time to get a job, a real job, maybe in a factory or somethin', so they could get themselves a flat away from their parents? He suspected she just really wanted a way out of secondary school early. Playing house would do.

"You knew I was a musician when you met me," Ed said, tired of bein' nagged. She'd tried to hang off him, fawning, saying she was just going to miss him, but he shrugged her off. The cloud of doom that had descended upon them, late autumn 1958, was apparently contagious and he was not in the mood. At this point, felt like, it was Scotland or bust - Scotland or give up truly. Otherwise just another year of slogging through the Liverpool clubs, the same two fans showing up at every show. This, at least, a *tour*. Some real, tangible progress - and, really, their only option.

Well, maybe not their only option. There was a friend of Jessamine's who was always hangin' around his club, the Delph. Albert Ball was his name, like the fighting ace, only he mostly seemed like a drunk lump of a schemer, a failed musician who'd lived in the states for a time until his money and luck had all run out. But he'd been telling the boys he had ideas for the Saffron Dervishes, that he had contacts in US and on the continent. A friend in Hamburg, whose club - a tasteful establishment, he said - needed a house band. Peck and Waller wanted to do it. Baron was dead against it, said "manager" was nothing more than a synonym for "vampire." Ed? He wasn't sure. Thought they might as well try to put together a tour on their own, first. See where it might lead them. If the road took them right back to Liverpool? No harm done, then, right?

The tour would happen over 6 days across the Christmas holiday. Ed really heard it from the family and the little woman on *that* count. What would they do without him playing piano during their Christmas party? They helpfully pointed out that Dad's arthritis was too bad to do it no more. He suspected the whole shebang had more to do with the fact that he was falling down drunk, lately, most days, than the pain in his hands.

"You can put on a record or the radio like a normal family," Ed told them. Christ. Everything was always falling apart without him. It was a Sunday, just a week before they were to set off on their travels, and most Sundays his family all went to his Auntie Lil's for dinner. But Ed sagged off. Decided to head to Baron's instead. Couldn't call first, of course. His poor sodding family still didn't have a phone.

When he got there, he stopped at the gate. There was Baron standing in the front door, pressing his body up against Sue Grasso. Giving her small kisses, or maybe several long kisses, maybe interminable kisses, until Ed, standing there, his fiddle case in hand, cleared his throat. Sue pulled back. Looked away. Laughing at Ed.

"Sorry, was just saying goodbye."

Ed forced a vague, vague smile. "Mm, yes. Wouldn't want to get between the young lovers." He could hear how peevish he sounded. Couldn't help it. Baron was staring at him, just over Sue's shoulder. A smoldering sort of glower that made his stomach ache.

"Bye, Sue," Baron said dryly, then waved Ed inside. "Come on, Hammy. Let's see what you've got for us."

Sue streamed by Ed, stopping to kiss him on the cheek so quickly that he almost didn't register that it had happened until after it was done.

"T'ra," he said. Ed hefted his guitar case up the stairs and followed Baron inside into the gray dim space of his home, late autumn, late afternoon.

* * *

No one was home for once, not uncle nor auntie, which Ed supposed was why Sue had been there at all. Sue, Ed thought, and not Eddie. Well, not like he could have expected it. When did the two of them ever spend time together alone anymore? Only when they were writing songs or when they could have the pretense of writing songs, and even then, those were thin, thin bands of tender time. Because Aunt Deedz was out, they could go up to Baron's room today and not the sun room where they were usually banished. Ed followed Baron up the stairs, smelling the unwashed, musty, animal smell of him, like a perfume, trailing after.

"You shag her?" Ed asked, sounding more wounded than he really wanted. Baron let out a dry sound.

"Jealous, mate?" Baron asked. Baron threw his bedroom door open. If the shagging hadn't been apparent before, it surely was now. The covers were half torn off the bed completely, and it smelled like sex all around. Ed put his guitar case down, knelt before it. Opened it up.

Madly, he thought, but only shrugged. "I'm only curious," he said.

Baron threw his body down on the bed. Funny, because for all of Baron Templeton's shortness, it always felt to Eddie like he took up an inordinate amount of space. Not only physically, but in terms of how he sucked all the air from the room as well.

"Shagged," Baron said, shrugging back. Then he held fingers in a v shape against his mouth and licked wildly. "Among other things."

Well, that explained the smell. Ed grabbed his guitar. Sat down. "Mm," he said. Baron was grinning at him.

"Has Genie let you do it yet?"

"Christ," said Ed. Tuning up. "No. She barely lets me stick it in her lately. Haven't been able to get any condoms and she doesn't want a baby."

"Why don't you just pull out?" Baron asked. Ed frowned.

"What?"

"You know, just-" He made a gesture. "On top of her. Not inside."

Ed felt himself blushing bright red.

"Dunno if I'd be able to last long enough to do that," he said.

"Poor, tortured Ed," Baron said. "You raunchy?"

Ed looked down, frowning. Yes, actually. All the time, actually. But it wasn't like he wanted to talk to *Baron* about it. It wasn't as though *Baron* weren't largely the source of the problem. So he started to play it instead, turning it into a joke. Y'know, the song. "Raunchy." The Ventures. As soon as he started playing, Baron's hard, teasing smile softened into a grin. He was snapping his fingers. Enjoying himself.

"Yeah," he said. "Rock 'n' Roll, Hammy."

Ed stopped, just as abruptly as he began.

"You gonna get your ax or not?" he asked. "We have *songs* to rehearse. Scotland in a week, y'know."

"Yeh," Baron said. Sitting up so that his legs dangled off the edge of the bed. "We could do that. Rehearse. Sure."

But he didn't move. He was looking at Ed intently, as though something was on his mind.

"Or?" Ed asked.

"Well, I thought maybe I could help you with your problem, pet," Barry's smile, wormin' its way into him, and Ed straining his trousers already, but still sitting there, guitar on his lap.

Because that thing that had happened between the two of them on the day that Baron's mum died? Well, it had only happened that once. And they'd said to each other - they *said* it, it had *happened* - that they loved each other that day. But it still hadn't happened again. Sure, sometimes it seemed like Baron touched him more, now. Throwing an arm over his shoulder, kissing his cheek, grabbing his arse and cackling like a madman. And all of that in front of the other lads, like it was some grand joke. But they hadn't kissed properly again and they hadn't shagged (was that what they had done? Shagging?) and they hadn't wanked, even, even as both of them seemed to constantly be endeavoring to spill their seed into their *girlfriends*. Ed had thought that what had happened had mattered to both of them in the same way, but… well, whatever it was between them, maybe it was just a one-off. Except he'd known that Barry had shagged or at least been shagged by Dickie Ashby and the two of them hadn't even *done* that. Maybe he had been wrong. Maybe that day had just been a laugh for Baron. That's what Ed had told himself. All these months. Not knowing how to make it happen again. And now, here it was, presenting itself. And Ed just sat there frozen, unsure of what to say.

"Ed?" Baron asked, looking amused by Ed's silence and Ed leaned back. Drew in a sharp breath, one that almost hurt. A sharp, shaky breath.

"Yeah," he said, the words sounding pinched. "All right."

Baron, lips parting. Still looking amused. "Put down the old viola, Hammy," he said. And carefully, Ed put it on the floor. Knowing his arousal would be obvious, and judging from where Baron's eyes went, it was. Forced himself to stay steady in his gaze, to not feel quite so… undressed by it. Why was this so hard? It wasn't with Genie, where he was always wanting it so bad and she was always pushing him away. With Genie, he practically couldn't wait to pull out the old turtle. Even though she treated it mostly like it was a repulsive thing. But Barry… did not look repulsed. He'd put it in his mouth once, hadn't he? And yet part of Ed wanted to hide, to shrink down away to nothing.

Baron said nuthin', really, just slid his body down off the edge of the bed. And practically… crawled to where Ed sat. Coming closer, closer, sliding one hand up against Ed's cheek, just a little bit rough, because he hadn't had time to shave that mornin', and at first Ed pushed his face into Baron's hand,

and then Baron was turning him toward him, both of them sort of breathing on each other, and Ed could really smell Sue Grasso all over Baron now, mixed up with his usual perfume of BayRhum, armpits, and Royal Crown, maybe a bit of his uncle's gin, too, and he *hated* that he smelled Sue on him, if he was honest with himself, but what was he s'posed to do about it, anyway? They were breathing on each other, and then they were kissing, hard, hungry kissing, and just a moment later there was Barry's hand against his throbber, first rubbing it through his trousers, knuckles against the head, and then a moment's fumbling, button open, and gripping him hard inside his pants. Ed felt himself make a noise, a long, animal, humming sort of noise, his mouth against Barry's still, but not really kissing but rather grimacing, for how much he wanted it, and he was wriggling there on the threadbare old carpet, Barry's hand tightly squeezing and jerking, jerking, and then -

"Baron?"

A voice from downstairs, so faint that Ed almost wasn't sure he heard it, but Baron heard it, and yelped out, "Fuck!" In a flash, he pulled his hand away from Ed's cock, grabbed Ed's guitar, chucked it on top of him, scrambled back onto the bed, where he grabbed his guitar, too. Holding it down flat over his lap. Hidin' himself.

"Up here, Deedz," Baron said, wincing, and Ed's chest was moving fast and he could see that Baron's was, too. Baron was scrambling to smooth his hair back with his hand, then put his hand under his chin, holding up the wobbly, maniacal grin there, and Ed listened for the footsteps on the stairwell, his pants still open, his throbber pressed up against the guitar's cool back, but hidden, at least, and he tried not to let his eyes get wide when Baron's auntie threw the door to his bedroom open.

"Afternoon, Deidre," Baron said sweetly. Aunt Deedz looked around - confused, dismayed.

"Baron, what happened to your room?"

He shrugged.

"For goodness' sake. You're eighteen years old! Not a child anymore. And what-" She sniffed at the air, looking disgusted. "What on Earth is that smell?"

"Think one of your cats must have sprayed in here," Baron said, mock-seriously. "We should have old Doot sentenced to death for it."

Deidre rolled her eyes. "You're teasing me. Hullo, Edmund," she said to Ed. It had taken her about 18 months, but she finally reliably knew his name.

"'Llo," he said in a tone that was just that. His throbber still pressed to the guitar, painful, and he felt the blossoms on his cheeks spreading even lower, to his neck and chest.

"How's your father?" she asked carefully. Christ. Hammond patted the back of his neck with his palm.

"Fine," he said. "He's fine. I'll let him know you said hello."

Her pinched, displeased expression suggested that she really *hadn't* said hello. But she let out a small "Hmm," anyway.

"Baron, I'll need help bringing in the groceries. And clean up in here when you're done. It's a sty."

Baron pushed his nose up with his finger, snorting. But after a moment, he put down his guitar, and started to follow Deedz from the room. Paused at the door, rearranging himself. Winked at Ed.

"Sorry, Love," he said. "This should buy you a few minutes at least if'n you need to -" Another gesture, a jerking, then an exploding, complete with sound effects.

"Baron!" Deidre called sharply. So Baron, giving a wink, ducked out of his room.

Ed waited until the door shut. Then fell backward on the floor, his hands over his eyes, groaning.

* * *

Ed met the rest of them outside of the Delph on Christmas Eve Eve, late in the day, just as the sun was sinking. Snow swirling, dirty and gray, all around. Suitcases and guitar cases gathered on the curb. Baron and Liam and Charlie stood around sharing cigarettes. Ed took one look at them, shook his head, and went to help Jessamine load up the van.

"Thanks, mate," Jessamine was saying, in his strange, heavy accent, which was half Dingle and half somewhere else entirely. "Ey, wot you think of this?"

Standing in the back of the empty van, he pulled out a yellow flier. The text was all fat and bubbled and there were spiky little stars beside every line.

*HURRY! BUY TICKETS NOW!

* SAFFRON CHRISTMAS TOUR! *

* LIVERPOOL'S BEST ROCK 'N' ROLL *

. . . and then the dates, down beneath. Ed took it, frowning down at the blue text.

"But we're called the Saffron Dervishes," he said. "What kind of name is Saffron?"

"The other one was too long, innit," Jessamine said, jabbing the paper. "I couldn't fit it."

Ed sighed. He glanced back, to where the others waited in the street. Not helping. Just watching him.

"Lads," he called. "He renamed us."

He held out the flier. The rest of them just stood there, looking nonplussed.

"We know, Ed," Liam called, stamping out his fag. "He told us before you got here. If you hadn'ta been late… "

Ed frowned. He hadn't been *that* late, anyway. And what was he supposed to do? Had found himself in an empty house, for once. Had needed to take care of things. Lately, it wasn't helping, all that wanking. Sometimes felt like it only made things worse. But six nights in a van with the four of them? Seemed important, to get it out of the way.

"Yeh, but -" Ed glanced back at Jessamine. He didn't want to *offend* the man. But Jessamine didn't look at all offended, only amused, as Ed's cheeks heated red. "The name 'Saffron' is a queer name for a guitar group."

"'Sfine," Charlie Peck said, shrugging. "The Saffron Dervishes was just as queer to us."

"Didn't want to tell you," said Liam. "In case you were a baby about it."

His expression suggested that Ed was being a baby about it.

"Baron?" Ed asked, a bit of begging in his voice. Baron's cigarette dangled between his lips.

"Sorry, Hammy," he told him. With that, as if by fiat, the three others stepped inside the van with him. "Just don't care what we call ourselves. We should get on the road, yeh?"

Peevishly, Eddie waved Baron's cigarette smoke away from his face. "Fine," he spat, and hoofed it into the front seat. Put his feet up on the dash. Closed his eyes. Waited to go. Angry. He was angry. Angry at Jessamine. At Baron. Angry at the whole damned world.

* * *

Ed stayed quiet the whole trip up, while the others played with a deck of cards in the back. The van was unheated. Ed's toes were freezing by the time they got to Blackpool, just after the soupy dark had descended upon them. The first show was 50 pounds and a plate of fish and chips shared between them at a pub, a pint each that Ed didn't bother with but the others did. He was feeling mean and surly by the time they got on stage, particularly when the bartender got up and introduced them as "Saffron?" with a question mark, just like that. The place was mostly empty at first, just a few old drunks trying to escape their families. But. But. After a few songs, a cluster of birds came in off the street, snow in their hair, looking bright-eyed and hungry. And then a few more. Maybe, Ed thought, not really thinking *sanely* at all, they weren't so doomed, after all. Because after all, there were birds at least, and they looked happy to see them. Whatever their band was called. They were boys, musicians, and the girls were *girls* and they wanted to dance and giggled to each other about the pretty boys and their songs and they weren't the most beautiful girls he'd ever seen. But they were girls.

After a few hours playing, the band were all sweat-slicked, jangly, alive. Ed blew all his money getting the birds drunk and didn't care, for once, about money at all. They were on tour. He was going to make the most of it. Desperate. Desperate. Necking with one of them in the booth, not really caring which one, until she took his hand and led him to the WC and she shoved him down on top of the toilet and climbed on top of him, grinding her fanny against him, and they were still fully dressed but he could feel how he was practically inside of her, and he was close, almost immediately, and she was gasping and crying out in a way he suspected was fake but didn't really care but but but

A knock on the door, not a polite one, which turned into a pound, which turned into bellowing.

"EDMUND MATTHEW HAMMOND THREE GETCHERASS OUT HERE!"

Ugh. Fucking. Baron. But but but the bird grinded a minute longer before peeling herself off him, because the pounding was pounding on and on, and it was too late by the time she did, he was too far gone, spilling into his trousers, moaning, halfway unsatisfying. Fuck. While the bird, her hand on the doorknob, just watched. Almost like she'd intended to do that to him, to get him so wound up. Fuck. At last she let the door fall open, and squeezed out past skinny dark Baron, who rested a hand on the door jam, watching Ed, a smug look upon his face. Ed cast about uselessly for toilet paper, which they seemed to have none of in Blackpool, apparently.

"Fuck! Baron!" Ed snapped, putting his arm across the mortifying wet spot on his trousers, as if he could hide it, as if Baron hadn't already seen.

"Van's leaving, mate," Baron said. Waited a beat. Still looking smug. "Besides, what about *Genie?*"

"Fuck you," Ed said, standing. Untucked his shirt, hoping it would cover it all up. Hide it from the others. Glanced in the dingy, scratched mirror. The poppies were bright on his cheek, but that was really the only sign. Baron was standing behind him. Watching. That's when he noticed a dark bruise on Baron's neck, like a flower.

"'Sides, what about *Sue?*" he snapped, glaring at that bruise. Baron laughed.

"We have an *agreement*," Baron said.

"Do you now?" Ed asked, running the water, splashing it over his face. Trying to get his heart to calm down, his anger.

"Yeh," said Baron, stepping closer, and Ed felt himself tense more. Terrible, how tense he was. "But don't worry. I still love you best."

Baron was standing behind him. Close, very close. When they both heard a shout from the back of the bar. Little snotty Liam Waller, calling to them.

"Oi, you pansies! Van's leaving."

"C'mon, poppet," Baron said, putting a hand on Ed's shoulder. Leading him away.

***

By the time they reached the hostel in Carlisle, they were all half frozen, and it was nearly dawn. The sky outside was streaked with color. Purple and orange, dotted with pinprick stars. Ed stood outside the van, taking it in, feeling the cold upon his face.

"Christmas Eve, Hammy!" Baron crowed, clapping his arm around Ed. In the silence, they stood there for a moment, watching the dawn come in. And Ed, for a narrow moment, felt alright. *Well*, even. Standing there beside Baron. Both of their hearts beating, their warmth fogging the air. Young and alive and on their way, full of spunk and vigor. Standing next to each other, their bodies touching, Baron's arm like a cloak over him, warm and thick, and the sky growing brighter and more golden with each passing moment. Not dead. Here, together. Loving each other.

"'Ey, you queers," Liam called from the hostel steps, with just enough gravity in his voice that Ed felt a jolt of fear go through him. Even though it was just the sort of joke they all made, all the time. Boys, being boys, sniggering at queerness. Still, too close. Ed shrugged off Baron's arm. Rubbed his hands, frantic and worried, over his worried face. "You comin' or not?"

He felt Baron beside him stiffen up, as though his very soul was hardening

"Yeah," he said, glancing at Ed. Was Ed mistaken, or was a wound there, behind Baron's dark eyes? Nothing to say about it. Nothing to do. Ed watched Baron go up the stairs alone, his shoulders sloped under his leather jacket. The lean jagged darkness of him. Lonely. Felt his own loneliness too. Ed sighed, his breath forming a cloud in front of them.

"Yeh," he muttered, "Coming." And he walked up the stairs, hoping he was tired enough that sleep would come on fast.

* * *

The next show was a dud. No birds. No birds at all. And who could blame them? Ed thought, because it was Christmas Eve and any sane bird would be with her family, or maybe her beau. In the little subterranean pub, the others got drunker and drunker as they slogged through their set. At some point, Baron slinked off to the khazi, leaving Ed to do the throat-tearing vocals on "Rip It Up." From the way that Liam was grimacing as he glanced over, Ed could tell that he was *bombing*, and no wonder. It just wasn't right, just wasn't his range, but what was he supposed to do, anyway? Nothing to be done, especially not when Baron came out of the WC with a toilet seat slung over his neck like a yoke.

"Cor," Ed muttered into the mic as the song ended, not even thinking about it, "What are you doing, Barry?" And that's when the bartender looked over, and shouted something Ed couldn't understand, and before he knew it, Baron had launched himself over the bar, slamming fists into him, and Liam and Charlie abandoned their sticks and axes and went and pulled them apart and before they all could really think about it, they were packing up their guitars in a rush, going—that is to say, leaving. Without pay. Hefting instruments out into the cold. Jessamine was shouting at them to hurry up as he turned the van's engine over and they all ran in.

"Hilarious, boys," Jessamine said, lighting a cigarette, as they rattled down the road and Liam and Baron and Charlie were all laughing, but not Ed, who was too sober and too randy for this, whose throat hurt, whose pockets were bare.

"You forgot something, Barry," Ed said, peevish. He reached over and took the dirty old toilet seat off from around Baron's neck, handing it to him. Baron just cackled.

"A souvenir!" he said, "From our first tour. Wouldja treasure it forever, pet?" He offered it back to Eddie. Eddie shied away. He could *smell* it. Revolting.

"Get away from me," he scowled. The rest of them were laughing still, but less, as they moved on down the road.

* * *

The plan was to drive all through Christmas day, and reach Aberdeen by dinner. And perhaps all would have been fine if they'd just *done* that, stuck with their plan from the outset. But no, life could not have been that simple. Because they drove through Edinburgh just as the church bells started *ding donging* and Charlie, of all people, started needling Jessamine about wanting to stop.

"C'mon mate," he said. "Have a little Christmas charity in your heart. We can't just spend the day stuck in the *van*," and Jessamine sighed and fingered a small silver cross that was on his neck, like he was thinking about it, and they decided to put it to a vote. Waller and Peck and Jessamine wanted to stop. Baron, his feet up on the dash in front, loudly declared, "*Foock* God!" and Ed abstained from voting, unsure of what he wanted. In truth, for a long time, he'd shared Baron's sentiment. Fuck God! Who had probably abandoned them, if he'd ever been real in the first place. But it seemed rude to put it so plainly, and Ed had been raised not to talk about religion in polite company, anyway.

So Jessamine found a spot near St. Mary's and the others got out, while Baron spread himself out in the back of the van with his guitar and a bottle, like he meant to spend his Christmas day sitting about, playing it.

"No way I'm setting foot in there," Baron said. "I'm like a vampire. I'd burst into flame. You gonna stay here with me, mate?"

Ed's eyes went to the spot in the van beside him, between two drum heads. Could see it then, taste it. Time alone with Baron. Here. In the van.

And Ed felt his belly pulse, his throat throb. Glanced back at the wide open van doors, which were letting the cold air in, glanced back at the others, who were waiting for him. Glanced back at Baron. And it would have been so simple for him to hang back, to do what he wanted - what he'd *always* wanted to do. To be alone with Barry. Just the two of them. But. It would have looked queer, wouldn't it? The two of them, alone together? With the rest of them at bleedin' *church*?

"Nah, Barry," he said, raking a nervous hand through his curls. "Thought

I might say a prayer for our poor dead mums today." Wasn't sure why he said it. It was too close to the truth, really. But fine. It was said. He watched as Baron got out a ciggie and started to smoke.

"Suit yourself," he said dryly, barely looking at Ed. Looking at the cherry of his cigarette instead. And was Ed mistaken, or did he recognize a drop of disappointment there, in the set of Baron's lips, in the tug at the corner of his mouth?

Well. Nothing to be done about it.

Ed left Baron in the van alone.

* * *

Standing there in the Catholic church, trying to feel something. This was his mother's religion, his mother's way. Rosary beads and holy communions. The smell of incense. The taste of red wine. Ed had always felt drawn to it, at least before. The very *idea*, ceremonial and ancient. But today? He felt nothing. Angry. Hard. Lonely. A little randy, even. There was no holiness here. No holiness anywhere, he thought. In the whole damned world.

* * *

By the time the mass was over the snow had come on thick. Huge white gasps of snow, swirlin' all around. Jessamine suggested they find someplace open to eat first, that maybe the storm would blow over. Bought some chips in a shop (miracle they found one open), ate in the van. No luck, though. By nighttime, it was even darker, the storm even more thick.

"Well, guess we'll move it along anyway," Jessamine said, balling up the paper from his food, tossing it in the back of the dingy van. Ed stared out the window, contemplating it.

"Are you sure we shouldn't tuck in here for the night?" he asked. Jessamine shrugged.

"Only if you don't mind missing our Boxing Day arrangement."

Ed grunted. He *did* mind, of course. Days into this odyssey and not a pound to show for it. Just cold-numbed toes, a restless mind.

"No," he concluded. "It's fine. Waller, you want the front seat?"

Waller did. As Ed went into the back of the van, where their luggage and their garbage and their guitars and drumheads were kept, he sat down between Baron and Charlie. Realized how separate he'd felt from them this whole trip. Like he wasn't one of the band at all. He reached out and grabbed a Gauloise from Baron's pack of fags, lit it. Was acutely aware of Baron watching him. Ignored it.

"Deal me in," he said, gesturing to the cards. There was a liter of Scotch on one of the guitar cases. Ed took a draw of that, took a swallow. Trying to make himself feel looser, better, brighter. A familiar feeling, forcing it. It was Christmas, after all. And didn't he always have to force it on Christmas?

The cards went round, the pocket change, the bottle. Singing and smoking and drumming on guitar cases. Happy, for a moment. Real loose. Like there was hope there, somewhere, buried in frozen flesh.

By the time the night came they were all cloudy with cigarettes and drink. They huddled together under their coats in back, all four of them, their hips pressed together for warmth. Well, the booze helped at least, Ed thought, feeling himself rattle around in the van like a stone in a tin. The wipers were moving furious up front, and he heard Jessamine curse about making a wrong turn. Waller made a joke, and even though he was right up against Ed, Ed realized how *drunk* he was. It was like the voices were coming through a long tunnel, like everything was foggy, jangly, and above all *cold*, as Jessamine squinted through the dark in the front seat and took a slug of the bottle someone had given him and they were all laughing at something - God knows what. Baron was beside him, humming a little. Something familiar. What was it? Oh, that song Baron had written for him. Their *secret*. The one they'd tucked away, for future days past.

And Ed found himself thinking *A dream, it's all a dream*, because Baron wouldn't have been humming it if he were awake, and that's precisely when it all went wrong, Jessamine calling out - *Crap!* - and jerking his hands to the side and the van tipping sideways and bodies falling to bodies and suitcases and guitar cases and drums everywhere and in that moment, as Ed's body went sliding across the floor of the van, as something struck him hard on the side of his face (was it the wall? The floor? He could no longer tell one from the other) he found himself thinking *Well, here it is. That moment you've been waiting for, for such a long time.*

A crunch, and everything crashed onto the ground, including Ed, and there was a long, long muffled silence after. Everything quiet, cottony. But that's what he had expected, wasn't it? From dying.

Funny, then, To hear breathing. Rapid, hard, beside him. He looked over. It was Baron, his face smushed to the floor, his black eyes wide open. Those eyes boring into him. There was blood on Baron's cheek. It took him a moment to realize that he could reach out, touch it. That his body still contained a pulse, oxygen, impulses. Baron winced as the pad of Ed's finger touched his split skin.

"Everyone alright?" he heard Jessamine call from the front seat and there was a pound of footsteps, then a groaning. Charlie's voice, and when Ed looked over his own neck let out a scream of protest but he turned, anyway, looked anyway. Charlie, half-buried beneath a pile of equipment, clutching his head.

"Been better," the older man said, scowling. And Ed heard Liam cackle a little, saw his dark head pop up from behind the equipment, and he didn't know how glad he was to hear that sound, to see that zitty face, until he did. His oldest friend. Our kid. At the very least, not dead yet.

"We're okay," Ed said, which is when he realized his hand was still resting on Baron's cheek, feeling Baron's hard breath. He withdrew. Sat up. Beside him, Baron struggled to sit up, too. Ed reached out a hand. Helped. Felt right. Felt natural.

"Christ," Jessamine said, stumbling into the back of the van. Ed realized the floor were tilted, like the floor of a ship that had been tossed up on a wave. "Sorry, boys. Thought I saw a fox on the road…" Jessamine pawed the back of his neck, looking half-pained, half-sheepish. That's when Ed realized that Jessamine couldn't have been much older than the lot of them. Seven or eight years, maybe. A kid, sort of, too. And that's when he figured what this trip had been for Jessamine. A holiday. A lark. *Fun.* Nothing serious. Even though it had just become, well, more serious, just then, on the dark Scottish road. Jessamine went to the rear door, pried it open with his hands. Ed turned back, wincing again, watching the snow swirl bright in the pitch blackness.

* * *

The van was half-lodged in a ditch, wheels spinning. The snow still swirled around them in heavy gusts. The darkness beyond was whistling and misshapen, craggy, dark. Just beyond the road's turn was a sign - Kingcausie, 6 km. The name imprinted itself on Ed's brain.

"Can't we just sleep in the van?" Liam was whining. Out of the corner of his eye, Ed watched Baron grimace. He, too, had been surveying the scene.

"No," he said. "We'll freeze to death if we do that."

He said it with such assurance that no one argued with him. And really, he was probably right. It was bitter, bitter cold, and they were drunk, with nothing but their coats to keep them from freezing.

So a few moments later, the four of them were pushing, while Jessamine tried to reverse back out into the road. Ed couldn't tell if he was sober now, or the adrenaline from the crash had just made him *feel* it. Now he seemed to perceive every moment of the night, black and endless. The strain of his hands on the paint-peeling bumper. The smell of diesel fuel. The sound of the engine, pointlessly *whirrrrrring*. And then beside him (always beside him, Ed noted), Baron grunting. A vein of bright red blood still trailing down his face.

"Harder!" Baron barked, and they all heaved at once together, and the van lurched, then spun back. The rest of them let out a collective cheer, but not Ed. The night was too dark for it. His fear was still thick on his throat. This trip had been cursed, and - the way he saw it - there was no guarantee, still, that they would make it through the night. Jessamine was still pissed. The night was still endless, black on white on black.

They went back to the van together. The others jovial. Ed, contemplative. The door didn't quite shut right now as he pulled it closed behind him. It let in a shaft of air, Bitter cold. The other three went to start another game of cards. But it didn't seem worth faking it, to Ed now. They were different from him. He was a ghost. He found his coat and laid out on the floor behind them and pulled the coat up over him. Tucked his arm beneath his head. Half-slept, as Jessamine drove, weaving and dodging. Every few minutes, the van would give a lurch and Ed's eyes would jerk open, and he wondered if he'd died.

Eventually the others grew quieter. Ed thinly heard the nighttime preparations. Charlie went up to the front seat with Jessamine, to keep him company, to keep him awake. Liam and Baron would join Ed on the floor. Ed's eyes were still closed when Baron laid out his body in parallel to his own, as Liam laid down just a yard or so away. The three boys lined up, like sardines in a tin.

The van wove through the Scottish roads. The wipers went ka-chuck, ka-chuck. Ed heard the low tones of Jessamine and Peck's conversation. And the jagged sounds of Baron barely breathing.

We're alive, Ed thought, still almost not believing it. *Baron's alive. You're alive.* And just inches away from each other. Lying so their feet were touching, just a little. Not that Ed noticed.

There was a cold burst of air through the gap in the door. Ed found himself turning toward it. Imagining that the door might go flying open, his body tumbling out onto the asphalt beyond. Escaping this life, and all of its temptations.

Behind him, he heard Baron shift, too. Turning over. The sound of Baron's breath, closer again. Behind him. The sound of Baron's body inching closer to his own.

And he knew - he *knew* Liam was right there. Right there. And he knew Charlie and Jessamine were still awake, talking low in the front seat. But. When Ed felt Baron's hand fall on his belly, he let it.

They were alive, they were alive, both Baron and Ed were alive. That's what Ed realized in that moment. He put his hand on top of Baron's freezing hand, found himself pulling himself closer to Baron, or maybe Baron was pulling himself closer to Ed. Until they no longer ran parallel but intersected entirely. Becoming one line.

Ed felt Baron's throbber against his back, right through all that cotton that lied between them. He felt Baron's cool hand on his soft, warm middle. Felt his own adrenaline coursing through him, his shock at being alive, still, somehow, on this night. Felt his cock, rock hard already, and the cold air on his face. Found himself leaning against Barry. For warmth. For sustenance. Found Barry pressing silently into him.

And for a moment, they were still like that. Not really *doing* anything. Until the van went over a pothole, and their bodies lurched into each other. And he heard Baron's breath hitch, and then suddenly, almost violently, Baron's hand was fumbling with the button of Ed's jeans, yanking them open and down, just a bit, so that Ed's cock was out in the open air and the top of his hips, his back, his arse, exposed. Ed gasped, as Baron gripped him, and as Baron pressed his cock up to the cleft of Ed's body, and began wanking him - irregular, wild movements - and pressing against him, irregular, wild movements and a different sort of quiet had descended in the back of the van. Ed felt sure, in that moment, that Liam was listening. But couldn't stop, didn't want to stop, his cells lighting up like fairy lights and twinkling faintly.

Why was it that this felt *so different* to him than Genie? Or any other bird? This thing, which he somehow kept just falling into doing, like it was the most natural thing in the world. Whereas women took planning. Scheming. A different sort of intent. This was instinct. This was their bodies melting down to become one body. Ed squeezing his eyes shut, trying not to cry out. Baron's ragged breath against his ear, hot and musty. The two of them twitching. Rubbing. All cold except for places that they were very, very hot. Against each other. In each other's hands. Faster, and faster still, and Ed feeling his hips buck into Baron's hand and Baron's mouth must have fallen open and let out a guttural sound, strangled, wild, and Ed felt the explosion against him, felt his own body tense, tremble, and explode, and for a moment they were still like that, frozen together. Until Ed heard Baron's breath slowed against his ear, until Ed felt Baron's vise-grip loosen from Ed's cock, felt his hand retreat. But before Baron could turn over, individuating their bodies again, he left a kiss, quick and silent, against Ed's jaw. A thank you, or a you're welcome. Hard to be certain which.

Ed lie there for a moment longer, still and empty. But a new kind of empty. A better sort. At last, he stuffed his cock back into his blue jeans, pulled his coat back over him, and forced himself back to sleep.

* * *

Sweet, empty morning. Boxing Day. Ed woke up aching in the thin light of the van floor, the heavy weight of Baron's hand still there, a dead weight, against his belly. He sat up, scratching his head. Must have been the first one up. He picked up Baron's hand, gave it back to him. Baron just curled in on himself more, smacking his lips.

Ed, for a moment, watched him. That sweet boy.

He got up. Opened the van door. And so it seemed, they had made it to Aberdeen, by some miracle or favor, he couldn't be sure. They were parked in an alleyway. Ed climbed out, glanced about. Moved to the back of it, behind some garbage cans. Unzipped himself. Put a hand on the wall. Started to piss.

Mid-stream, he heard the van door open again, then slam shut. Baron came whistling over.

"Allo," he said to Ed. Ed glanced at him. Grinning a bit. As Baron unzipped and started pissing, too.

"Morning," Ed said.

"Seems we made it through the night," Baron said.

"Yeah," said Ed, shaking himself out. "No thanks to you."

They grinned at each other for a moment.

When the pissing was all done, they walked together over to the van. Baron leaned his weight against the dented back bumper. Ed stood there beside him, his arms crossed. Watching the foot traffic at the mouth of the alleyway, all those old grannies off to do their shopping.

"You've been a real cunt lately," Baron said suddenly. Ed looked over, eyebrows raised. Feeling surprised. But not exactly wounded. Baron added,

"Why?"

"What do you mean?" Ed asked.

"Y'know," said Baron, getting out a pack of ciggies. Shaking one out. Offering one to Ed, but Ed said no. "One minute you're acting all libidinous. The next, yer drunk off yer rocker. The third, you're a sullen girl. Why?"

"Oh," Ed said. "That." His arms were still crossed over his body. He was silent for a minute, thinking about it. Wondering if he should tell. Then suddenly, telling anyway. "Me mum died today. Boxing Day. Three years ago."

Baron looked at him, his cigarette dangling between his lips. He took it out. "Oh," he said.

"Every year," Ed went on, "I feel it buildin' and buildin' and buildin'. Inside of me, like it has to explode. All this *grief*. Y'know, the memories."

"Yeah," Baron said, his voice dry. Pain there, behind that one syllable. Ed heard it, knew it was there. And why.

"Y'know," Ed said, wincing, "Me dad never cried when she was sick. Or after. Once I heard him, in his room. Just after it happened And I'd thought, Dad's the only one in there. He has to be crying. But otherwise? Not once. He turned his feelings off, like a switch."

Baron took a break of his cigges, exhaled. Said nothing.

"And I just keep wondering," Ed said. He heard himself give a sniffle, but almost didn't feel himself do it. "When I die - and I know I'm gonna someday, because we all do - who's going to cry for me? That old fart won't. My brothers? Probably not. Who, Baron? If me own old man can't cry. And if I've got no mum."

No answer for a moment. Baron sighed.

"We orphans hafta stick together," Baron said at last. And then he reached up. Took Ed's hand in his. Warm. Firm. Comfortable. "I'll cry for you, Hammy."

Ed felt himself smile. They just stood there, for a moment, holdin' hands. The moment stretched on. Then Ed added: "I think when we get home we should let Allie Ball manage us. I'm tired of struggling, Baron. I want things to be easy for us. From here on out."

Baron looked up at him. Looking tired and beautiful. Nodded. Squeezed his hand.

"Alright, Hammy."

The pair of them watched the sun come up over Aberdeen.

214

Reunion IV

Took awhile for Ed to look into that nutter's claim.

They stuck around New York for three weeks after the award, for Helen's grandkid's graduation party. Ed schmoozing, playing the granddad role, even though he'd never felt like much of a granddad to her, to any of them, really. This new, other family, who hated dancing, who listened mostly to NPR while washing up, who had no instruments in their home. Oh, the girl was a nice enough sort, and there was always a certain amusement in watching a child grow from a fat toddler into some semblance of a *person*. But truth be told, Ed often felt like the whole affair could have been done via a phone call. Oh, well, they were expected there, and it meant something to Helen, and he got to be the hero with the fat checkbook, and he managed to squeeze in one last visit with Little Ed and Matt before they tucked it in for the airport.

Matt, happy now. Nice to see. He'd been so miserable, for so long. Now he had this wild glow around him. Must have been Baron's girl who had done it. Ed had hoped to see her again, but Matt said she was gone off on tour.

"An' you're all right with that?" Ed asked, sitting at Matt's little kitchen table, where he was helping the little one with his maths. "Her going off without you?"

Matt, bent over the dishwasher, blushed bright red. "Yeah, Dad, it's *fine*. It's not like we're even dating."

"Hmm," Ed said. Matt stood up straight.

"What?"

Between them, Little Ed snickered.

"Not you too," said Matt, and the two Eds grinned knowingly at each other.

"She was over here every night last week," Little Ed said. "I had to blast my noise machine to drown it out-"

"Okay, okay," Matt said. "That's enough."

Ed sat there, his eyebrows raised. His grandson, across the table, wearing the exact same knowing expression.

"Anyway," Ed said. "I hope you'll write her."

"Dad," Matt said, shaking his head. Shutting the dishwasher firmly, "this isn't 1957. We have cell phones."

"They *sext*," Little Ed said, snickering. Ed watched, amused, as his son gave his grandson a flick of the ear.

Anyway, the boys dropped he and Helen off at the airport, big hugs and promises to see each other at Christmas.

"Bring her," Ed said, as he held his son against him, and he didn't need to explain, and Matt didn't need to ask, who he meant by *her*.

* * *

In London for a week, producing Harry Styles' new album. He'd promised the missus he was out of that game, but Harry was a talented kid, that one, and for Ed, being in the studio helping a beautiful boy make music was the next best thing to *bein'* a beautiful boy, making music yourself. Sitting there behind the mixing board, listening to the rough cuts on headphones together, he found himself contemplating the child's jawline, his wrists. He was wearing some kind of bleedin' *blouse* or something - the sort of thing that would have gotten you beaten to a bloody pulp, when Ed was a boy. But the world had changed. Hell, they'd helped change it, back in their hippy days. Now, looking at him, he found himself thinking about how nice Harry looked in it. How lovely. Felt something else for a minute, too, watching Harry lick his lips and groove to his own music. An old stirring. But it had been a very long time since he'd made it with a kid so young. Ed couldn't even figure out how to start it. If it would be *wanted*, or if he'd just be rebuffed. He tabled the thought, decided he'd take the fantasy home with the missus. That night he fucked her silly - something they still did, on occasion, thankyouverymuch - and she blushed and giggled and wondered what had gotten into him. But there was no way for him to explain it, not really. That was an entire self he'd never shown to any woman. Any wife.

In London for a week, wrapping things up. Then out to Sussex for a few. Watching Helen ride her horses. Reading the paper together. FaceTiming Shelagh's kids. Taking the dogs for a walk. Trying not to think about what was waiting for him in a closet in Kingcausie. Surely, he told himself, nothing at all.

A breast cancer fundraiser. Ed, with a pink carnation on his lapel, talking about his Mum, about Genie. Tryin' not to cry. He'd become such a sap in his old age. Once, tears were mortifying. Well, what was the use of shame, and at *his* age? Mortification meant death, didn't it? He'd spent years thinking about dying. Fearing it. All those songs he'd never write, the albums he'd never buy, the kisses he'd never steal. His death had been with him all this time, and now, closer to it than he ever was (though wasn't that always the truth? That every day was one day closer?) it felt almost like an old friend. No shame in tears, he'd decided. Not when they were tears worth crying. His mum had been worth crying about. Genie, too. She'd been a good wife, a good woman, though he knew on some level that he'd never been able to love her like he *should*. And that was part of the grief of it. Standing there. Talking about the latest research developments. Because he'd tried and he'd tried to make himself love her right, but never quite *gotten* there. Maybe if he'd just had more *time*.

Sitting in the back of the limo with Helen later, feeling wrung out. Hadn't even noticed the *mood* she'd been in all night, had been too preoccupied with the memories. His mum, talking in low tones to his Auntie about something the doctor had said. His Dad, crying behind closed doors. Ed crying behind closed doors himself, hoping the kids didn't hear. The shame of it. Thinking about all of this at this gala, while they danced and schmoozed. Hadn't noticed the sour look on Helen's face, the short answers. Until she shut the limo door behind her and made it clear what she'd been holding in.

"I spoke to Kara last night," she said. Ed looked up.

"Oh?"

"After you went to bed."

Ed looked at her, shruggin'. He always went to bed earlier than she did. For Chrissake, he was twenty-two years older than she was.

"She said that Five told her that he walked in on you kissing some woman when you were in New York."

Ed winced. Oh. That.

"Oh," he said. "That."

"Yes," she said icily. "*That*. He said it was that musician, from the '90s."

"Cymbeline," Ed said, not trying to hide or deny it, because what was the use? He was already caught, even if he didn't *feel* particularly caught. Even if he didn't feel like he'd done anything wrong.

"Did you kiss her, Edmund?"

"She kissed me," he said.

"A convenient way to frame it."

Ed shrugged.

"She's forty years younger than you are!" Helen said. She was pulling her coat around her shoulders, as if she could shield herself that way from the terrible, terrible things Ed had done to her. He glanced behind him, to where the driver was pretending not to listen.

"Can we talk about this when we get home?"

"Fine," Helen said icily, fixing her gaze out the window. Sighing, Ed just did the same.

* * *

He stood over the wet bar in the den, pouring himself a Scotch. What he really needed, he thought, was a fat spliff - but Helen hated marijuana and he'd given it up when they'd gotten married. The world, it seemed, was always so much harder without it. His anxiety sharper. The chords more discordant. Everything closer to the surface. Oh well. Scotch would have to do. He called up to her.

"Do you want a drink?"

"No," she said back, after a pause. "I want you *not* to drink."

Christ. Fuck it. He drank his Scotch down and went upstairs.

She'd already taken off her coat. Her earrings. The tasteful silver necklace she'd worn with a jade pendant, which he'd watched out of the corner of her eye all evening, as it had dipped into her tits. She was a lovely woman, had lovely tits even if they were a bit sagged, and he loved her neck and her collarbones and her body. Even now, as she vibrated with rage. She was standing in the downstairs powder room, taking off her make-up.

"Do you need help?" he asked. "With the zip?"

She sighed. Put her hands on the edge of the sink.

"Yes," she said.

He unzipped her. Revealing whatever strange corsetry passed as underwear these days.

"I'm going upstairs," he said. "Getting out of this monkey suit. We'll talk then, alright, love?"

She sighed again. Didn't say anything. So he didn't either. Trudged upstairs.

He knew, in a way, what he was doing. What he had always done. Being cute and sweet and helpful was a sort of a shield, wasn't it? And he knew, deep down inside, that she had a right to be hurt. They all did, the women. Genie and Helen. The ones he met on tour, who had written him after. Who had wanted something from him. Wanted more. He took off his tuxedo, draping the pants and jacket from a hanger. Unbuttoned his shirt. Tossed it in the hamper. There were mirrors lining the far wall, and he turned and looked at himself in it.

Flabby, age spotted body. Lumpy and sparsely haired. Well, Ed thought, age catches up with us all, eventually. Or, he thought, not. And the last thought was almost thought in Baron's voice, inside his head. That wry, laughing baritone. He wondered what skinny little Baron would have looked like as an old man. Was a painful thought, like it always was. Because he thought of it all the time. That he was forty now, then fifty, then sixty. And

Baron had just stopped somewhere short of all that. They'd had such little time together. The ultimate injustice.

Helen came in dressed in some silky pajamas. Ed grabbed his dressing gown, put it on. He could hear her sighing at him again. She hated when he slept in his underpants. Well, it was his bed. His body. He'd sleep however he pleased, he thought, but it was a thought without much oomph behind it. He sat down on the bed, up among the pillows.

"Let's talk, love," he said.

Mad, still. She sat as far away from him as she could, in a plush revival chair in the corner.

"I really don't know if I have anything to say," she said. Ed sat up a bit. Sighing.

"That woman who kissed me is a nutter," he said. "Off her gourd. I asked Mattie about her. Said she had a brain tumor. She wasn't making any sense."

Helen was staring blankly. Blinking at Ed. "Five told his mother that you seemed to be enjoying yourself."

Yes. Well.

"It's complicated," Ed said gruffly, because there really was no way of explaining it.

"Complicated that you enjoyed kissing a woman half your age?"

"It wasn't about that," Ed said, rubbing his jaw. Knowing it sounded unconvincing. Christ. Of course it did.

"What then, Edmund? I swear, I spend the first fifteen years of our marriage in the shadow of Saint Eugenia, and now this."

Ed winced. "Don't *call* her that," he said.

"This is exactly what I mean," Helen said.

"She was the mother of my children," Ed said. "I don't give you a hard time about Louis-"

"Louis lives in Cincinnati! You know he's no threat to you."

Well. That was true. Helen had always made it abundantly clear that Ed was the love of her life, no matter how late in life they'd met. After all, she'd revealed on their first date that her adolescence was spent diddling herself to his records. Like it was fated, she said. But what was fate? She was far from the first one who had told him such things.

"Have you ever been faithful to me, Edmund?" she asked, the words falling down swift. He felt himself frown. He had, of course, occasionally had dalliances. Occasionally. Less, lately. Too tired, too old for all that. But when you're Edmund Matthew Hammond III? Opportunities present themselves. An occasional lass. An occasional lad. Not many, through their relationship. Not as many as when he was with Genie, when the numbers were in the hundreds. The thousands, maybe.

Though not a single one had meant anything.

"I see," Helen said.

"It's just sex," Ed said softly. "I mean, I've always -"

"Yes," Helen said stiffly. "Groupies, I'm sure. You were in *Saffron*." She said it like it was a joke.

"We called them something else back then," he said bleakly, as though it even mattered. "Not groupies. Something else."

"And did Eugenia know?"

Ed sat forward. Put his head in his hands. Somehow, selfish oaf that he was, he had never even considered that question. *Did Eugenia know?* About the *birds*? That had never once been his worry. And sure, maybe it should have. He heard an echo in his head now, something Baron had said a whole lifetime ago. *Me and Sue have an arrangement.* There had never been an "arrangement" for Ed and Genie. Never a conversation. Only talking around things. But.

"I think," Ed said carefully, "On some level, she must've. Sometimes birds would come around Kingcausie. Hitchhike over. Because they were sotted over me. After we… Well, and sometimes they'd come up at events. Try and draw me away. She never seemed to care, much. I was with her, y'know? We were *babies* when we got together and… "

He trailed off, because he realized he was talking too much. Sharing too much. He felt queasy, even saying as much as he had.

"How *elevated*," Helen said. "Did it ever even cross your mind to *talk* to her about it? Or to me?"

He dropped his hands. Looked at her, miserable.

"Hel," he said, "You grew up in a different *world*. When I was a lad, you didn't… couldn't… "

"Yes," she said, stiffly. "I'm sure."

"Look," Ed said, hands worrying his brow, "If you don't want me to screw anyone else, I won't. And if you don't care, well then, I'll tell you when I do. It doesn't matter to me. It's just screwin'."

A long pause. A sigh. "I'm not sure I care, either," she said, sounding dulled, like the wind had all been let out of her. "About the *sex*. What concerns me is the lying. How can I trust that you even care about me if you lie to my face?"

"I do care!" Ed protested. Dropped his hands. "Right now, you're the only one in the world that I love like *that*!"

And it was true. He loved her. He did. Their small, lovely lives together. Sweet sex and tele in the morning and talking about books together, going for walks together. Holding hands like kids might. The comfort he took in her. Maybe it was no great love affair. But it was something he'd always wanted, from his youngest days.

Even if, in those days, he'd wanted it with someone else.

"Right now?" she asked, without certainty. And he cringed. Because he hadn't thought that *that* would be the thread she pulled at. But pull at it, she did.

"W-well," he stammered. "There was Genie… " A pause. Long and terrible. And she *heard* it. She *knew*.

"And?"

"And someone else!" He spat it out, like it was hateful, like he was ashamed. Not knowing if he really was, or wasn't. Hating himself, hating her, for making him say it. "And someone else, the whole damned time I was with her but you don't have to worry about that now, because they're dead too!"

He cradled his face in his hands. Not crying. Shaking with the effort, shaking with everything that had been taken out of him. To say even that much.

"The love of my bleedin' life," he muttered into his palms. Horrified, inside, that he was still, somehow, talking. "But they're dead so you don't have to worry about it *ever* because they aren't ever coming back."

Shaking. Shaking. His whole body felt like it was going through spasms. And the silence was thick and long and Ed heard Helen rise from the chair and come close to him. Sitting on the bed beside him. Reaching out. Putting her hand on his knee.

"Edmund," she said very slowly. "Who was it?"

Ed only shook his head into his hands. Couldn't say it. Wouldn't. Couldn't. It had been too tightly locked inside him for far too long. It would kill him if he let it out. All that truth.

"I can't," he told her. "I can't."

She sighed. Wrapped her arms around him. Drew him close.

"Okay," she said softly, rocking him, and he wasn't sure why, until he realized he was crying, big fat tears right down into his hands. "Okay."

*   *   *

She wasn't mad anymore, in the morning. In truth, it seemed almost like she was afraid of hurting him. Tiptoeing around him. Making him tea. He sensed that there were questions she wanted to ask, but wouldn't. He certainly wasn't going to volunteer. Hadn't that been how he'd gotten through all these decades? Holding his cards close to his chest? He'd outlived his father already, most of his brothers. However he was going to close out this life, it was too late to change. Too late to start tearing himself open just to let those old wounds bleed.

They settled back into their rhythm. Horses. Dogs. Books. Radio. Phone calls and emails with all of the grands, and lunch with them, when they passed through town, and things felt normal again, but there was a tenderness there. A scab that neither was picking, but that just wouldn't heal, anyway.

A few weeks later, they went out to Kingcausie. It was almost a concession on Helen's part. She'd never loved the place, precisely, not like Genie had - but then Genie had raised three bonnie babies there, and it always felt a bit like her ghost was all around. Maybe that's why Helen had always been reluctant, Ed realized. He'd never thought about it before. Never really inhabited that space, those brainwaves. The life of a bird. Well. Still. It was one of Ed's favoritest places in the whole wide world, and even if she felt a bit tender about it, she understood, on some level, how he needed it. Even as old as he was. Wasn't going to go out and shear the sheep himself anymore, or dig fence posts, but he had it in his head this lovely autumn that he'd like to give the back patio a good sweeping and maybe put a fresh coat of paint on the front door. He hadn't decided the color yet. Maybe blue.

His eyes were too bad for him to drive them out there himself anymore. The roads too twisted. When they passed the sign that said *Kingcausie - 6 km* he thought, as he always did, of that first trip up. 1967. He'd been searching and searching for weeks for a place for he and Barry, but nothing was perfect, nothing was right. Couldn't have looked together. Would have raised too many suspicions. Besides, he had wanted it to be a surprise. It hadn't been until he'd seen that sign that he felt a little spark inside. Once, they had been going somewhere on this road, together. And though in that moment, he'd been sure he was on the verge of death, it had been a lie. The truth had been so much deeper, and more complicated, yet. That hadn't been the end, but the very beginning. Perhaps, he'd thought, back then, this would be a beginning too. He'd toured the old decrepit farmhouse, imagining the lives they'd lead in it after they got it all fixed up. It wasn't perfect. Far from it. Water damage and old peeling wallpaper, bats in the attic, rats down below. But from the very beginning, he knew, he knew, it had to be theirs.

Of course, that hadn't been the case. But he never could have known it back then.

The first few days, he didn't even think to go looking. Too much to do. Check in with the caretaker about the flocks. Meet the newest litter of Coricopats. See the damage that a storm had done to the barn, agree to let them patch it up. Used to be that he was a farmer, truly, in between albums. Now he felt more gentleman than farmer. 'Sokay, Ed told himself. He'd earned his retirement. Someday this place would be Matt's - the girls sure didn't want it - and he felt some satisfaction imagining Little Ed learning how to hammer a nail here, to dig a post there. All the important parts of manhood he hadn't gotten yet, living in the city, in the states. Maybe this summer would be the one he asked Mattie to send Five out here, now that Ed was retired. They'd spend the whole season with their shirts off getting sunburnt, building something, or nothing at all.

By the third day in Kingcausie, he knew he was dragging his feet. Kept thinking about *it*. That guitar, down in the closet. The one he always told himself he'd forgotten. He was dragging his feet because he didn't want that nutter to be wrong about it. Or maybe because he didn't want her to be right. Easier, he thought, that night as he was up late reading in bed next to Helen, or at least pretending to read, to live in this in-between space. The not knowing.

When he was a boy, he'd believed in angels. In ghosts. In God. Had prayed every night that school would burn down and that he'd become famous and he'd finally get laid. Somewhere after his Mum died, it all had stopped. All that hoping and wishing. The world had proved itself to be substantial, and by that he didn't mean *a lot*, though it was also that. No, it had proved itself to be of substance. Immutable. No magic here. Nothing surprising.

And, well, after all, Baron was a non-believer. And he loved Baron, knew, somehow, deep down, that Baron was the sharper of the two of them, even though he wasn't really sure which of them was more *talented*, even though he knew (deep down) that he was the pretty one. But Baron was clever. His bright, sparking brain seemed to make more connections than Ed could ever figure. Beautiful leaps from A to B right to Z. If Baron said God was a lie, that there was nothing waiting for them, after death, well, then, Ed figured, Baron was probably right.

But. But. That *bird*. Her *kiss*.

The next afternoon, Helen went for a trip into Aberdeen to go shopping. The cook was puttering about somewhere, but Ed didn't care. No one would ask why he was hiding away in his recording studio. It was *his* farmhouse, at all. He was entitled.

He went downstairs. Pausing by the shelf there, and for good luck, like he always did, he touched that old brick, the radio, the red cap from a bottle of

Beefeater's long since drunk. But then kept going. To the closet, which was full of Christmas decorations, because they always spent Christmas here, all of them, since the kids were little. He knelt on his old knees and started dragging out the fairy lights, the garlands. Setting them aside.

There it was. Way in back. A cardboard box, battered, guitar-shaped. Covered in too much tape. Ed crawled in and grabbed it and dragged it out. He'd cut the tape open carefully years ago. Hadn't thought much about it since. Once, twice, peeking at it. Before putting it back away.

Laid the box down. Opened it.

There it was. Old Ed. Poor thing. By the 70s, the dark green paint that Baron had coated it with had started to come off in huge flakes, revealing the pale wood beneath and large fleshy flashes of pink. The colors were odd together. Discordant. But somehow right, too. Even if Baron had never painted it, there really was no other guitar like this that Ed had ever heard of. Weird hollow bodied Ricky. With the big heavy Japanese tremolo that you could barely use if you wanted to keep it in tune, but Baron said he liked the way that it looked, so it stayed. The bronze pickguard, the pick-ups, the knobs all crusted with red rust. Time hadn't been kind to them, either.

Ed sat back. Holding it. Without even thinking, he did what he always did with a guitar. Set it on his knee. Started to tune. Christ, it was a strange one. Tiny little neck that made Ed's arm and hands feel enormous, and the light, jangly strings that Baron had favored didn't help any. He'd have to change those out. Would clip the ends of them, too. Maybe. Baron never bothered. Left them long and curling, like ribbons. Or maybe Ed would leave the new ones long - in honor of Barry.

For a few minutes, he played. Ancient songs, early songs. *Rock 'n' roll, Hammy,* just like Barry had always liked it. His fingers hitting the dry, worn spots where Baron's fingers had hit. Like holding hands in a way. Of course, he'd never been much for rhythm guitar, not like Baron was. He remembered a moment, early on, in his room with brothers snoozing and Baron with his old Antoria on his knee saying, *Not going to play those scales Liam showed me. Can't see any fun in it. Rhythm, my Ed, that's what I want to play. Getting that beat inside you. It's like foockin', innit?*

Had been early on enough that Ed hadn't known what it was like to fuck, hadn't understood. Baron always had, intuitively, somehow, even though Ed had figured out, somewhere, along the way, that Baron was a virgin, too. But now, as an ancient old man, Ed knew precisely what he meant. You had to feel it more than think it. In fact, if you thought about it too much, it'd all go wrong.

Ed threw the strap - floral, worn, some woven sixties thing Barry had got who knows where - over his shoulder and walked back into the studio. Plugged her in. Started doing a bit of the Chuck Berry shuffle, thinking about how Baron would have liked that. But as he fiddled with the dials he remembered: pick-up, the lower one. Broke. And he stopped, and stood there, still for a moment. Remembering why he was here.

Unplugged again. There was a table in back that served as a desk sometimes, a place to change strings or sit down and jot lyrics once, when he'd still been writing and recording on the regular. A place for the kids to sit and draw when they were bored mostly, when they were young. Ed went and set the guitar down on it. Went digging around in the drawers there for a screwdriver. He knew he had a soldering iron, but wasn't sure about the solder. Maybe, probably, out, or had walked off somewhere, as things like that tended to do. He found the skinny little Philips head, tucked it behind his ear. Started loosening the strings and shoved them out of their place in the trem. Pulled off the knobs. Began fiddling with the screws. There were so many of them, and his hands weren't as still or as strong as they once were. Felt like it was taking him forever.

At last, he had the pick-up rings off, the screws all out. Lifted up the metal pickguard, set it aside. The lower pick-up wasn't wired in at all. There was a blob of messy solder that had dripped into the guitar's pink body, useless. Ed shook his head. That Baron. Never did know what he was doing with guitars.

And then he turned, saw something glinting on the back of the pickguard. Stopped.

It was words. Carved into the metal, or scratched in with pen, or written with marker. So many words, covering the inside, the back, of the whole damned thing. Or, well, the same words. Three words, and then a date after it, to show Ed when they were written, because clearly they were meant as a message to him. A sort of a love song. The same love song. Over and over again.

Baron loves Eddie 17.1.59

BCT loves EMHIII Feb 78

Barry loves Hammy, 1961 and a heart behind that one, with an arrow in it. *Baron loves Eddie* and *Baron loves Ed* and girlish, sweet *BT+EH3 4ever.*

Ed stared, still bent over that guitar. Ed read. Ed contemplated.

Baron loves Ed. Baron loves Eddie. I fucking love you, mate - Baron, '69, and he smiled, a bit painfully, to see that one, because he'd doubted it back then, back when they were murdering each other on the daily in court. *In 1964 I will always love you more,* and *Baron Loves Ed, 1971* and some had places on them, too. *London, BT+EH, 6/4/65* and Ed reached out and put his hand on that cold metal pickguard, not really believing what he was seeing, reading. Thinking about how many times Baron must have made this tender surgery. Taking his strings off. Removing screws. Ed thought about how Baron had carried this with them, on tour, in the studio, and then carried it alone - over oceans, to new homes, on new adventures, all those years. Ed sat down at the table, taking that pickguard in his hands. Staring at it. Trembling.

And bent over, suddenly, and started to cry, and couldn't stop, couldn't stop at all. Remembering Baron. Remembering how it felt to be loved by Baron, how tangled up and hard it had been. Baron. Baron. The secrets they carried, in their guitars and their pockets and their hearts, and he felt the ugliness of the world against them, against something so simple and so pure. Two boys who should have been men together, loving each other. A marriage like any other. But it had been impossible then, dangerous, and so it became a secret, a delicious one. Eddie loving Baron, more than anyone else, ever, too. Whether in 1957 or 2022.

Didn't notice the racket he must have been making with his keens, or remember the open door to the studio. Didn't hear the voice at the top of the stairway with his head bent, the pickguard in front of him, the tears flowing down.

"Ed?" came Helen's voice just behind him, and he felt her hands on his shoulders, and if it were any other time in his life he would have hidden it. Rushed to cover it up, those words, too honest, obvious, true.

I Baron Clement Templeton will love Edmund Matthew Hammond III to my dying day and every day thereafter, 9 August 1967. Helen was taking the pickguard from him. Reading it. And he was too sodden and sloppy to stop her. And maybe, maybe, maybe for once he just couldn't even begin to care.

Had always worried, when this moment would come, that she - Genie, Helen, either one, really - would have shoved him away, revolted by him. But that's not what Helen did. The world had changed, or else they had. There, in the little dug out basement in Kingcausie, Scotland, all that happened was that she put a hand in what was left of his hair, stroked it gently. And he threw his arms around her, and hugged her, and it wasn't Baron, but for the first time, Ed realized, it would be alright, anyway.

Here, Now

Baron was west that summer; the long, hot summer; the summer of love. 1967, when Baron went completely off his bloody head. Sitting in the recording studio, watching Ed set down take after fastidious take of the songs they'd written at his house or Ed's house, songs that were weird, silly, sprawling, songs with their feelings tucked inside of them, set in code. Baron would watch as Ed's tender, familiar mouth would grace the soft end of the microphone, would watch Ed's eyebrows raise, would watch as Ed's eyes fixed on his eyes. Pressing. Public. And Baron, for once, would be the one who looked away. Cracking a joke, maybe, for Charlie's benefit or Allie's benefit or Liam's benefit (did Liam not know, still? Or did he? Baron had never quite worked it out, and asking Ed would have been to admit to a vulnerability. To say that he *wanted* to know. That he cared.) Somehow, he was unpeeled that summer, made raw and sinewy and rearranged. Sotted, as in drunk, because he felt drunk all the time now even when completely sober, but also sotted as in *be*sotted. All over stupid, perfect Ed.

"It looks stranger, you know," Ed said to him one night as they walked back from the studio to Ed's townhouse. Their knuckles touching, just barely, as they walked. They'd found they could walk in evenings if they were quiet about it and be trailed by only one or maybe two fans. It was an anonymity they would not have enjoyed only a year or two prior, but their fans were growing up, and so were they. "When you look away from me. You never would have, before. You would have flirted right back. You would have been the one making *me* blush."

230

One of the girls outside Ed's gate chirped a bit of a hello at them, or at Ed, really. The birds were always soppy over him, more than they were over Baron. Baron had his fans, but they were as many troubled boys as there were birds, boys who wrote him letters, mostly, after the albums came out, interpreting his lyrics like some kind of ancient text. Wrong, those boys were always wrong, but it was amusing to see the patterns they found. Felt good, in a sense, to be read - even wrongly.

Baron waited outside the gate as Ed fumbled with his keys, ignoring the camera that flashed as they slipped inside. *What did the birds do with the pictures?* He'd asked Ed once, because the fans outside his gate were always taking pictures. Ed's smile at Baron had been winking, knowing. *Well, yes, that, surely,* Baron said, *but after they touched themselves, what then?*

Baron stayed silent up Ed's front walk. Head down, hands in pockets now, dizzy, defensive. He waited for Ed to open the door. Stepped inside, standing there as Ed closed and locked the door behind them, threw down his keys on the table by the entryway. Standing there as the cats circled their legs, mewling for attention. Was frozen for a moment, still feeling the pressing eyes of their bandmates upon them. Still feeling the pressing eyes of the birds. Still feeling the pressing eyes of the world until he gave one last glance back to the closed door, and then, satisfied, sprung on Eddie, his hands cupping either side of his face, his mouth hungrily enveloping Ed's mouth, the weight of Baron's lean, lithe body throwing Ed off balance and back, against the table, the tasteful nick-knacks there going jingle jangle, like a bell.

"Whoa, Barry," drawing back. Putting his hands on Baron's hips. Slowing him down. "What's gotten into you?"

Baron didn't want to talk about it, not really. Baron didn't really want to talk at all. He didn't know how to be a normal person anymore, to have normal person conversations in normal person company. This summer had been rearranging him, cell by cell by cell. The only time that he felt steady, himself, was when they were fucking, or maybe when they were deep inside a song. Then, he could just follow his own impulses, sure that those impulses were wise and safe and correct. But the rest of his life? Full of dangers and traps.

"You've gotten into me, ya tease," Baron growled, and he licked at Ed's soft pink neck, aggressive, like a tiger, and then kissed and bit downward, hearing Ed let out small laughter, and Baron felt Ed get both softer and harder, all at once.

"All right," Ed said, lacing his hands through Baron's hair as Baron kept on kissing him. As Baron opened Ed's floral shirt, finding the softness of Ed's body beneath. Bruising it, with his teeth. "But we can go upstairs and fuck in a bed. Like *people*."

Ed must have known that Baron wasn't a person. Not anymore. That he needed *leading*, shaping, guidance. Because Ed pulled away again, stopped Baron again, tangled his fingers through Baron's hand, tugging on his arm, leading him up the stairs.

They went up to Ed's third floor bedroom. Ed turned, busying himself by the dresser, humming as he took off his watch, finished unbuttoning his shirt. Baron contemplated shoving Ed up against the dresser, grinding his cock up against Ed's arse. Scattering the loose change, the jewelry, the cuff links. Decided against it. Ed hated a mess, and besides, Ed had made it clear that they were going to be *human beings* tonight, not snarling, growling animals.

So instead he tossed himself into Ed's bed, snuggling up by the bookcase headboard. Silent. Waiting. Behind him were Ed's slim volumes of Important Poetry. Once, he'd teased Ed about them - how he never really knew if Ed *read* them, or just collected them based on how impressive they would look on a shelf. He didn't tease him about it now, though he still wasn't sure. Poetry? Ed? Really? Anyway, it was like Hammy had said. No more teasing, not lately. Everything felt too fragile, too fierce that summer, like the slightest wind might break him.

When he touched himself, it was almost an automatic movement, detached from his thinking, feeling self. He stuffed his hand in his trousers, started wanking. Enjoying the long-awaited sensation of flesh against his cock, even if it was only his own.

"What are you doing, mate?" Ed asked, eyeing Baron in the mirror. One eyebrow cocked. Baron heard himself scoff.

"Oh, we're mates now, are we?" he asked. Ed's smile grew cocked too. He turned to Baron, hands on hips. Standing there in his y-fronts, all pink skin, white cotton. Our kid Ed. Baron felt himself come back to Earth a little, come back to his body a little. Despite himself.

"Pet," Ed said, blushing slightly. When Baron only stared, stared and stroked, Ed added, more succinctly: "*Love*."

"That's more like it," Baron said, the warmth building in his hips and his belly. But the smile that finally wormed its way over his face, he knew, somewhere, deep down, was forced. *Love. Love.* The word he was always thinking. The word that seemed too precious, trembling, false. If Ed knew Baron's thoughts, if he had any idea, he gave no sign. Ed had knelt at the end of the bed and then started crawling toward him. On all fours. Well and truly crawling. Baron stroked faster, harder, reaching out his free hand to touch the length of Ed's back, his belly. Trying to forget. Trying to *feel*, simply feel, instead. His fingers registered warm skin, velvety texture. Its richness. Its electricity. Feeling that spark, Baron let himself let go of everything but Ed. And Ed - well.

Ed sank himself down over Baron, his warm, smooth body covering him. He smelled a bit ripe, actually. The sweat of summer. Baron didn't mind. Actually made him harder. His hand wanking and wanking in between them as Ed kissed his jaw, his neck.

"I think I'd like to fuck you tonight," Ed was saying thoughtfully, only he said it at the exactly same time Baron said the wrong thing, the weirdest thing.

"How long d'you think it'll take the rest of them to realize I've slept over here every night this week?"

Ed drew back. Frowning.

"Is that really what you're thinking about?" he asked, his eyes going pointedly to Baron's crotch. To Baron's hand still moving, moving, moving in his trousers.

It was a good question. Because from the live wire way that Baron was feeling, it seemed like Baron *wasn't* thinking about that, or at least should not have been. It was the wrong thought. The unsexiest thought of all. Like something his Auntie Deeds might say. *What might the neighbors think?*

"Forget it," Baron said, biting his lip. Still wanking. Wank wank wank. "I like what you said better."

Sitting back on his knees, Ed looked at him. Biting his lip, too. One eyebrow raised. So fucking sexy. Like a plump little angel. And Baron knew that Ed could have pressed. Could have picked at it, that loose thread. Baron's insecurity, a thing that Baron Templeton was not ever meant to possess.

But Baron was only human, wasn't he? Ed must have known that. Because, in that moment, for both of them, he chose to let it go. Reaching out and unzipping Baron's trousers, revealing sticky cock and sticky hand. Lowering his golden head. Going down on Baron. Getting him ready. Forcing Baron's mind, kicking and screaming, back to the places it was meant to be. Ed's hot mouth around his rod. Ed's fingers worming their way inside. Soon, soon, Ed's cock stuffed up in him. Both of them going off like a pair of firecrackers. Making Baron almost - *almost* - completely forget.

* * *

Dawn was humid and gray, like August dawns sometimes are. The London air warmish, a feeble threat of rain. Baron woke up the little spoon, a slow waking. Saw their legs, bare, stretched out in front of them, and Alonzo sleeping at the end of the bed. Baron, the only thing awake in the whole wide world, and Ed snoozing behind him - snoring a little, really. And Baron, lonely in the moment, his belly hungry and empty, conflicted. Whenever he was happiest, why did he always have the feeling like his happiness was doomed to end?

Distraction, then. He pressed the bottoms of his feet to the tops of Ed's feet, drew his body up against Ed's. Felt Ed's cock, soft now, against his arse. Pressed himself deeper. Rubbing himself there. Closed his eyes. Thought *Scotland.* Felt Ed's cock grow harder, his breath hitch. Still sleeping. But horny sleeping, now. His hips moving with the tide of Baron's hips, his cock pressing deeper, harder against him, and Baron was hard now, too, and Ed must have been awake by then, because he kissed the back of Baron's neck, his shoulders, wrapping his soft, strong arms around Baron, drawing him even closer, both of them wordlessly moaning.

And in that moment, as Ed pressed Baron's body down against the mattress, as Ed pressed Baron's cock up against the mattress, too, his own cock reaching the soft-furred cleft of Baron's body, Baron thought that perhaps he really *could* make this moment stretch out forever. That moment just before day breaks, that moment just before waking, this moment just before fucking, that moment that both of them were young and beautiful and would never die and they were about to finish this album that would change the universe and they were about to move up to Scotland together and they would love each other forever like this, every part of them sweet and sticky, tender and alive, that they would both always be *here*, in Ed's bedroom, the cat watching them like a nosy interloper, and maybe the world would hafta erect monuments around them as the ages around them passed on and on.

Baron was close already, humping the mattress, and it seemed Ed was close, already, too. Didn't get it in Baron. Just pressed one hand to his lower back, and then reached down and wanked himself. Letting out a sound more animal than man as he spilled himself across Baron's arse, his back, and stayed there for what felt like an entire eon, trembling over Baron's body.

Then at last, collapsing against him, never mind the wet sticky between them, laughing a little, kissing a little, and Baron thrust a few more times into the mattress until he came, too, Lights going off, everywhere - or maybe on. The world waking up around them. All at once, just like that.

And then all at once sleeping, in their own sticky mess.

* * *

Ed woke alone, in the cool damp spot, the covers cast back and tumbling down onto the floor. Would have been cold, had it been a colder season.

But it was summer, then. August then. Stretching on and on, and so no matter if Baron somehow managed to strip the bed half naked (to strip Ed half naked) every time he slept inside it.

Laid there for a minute listening to the shower going in his bathroom. Listening to Alonzo whining around the door of the WC - crying for his brekkie, crying for Baron. Ed was warm and sleepy and satisfied and saw no use in crying. Only scratched himself, feeling spent and happy. Thinking about the day before. Had been something, to record those songs together. The ones they'd written, more love open and throbbing between them then they'd ever had at any other time in their lives. Sometimes he thought that they all musta known. Charlie and Liam and Albert and every engineer, as Ed watched Baron slide his eyes closed, hands clamped down on his headset, feeling the music that had gotten all up inside him. Good thing, then, for psychedelia. For the drugs the engineers were always smoking, openly, right there in the booth. These were not the days of white hot amphetamine anger, nothing like that. This was a warm summer, a summer to eat mushrooms and go walking barefoot in the park. Maybe not as soft and wild as what Ed imagined San Francisco must have been like, but soft enough. As soft as British blokes got, at least.

Still, he thought, yawning, stretching his toes, hadn't there been something else different lately? He'd grown looser, more comfortable. Bringing Baron to his flat every night. Having his way with him. Making him an eggie in the morning. But Baron. Well. Something seemed different, odder, about Baron. Not that Baron wasn't always odd. He was, of course. And it was a time of oddities - the riots on the telly, which Ed hated watching but which Baron could not turn away from. The scent of change in the very air, which no longer smelled like hair tonics and aftershave but rank sweat and sometimes urine, as Ed walked down the street at night.

Feral delights, Ed thought. *Floral delights.* And he smiled to himself about his own rhyme and resolved to tuck it away into a song, later.

Anyway, he told himself, Baron was fine. Baron was only Baron.

Ed got up and went to the door of the khazi, letting Alonzo Kittycat tangle up his bare legs, ignoring him. Pressed his ear against the door, listening.

Baron, he knew, normally could not resist singing in the shower, or at least whistling. Letting his voice echo and boom against the pipes and tile, brighter and more resonant than it sounded usually, when it was unadorned. Some days Baron begged the engineers: *Give me a bog voice. Make it really soapy.* The other lads hated the sound - Ed included. Baron's voice was perfectly alright the way God had given it. But it wasn't the sort of thing worth fighting about, Ed knew. They'd fought through so many stupid battles already as a band. As a… couple? Was that right? Well, a coupla something.

Ed waited. Listened. Frowned. No song, then. Just the steady *hsssssssss* of running water.

"Barry?" he asked. Knocked once. No answer. Well, his shower anyway, wasn't it? So without waiting to be invited in, Ed stepped inside. The glass door was all steamed up - Baron was simply a series of brown blots inside gray. Ed opened up the door, without much thinking about it, said, "Barry?" one last time, simply, like that.

Baron let out a ragged yelp.

Startled, Ed startled back, one hand to his naked chest. He laughed a little.

"Barry, you almost gave me a heart attack." But the look Baron gave him was not laughing. The shadows under Baron's eyes were like dark bruises. His mouth was down-turned, perturbed. When he looked at Ed, it was with a furrowed brow.

"I'm almost done," he said peevishly. "I'll be right out."

When Ed had stepped inside the steamy room, he'd imagined slipping inside the shower with Baron. Soaping him up. Washing him clean. Dirtying him again, maybe. Now, he just cleared his throat.

"Alright," Ed said softly. "Just wanted a piss."

He went and sat down on the toilet, taking one. Watching Baron grab for a towel and sop himself off. Baron wasn't looking at him. It was almost pointed, how Baron was *not* looking at him.

Tired, Ed told himself, he's just tired.

When Baron left the bathroom, the towel around his waist, Ed followed. Feeling a little bit like a demented puppy dog.

"I thought once we lay down 'Knapsack,' we could start on another one I've been working on. I think you'll like this one. It's-"

"Christ, I need a day off," Baron interjected. He'd grabbed his own shirt off the floor and was tugging it over his head. "They don't need us mucking about in there while they're laying down the orchestral shite."

Ed swallowed. Frowned. Staring. They never took a day off the studio, any of them. That was one of their rules - unspoken, sure, but it might as well have been set down in stone. They were the biggest band in the *world*. None of them ever left a track to *chance*.

"A day off?" Ed said dumbly. "But I thought this weekend… I thought we could go to the Speak this weekend. Jimi-"

"No," Baron said. Shook his head. Pulled his dirty trousers on, like he was in a real hurry. No pants, but then, Baron often didn't wear them. "Need to head home this weekend. The cats have probably eaten each other."

"But your housekeeper -"

"She doesn't love them like I love them," he said, which was, of course, true. No one loved a cat like Baron Templeton loved a cat. And Ed, still naked, still sticky, wasn't really sure what to say. It was like a door had shut between them, firmly, abruptly. But he couldn't see no *reason* for it to have shut. Hadn't they been fine the night before? Hadn't they?

Baron must have seen the look upon his face. He sighed, said "Aw." Came closer, kissed Ed. Breath all stinky. Ed leaned into it, but there wasn't to be any lingering. Baron only drew away.

"Don't look like someone put your puppy down, Pet," he said. "I still…" He trailed off. Paused. A knife in the gut, that pause. Before finally concluding, "I still love you. Just need some time. If you're not too hungover after Jimi and the Speak, come see me Sunday, okay, Love? We'll work on that song of yours. Get it all ready for the studio on Monday."

"Yeah," Ed said, hugging himself. Nodding. Hating how he sounded. Like a needy little girl. "Okay. Sunday."

"Right," Baron said. He'd laced up his shoes by then, gotten all ready to go. At the top of the stairs, he paused, and Ed still felt stupidly, helplessly hopefully that Baron might have changed his mind. That he was staying.

For the session. For Ed.

But instead, Baron just let out a low whistle. "Come on, Alonzo. Let's get you some breakfast."

The two of them walked down the stairs together, leaving Ed alone in his bedroom.

* * *

Strange, to be without Baron in the studio. But almost… well, nice. Barry could be a right arse to the engineers, who hated the broad, sloppy way he talked about instruments, how Baron couldn't, after all these years, communicate *anything* about a key or a time signature. How he insisted on calling their equipment "boondogglers" and "whardoodles," no matter how clearly it annoyed them, or perhaps *because* it annoyed them. Now, without Baron there, Ed was free to move about the cabin. Telling the string quartet when to come in, directing them. Before that moment, because of Baron, he'd always hung back. There had been a few times when, drunk, in the studio, Baron had lost it, upsetting a chair, knocking a guitar or two over with a clatter, and so Ed had given him a wide berth, had given them all a wide berth. Biting his tongue. Biding his time.

But hadn't I been born into this? he thought, sitting down to make notes on the producer's sheet music. His father had been a musician before him. Those notes, and the precisely right way to play them, were written on his soul. Ed noted the guarded, skeptical way the musicians watched him when he first handed back the pages. After all, the public lie was that none of them even knew how to read music. But after the quartet played it through the first time, nobody objected. He was right. Of course he was. He was Eddie fucking Matthew fucking Hammond the *third*, and he knew a thing or two about the right way to write a song.

"You're an animal," Liam told him, as they shared a ciggie in the alleyway out back between takes. A comfortable fag, a comfortable conversation. Good old Liam, his oldest friend besides Baron, besides his brothers - and those weren't really friends at all.

"What?" Ed asked, taking small puffs. Pretended he had no idea what Liam was talking about. But Liam would not let him be coy. He leveled eyes, black as the coal his family had once mined, on Eddie.

"Holding out on us, for all these years," he said. "The music could have been better, and you know it."

"Tell that to the gold records on your wall, mate," Ed said, ashing. Handing the ciggie back. Liam took it, sucked furiously.

"I can't believe you," he said. "Dancing around Baron all these years in the studio like you're some tart who's afraid of doing the ironing wrong because his fist might go off."

Ed felt the anger like thick bile rise in his throat. The gall. The invalidation. *Like you're some tart.* "I'm not afraid of him," he leveled back.

"Well, then you're completely off your head. Moonie. Gone soft, mate. Softer. Over bleeding brown Barry Templeton. You think we don't see it? All of us?"

Would have been easy to be angry, normally. Hadn't he always defaulted to fists whenever anybody had called him soft or even implied it? And to be a lad as pretty as Ed, the implication was often made. That he was more girl than boy. More sweet than sour. And he'd blackened an eye or two or three over it, certainly.

But this… this was Liam. Looking at him pointedly, smoking that ciggie down to its butt, stomping it out under the toe of his plimsolls. Liam, who already knew Baron and Ed shagged. Much less the rest of it.

Ed felt his spine straighten, one vertebrae at a time.

"The music is better when we're together," Ed said firmly. He couldn't let any light out, any small chink of truth. "It all is."

He took his time lighting another cigarette. Inhaled slowly, his eyes fixed on Liam's eyes. Exhaled, right on him. Unwavering. Squinting, Liam waved the smoke away.

"You're a fool," Liam said, but there was a dollop of resignation in his voice as he turned on his heels and left Ed in the alleyway, smoking alone on his cigarette.

* * *

He stayed later at the studio than *any* of them, making sure the piano was right. This, too, was a new novelty. Usually, he and Baron sauntered away from the studio together, satisfied by whatever point the music had reached by dinnertime, motivated toward satisfaction by their mutual need to meet body to body. To, well, fuck. Well. Fuck. There would be no fucking tonight, so why not make sure every bleeding note was perfect? The engineers looked positively ghastly by the time that moment came, wan and haggard, with bags under their eyes. Ed was sure he only looked a mite better. But, oh, when they played the tape back that final time, how it was worth it. He had waited for years for this feeling to hit him in the studio, that wash of, *Oh, perfect beauty*. For the sensation that, at last, the music sounded as it did to him in the head. Yes, yes, of course, he liked their albums well enough. They'd made him bloody rich, hadn't they? But they hadn't been *right*. They hadn't been *satisfying*. This was almost like a wank, like a climax. The ecstasies of art done your own way, and for you yourself, and no other pressing matters to distract from them.

At the end, Bruce's voice in his headphones. "Brilliant, Ed. Fucking brilliant." There was a sort of silence in his voice after, a hush, inside which nothing needed to be said at all. Ed hadn't had a reaction like that since he'd first whipped out "Cymbeline." And that hadn't been his song, even. That one had belonged to Barry.

Now, Edmund beamed his bright, secret smile and left the studio alone. Not walking. Flying.

He intended to go see Jimi that night. Really, he did. Wanted the musical ecstasies to continue, to roll on and on for hours and hours more and maybe he'd snort some cocaine or find a bird or even call up Genie- should call up Genie, really, had been meaning to, was mean, how he'd been ignoring her - and plunge himself into the sort of body that didn't make him feel murky and confused and, well, awful sometimes. He intended to, truly. But when he returned to his flat to shower and put on something appropriately psychedelic and for the Speak, he found a slip of paper on the table just inside the door. As the cats circled his ankles, he picked up the note from his latest housekeeper.

Call from your real estate agent. There is a place in Scotland she wants you to see this weekend - King Cozzy?

Ed smiled a bit, grimly. The help always seemed to have atrocious spelling. He brought the note into the kitchen where the phone was, doing his best not to trip on the cats on the way. Picked up the receiver, and started to dial.

* * *

The twisting path his driver took was oddly familiar, looping through sheep pastures and rolling wildflower fields, the earth shadowed by aimless clouds. Ed stared out the back window of his Royce, quiet, not sure what he was thinking, or feeling, or even *if* he was feeling anything at all.

Maybe. That was the word that kept flying through his head. Maybe maybe maybe. Maybe someday soon, he and Baron. Maybe the album. Maybe the music. Maybe better off not, then. Maybe. Eventually, after hours of maybe, it seemed, the driver rolled off the paved road. Drove all along a broken fence. In the distance, Ed saw a shadow, a man, prowling the countryside, a flock of gray clouds trailing after him. Shepherd, he thought. Maybe. Sheep. At last, his driver pulled up alongside a barn that looked like it was built more from moss and rot than it was from wood. Ed got out, and immediately regretted his expensive leather shoes when his feet sank into the muck. He squinted into the fresh new afternoon light, glanced about until he saw his real estate agent rushing toward him in her wellies. Waving wild hands.

"Edmund, isn't it a gem?" she asked, tucking her little hand into the crook of his elbow. "It's the very thing you and the little lady need for a retreat away from the world. Now, keep in mind it may all take a little sweat equity to bring it up to her tastes, but for a young lad such as yourself it should be no trouble."

As she pulled him up the soggy path, he couldn't help but smile at all the euphemisms - those she knew she was using, those she didn't. *Little lady,* as if Genie would ever see this place. It was for Barry, who, he was sure, would prefer the place rotting and Byronic. *Young lad*, for loaded, as in stinking fucking rich. But she knew better than to drop a reference to hiring workers directly. Better, Ed thought, to appeal to his sense of enterprise. Adventure. A man, young as himself. Still, as he stepped through the front door and into the dusty, dim space - saw the peeling wallpaper and the unfinished, splintery floors - it was easy to imagine himself up on a ladder, peeling off paper. Or maybe down on all fours, hammering nails. And maybe. Maybe. Maybe, he thought, standing in what might someday be a front hall, looking around at all the cobwebs in the corner, Barry, there beside him. Painting, with his shirt off. A little drunk. And beautiful.

"Oh, you *must* see the kitchen," she was saying. Grabbing his hand again. Dragging him forward. "It's just the place you can imagine a family sitting down for breakfast."

The threshold to the kitchen was a little off-kilter. Ed almost stumbled as he stepped down into it. Floors a mess, still. Asbestos tiles peeling off, revealing what looked like pure dirt underneath. But the summer light through the kitchen had a yellow loveliness. There was a table there in the middle, heavy wood. Knotty.

"What's this?" Ed asked, touching the oak top. Needed an oiling, maybe. But it wasn't bad. Maybe even usable.

"A table," she said, and Ed grinned a little, because he *knew* that. "The last owner's children left it. Couldn't fit it through the door. There are some wardrobes upstairs, too. They come with. I'd assume you could take them apart, if you want. You'd probably like something more modern, wouldn't you? More to your own tastes."

Ed laid his hand on it. It was the kind of old furniture his parents might have had, handed down across generations. Not to anyone's *tastes* but essentially immortal. Almost felt like he could hear the heartbeat beneath it. He saw the light spilling over the knots. Imagined Baron sitting there, his shadow falling harsh against Ed. Imagined Baron sitting there, scratching Alonzo or Lady Bo or maybe even a new cat, one they would buy together or else tame from ferality with the promise of tinned foods. Baron, sitting there, smoking and drinking and joking and saying not much of anything.

"Yeh," he told the real estate agent, not feeling the need to share any of this. It was private, like most of his life was private. "Maybe."

* * *

Tucked in early, then woke up early, too. Fed the cats. Put on something loose and appropriately counterculture, something that he knew that Baron would like. Those old seafarers, probably once owned by a sailor. Sometimes, when Baron got a faraway look in his eyes, he would talk about his father, lost at sea somewhere, how he sometimes wanted to get lost at sea, himself. Over top that, a floral shirt. Light and blousy. His trainers. Casual. Baron usually didn't like it when he got all gussied up. *You're not a bird, Ed,* he would say. *You're* you.

Put his acoustic in a soft case on his back, the one with the straps like a backpack. Put on his helmet, dented still, but those dents were like a badge of honor now. Yet he rode his moped carefully up the road from London. Obeying local speed limits. Head clear and sober. Couldn't risk getting pulled over. Not again. Not today.

When he got to Baron's house, he parked alongside Baron's psychedelic Rolls. Once, their cars had matched, but Templeton wore his hippy heart on his sleeves these days. Literally. Figuratively. Liked to talk like a guru to the straights sometimes, just to confuse them. Ed didn't like anyone to know he had dropped acid or puked his brains out on shrooms or read the Bhagavad Gita. A floral shirt was one thing. A grand statement on the oneness of all beings? Too much of a risk. In interviews, Ed was still the friendly one, the slick one. Let Barry be the gamboling jester. Ed would smooth it all over with the press later.

Not whistling, not humming, Ed headed up the walk. But when he knocked, it was the housekeeper who answered, a plump little woman who seemed like she was out of a Victorian children's novel.

"The mister's still asleep, love," she told Ed. "Shall I tell him you called?"

Her eyes, a bit cautious, a bit questioning. She must have known. Ed had spent the night often enough, had left his clothes all around, only to find them folded, separate from Barry's, later. But she never *said*, never *asked*, which is what Ed liked about her. His own staff was always sniffing about, riffling through his things. Nosy. He'd fired more help than he cared to admit.

He hesitated, shifting from foot to foot. "No," he said. "Do you think it's all right if I wait for him by the pool? He asked me to come," he added, as if to reassure her that he had a right to be there at all. She, too, hesitated. Grunted.

"Yes," she said, a little skeptically, "If you insist."

She opened the door, let him in. He followed her through the grand marble entryway, his trainers squeaking on the floor. No signs of Baron or even his cats. A house like an empty tomb.

And then, through the kitchen, and the sun porch - littered with newspapers and record sleeves, like always - and back out again. She left him there sitting at the edge of the kidney-shaped pool on a deck chair. He did the same thing he always did when he had a guitar and a moment. He opened the case, set it on his knee. Tuned it up. Played idly, contemplated trying to fit a song together in the ten minutes or two hours or however long he had until Baron rose from his slumber. Decided against it. Played something by Little Richard instead. "Rip It Up." His old first love, made looser and softer by the acoustic strings. The day was warming up to brightness, and he felt good for a minute, truly good, as the music squirmed its way inside of him.

And then a shadow cut down over him, and he turned, and he saw Baron there, in his dressing gown, looking disheveled and sleepy still. One arm was crossed over him, the other holding a cigarette to his puckered mouth.

"How was Jimi?" Baron asked him at last. Ed looked up, examining Barry's expression. Guarded. That's when he realized what the problem was. What the problem had always been. Baron Templeton was *afraid*.

"Didn't go," Ed said simply, smoothly. He tucked his hands along the top of his guitar and then put his chin on top of them. Smiling a little. Thinking, *Calm down, child, you're safe with me.*

"No?" Baron answered, smoking more. Too fast. Coughing, then tossing the butt into the pool. "Did you call up Genie or some other tart then?"

Ed let out a snort. "Christ," he said. "No. I had an errand to run yesterday, early. I went up to Scotland, you know. Found us something. A little farm. For your sheep."

Baron blinked at him, face still hard. Didn't say anything at first, then finally blurted out, "I know you, Ed Hammond. And I know you can't promise me you're not going to leave me. Everyone does, in the end."

Ed sat up straighter. He put his guitar down, then, on the concrete next to him. Gestured to the empty deck chair beside him, offering Baron a space. Baron hesitated a long time, as if he wanted to make Ed suffer the same way that he was suffering. But Ed didn't waver, and he didn't take it personally, either. Couldn't. Wouldn't do neither of them any good. At last, Baron sat down beside him. His hands clasped. Looking away, out into the blue pool water.

"I can't promise you," Ed agreed softly. "I can't predict the future, can I? So any promise would be a lie."

"Well, then," Baron said. Hands still clasped, jiggling a leg. "What good is it, then?"

Ed sighed. Held out his hand to Barry, leaving it hovering there for a long moment.

"I'm here now, aren't I?" he asked. "That must count for something."

Baron snorted hard. Laughed hard, too. But then Ed neither snorted or laughed, and they were both quiet for a moment, the only sound the pool filter kicking in.

After a moment, Baron slid his hand against Ed's hand, and they were frozen there together, at the edge of August, at the edge of the impossible blue.

Reunion V

Five slept the fathomless sleep of the young, an endless tumble of dream upon dreamlessness, gray, and his limbs were heavy, until, all at once, he was slammed back into the same body, the same soul he'd always had. As always, it took him a moment or twenty to deduce where he was, exactly. No, not the palatial bed in his mother's West Egg suburb, the second master, which he'd been given after the all-but-divorce as some sort of consolation prize. Lost home, lost dad, but here: have a private bath and a bay window because mom, as a girl, had always wanted a bay window. Lost school, lost friends, but at least when you get off the bus you can bring the snack the nanny left you up here and you can watch the dog walkers going by. No, no, today he did not wake up there.

And not a trundle bed in an old farmhouse in Scotland. And not an ex-London manor home. These were all possibilities, but not today. Today, Five woke in the narrow loft bed and he stared, sighing, at a popcorn ceiling only a few short feet from his face (*Don't pick it,* Dad had said once, *I haven't been able to figure out if there's asbestos in there.* And then a pause, *Don't tell your mother I said that.*) Really, he should have known, should have expected. This year, sixth grade, this had become his most frequent locus of waking, a reversal of the usual rhythm. For years this had been an only weekend, or every-other-weekend-at-best spot, and now, it was something else. Dad had been the one to insist on it. The middle school where he worked had a *halfway decent* music program, he said, unlike the school out on Long Island where he would have normally been enrolled and where everyone was booked up in travel sports and they didn't even assign band instruments until sixth, and his father wasn't going to see his son's talents buried, he'd said - and Five, only in fifth grade, then, not really more than a little kid, and definitely not adult enough to be *asked*, had found himself retreating in on himself, collapsing. Shutting down. Bracing himself for the fight he felt was sure to come - but for once, his mother only sighed. Looked sidelong at her son. And agreed.

Only when she did, did Five realize how terribly badly he'd wanted it. Wanted this. Before then, he'd felt too timid to hope, much less give voice to that hope.

Now, a Thursday, like all other Thursdays, but also somehow not, Five kicked his blankets aside and scurried down the ladder in his boxer shorts. Stood, scratching himself for a moment, before he turned off the blaring alarm. Looked at the phone, plugged in there. Noted the event notification that blinked to life on his phone. *Practice Room Reservation: The Mutineers 3:35 - 5.* He felt something, a shiver of something. Fear or excitement. Both. Neither. Quickly, not wanting to feel anything, he swiped away. Before his dad could wake up and stink up their tiny shared bathroom, he rushed off toward the shower. Most days, he sang in here - it had the best reverb of any of their bathrooms in any of his homes, all subway tiles, everywhere, even on the ceiling. But today, it felt like the notes froze on his still-unchanged vocal cords (that would come later, his doctor said, after T). He could hear them but he couldn't give them voice. He wondered for a minute if it wasn't a bad portent of what was to come. He'd never had stage fright before. But he pushed that thought away, too. Best not to dwell, to let something like that become too big, too real.

By the time he got out of the shower, his dad had already come in. Sitting on the shitter, staring at his phone. Five hastily covered the in-congruent, embarrassing parts of himself with a towel - not that his dad hadn't *seen* them before, but still - and hustled out, before his father could even mutter a single, mortifying, "Morning, bud."

Was it dorky? Five wondered, as he began to get dressed, *That he'd set out his clothes the night before?* His favorite old jeans, torn at the knees, the ones his mom was always trying to throw out and so he'd started to leave them here though he was worried he'd outgrow them soon. His second-favorite t-shirt. Not his favorite - that was one of his dad's old tour t-shirts, from one of his grandfather's tours, which felt like bragging, which felt like cheating, on a day like today. But a still-pretty-good t-shirt that he'd gotten from Target with a gift card last Christmas, a shirt with David Bowie on it. David Bowie was always cool, right? Five pulled it over his head, convinced himself that he was. Well, he'd heard on a TikTok that Bowie was kind of faschy, but also Five *felt* something when he looked at him, a certain kind of kindredness, and that mattered. That was important. He and his Dad didn't have any religion (Mom had her weird witch stuff, which Five couldn't stand). But sometimes Five felt like he still had saints, and Bowie was one of them. St. David, St. Roberts, St. Jones, patron saint of the genderbent and the musical. He needed that today, need to jam good, right? With Weird. With Gilly. With Arji.

He'd been smoothing his shirt down, but he stopped when that name flitted unbidden through his brain. He hadn't meant to think it, had meant to keep it at arm's length. But there it was. Arji. Arji who was an eighth grader. Arji who didn't know he existed. Arji who maybe would, soon? If the saints allowed. Praise be to Aladdin Sane. Five swallowed hard.

Please let this go okay today, he thought, and he wasn't sure who he was asking. David, he supposed. He looked at the man's make-upped face in the mirror. Looked at his own face. A face still composed entirely of youthful androgyny. Boy's hair, yes, boy's soul, but still. Still. Not there yet. It would come someday, and then maybe it would be easier to get the other guys to take him seriously and then it wouldn't be so scary, so terrible, a day like today. But. But.

Stomped the thoughts out. Went out to the kitchen, pantomimed getting his things together. Put his Jazzmaster in its case by the door, which his dad was bound to ask about, but he did it anyway. Made them both coffee, put them in to-go cups, like he always did. They never had enough time for breakfast.

"Thanks, bud," Dad said as he came out of his room, tightening his tie. Bud, Bud, Bud, it was always "Bud" with Dad, ever since the name change.

Five had told himself that his father meant it to be affirming, or something, even though he would have preferred if his Dad would have just called him Five, or maybe even Eddie - the name they shared but neither really used. Still, it was better than Mom, who had stuck with "Sweetie" no matter the changes and no matter how hard she'd fought them.

What? You're still my sweetie, she was always saying, swiping back Five's hair from his forehead, and he knew it could have been worse, because she could have been dead-naming him, but it also could have been better.

Anyway, Five put on his sneakers, his light spring coat, his backpack, and then, pressing his lips down flat over the sharp edge of his teeth, slung the soft guitar case over his shoulder, too. They were halfway down the elevator, sipping their coffees in silent unison, when Dad noticed it.

"Jazz band's Friday, bud," he said. Five slid his gaze away, felt how his cheeks were heating, hated it, ignored it.

"I know," he said. "I thought I'd stay after today. Use the practice room."

"Mm," his Dad said. See? This was the problem, with his Dad being the music teacher at his school. He knew too much, was too involved. "I think the eighth graders have it reserved today."

"Yeah," Five said blankly. His hand around his coffee cup was suddenly numb. He ignored it. "I know."

A long pause as the doors slid open and let in the light of the lobby, the bright light of the day.

"Okay," his Dad said. "You want me to stay out of your hair?"

Hands still numb, face still searing hot, Five stepped out of the elevator. His eyes trained ahead, toward the busy street.

"Yeah," he said simply, a little more meanly than he intended. "I would."

His father made a noise, low, in the back of his throat. "Sure thing," he said brightly, though it sounded fake, and then added, as though he'd forgotten it, "Bud."

* * *

Before Arji Iyengar, Five had been the best musician in their school.

I mean, at the winter concert, Five had surprised everyone - even Dad - by getting down on his knees and playing his solo with his *teeth*. There had been a moment of silence, and then howls, girlish, validating, from the audience, and Five knew then - even before the celebratory trip to the diner after, his Dad beaming at him, and the call to Grandpop to tell him all about it - that all those hundreds of hours practicing alone in his room in secret with his amplifier headphones on, letting his Dad think he was playing video games - had been really, truly worth it. Technically, "Five" had been born three years before, but it felt like it was that moment, the moment he felt the splintered wood boards of the old school stage bite at his knees, that he was *truly* born - fully formed from the head of Zeus, like a boy should be. No struggling. No effort. Just pure instantaneous dominance, over all of them.

But then winter break. And then the new kid. A tall, gawky eighth grader who wore black t-shirts with bad jokes on them, nothing to really even think about, at first, until he overheard his Dad one night telling his girlfriend on FaceTime all about his latest student.

"You should hear this kid," he was saying, "He plays bass better than my Dad does. He could be a professional. Not later. Like, *now*."

Dad's assessment had been innocent enough. Just small talk, really. He often gossiped with Naomi about his students. But that was mostly complaining. The flute girls never practiced, and the drummers spent too much time goofing off, that sort of thing. This was different. This was his father *respecting* someone, the way that, Five felt sure, he would never be respected. Because his Dad knew his whole embarrassing history, had wiped his ass, knew he'd had to come home from Girl Scout camp that first year because he was homesick, had been the one to *teach* him how to plug in his guitar and make it hum. And where could there be respect in that? There couldn't be, really. Not like this.

Arji was in his gym class, and after that, Five started paying attention. Quietly, subtly listening in on the conversations Arji would have with his friends, mostly about bands and girls. Five would take the long way to his next class so he could follow them. He was hoping that the older boy would drop some tender morsel, chat about what he was listening to or how he'd gotten so good. But he almost never talked about music. In fact, he mostly made crass jokes about sex, about touching himself, about his erections, and his friends would all laugh and clap him on the back and it was clear, then, to Five, that they were a pack. The bio-boys, who put their hands in their pockets, jiggling things, and discussed how to hide their arousal. Problems that Five didn't have, and likely never would.

Five had never even heard him play the bass, not at first, because Arji had told Dad, and Five had learned from listening in to Dad's dinnertime conversations with Naomi, that Arji thought jazz band was just kid stuff and he was a lot more serious about his *career* than that, and so Five was stuck plodding about with the jazz band crowd, with their boring adulation and even more boring covers of Chicago's "25 or 6 to 4," because what choice did he have? None, really.

But one Thursday afternoon Five had wandered into the band room from his after-school art club to ask his Dad if he'd remembered the form for the art club trip to the Met, and that's when he heard them for the first time. The Mutineers. At first it was… nothing. Pretty terrible, really. The drummer was off-beat and the guitarist was only playing cowboy chords and Five kept walking back, to his Dad's office, when something tugged at him. He stopped behind the risers and peered through the chair legs, because he *heard* something, essential as a pulse. Arji, eking notes out of that slim neck, the fat, tender strings, and *ohhhhh,* yes. Dad was *right.* Arji was *good.* Five watched him in secret, saw the dark flop of Arji's hair and how it hung in his eyes, saw the look of absolute concentration. The tongue darting out between the lips, a thin pinkish red edge, while his fingers went *bomp ba bomp bada bomp bomp* and so did Five's heart.

But then the song ended in a scratchy explosion of amplifier static and the boys in Arji's band (of course it was all boys, only boys) were all laughing, and even Arji wore the hint of a smile, as he lifted his eyes from his fingers and, on his way to smiling at his friend the guitarist, Arji's eyes hit Five's eyes, and they were looking at each other for a moment, Arji frowning. Five, stunned and owlish, staring back.

Hastily, he'd hustled out of there, forgetting entirely the stupid art club form, why he'd even come.

* * *

Sitting in civics class, trying not to think about how his Jazzmaster waited for him in his band locker, like a second, secret heart, Five drew spirals in his notebook margins and practiced his introduction in his head.

Arji. Hey. Heeeyyyyyy. Arji.

Hey.

You guys don't mind if I, like, jam with you?

(Did people, cool people, cool *guys*, eighth graders, say *jam*? Or did they just take out their guitars, the jamming implicit?)

You guys don't mind, right?

I think you're missing something. I think there's some essential element...

You know I'm the best guitarist in this school, right, you dick?

No, no, I didn't mean anything by it. I didn't...

If this were a movie, the teacher would have called on Five, who was so obviously occupying another plane of existence entirely. But it wasn't a movie. Five was invisible, like he mostly always was since Arji Iyengar, and the loop-de-loops covered his margins, and his mind went round and round.

Hey. Arji. Hey.

Hey.

* * *

The last bell of the day honked out its muffled, nasally sound, and Five snapped to action almost immediately - stuffing his books into his backpack, racing downstairs. Forgot, even, to stop by his locker for his coat, but maybe it didn't matter, though part of him wished for the warm, familiar hold of it around him. A cloak. A shield. Oh well. In his David Bowie t-shirt, he went to the music room, ignoring the clarinets who streamed out behind him, went right to the row of ancient lockers at the back and took out his guitar case. In a way, he knew it was too cheesy, too much, to be here so

253

early, and when his dad poked his head out of his office and chirped, "Hey, Buddy," Five blushed up to the tips of his ears.

"Hey," he muttered, looking down at his Jazzmaster, his old friend, seeing his own face, disembodied, in the artificially distressed teal finish. It had been a gift for his last birthday, begged for, drooled over on his phone a million times, and he'd felt something when it had finally arrived, a gift from Grandpop, naturally. Anodized pickguard and burnished chrome fixtures, but it hadn't been the feeling he'd expected. An emptiness, really, almost like disappointment, but he told himself to stuff it down. Most kids didn't have a rich grandfather that would understand what exactly the right guitar would even *look* like, and he was lucky, wasn't he? To be so gifted, so privileged, so blessed. To ask for what he wanted, and to get it.

Anyway, he and Rocket - he'd named it Rocket, for some reason, because it just *felt* right - had learned to appreciate each other in a different way, slowly, through bleeding nail beds and built-up calluses, and eventually it became *his* guitar in the very same way the old ax of Dad's he had stolen most frequently before all this (a shitty heavy awkward Gibson with a glossy neck that made his hands sweat) had been his and now, mostly, he could imagine playing on no other even though, in a way, Rocket had been his first real lesson his heartbreak. The first time he'd gotten exactly what he wanted, and realized that deep down, really, truly, and in all actuality, perhaps he actually needed something else. Who knows what.

Five braced himself for more from his father. But it never came. Instead, after a moment's silence, his hands in his pocket, his Dad strolled away, back into his office. Five slung his guitar strap over his shoulder, zipped up his case and put it away. Holding one of his picks between his teeth - the thick red kind, Grandpop's favorite, too - he walked out to the music room. Went to the stack of amps that were set up in the corner, and started tuning up. It felt like time was passing more slowly now, almost stuttering, and when the door finally swung open and Arji and his friends streamed in, Five found himself breathing again. He hadn't realized he hadn't been.

"What's this?" Arji's friend, another eighth grader named Mark Thomas, asked, standing, staring at Five, his hands on his guitar straps. "Who's the little kid?"

Five cringed. Blushed. Kept tuning. Didn't look up. He heard someone say, "I think that's Mr. Hammond's kid… " And he thought it might have been Arji, but he wasn't even sure, really. There was a weird pause, and a snicker from back behind the risers, and Five wondered what they were saying. He could maybe guess - all his fears exposed, something about how he was *really* a girl or whatever, but whatever it was, they were out of earshot, past the fuzz sounds of the amplifier. Another excruciating few moments, and they all sauntered back out slowly. First the drummer. This kid Hayden. Who messed with the kit a little and then sat down, staring at Five, and then Mark.

"Hey!" Hayden said, not really a question. Half a shout, really. And then said it again, *"Hey!"* until Five's eyes snapped up.

"Yeah?" he asked, forcing a smile even though he could still feel himself blushing.

"We reserved this room. You can't be here."

He could feel, nebulously, a disapproving presence, just within the periphery of his vision. Mark. Who had *his* guitar, a shitty Strat copy, slung over his shoulder. He wore it low down, over his pelvis, like he was hiding something. Whereas Five had always worn his guitar high up, almost near his chest. Because he was small, with small hands, but also because, okay, yeah, he was *also* hiding something.

It was a long moment, the world's longest moment. Mark and Hayden, staring at Five, and Five chewing his lip back. They were taller than him. Older than him. They'd had it harder, almost assuredly - parents who struggled with rent and to keep them in good schools and maybe they'd worked *jobs*, actual *jobs* to get themselves those instruments. They thought that made them tougher, too, even though Five knew that he was plenty tough in certain ways. He knew how to shear a sheep, for one thing. How to hold them still while Grandpop clipped their hooves. In his wild girlhood days, Five had learned to build a fort with the ties firmly lashed. And then, of course, there was how, at age eight, he'd gone to his parents and told them the worst, most hidden truth about himself, and weathered the storms after, the psychologist appointments and the arguments with Mom, the cuts on his inner thighs that he hid beneath the pantyhose at his grandmother's funeral, the four days in the hospital after Mom figured out what was happening, the zoom doctor visits, the way his old friends had fallen away after he had come out - the way that new friends had never really fallen back. He'd been alone, and he'd fought, and he was strong in his own way, even if it was not the usual way.

And he did not wither now, not yet. Even if he was small enough and different enough to know that the best response was no response. To stay there, silent and unbudging, staring back.

Mark made a noise. He went over to the amp, and, without asking, unplugged Five's guitar. There was a pop and a crackle, and Five turned to watch Mark plugging himself in, instead. Didn't really know what to say. Not at first. Just watched.

"I told you," Hayden muttered, behind them. "We reserved the room. Go ask Daddy if you don't believe me."

Then the worst thing happened, because Five blushed up to the tips of his ears. A physiological response - but a losing one. He heard himself let out a little sigh. On shaky legs, he went and sat down on the edge of the lowest risers, where the flutes sat during music class. Put his butt right on the carpeted floor and sat. Watching.

Arji came out with his bass. He didn't seem to even see Five at first, as he said something, soft and laughing to Mark, and plugged himself in. But when he turned around, he saw Five there. Glanced at Mark first, then Hayden. Said, "Who the hell is this?"

"Hammond's kid," Mark said, grabbing the nearest microphone in one hand like he was afraid that Five was going to take it. Five felt himself laugh a little bit at that. As if he were any kind of a real, credible threat. They all knew - well, thought they knew, at least - that he wasn't.

"Oh," Arji said. He was tuning up his bass, only half-paying attention, it seemed like, and when his thickly-lashed eyes flickered up it was almost as if it were an accident. Almost like it didn't happen. Not really. Except he looked at Five again and turned on the microphone, and his lips were curling when he said into it, "Nice shirt."

Blushing. More blushing. Mortifying, humiliating blushing. And Five was so preoccupied on the inside with figuring out how to stop it that he almost wasn't even there in that music room, as the three boys began playing their awful, disjointed music. Some hackneyed thing, all power chords and distortion to cover up how poorly they played. Except part of what made it so bad was that it *wasn't* all awful, because Arji was good, damn it, and his notes sort of floated out, separate and individuated from the rest. None of it matching. None of it meshing.

Five scrunched up his nose. With his Jazzmaster on his lap, he sat watching, and making a face that he couldn't hold back at all, and the whole thing went on for like an entire fifteen minutes - though they only got through two and a half songs or so - before Hayden quieted his drums and loudly announced, "I HAVE TO PISS," and Arji laughed, said, "Okay, let's take five."

And Five perked up, and then blushed again. Mortifying, too. He put his face in his hands and groaned into them as there was amplifier noise, and then nothing. Instruments, turning off.

But then. But then. A weight on the step next to him. One he hadn't expected, and a sweet smell, half sweat and half fabric softener, the nice kind, and he dropped his hands and opened his eyes and was shocked to see Arji sitting there. There, right there. Blue jeaned hip next to Five's blue jeaned hip. Next to him.

"So," Arji said. "You think we're terrible, huh?"

Five's eyes went wide. "Ah," he said. Scrunched his nose again. Tried to stop. "Well…"

"I've heard about you, you know," Arji said. "Well, I mean, your dad's told me a bit. But I Googled you, too."

"God fucking damn," said Five. He wanted to bury his face in his hands again, but thought it might make him look even weaker, squishier than he already did. So instead he just sat there, his hands draped over the top of his guitar.

"Bowie, huh?" Arji went on. There was something strange about his voice. Not unkind, but pressing. Testing. "Would have half expected you to wear a

Saffron shirt."

Don't blush, don't blush, Five thought, and somehow successfully willed himself to blush *less*, at least. "Yeah," he said, "Well." A long pause, too long. "That'd be kind of cringe, wouldn't it?"

It wasn't the type of slang he usually used, but he thought Arji might understand. Nobody wanted to be *cringe*.

"I dunno," Arji said. "If my grandfather was the last living legend of the rock and roll era I might not care if it was cringe. That's, like, I dunno. Pretty base. If you ask me."

"Yeah?" Five asked, tilting his head up toward Arji. Looking at him. Christ, he was *pretty*, wasn't he? Five hadn't really noticed that before. The glossy, loose curls. The curling, clever lips. He'd so far been too preoccupied by wanting to murder the other boy and run around with his skin as a new set of clothes to notice.

Five blushed deeper. Only a shade.

"Yeah, I mean, he *met* Little Richard. Little fucking Richard!"

"Yeah, I guess."

"I've always liked Templeton more, though."

"Is that allowed?" Five asked. Arji laughed.

"Why, because of the whole toxic masculinity violent murder radical cult problematic thing? I dunno. I don't listen to all that TikTok shit."

Now it was Five's turn to laugh.

"No," he said. "Because he's not a bassist."

"Oh," Arji said. He sat back a little, staring forward, smiling, and Five couldn't be sure, but did *Arji's* complexion darken a shade?

Five only hesitated a moment before what came next. Usually, he hesitated more. Usually, it was clear he couldn't talk about this stuff. It was too close to bragging, too *cringe* - and about something most kids didn't care about at all. But it seemed like Arji wanted to hear it.

"Grandpop told me once that Templeton was a terrible bassist. Or maybe he just found it boring. He'd fuck things up on purpose just to make sure they'd never ask him to play. Grandpop didn't really *want* to play the bass, but he had to, because no one else would. But he ended up liking it. I don't think there's an instrument he doesn't like, though. You could hand him - I don't know - an oboe and give him fifteen minutes and he'd be able to figure it out."

"Man, it must be awesome to be that talented," Arji said, and that was all he said. Quietly.

"Yeah, I dunno," Five went on. "Dad said Grandpop never used to talk about that stuff. Saffron and Templeton and all that. Maybe it's because he's old as fuck or maybe it's just because I ask him, but he tells me about it all the time. Like there's this one story he told me about a chocolate bar-"

"What about you?" Arji suddenly interjected. Five glanced sharply up.

"What about me?"

"Sorry, I wanted to ask, what instruments do you play?"

Five looked down at the guitar in his lap. Shrugged. "This. Well, mostly this. I fuck around on harmonica a little bit, and Dad's trying to teach me piano but it's boring as fuck. But I've played the guitar for as long as I can remember."

And for a moment, he did remember. One of his earliest memories, old enough that Mom and Dad had still lived together in their apartment downtown. Standing up on the white sofa, reaching for one of the guitars on the wall. The way his whole small body had seemed to hum beneath the hollow dreadnought when he played it. Tunelessly, then. But that hadn't lasted very long.

Listen, his Grandpop had told him that Christmas, Here's the secret about guitar. Just play it like it sounds in your head. You'll mess up at first, but just keep trying. Keep going. It feels like faking it, but it's not. It's how it works.

Even then, at four, at six, from the very start Grandpop had talked to him like a grown-up when it came to music. Mom had wanted to shuffle him into voice lessons and Suzuki violin, but that hadn't been Five's scene. No, what he had wanted - what he had wanted from the very beginning - was to be a grown-up music maker, among grown-up music makers. He had wanted to be taken *seriously*. There was no point in anything else.

"Any good?" Arji asked. And Five felt his eyebrows lift, and he had to stifle a smile, because what the hell kind of question was that? He was Edmund

Matthew Hammond V, and certain questions were rendered absurd upon asking. That one, especially.

Better not to speak. Better to play. He stood up, went to the amp, and wordlessly plugged in.

He wasn't nervous. He didn't need to be. And maybe it was a dick move, but what he did was simple. He didn't play a Saffron song or a David Bowie song or even one of his own creations. He played the last song Arji and his friends had been playing. Except, you know, better. Except, you know, good. Just a little flash in the solo. Not too show-offy. No getting down on bended knee to play with his teeth or anything like that. He jazzed it up just enough to demonstrate that he knew what he was doing, that he was holding back, too. That he could be even better, if Arji wanted him to be better.

His eyes right on Arji's eyes. Blue glassy lasers. Two.

After, Arji stood up. He clapped, and at first, Five's back tightened - unsure of whether he was being mocked. But then Arji touched Five's shoulder, a warm gesture, like the way men touched each others' shoulders, and Five felt himself relax a little. Arji meant it - whatever it was he was about to say.

"That was awesome. Damn. I figured you would be."

"Thanks," said Five, and he realized he spoke a little breathlessly when he did.

"Gotta say, though, I was hoping you'd tell me you played the tambourine or something."

"Huh?" asked Five.

"Mark's going to be *pissed* when we kick him out of the band for you."

"What am I going to do now?" A voice came from back behind the risers. Five and Arji both turned to see Mark standing there, his complexion wan, his guitar slung low over his shoulder.

"Nothing, sweetie," Arji said, his voice dripping with sarcasm. He clapped Five on the shoulder again, and Five let himself let out a little snicker. "Don't you worry your pretty little head about it."

At first Arji's grin was cutting. But then he looked at Five again - hand still on shoulder, the secret invisible circle drawing together around them -

and his mouth softened, just a little.

"Hey," Arji said, in a lower voice, meant only for Five, "You don't write songs, do you? There's one I've been working on. Could use a hand."

"Yeah, sure," Five said. Shrugging. Cool. Cool. "I could take a look."

Chip Shop

They knew *of* each other, even if they did not *know* each other. Of course they did. The stupidest part of the myth, Ed would later think, that they were strangers on the day they met in 1957. Because what was a stranger in Liverpool? Their aunties had stood in the ration lines together during the war. Everyone knew exactly how much everyone else's father was drinking. You saw one another at church, or at scouts, and if you did not see one another at church or scouts, that was a topic of conversation too. Small town world, small town politics, and he'd been hearing rumors for years that Deidre Peters' boy was trouble, been hearing all about that Lost Boy whose wanton parents had left him on Didi's doorstep, the boy with the sticky fingers who was always getting caned at school. Had even seen him a few times on the bus. Hair piled up high like a ted and eyes all squinty, like he was spoiling for something, a fight, probably. If their eyes ever met, Ed sank low in his seat.

Ed knew all about it. Of course, he wasn't thinking about it, then. Not yet.

It was spring, almost summer, and Ed was eleven, but almost twelve years old. Ed had other problems on his mind. Cracks had begun to appear: his parents were whispering together at night when they thought the boys were asleep, and though most of the boys were asleep, Ed wasn't. He took useless trips to the khazi, pressing his ear to the thin wall between the WC and his parents' bedroom. *Whisper whisper whisper* they were saying, and he couldn't make out the words, but he heard them, their worried tone. Ed began to put together the clues.

Hadn't his father been working less? Hadn't Ed skipped school one day with Liam and seen his dad in Ye Cracke? A pale shadow drinking in darkness past fingerprinted glass. Ed had stopped, stared for a moment, before Liam urged him on.

Even if that is your old man, Liam had said, *Do you want us to get a hiding?*

Ed thought about this. About all the mouths his parents had to feed, about the pounds being drunk down to nothing, about the stress of it all. He couldn't talk to his brothers about it - he knew, most assuredly, that each and every brother would somehow make this problem about his very own self. And that was the last thing Mum needed, wasn't it? She always came home so *tired* from her days with the nuns and the nursery children and it used to be that Ed would offer to rub her feet for her but lately even that didn't seem to help. No, no, Ed knew, it was time for him to become the man of the house, if none of the other boys - dear old daddy included, of course - were willing to do so. No one was asking. It was just natural, and right. The job would fall on him.

That's how he ended up with the job at the newspaper stand outside the chip shop. Sometimes he'd ride his bicycle around and deliver the heavy stacks of paper, both before school, and after, when the other boys hadn't shown their faces there - no sense of responsibility, not like Ed. And sometimes Old Man Parker would wander off to the pub himself and leave Ed collecting guineas for papers and magazines until the sunlight started to fade. Once or twice Liam came by, and whined at Ed to let him see the dirty magazines, the ones tucked behind the highest rack, but Ed couldn't risk his employment even for his worst best friend, and so he chased him away and told him that he'd see him later. Soon. Of course, Liam wasn't the only troublemaker. There were other boys, and even a man or two, who tried to nick a magazine in a waistband or, in the cold weather, under a coat. Once or twice, Ed chased, and he was fast, but relieved, still, when he didn't catch them. Mostly he ignored it. Until. Until. Until.

A gaggle of boys one Friday afternoon, older than him. Mostly all looking pretty much the same, halfway like good boys, halfway like teds, the way older boys sometimes did when they were trying on a new set of clothes like a new identity. All wandering over, chewing gum, smoking stolen cigarettes. Half of them wandered into the chip shop. But two stayed behind. A ginger lad, and a duskier one, and the names lazed about through his head. *Dick. Baron.* The pair stopped, and the ginger one reached up for one of the music magazines, and they stood paging through it, chewing their gum together.

Ed watched them. Remembering what he'd heard about Baron Templeton. His mother, warning Paulie, who was the same age. *Stay away from that one. He's given his auntie no end of trouble.*

But really, was he that bad? Baron was small - barely taller than Eddie, though older, clearly, a few more acne marks, maybe the shadow of a mustache. His hair was so greasy it basically shone, the only shining thing on this gray day, and Baron was saying something to Dickie and they laughed softly together, and kept turning pages.

But Ed was a good boy, and his job was important - not just to him, but to his family, too. The pennies he took home, he told himself, keeping them all afloat.

"You need to buy that," he said, and hated how girlish and high his voice chirped out. Baron looked at Dick, who looked at Ed. Ed cleared his throat. "I mean, you can't just read it. You need to buy it."

It was the ginger who let out a snicker at him. Dick. *Dick.* What a name. But Baron was looking at Ed now, and the words *not so bad* once more occurred to Eddie. He had long eyelashes, that Baron. Kind of wasted, weren't they? On a lad? That's the sort of thing Ed's mum would have said.

(*Only no. Not really wasted. He's a beautiful boy, isn't he?* Ed thought, and knew it was queer to think it, in every sense, only he wasn't sure he actually cared, because it was true. And wouldn't it have been even queerer, to deny that another boy was pretty, when it was so bleeding self-evident? Ed, after all, had nothing to prove.)

Ed stared. Baron stared back. And then, after a moment, the corner of Baron's mouth curled. He reached up, putting the magazine back into its place. His shirt came a bit untucked when he stretched, showing a stretch of brown belly. Ed did not bother to look away, staring still.

"Let's go, Dick," Baron said, though his eyes were on Ed. "They're waiting for us."

Dick sniggered again, as though a joke had been told, although it hadn't. Ed's eyes stayed on them, hard, until the pair of boys disappeared into the chip shop.

He waited a moment, watching their heads move beyond the window glass. Then he went over to the very space Baron had just occupied, and fished out the music magazine for himself.

Down Beat Magazine, it was called. An American magazine, price in cents on the cover. Sold some issues to sailors on occasion. Not many. Pink and gray and white cover, a man holding a trumpet between his knees. *R&B Concert Package Set* the cover read, and Ed touched the square, bold letters. Waited to feel transformed. Began to read, idly. Reading was the one excess he permitted himself on his newsstand afternoons, though so far it had always been comics for Ed. Hm.

He almost didn't notice when the chip shop door opened again. Not until he heard the footsteps, squeaky, soft, Baron's plimsolls on hard pavement. Blushing faintly, Ed looked up from the magazine. Trying to pretend as though his reading habits had nothing to do with the boy in front of him.

Baron was alone this time. No pack of boys. Not even Dick.

"Shouldn't you be eating with the rest of those pigs?" Ed asked, more harshly than he'd meant to. Baron shrugged.

"Don't have the cash," he said, and he spoke with a strange, fake-American accent, all nasally. Caaaaash. Ed saw something in Baron's hands then. A flash of paper and foil. A chocolate bar. Baron was breaking pieces off, stuffing them in his mouth. But he stopped. Looked down. Broke what remained in half, and offered that half to Ed.

"No, I'm-" Ed started to say, because he wasn't supposed to eat on the job. But Baron shrugged. Pushed the half of the chocolate bar forward.

"Go on, son," he said, and grinned, and Ed could see how that pretty mouth was all mucked up with chocolate.

"Thanks," Ed said simply, and took it. They stood for a minute on the street, eating quietly. Best chocolate bar of his life, actually, though Ed wasn't about to admit that.

Baron, smiling faintly, at long last said, "Don't damage the merchandise, son," in that faux-American accent again, and Ed glance down and realized how he'd left fingerprints on the magazine. He cursed softly. Tried to wipe it off. Baron laughed a little, but it wasn't a mean laugh.

"Here," he said. "I'll buy it. Wanted it, anyway."

Baron reached in his pocket and pulled out some coin. Ed took it. Handed over the magazine. Baron tucked it into the waistband of his pants.

"Thought you didn't have the caaaash," Ed said. Baron shrugged. Vague, vague.

"Wouldn't want to get you in trouble with your boss," he said. "Seems like the right thing to do."

Ed frowned. Tried to figure out an answer to that. Failed, but it didn't matter. Because in another moment, the chip shop door swung open again.

There were the other boys. Bigger, stronger. Dick clapping Baron on the shoulder.

"You alright?" he asked, and his glance at Ed was pointed.

"Yeh," said Baron. "Wonderful."

And then - did Ed imagine it? - Baron winked at him.

"Ta," he said to Ed. Ed's voice came out faint back.

"Of course."

He watched as the gaggle of lads departed, leaving him alone at the newsstand. Clutching Baron's coin.

And isn't it strange? For all it stuck in Ed's head, for years and years after. For all of its trembling significance - the dreams he had, the way he had nudged Liam in the days after that into wanking with him so he could close his eyes and think of the boy who had shared his chocolate and bought a silly American music magazine from him, he and Baron never talked about that day, not once, not to each other. Even though they both held this memory in common - even though they both, individually, thought of it often, more often than they cared to admit. Perhaps neither of them wanted to learn that the other had forgotten. Perhaps that's why neither of them asked.

It was only years later, after Baron was dead and gone, that Ed dared to speak of it, maybe, to a grandkid or two. Once or twice, to a hungry musician who wanted a tender tidbit, and Ed, feeling magnanimous, let the story go. In a new century, a new lifetime, Ed permitted himself to talk about it in whispered tones, like a secret. Admitting that this was the beginning of it all, how it *really* started. Not at a church, but on the suburban streets where they grew up, where everybody knew everybody. He shared then, later, in Baron's absence, how Baron Templeton had wormed his way into Ed Hammond's heart. Not simply because Baron Templeton was good looking, which he was, yes, Ed thought, right from the very beginning. No, no, Baron Templeton had sealed himself to Ed Hammond in that moment because Baron shared a chocolate bar with him. Ed loved Baron not merely because he was beautiful. But also, above all, because he was kind.

Playlist

Listen on spotify: https://open.spotify.com/playlist/14EtQAsuwRFD3j2op ynWQk

1. Bambi Kino - Wild Cat
2. The Dixie Cups - Chapel of Love
3. Lou Reed - Kill Your Sons
4. Little Richard - Rip It Up
5. The Who - My Generation
6. Harvey Danger - Wine, Women, and Song
7. The Shirelles - Will You Love Me Tomorrow?
8. The Stooges - I Want To Be Your Dog
9. Ben Folds - Zak and Sara
10. Wings - Let Me Roll It
11. Hefner - I Love Only You
12. Generation X - Dancing With Myself
13. Roxy Music - Jealous Guy
14. Ultimate Fakebook - Roll (Electric Kissing Parties, Part 1)
15. Ann-Margaret - One Boy

About the Author

From their home in the Hudson Valley, F. Fox North (call them Fox) saves Girl Scout camps, writes songs, climbs trees, and has better taste in music than you do.

Feel free to reach out to them, but only to talk about the queer hidden subtext in Beatles songs. Metaphysics and dick jokes are okay, too.

You can connect with me on:

🌐 http://linktr.ee/FFoxNorth

Subscribe to my newsletter:

✉ https://www.patreon.com/FFoxNorth

Also by F. Fox North

Still need more of the Saffron universe? Find out what happened when the world learned of Naomi Templeton...

The First Feast of Naomi Templeton
She was Matthew Hammond's best-kept secret. But this Christmas, the world, his girlfriend, the Saffron kids, *and* his sisters are going to learn about Baron Templeton's firecracker of a daughter in this Amazon exclusive e-book short.